<u>THE MORGUE</u>

THE MORGUE

by

Dennis N. Griffin

ISBN 1-58500-034-5

ABOUT THE BOOK

THE MORGUE is the story of the investigation of a Medical Examiner's office in upstate New York by the New York State Department of Health. The ME, Dr. Robert Franz, has been accused by his colleagues of a litany of misdeeds, including illegally harvesting research tissue from dead bodies without the consent of the next of kin. Dr. Franz denies the charges and labels his accusers as disgruntled troublemakers. John Grant, lead investigator, is assigned to find out the truth about what has transpired in THE MORGUE.

Follow the efforts of Grant as he confronts Dr. Franz, county government and sabotage from within his own department.

CHAPTER ONE

July 1989. The noise was the first indication Joan Morris had that something was wrong that afternoon. The piercing scream of tires sliding across the hot pavement shattered the tranquility of the upstate New York village of Oriskany.

That sound, and what it might mean, interrupted Joan's knitting. She jumped from the chair on her front porch, looking in the direction of the noise. It had come from the west, up the hill toward the village line. The same direction that Timmy, her twelve-year-old son, had pedaled on his bike a couple of minutes earlier. In a near panic she ran to the road and started up the hill, two hundred yards away.

As she approached the top of the hill Joan saw a black Bronco angled off on the shoulder of the road. Other cars were stopping on both sides of the highway; a crowd was forming around the Bronco. As she got closer she was overcome with gut wrenching fear, somehow knowing what she was going to find.

"Timmy! Timmy!" she hollered as she tried to get through the mob. A man grabbed her and tried to stop her. She twisted from his grasp and made it to the Bronco. Protruding from under the vehicle was the front wheel of her son's bicycle, and a leg, Timmy's leg.

After that her mind shut down. She wouldn't remember the wailing sirens. She wouldn't remember seeing Matt Cavanaugh, the twenty-seven year old driver of the Bronco. The man who had been doing seventy miles an hour as he crested the hill into Oriskany and its forty mile speed limit, the man who lost control of his vehicle, panicked and slammed on the brakes. The same man whose eyes locked with her son's in the instant before Timmy and his bike disappeared under the Bronco.

1

Five hours later Dr. Robert Franz, Oneida County Medical Examiner (ME), had just completed his autopsy of Timmy Morris. He turned from the autopsy table and glanced at the deputy sheriff, standing rigidly next to the exit door, about fifteen feet away. He was a young one who Franz had not met before. One look at his ashen face confirmed that this was his first autopsy. Franz suppressed a smile at the deputy's obvious discomfort. But he could understand it. The room reeked with the smell of various chemicals and body fluids. In addition, the dead body itself and what happened to it during autopsy was repulsive to most.

"Clean up will you, Bill?" Franz said to his assistant, Bill Maxwell. He then went to the sink, stripping his gloves along the way and tossing them into the medical waste disposal bag. After washing he shed his surgical greens, revealing a blue sport shirt and gray slacks, no tie. He dropped the greens in the laundry receptacle and headed for the door. "Come on," he said to the deputy, "I'll buy you a cup of coffee."

Leaving the autopsy room they went down a hallway, through the main office and out a door on the other side of the room. Twenty feet down another corridor they came to a combination conference and break room. This room held a conference table with chairs for ten. A large bookshelf served as a room divider. On the other side of it was a kitchen area with a sink, stove, refrigerator, microwave and coffee maker. Franz fixed two cups of coffee, then joined the deputy at the conference table.

The surroundings were more normal here and the odors were different. The smell of coffee and the faint aroma of microwave popcorn seemed to agree with the officer. His color was almost back to normal.

"I'll tell you something," Franz began, shaking his head sadly. "This was a healthy boy. I found no indication of any medical problems. We're sending some tissue specimens to the lab for testing, of course, but I don't expect any surprises."

"What actually killed him?" the deputy asked.

"Do you want me to be technical or will layman's terms do?" Franz asked, a slight smile on his face.

"Layman's terms please, doctor," the deputy smiled back.

"Then I'll be brief. Massive head and internal injuries.

With the damage he sustained it's merciful that he didn't survive." After a short pause Franz went on. "What about the driver? What do you think will happen to him?"

"He was in shock and admitted to St. Lukes for observation. I've already been informed by his wife that he has a lawyer. I don't know when I'll be able to interview him. There were no witnesses. The physical evidence at the scene indicates speed was a factor. His DMV record shows a history of speeding and reckless driving charges. He's had some DWI problems also. Anyway, an accident reconstruction specialist has been assigned to the case. I'll know a lot more when he's finished. It's my guess there will be an unreasonable speed charge now and probably vehicular manslaughter later."

Franz stood up. "My preliminary report will be ready in a couple of days. If you need a copy just call the office and the girls will take care of it for you. Now, if you'll excuse me I have some other pressing matters. You're welcome to stay and finish your coffee."

"No thank you, doctor. I've got a lot to do myself," the deputy said, getting to his feet. He followed Franz back to the main office and continued out the door.

Franz watched as the door clicked shut and locked. Then he turned toward the hallway leading to the autopsy room. Before he could take a step he heard a familiar voice call his name. He swung around quickly, startled. He saw Melvin Kemp, morgue attendant, perched on the corner of one of the secretaries desks.

"I'm sorry if I startled you, doctor," Kemp said, getting up from the desk. "I thought you knew I was here."

"Well I didn't!" Franz snapped. "What do you want?"

"I need to talk with you, doctor. In private."

Franz glanced around the office. "The girls have gone for the day. We're all alone, go ahead," he said sarcastically.

3

"Mr. and Mrs. Morris are in the back conference room," Kemp explained. "Can we go to your office?"

Franz arched his eyebrows quizzically. "Okay," he said. "Come on." They left the main office and turned left down the hall, heading away from the conference rooms. They entered the first door on the left, Franz's office. The room was small and cramped. A desk and chair were at the far side of the room facing the door. A computer table occupied the right wall, and a bookcase the left wall. Two chairs were in the center of the room facing Franz's desk. There was about four feet between the backs of the chairs and the door.

As soon as they were in the room Franz closed the door and walked to the front of his desk. Kemp positioned himself between the bookcase and door, facing Franz with the chairs between them. "Well, what is it?" Franz asked irritably.

Kemp tried to meet Franz's stare, but in a few seconds he switched his gaze toward the floor. Franz was forty-three, five feet eight and a hundred and sixty pounds. His physical stature was not particularly imposing. But his face, the red hair and green eyes, eyes that seemed to shoot sparks when he was angry, and his air of complete self-assurance awed Kemp. He was twenty-five, bigger and stronger than Franz. He shouldn't be intimidated by him, but he was. And right now he was damned scared.

"Damn it to hell, Melvin, spit it out! Don't you think I have anything better to do than to put up with your foolishness?"

"I couldn't get the Morris's to sign," Kemp said without raising his eyes.

"What?" Franz said, his voice rising. "What the hell do you mean they wouldn't sign?"

Kemp looked up now. Franz's face was turning a dark red. "I tried, doctor, honest," Kemp stammered. "Three times I asked, just like you taught us. I think the wife might have agreed, she's kind of out of it right now, but the husband said absolutely not. He started to get really mad so I backed off."

"That's no excuse!" Franz raved, pounding the edge of his fist on his desk. "These people are vulnerable at a time like this. Especially with the unexpected death of a child. I've told you that I want consents signed in all cases, and especially when the deceased is under eighteen."

Kemp wished he could leave, or at least move farther away from Franz, but there was nowhere to go. "I know, doctor," he whined, voice trembling. "But I did convince them to stay so you could talk to them. And you know my record for consents is good."

Franz saw Kemp's bottom lip begin to quiver. He knew he had to get control of himself or he might push Kemp over the edge. Kemp was a good employee. He did whatever he was told without question. And that was important, very important. Before he was finished all his people would be like Kemp, totally loyal and obedient.

He forced a smile and stepped around the chairs to stand in front of Kemp. Reaching out with both hands he grasped Kemp's shoulders firmly. "I know you're a good employee, Melvin. And I really appreciate your loyalty," he said softly. "It's just that we need to get the donation consent forms signed in all cases. Now, introduce me to the grieving Morris's. I'll see what I can do."

He let go of Kemp's shoulders, opened the door and headed toward the conference room. Kemp fell in behind him. Just like a puppy, no amount of abuse could shake his dedication to his master.

The conference room where the Morris's were waiting was large. It contained two-conference tables positioned end to end. Twelve chairs were arranged around the tables. Storage shelves were attached to the walls about six feet above the floor. They were loaded down with cardboard boxes of various sizes. This room tended to have a musty odor and was routinely sprayed with a room air freshener prior to use. Kemp had remembered to do that before he brought the Morris's there. It now had a very pleasant pine scent. As with all rooms in the morgue, except the main office area, it was windowless.

Just outside the door to the conference room Franz stepped aside to allow Kemp to enter first. Kemp stepped inside and found the Morris's where he had left them, seated at the conference table, their backs toward the door. Mrs. Morris was still staring at her hands folded on the table in front of her. Her husband was another matter, however. As soon as he heard footsteps he swung around facing the door. He glared at Kemp as though he'd like to punch him. A snarl formed on his lips. "What the hell are you trying to pull, leaving us sitting here all this time?"

Kemp quickly moved to his right without answering, revealing Franz's presence. He extended his left arm toward his boss. "This is Dr. Robert Franz," he said proudly. "Doctor, this is Fred and Joan Morris." He then backed up and stood by the wall next to the door, his job finished.

Whether it was Franz's title or bearing, the hostility seemed to drain from Fred Morris. He stood up and faced Franz, extending his hand. "Doctor, please excuse my show of temper. I hope you can appreciate that this is a very difficult time for us."

Franz took the hand and gave it a brief but firm shake.

"Please, there is no need to apologize," he said, a compassionate smile on his face. "I've never personally experienced what you're going through. I can only imagine the pain you must be in. Please be seated, Mr. Morris. I'll only keep you a few minutes more."

Franz walked around the table and sat facing the Morris's. He didn't speak for a few seconds, studying them. He had read the information on the Case Data Sheet before he autopsied their son. He knew they were in their early thirties. He worked in a furniture factory, she was a housewife. Timmy had been their only child.

Fred was seemingly composed and alert. His wife had still not looked up from her hands. She was plain but pleasant to look at, even in her grief stricken condition. For a fleeting moment

Franz wondered how she'd be in bed. He quickly cleared the thought from his mind; there was business to be taken care of.

"Is your wife all right, has she been seen by a doctor?" Franz asked Fred, concern oozing from his voice.

"I think she's okay, under the circumstances."

"I can arrange for someone to look at her," Franz offered. "It will be no trouble at all."

"I appreciate that, doctor, but I'll get in touch with our family physician after we leave here. Maybe he'll want to see her." Fred then turned to his wife. "Honey," he said softly, "this is Dr. Franz. Please say hello to him."

Joan Morris raised her eyes to Franz's face and stared blankly. Franz rose slightly and leaned across the table toward her. He briefly placed his right hand over her hands and squeezed gently. He withdrew his hand and settled back in his chair. Without word or reaction her eyes returned to the table in front of her.

Kemp, still positioned against the wall behind the Morris's, watched Franz's performance. He waited with anticipation for Franz to raise the donation issue. His wait was short.

"The reason I wanted to talk with you is to discuss the possibility of donating some of your sons tissue. It's too late to consider transplant, but a donation can be beneficial in other ways. I'll take a minute to explain what I mean," Franz said.

Fred Morris's anger returned in a fury. He rose from his chair, face flushed, and slammed his right palm on the tabletop. "The hell you will," he hollered. "Can't you fucking vultures understand English? I've said no three times and I meant it. Nobody is going to do any more to my son than what has already been done! We're leaving. Boyd Funeral Home will be picking Timmy up." He grabbed his wife's arm and roughly pulled her from her chair. Towing her behind him, Fred charged down the hallway, through the office and out the door. Franz made no effort to stop them.

When their footsteps had receded Franz got to his feet and started out of the room. Kemp was experiencing a twinge of pleasure that Franz hadn't done any better than he had.

Franz must have sensed it. Never one to apologize or admit failure, he took a parting shot at Kemp as he walked by him.

"He'd have gone for it if you hadn't pissed him off."

Kemp stood still for a few seconds thinking about what Franz had said. Did Franz really believe that this whole thing was his fault? He gave a shrug, went back to the office and made an entry in Timmy Morris's Case Data Sheet. "Parents asked to make tissue donation by M. Kemp and Dr. Franz. They refused."

Franz poked his head in the autopsy room door just as Bill Maxwell was putting the last of the freshly sanitized instruments away. As always, Maxwell had cleaned his work area with enthusiasm. He took great pride in his work. His official title was Morgue Superintendent, but his favorite job was assisting in the autopsy room.

"Bill, I'm going to change and be right back. Get the boy out of the cooler, will you?" Franz said. As he started to shut the door he heard Maxwell respond. "What the hell for? You just finished the autopsy and I'm all cleaned up!"

Franz stopped dead in his tracks. He didn't tolerate being talked to like this by very many people; Maxwell was one of them. He tolerated it, but he didn't like it. "I'll be back in a couple of minutes and we'll talk," he said as he let the door close the rest of the way.

Maxwell stared at the closed door. He was fifty-two, tall and lean. He worked out regularly. He had retired from the navy in 1985 after thirty years service, with the rank of Senior Chief Petty Officer. Starting his career as a corpsman he had risen through the ranks, finishing as assistant to the administrator of a large military hospital. He wasn't intimidated by Bob Franz, or anybody else for that matter.

He had been the first person Franz had hired after taking over as ME in '85. They had hit it off great at the start. Franz was a skilled forensic pathologist. It had been a pleasure to work with him. But things had deteriorated gradually over the last couple of years. It seemed to him that Franz had changed into a power hungry egomaniac. He now had little regard for ethics, or even the law.

The door swung open and Franz entered, again clad in surgical garb. He walked over to the flush sink where Maxwell was standing, but kept a respectful distance. "What's wrong with you lately, Bill?" he said in an even voice. "You question almost everything I do and every order I give. Why?"

Maxwell didn't answer right away, gathering his thoughts. "Before I answer your question tell me why you want the Morris boy back out," he said finally.

Franz answered immediately. "I'm going to take his testicles and bladder."

That was about what Maxwell had figured. "Why didn't you take them during the autopsy, Bob?" This time Franz didn't answer at all. After several seconds Maxwell went on, "Because the cop was standing here, right?" He continued the offensive without waiting for an answer. "And you knew the cop, even a rookie cop, would know something wasn't kosher. What do you need the kids testicles and bladder for? Do you have permission from his parents to do what you're going to do? Do they even know about it? What about the stuff you've been taking from other people? Does anybody know what goes on in this place?" Out of questions, Maxwell shut up.

It was Franz's turn to hesitate. He had a strong urge to fire Maxwell on the spot. But, down deep, he knew that Maxwell was a valuable asset. He didn't want to get rid of him unless he had no other choice. When he was sure he wouldn't say anything he'd regret, he responded. "When you first came on board with me here I told you what my plans were. I said I was going to make this office the largest forensic center in the state outside of New York City. You were excited and I thought we shared the same dream. What's changed?"

"I'd still like to see those plans come to fruition," Maxwell answered. "It's the change in you that bothers me. I think your ethical standards have slipped. I'm not even sure that everything we do here is legal. But you haven't answered my questions yet. How about it?"

Franz had heard enough. Maxwell had pushed him as far as he could allow. "Let's get something straight," he said. "In case you've forgotten, I'm the boss here. I have no intention of letting you interrogate me. The questions you asked are not your concern. I'm well on my way to reaching my goals, and you're welcome to come along with me. If you do, it will be as a team player, and without your present attitude. This is something you need to think over and then decide what you're going to do, and soon. Now, get the boy on the table, and that's an order."

Maxwell got the message. Reluctantly he turned and headed for the coolers.

CHAPTER TWO

March 2, 1993. John Grant, investigator for the New York State Department of Health (DOH), was at his desk in the state office building on Genesee Street in Utica. It was ten minutes before 8:00 and he was the first one in the office. Sipping his morning coffee, he was just about to flip open the early edition of the Oneida County Observer when his phone rang. In the quiet of the empty office the ring seemed especially loud. Startled, he involuntarily jumped, the coffee cup in his left hand tilted, the hot black liquid spilling on his fingers. Stifling a curse he put the cup down and grabbed the handset. "Special Investigations Unit," he answered.

"Good morning, John," said the voice of his boss, Linda Ludwig. "I've got a little job I'd like you to do for me today." Grant knew there was no such thing as a "little" job when it came to Linda. He reached in his desk drawer for a note pad and pencil, just in case. Whatever was coming must be important, because Linda normally didn't get into her Albany office until nine o'clock.

"Certainly, Linda," he said. "What is it you want me to do?"

"What do you know about the medical examiner there, Dr. Franz?"

"Just that, he's the ME. I can't think of anything else that I know about him. Why?"

"All those years you were with the sheriff's department you never had any dealings with him?"

"I was with Madison County, not Oneida," Grant reminded her.

"Yes, of course. Well, anyway, I got a call late yesterday afternoon from a Dr. Donald Johnson, an assistant to Dr. Franz. He told me that he, another assistant ME named Harrison Samuels and Matthew Porter, Chief Toxicologist, were holding

11

a press conference at six last night. They were going to expose unethical practices, and possibly criminal activities involving Franz. They suggested that we have somebody attend. I knew that you had already left for the day, so I told him we couldn't respond with such short notice. He wasn't happy, but we did have a twenty minute chat."

"And?" Grant prompted.

"According to Johnson, Dr. Franz has been doing all kinds of nasty things, from dicing body organs and flushing them down an open commode to illegally harvesting research tissue."

"This sounds very gory, but what does it have to do with SIU? We handle laboratory cases, not MEs' offices."

"Very true, John. It just so happens that Dr. Franz is the director of the county clinical and environmental labs. We've issued him our certificates, and, as you know, one of the requirements to get and retain certification is that the licensee must be of good character."

"Agreed, and in the past we've let whatever division handles the particular complaint do their investigation. If they bring a successful action we use that as a reason to deny issuance or renewal of a certificate. Are we going to do something different in this case?"

"As a matter of fact, I wasn't the first person Dr. Johnson spoke with here yesterday. His call was switched around all over the department, trying to find someone with the appropriate jurisdiction. Believe it or not, John, nobody in the department regulates medical examiners' offices. Apparently we're the only ones with any kind of a hook at all."

"What about the Medical Conduct people? This guy's a doctor and that's what they handle."

"These allegations don't involve malpractice or patient abuse. Franz doesn't have any patients in the traditional sense. Look, John, there may still be somewhere else to get rid of this thing, I'm working on it. In the meantime I've been given my marching orders."

"Okay, Linda. I'm not trying to give you a hard time. It's

just that I think this is a stretch. Now, what do you want me to do?"

"Johnson and his friends had their press conference outside the county office building on county property. In order to do that they had to get permission from the county. They got permission, but with the advance knowledge the county planned an immediate response. Johnson said that Franz and some other county officials are holding their own press conference at 4:30 this afternoon. It'll be in the auditorium of the county office building. I'd like you to see what you can find out about what Johnson and company had to say yesterday, maybe there will be something in the paper. Then I want you to stop by the county building this afternoon and listen to the response."

"That sounds simple enough. Then what?"

"Nothing. Call me tomorrow morning and let me know what you think. We'll go from there. Maybe we'll be able to pass it on to somebody else by then."

"One more question, Linda. Who gave you your marching orders?"

"They came from the fourteenth floor," she said.

The fourteenth floor of the DOH office building in Albany housed the commissioner, deputy commissioners and other higher ups.

"Why is this important enough to draw the attention of the big boys?" Grant asked.

"Dr. Johnson is also alleging that the county is covering up for Franz. If somebody doesn't act on his complaints he says he'll go to the governor and every media outlet that will listen to him. The people here seem to believe he'll do it."

"This Johnson sounds like a loose cannon to me," Grant said.

"That's probably true, but he and his friends are making some serious charges. If there is any truth to them, especially about the county looking the other way, then this could be a real hot potato. I suggest you keep a low profile at the press

13

conference this afternoon. Just sit in the back of the room and observe."

"Okay, Linda. I'll give you a ring in the morning," Grant said and hung up.

He grabbed the Observer and scanned the front page. The article by reporter James Doyle was on the lower right. "Medical Examiner Under Fire Again" the headline read. Grant quickly reviewed the story. It was pretty much what Linda had said, numerous charges made by MD's Johnson and Samuels and Ph.D. Porter. Most of the allegations had to do with Franz ignoring the safety of his employees in an effort to expand morgue operations. He supposedly was seeking to do autopsies from other counties and state correctional facilities and charging a nominal fee for the service. Unfortunately, many of these were TB and AIDS patients. The assistant ME's objected to being exposed to these risks unnecessarily. They also questioned Franz's treatment of employees. Grant didn't see any way he could, or should, investigate those matters. The allegations of the improper disposal of medical waste and harvesting tissue without consent were another story, however. Someone from DOH should probably look into them.

Grant put the unused note pad back in his desk drawer, got up from his chair and walked over to the window. He stared down at the street three floors below. A steady flow of state employees streamed toward the building from the parking lot a block away. In coats, hats and gloves they gingerly stepped around patches of ice and snow on the sidewalk. He promised himself that someday he'd move to someplace where he wouldn't have to contend with winter.

Grant was forty-seven. He had left his job as a deputy sheriff after eighteen years to take a position with the state. It was the same retirement system and represented a substantial pay increase. That was seven years ago. He loved his job. The only downside was his losing battle of the waistline. No longer having to get into a uniform had its pros and cons.

He and Linda Ludwig had a great working relationship. She was a year younger and had been with DOH since she was eighteen. She had a strong administrative background, but little investigative experience. They complimented each other very well. She had enough confidence and trust in him to assign him to work out of Utica, about a hundred miles west of Albany, with no direct supervision. They could speak their minds when they talked. Even if they disagreed, when it was over, it was over. Neither held a grudge.

Grant returned to his desk to clip out the newspaper article in case he ended up opening a case file.

At twenty after four Grant left his office and walked the two blocks to the county building on Park Avenue. The auditorium was on the second floor. He stopped in the hallway a few feet from the auditorium door and eyed the handful of people standing in front of the door talking. He had only been assigned to Utica for a few months and hadn't met many people outside his own office. He didn't anticipate bumping into anyone he knew here. Sure enough, they were all strangers. That was good, he wouldn't have to explain away his presence.

The auditorium was a large, high ceilinged room. There were theater style seats for about three hundred people. The stage was empty except for a podium in the forefront and several chairs against the right hand wall. The seats directly in front of the podium were fairly full for the first eight rows. Grant spotted an empty seat in the middle of the last occupied row and headed for it. As he walked he glanced at the people around him. Again there were no familiar faces.

Seated, he removed his winter jacket and placed it over his lap. His black pull over shirt and gray slacks blended in with the rest of the casually dressed audience.

It was three minutes before the press conference was scheduled to start. Grant tried to determine the makeup of the crowd. Several had notepads and were presumably reporters. A crew from Channel 3 arrived and set up their camera against the far right wall about ten feet in front of the stage. A few last minute arrivals took up seats in the row behind him.

Promptly at 4:30 four men entered the stage from a door in the left-hand wall. Three of them walked across the stage and took seats in the chairs along the right wall, the fourth stopped at the podium. All were dressed in suits. Grant didn't recognize any of them.

"Good afternoon, ladies and gentlemen," the man at the podium said. "For those of you who don't know me, my name is Dr. Morton Massey, Oneida County Health Commissioner. We're here this afternoon in response to the recent allegations made against our medical examiner, Dr. Robert Franz."

Dr. Massey appeared to be in his late fifties. He was average in height and build, with salt and pepper hair. He wore a charcoal gray suit, blue shirt and maroon tie.

"Let me start out by saying that I hired Bob Franz in 1985," Massey continued. "During these past eight years Bob has built his office into the third largest in the state, outside of the City. Our morgue operation is the envy of our neighboring counties, many of which now utilize our autopsy and lab services. And he has done this at no additional cost to our taxpayers. The services we provide to other counties are, in fact, revenue producers. The morgue has operated under budget every year since Bob took over." Massey paused to let his last statement sink in.

"In closing, let me say that it is a sad day when a man like Bob Franz has to spend time defending himself against lies and distortions. I can't understand what motivates such people. I'll let Bob address the situation in more detail when he talks to you. Suffice it to say that Bob Franz has my complete trust and support. Now, I'll turn the podium over to Mr. Reginald Whitehurst, Oneida County District Attorney."

Massey left the podium and walked toward the three seated men. One of them stood up and shook Massey's hand in passing. He continued on to the podium. He was a big, barrel chested man, over six feet tall and at least two hundred-fifty pounds. In his early forties, his hair was light brown and he wore glasses.

"Good afternoon," he said with a smile. "I'm Reggie Whitehurst, the DA. When I heard about these most recent attacks against Bob Franz I felt it was my duty to speak in his defense. I've worked very closely with Bob since he was appointed ME. I can tell you that you won't find a more dedicated public servant. We've been at crime scenes together at all hours and in all kinds of weather, looking for the evidence that will put the guilty party in prison and off of our streets. The high percentage of homicide convictions in this county is due in no small part to the dedication and professionalism of Bob Franz. The people of this county can rest easier tonight, more safe and secure because of his efforts. I'm not going to let his reputation be tarnished by a few people who, for unknown reasons, feel they have an ax to grind." With that Whitehurst returned to his seat. After a round of handshakes another of the men approached the podium.

This man was a red head, about Grant's height, he appeared fit and trim. He was wearing a dark brown suit with a white shirt and brown tie.

"Ladies and gentlemen, I'm Dr. Robert Franz. I must tell you that I'm embarrassed to have to appear before you today because of the reckless actions of three of my subordinates. However, I couldn't in good conscience let their allegations stand unchallenged. Mine is a difficult business that is not understood by the general public. Because of that, it is easy for treacherous and disloyal individuals to spread false stories that the public finds revolting. I want to assure the people of this county that I have run my office as it should be run. Regardless of how repulsive some aspects of the operation may be, I have done nothing wrong!"

After a brief pause Franz continued. "I had originally planned to answer your questions relating to the current false allegations, but due to certain legal actions being contemplated that won't be possible." There was an audible groan from the reporters. Franz extended his arms toward the audience, palms out. "My attorney, Mr. Peter Gorsky, has advised me that it would be foolish for me to be any more specific until all my legal options have been explored, sorry. We'll get together again in the near future and I'll be happy to answer your questions then. Thank you all for coming."

Franz wheeled from the podium and headed for the door he had entered from. Massey, Whitehurst and the other man rose from their seats and followed him. A tall, thin reporter standing in the aisle waved his notepad over his head and hollered, "Pete, Pete Gorsky, are you going to sue Dr. Johnson and the others?"

The fourth man, the man who had not spoken, stopped and turned toward the reporter. Smiling, he shook his right index finger at him. "Good try, Jim, but you know a good lawyer never discloses his strategy." He then continued out the door.

Grant remained seated, waiting for the aisle to clear. "Bastards," he heard the man on his left mutter. Grant turned toward him. The man looked to be around sixty. He sat with his arms folded across his chest, staring at the now empty stage.

"Pardon me, did you say something?" Grant asked.

The man turned toward him, face flushing. "I'm sorry, I hope I didn't offend you. It's just that these people who are doing this to Dr. Franz ought to be crucified."

"You know Dr. Franz?" Grant asked.

"Yes. My grandson died in '91. Choked on a piece of apple, he was only two. Dr. Franz and his people couldn't have been nicer. They're always in my prayers. These jerks shooting their mouths off about him infuriate me!"

"I can understand how you feel," Grant said, extending his hand. "I'm John Grant, I'm very sorry about your loss."

"William Clinton," the man said, shaking Grant's hand. "No, I'm no relation to the guy in the White House. My grandson was named after me. I wonder how he'd have felt about having the same name as the president. Well, nice to meet you John, I've got to get going."

Grant left just behind him, he still had a fifteen mile drive to get home.

A few minutes after 9:00 the next morning Grant called Linda. "How did it go?" she asked.

"Well, according to the newspaper, the first press conference was just about what you said. The one yesterday was more of a statement, the speakers didn't take any questions. The bottom line is that Franz is a great guy and hasn't done anything wrong."

"Who all spoke?" Linda wanted to know.

"Dr. Massey, Franz's boss, the DA, Reggie Whitehurst and Franz himself."

"The DA spoke in support of someone who is alleged to have committed criminal acts?" Linda said in amazement.

"I was surprised myself," Grant admitted.

"So, what do you think?" Linda wanted to know.

"They were very impressive."

"I sense that you don't believe them, do you?"

"Not necessarily."

"Why not?"

"They're reaction was a little strong. And I can't discount the complainants. These guys are well educated and in positions of authority in their own right. They must have something on the ball. I don't think they can be dismissed as simply disgruntled employees. Besides, they work directly with Franz on a regular basis, Massey and Whitehurst don't."

"Good. Can you be here in Albany at ten tomorrow morning?"

"I can be, what's up?"

"This is going to be an SIU investigation, it's your case. Be here in the morning and I'll give you the details."

CHAPTER THREE

The main state office complex in Albany is located in the Empire State Plaza. There are five office buildings in the complex housing various state agencies. The DOH occupies the tallest of these buildings, the forty-four story Corning Tower. Wadsworth Center, the laboratory division, is situated on four floors in the basement of the building.

Grant parked in one of the pay lots and made his way to the main entrance to the Center. After showing his department ID to the receptionist he went down the east hallway to Linda's office. He was a few minutes early so he peeked in the door window to see if she was busy with someone else. Linda was alone, she noticed him immediately and motioned him in.

Linda was five feet seven, well built and well endowed. She wore her blonde hair shoulder length. She was a sharp dresser. For reasons Grant didn't know, or care to know, she was in the process of a divorce.

"Good morning, John," she smiled. "Here, have a coffee," she said, handing him a cardboard cup from the side of her desk. "It should still be hot, I only got it a few minutes ago."

"Thanks," Grant said, taking the coffee cup. He was anxious to find out what had happened to make Linda decide this Franz thing was definitely an SIU case, but he didn't want to be pushy. Linda got right to the point without any urging, however.

"Dr. Lynch will be joining us shortly, you remember her don't you?"

Grant remembered her. Samantha Lynch was a MD in charge of the Center's blood and tissue programs. She was one of the few in the department who supported aggressive enforcement of regulations. Grant had done a couple of investigations for her when he had been based in Albany. She had been a pleasure to work with.

"Yes, I remember her. I liked working with her, I'm glad she's involved with this."

Linda looked over Grant's shoulder toward the door. She waved Dr. Lynch in. She was an inch or so taller than Grant and very thin. She had light brown hair and a slightly turned up nose. In her mid thirties, she had a bright future with the department.

Grant stood up and shook hands. After exchanging pleasantries he sat back down, Dr. Lynch took the chair to his right. They sat looking at Linda across her desk, waiting for her to start.

"Dr. Lynch came to see me yesterday afternoon," Linda began, directing her comments to Grant. "She was attending a blood banking conference in Utica when Dr. Johnson and the others held their press conference. She saw it on the evening news, and is very concerned about the tissue harvesting allegations. You see, although we don't oversee MEs' offices, the morgue has applied to her program for a license as a non-transplant anatomical tissue bank. Dr. Franz is listed as the director. This puts the most serious allegation squarely in our lap. I'll let Sam give you the rest of the details," she turned toward Dr. Lynch.

Grant turned in his chair to face her. "The regulation requiring tissue banks to be licensed became effective on June 1, 1991," Dr. Lynch said. "All parties falling under the regulation were given until January 2, 1992 to submit the required application and supporting documentation. Provisional approval was granted based on the information in the application package. Permanent licenses will be issued upon successful completion of a facility inspection. During the provisional period the applicant is obligated to fully comply with the regulations."

"I take it Franz hasn't had his inspection yet?" Grant asked.

"None of the applicants have been inspected yet. They are all operating provisionally." She held up her hand and gave an embarrassed laugh, "Don't think bad things until I explain. My program has only one inspector. With the problems we've had with HIV contaminated blood getting into the blood banks he's been tied right up. Tissue bank inspections are a much lower priority."

22

"That's understandable," Grant said. "So where does that leave us?"

"Routine inspections are a low priority, complaints of this nature aren't," Dr. Lynch said. "I'm going to ask my inspector to schedule the morgue for an unannounced inspection as soon as possible. I'd like you to go with him."

"I don't know anything about inspecting a tissue bank. I just heard about the regulation this morning. I'd make a complete ass of myself," Grant protested.

Dr. Lynch and Linda laughed. "That isn't exactly what I had in mind," Dr. Lynch said. "I want you to go along posing as an inspector trainee, not an investigator. Let my guy handle the inspection. Between now and the inspection gather all the information you can on what tissue Franz has taken, where it goes and why. Is he selling it? With what you find out you'll be able to help the inspector determine what to look for, what questions to ask."

"Why the pretext?" Grant asked. "Why not just do an investigation?"

"Right now Dr. Franz doesn't know we're interested in him," Linda answered. "Assuming the accusations are true, if you go in and flash your badge I doubt you'd get past the receptionist. Franz would involve the county attorney before he let you see any records. A stall of just a few hours could result in a lot of stuff disappearing. And remember, the county supposedly backs this guy to the hilt. No, I think Sam is right. Go in with the inspector and snoop around before Franz finds out he's being investigated."

Grant mulled things over for a few seconds, Linda and Dr. Lynch staring at him, waiting for his response. They were right, he concluded. Under the circumstances it was the right move. The more he thought, the better he liked it. "I'm sold," he said. "How much time do I have before the inspection?"

"I'm not sure," Dr. Lynch said. "I haven't even mentioned this to Tom yet. You've worked with Tom before haven't you?"

Tom Fargo was the sole inspector for the blood and tissue program. He was very knowledgeable and a nice guy, although he hadn't struck Grant as being very adventurous.

"Yes, I'll be looking forward to working with him."

"Great. I'll tell him to call you to make arrangements. I expect it will be a couple of weeks anyway. Stop on your way out and get a copy of the regulation from my secretary, call me if you have any questions. Bye." With that Dr. Lynch left the room at a fast walk, which for her was a normal gait.

"Now, John," Linda said. "You understand that this inquiry between now and the inspection has to be very discreet. If Franz gets wind of it our plan goes up in smoke. I'd keep away from Johnson, Samuels and Porter, I think they're media happy."

"Do you have any suggestions for a safe contact?"

"No. You're the investigator, I'm sure you'll figure something out." Linda checked her watch. "I've got to run, I'm late for a meeting. Good luck." She was out of the office before Grant could say good-bye.

Grant got back to Utica a little before two. He shared a medium sized office with two other people, Velma Vadasy and Ron Burrows. Both worked as environmental specialists and were usually out in the field. As Grant approached his office door he knew that Ron was either in, or had recently left. The odor of cigarette smoke was in the air. Grant, a former smoker, didn't mind the smell. The problem was that this was a no smoking office. The aroma often brought the office manager, Sue Keller, around looking for the culprit. Sue was a talker and a bit of a snoop. Once she came in you couldn't get rid of her. Grant had pleaded with Ron to do his smoking somewhere else, to no avail.

He entered the office and was relieved to find it empty. He quickly closed and locked the door and settled down at his desk to read the tissue bank regulation.

After forty-five minutes he felt he had learned enough to have an understanding of what the basic requirements for Licensure were and what Tom would be looking for during the inspection. He had just finished reading when his phone rang.

"What's this all about?" a vaguely familiar male voice demanded.

"What is 'this', and to whom am I speaking?" Grant responded.

"I'm sorry, John. This is Tom Fargo. I just got back to my office and found a note from Dr. Lynch asking for a priority inspection of the Oneida County Morgue. I found that very odd in itself, but when I saw you were involved I got a little nervous. Can you tell me what this is all about?"

"Have you asked Dr. Lynch?" Grant asked.

"She's out. The note said to call you."

"Okay, Tom, I'll be glad to tell you what I know. There have been allegations made that Dr. Franz is illegally harvesting research tissue, among other things. Apparently this involves removing tissue without the consent of the next of kin. Dr. Lynch wants the allegation checked out. She figures the best way is to do it as part of your inspection. They know an inspection is required, so they won't be overly concerned about it."

"I'd look those tissue removal records over as part of my inspection anyway. Why are you coming along? It seems that I should go alone and do the inspection or you should go alone and do your thing. I don't see the need for us to go together."

"Perhaps I haven't done a very good job of explaining this," Grant said, his tone less friendly. "I'm going along posing as your trainee. We're not going to tell them that there is an investigation going on."

"What?" Tom screamed. "This is a shady deal and I don't like it! I'm not going to go in there under false pretenses. I'm not going to end up in jail, or losing my job, for you!"

"Listen Tom, we'd better get something straight right now. Using a pretext is an investigative tool. I've posed as everything from a phlebotomist to a patient in order to get information. You may not be comfortable with it, but we won't be doing anything wrong. And one other thing, this was Dr. Lynch's idea, not mine. You're a good man and I'd like to work this with you. But, if you feel you can't do it I suggest you inform her, not me."

There was silence on the line for several seconds. "So you say we won't get in any trouble for this?" a much more mellow Tom asked.

"That's what I said, Tom," Grant said, his voice softer. "The targets of these investigations usually don't appreciate these tactics, but Dr. Franz won't know what's going on until much later, if at all. When that time comes you won't be involved. Are you in?"

"When you put it that way, sure. And no offense, John, you're fun to work with. It's just that this kind of thing isn't my bag. I'd appreciate it if you don't mention my reaction to Dr. Lynch."

"There's nothing to mention," Grant assured him. "Now, when do you think we can do this?"

"I'll have to check my schedule to see what I can change around. I don't see any way I can do it for at least two or three weeks. Do you have any dates that you can't make it?"

"I'll make myself available whenever it's convenient for you. Go ahead and pick a date and let me know. Before I let you go, do you have time to answer a couple of questions for me?"

"I'll try. What do you want to know?"

"It's my understanding that organs for transplant have to be taken and preserved rather quickly. That would mean they'd have to be taken at the morgue. Franz has applied for a non transplant license, why doesn't he also need a transplant permit?"

"Good question. I have their application package right in front of me. Let's see here. Okay, the ME's people don't get involved with transplant removals. They have a clean room that the removing agency uses. Morgue personnel only wheel the body to and from the room."

"Who are these other agencies?"

"Primarily the Red Cross and Eye Bank."

"What does Franz claim he needs a non transplant permit for? What tissue would he take?"

"Well, there is a certain amount of tissue that is removed for lab testing as part of the autopsy. That's not what we're talking about here. The morgue would want to take tissue to send to research facilities. A brain might go to the Alzheimer Institute or a heart to the American Heart Association, for example."

"The morgue itself isn't a research facility is it?"

"No. It's a county operation with a specific function. They don't do research. Why, have you heard he's doing research there?"

"No. But if he's really taking this stuff illegally, I'm just trying to figure out how he's using it."

"Another good question. If it is true, maybe we'll find out when we do our visit. Anything else?"

"No, Tom, thanks a lot. And, Tom?"

"Yes?"

"Don't worry about this thing. It's going to be a piece of cake."

CHAPTER FOUR

"God damn it, Bob," an exasperated Peter Gorsky said, slamming his right palm on the conference table in front of him. "I've told you, and told you, and told you that I'm not going to commence a lawsuit against those people until you answer my questions!"

It was ten o'clock on Friday morning, three days after Franz's press conference. Gorsky and Dr. Franz were in Gorsky's office on State Street discussing how to proceed against Franz's accusers. It was a spacious office containing Gorsky's large desk, a conference table with eight chairs and two additional stuffed chairs facing the desk. Three of the walls were lined with bookshelves containing an untold number of law books. The fourth wall contained a large fireplace just to the right of the entrance door. The wooden furniture shined. The pleasant aroma of lemon scented furniture polish hung in the air.

"I think your questions are too ridiculous to warrant a response," Franz said calmly. He stared at Gorsky's face, looking for a reaction. Peter Gorsky was forty-four. His hair was prematurely gray, making him look older. He was just under six feet tall with a trim build. His piercing blue eyes and acid tongue had made many an opposing witness tremble. He had been representing Franz for three years. He had one of the most successful one man practices in the city. Franz needed him. He wanted to stand his ground, but not go too far in disagreement.

After a deep breath and a sip of his coffee, Gorsky started again. "Bob, you want to go after these guys for slander. That requires that they have defamed your character by making false or malicious charges. Before I can advise you on the best way to go, I have to know if there is any truth at all to what they've said about you. I'm talking about this medical waste and tissue business. I'll ask you again, is there any truth to these allegations, any at all?"

Franz answered Gorsky's question with one of his own. "What would you suggest as an alternative to suing?"

Gorsky didn't like that response. He was a good interrogator and knew what it usually meant when a person was evasive. "If they can prove you've done any of these things, I'd sure as hell tell you not to open a can of worms. You start an action against these guys you'll be giving them their day in court, a day that they most likely won't get otherwise. So, have they got anything on you?"

"You've been my lawyer for over three years, Peter, since these charges first appeared. But in the past they've been made anonymously. Oh, I was pretty sure who was doing it but we couldn't prove it. Now we've got these rats right in the spotlight, their words recorded in newspapers and TV news footage. I'm reluctant to let them get away without punishment."

Gorsky leaned forward, elbows on the table. "This stuff is true, isn't it, Bob? Can they prove it?"

Franz stood up, his face starting to redden. "How many times have I been through this shit? Three? Four? I've lost count. Every time these things surface the county investigates. Not one charge has ever been substantiated. You know that! That's why I find these questions offensive!"

Gorsky didn't reply right away. He leaned back in his chair and clasped his fingers behind his neck. "You're right, Bob, I do know about the previous accusations and investigations. I sat with you each time someone from the county attorney's office interviewed you. And those sessions amounted to them asking you if you had done anything wrong and you saying no. They never examined any records or talked with any witnesses, at least not any hostile witnesses. When it comes to being the target, you don't know what an investigation is. Now please sit down and let's try to resolve this."

With some reluctance, Franz sat back in his chair, his face back to its normal color. "I want to make sure I understand, Peter, are you saying that you believe them and not me?"

"I'm saying that I'm your lawyer, I'm on your side," Gorsky answered, leaning back toward the table. "I want to give you the best legal advice I can. In order to do that I need all the facts, I need you to tell me the truth, all of it. Since you apparently don't trust me enough to be candid with me, I'm going to advise you this way. If there is any chance, no matter how remote, that these people can prove their allegations, drop the idea of a lawsuit. It will probably come back to bite you. Now, what do you want to do?"

Franz studied the lawyer for a few seconds before answering. "I am a completely innocent man," he said finally, again rising from his chair. "But I believe all three of these men can be very convincing liars. Because of that I won't give them the opportunity to put on their case in court. You can never know but what someone might believe them. Good day, Peter." Franz let himself out the door and went down the hallway, leaving a very disturbed Peter Gorsky alone with his thoughts.

Seven blocks away John Grant was having a phone conversation with Linda. "You wanna what?" she hollered in disbelief. Grant was tilted back in his swivel desk chair, holding the phone six inches away from his ear. "I can't believe you said that. You, who doesn't trust reporters, and shuns publicity."

When Linda finished, he pressed the handset back against his ear. "You're right, Linda. But I'm under the gun here. Tom called me this morning and we're going to do the inspection on the eighteenth, that's less than two weeks. I've got to come up with some information quickly if I want to add anything to the inspection."

"But why contact this Doyle? I suggested that you avoid anything that might end up involving the media. Now you want to contact the reporter who's covering the story. Unless you can come up with some sound logical reason, the answer is no."

"I understand your reaction. But I've done a little checking on Mr. Doyle. He's been covering the morgue story since various allegations first surfaced in 1990. He's written a number of articles, many of them critical of Franz, and the county's support of him. He has a solid reputation for protecting his sources. If I can get him to share his three years worth of

31

information with me I'll be way ahead of the game. Why reinvent the wheel?"

Linda's opposition seemed to have softened. "If he's that interested in Dr. Franz, do you really think he'll give you information with nothing in return?"

"That's a valid point. He'll probably want a promise of receiving any hot information ahead of his competitors. I don't suppose the department would go for something like that, would we?"

"No way. It's the official policy of DOH that all media are treated equally." After a pause she continued, "Of course the department has no control over a reporters anonymous sources, especially if the anonymous source uses good judgment. Questions?"

"No. I think I understand completely."

"Fine. You have my blessing to contact Doyle. How do you plan to handle it?"

"I'm just going to call and ask if he'll talk with me off the record. If he says no, that'll be the end of it. If he agrees, I'll meet with him and play it by ear from there."

"Okay, John. Keep me informed. Oh, by the way, how enthusiastic does Tom seem to be about this?"

"He's chomping at the bit," Grant lied.

Grant called the main phone number for the Observer and asked for James Doyle. After a series of clicks and rings the phone was answered. "Doyle," a deep, pleasant voice said.

"Good morning, Mr. Doyle. My name is John Grant, I'm an investigator with state DOH. Do you have time to talk with me for a few moments?"

"Sure, John. I don't believe I know you. Would you be so kind as to give me a little better idea of exactly who you're with and what you do? Then we'll talk."

Grant had the uncomfortable feeling that Doyle might be activating a tape recorder. "Before I do that, I'd like your assurance that our conversation, the entire conversation, will be off the record."

There was a short pause before Doyle answered. Grant visualized the recorder being shut off. "I sense that you don't trust reporters," Doyle laughed. "Have some of my colleagues abused you in the past?"

"I wouldn't go so far as to use the word 'abused', let's just say that I know you have a job to do, but so do I. I'd like to help you with your job without jeopardizing my own."

"Fair enough. We're off the record, but I'd still like to know a little more about you."

"Okay. I'm with the Special Investigations Unit of state DOH, assigned to Wadsworth Center. That's the laboratory division. My primary responsibilities are investigating health care fraud involving clinical laboratories. SIU also investigates environmental labs. I've been on this job for seven years, working out of Albany for all but the past few months. I'm now assigned to the state office building here in Utica. I think that covers it."

"I've never heard of your outfit before, but God knows there's a lot of fraud out there. I wish you the best of luck. Now, what do you want to talk with me about?"

"I'm trying to get some background information on Dr. Robert Franz and the morgue. I believe you're very knowledgeable on those subjects."

"Wait a minute! I thought you said you were involved with health care fraud. What does that have to do with Franz? The people he deals with are past the point of needing health care."

"True. I said that was my primary responsibility. The Center also licenses tissue banks. The morgue has applied for such a license. I'm just doing a little background stuff as part of processing the application."

"Does this have anything to do with the most recent allegations made against Dr. Franz?"

"It could. We're certainly interested in any information regarding the character and business practices of the applicant."

"Is Franz the target of an official DOH investigation?"

"I don't want to spar with you, Jim. I've explained my position the best I can. Now, are you interested in meeting with me to discuss this further, off the record, of course?"

Doyle answered without hesitation, "Yes. When and where?"

"Preferably at my office, and at your earliest convenience. But I'd like you to bring copies of your previous articles about Franz. Will that be a problem?"

"No. I can be at your office at two o'clock. Is that okay?"

Grant was pleasantly surprised. He hadn't expected such an enthusiastic response. "That will be fine, Jim. I'm on the third floor. I'll tell the receptionist to expect you."

Doyle arrived at five minutes of two. Grant met him in the reception area. He immediately recognized Doyle as the same reporter who had attempted to question Peter Gorsky at the press conference. Wearing a gray sweater over an open collar white shirt, Doyle looked even taller and more thin, almost gaunt, close up. Grant figured him to be in his late thirties.

"I really appreciate you coming to see me on such short notice," Grant said after a handshake.

"My pleasure, John," Doyle said. His top coat was folded over his left arm, in his left hand was a sheaf of papers a quarter of an inch thick. "These are the previous articles you asked for," he said, handing the papers to Grant.

"Thanks, Jim," Grant said, taking the papers without looking at them. "Can I get you a coffee?" Doyle declined the offer. "Okay then, let's go to my office and talk."

Grant led Doyle down two corridors, past several cubicles that served as offices, and into his room. After closing the door he motioned Doyle to a chair at the right side of his desk, and set the papers down to his left, next to the telephone.

"If you don't mind, Jim, I'll read these later," Grant said, patting Doyle's articles with his left hand. "I'd like to take advantage of your being here to have you give me the background on Dr. Franz and his troubles at the morgue. I assume that will include what's in these," Grant again patted the articles.

"Let me start at the beginning. Bob Franz came here in 1985 from Dade County, Florida. He'd been an assistant ME there. This was the first time he'd ever been the head man. His reputation was good. He was supposed to be an extremely talented pathologist and a real go-getter. For the first several years, until 1989, he seemed to be doing a good job. He got high marks from the DA and the cops. The county fathers were pleased with him. There was nothing derogatory. Then, around the fall of '89, I began to hear rumblings that he was doing some weird things, and that he was getting power hungry."

"What kind of 'weird things'?" Grant asked.

"He supposedly got involved with providing tissue to research facilities. The rumor was that he took the tissue he needed with or without consent. Then he kept a body that was supposed to have been cremated and...."

"Wait a minute," Grant interrupted, a trace of excitement in his voice. "Are you saying he stole a body?"

"I'm saying that a body that should have been cremated never went to the oven. It didn't leave the morgue, at least not until much later. It's all in there," Doyle said, pointing toward the stack of papers.

"When did this supposedly take place, Jim?"

"In 1990. And I believe my sources. It happened, there's no supposedly about it."

"Did this kind of thing happen more than once?"

"Several times. But I think we're talking about the wrong thing. There's something more important."

"More important?" Grant asked incredulously. "Maybe it's just the nature of what you're telling me, the shock value, but it will be hard to top what you just said."

"I'm not talking about the specific things Franz has done. I can arrange for you to meet with an individual who had direct involvement in what went on at the morgue. I'm afraid you're

35

going to overlook a bigger question, why hasn't Dr. Franz been fired?"

"Hold on, Jim," Grant said, having trouble hiding his excitement. "I want to talk about this person with direct knowledge. Who is it and when can I meet him?"

Doyle smiled, "You didn't expect I'd be this much help did you? His name is Pat Murphy. He was the Director of Operations at the morgue from 1986 until late '91. He has first hand knowledge of about everything in those old stories. After you called me, I called him. He said that he'd be willing to talk with you if I felt this was going to be a serious investigation."

"Have you made that decision already?"

"The fact that you asked to see me, that you wanted the background information, impressed me. But I was more impressed that you didn't do the natural thing, go right to Johnson, Samuels and Porter. And if you had, I'd have been the first one to know about it, believe me. So, yes, I believe you're serious."

"I take that as a compliment, Jim, thanks. Why did Mr. Murphy leave the morgue and what's he doing now?"

"He got fired because he didn't agree with how Franz was running things. Officially, they abolished his position and put in a Morgue Administrator. That's a story in itself that Pat can tell you about. Anyway, Pat got a private investigators license last fall and opened a business called Forensic Investigations at 813 Hobart Street. He said he'll be in his office tomorrow morning if you'd like to stop by. Should I tell him to expect you?"

"I'll be there. I can call and tell him."

"I'll call him," Doyle said firmly.

Grant shrugged. "Okay with me. Jim, I don't want you to take offense at this, but I've got to ask. Do you or Murphy have a personal vendetta against Dr. Franz? Do you believe that your opinions, or those of your sources, are objective?"

"No offense taken. I'd have been disappointed if you hadn't asked. I have nothing personal against Dr. Franz. But, there are an awful lot of his activities that demand explanation. I believe that the previous and current allegations are substantially true. The county has investigated the morgue several times in response to the accusations contained in my stories. They've never found anything wrong. I have to wonder how hard they looked. No, there's no vendetta on my part. I just want to see the truth come out and let the chips fall where they may. I believe that Murphy and my other sources want the same thing. This is the first time that anybody other than the county has taken an interest. I think your involvement will generate a lot of enthusiasm, and cooperation."

"I take you at your word, Jim. Now, what's this 'more important' matter that you wanted to talk about?"

Doyle leaned forward in his chair, elbows on his knees. "What do you know about the politics in this county?"

"Strong Republican. That's all I know and all I care to know. I'm sorry, Jim, but I don't want to get involved in that stuff. My investigation is going to be confined to Franz and the morgue."

"I said I was afraid you'd miss the point, and you are. Franz is an appointed county official, the morgue is a county facility. Like it or not, you are investigating the county. You can't separate them. The best thing I can do for you is to give you the political lay of the land. If you don't take that into consideration you'll be in for a lot of grief, and maybe even failure."

Grant thought Doyle's words over for a few moments. He had no experience investigating a public official. Grudgingly, he had to admit that Doyle was right. Linda had said as much when she first told him about the case.

"I've got to agree with you, Jim, as much as I don't want to. Go ahead, educate me."

Doyle smiled, obviously looking forward to his task. "You were right, this is a Republican county. But the situation here would apply when either party has been entrenched for so many years. I want to concentrate on the office of county executive, but let me say first, in general, that whoever gets the republican nomination for any county office is virtually a shoo in."

"Now for the county exec," Doyle went on. "He's 'The Man'. Nothing happens in this county without his approval. When he tells a department head or legislative committee chair to jump, they ask 'how high?'. When Franz was hired the exec was Anthony Barone. You've heard of him I presume?"

"Certainly, Jim. I've lived in this county all my life, except when I was in the service and when I was based out of Albany from '86 until last December. It's just that politics isn't my bag. I don't follow it, I'm not interested in it."

"I understand. Politics doesn't interest everybody. At any rate, Barone was sixty coming into the '90 election. He'd already served three terms. He was going to do one more and retire, turn the reins over to his protege, Ronald Bronson."

"He's the exec now, right?" Grant asked.

"Right you are. Anyway, Barone was diagnosed with prostate cancer a few months before the election. Things didn't look good for him. He considered turning things over to Bronson then. But Bronson didn't wait for him to make a decision. I guess he didn't want to leave things to chance. Bronson's people made their move while Barone was undergoing initial treatment. He was weak physically and politically. A lot of Barone's supporters didn't want to jump ship, they didn't like Bronson's methods. But Barone's future was too uncertain, they ended up going with Bronson. Barone was thrown over, too tired to put up much of a fight."

"This is all very interesting, but I don't see what it has to do with Franz," Grant commented.

"I'm getting to that, bear with me. Anyway, Barone survived. Some say it was his hatred for Bronson that kept him going. Now he plans to take the nomination for next years election away from him. From what I hear he'll do it too.

"Now for the connection with Franz. The first allegations against him came during the Barone regime. Every time something came up Barone ordered some type of investigation or audit. As I said earlier, nothing was ever found. Many of us assumed that when Bronson took over things would be different. They aren't. Bronson backs him as solidly as Barone."

"Maybe they're just loyal to their appointees," Grant ventured.

"Running a county this size is a business, a big business," Doyle said, shaking his head. "In the private sector a manager with Franz's baggage would have been gone a long time ago. Here he never gets so much as a reprimand. Why? Why would two different county execs, who are arch enemies, both protect this guy? I think the question you're going to have to answer at some point is why is Bob Franz untouchable?"

"Do you know the answer to that, Jim?"

"Let's say I have a theory."

"I'd like very much to hear it."

"Okay," Doyle smiled, obviously pleased. "Barone and Bronson go way back, to when they were both county legislators. Bronson is ten years younger than Barone. I don't want to say that they had a father and son relationship. But they were very close, Barone treated Bronson as a younger brother. Barone was a mover and shaker with plans to move up the political ladder. He taught Bronson the ropes, and he was an eager student."

"Were you following politics when this was going on? I didn't think you were old enough."

"No, no," Doyle blushed. "When I became interested in this I did my homework. I talked with some former legislators who had served with them, and a few of the reporters who had been around for a while. I'm comfortable that my scenario is accurate. Anyway, a lot of wheeling and dealing went on over the years, especially back in the old 'smoke filled room' days. There is pretty much unanimous agreement among my contacts that palms were greased and favors were given. Rumors circulated from time to time about mob associated trash haulers getting county permits and contracts. There was also speculation that some campaign funds may not have been appropriately handled or recorded."

Doyle paused to catch his breath, then continued. "Based on that, I believe that Barone and Bronson know too much about each other for either to talk, kind of a standoff. Whatever got Franz his clout is something between him and Barone. Bronson can't afford to take the chance of dumping Franz and teeing Barone off any further."

"You said that Barone already hates him," Grant interrupted. "Why not get rid of Franz now to avoid any potential embarrassment, and see what happens?"

"Right now Barone is out to do a political hatchet job. If Bronson goes over the edge of what is considered acceptable political conduct, like reneging on a deal made by the very popular Barone, he could end up in legal trouble. Somebody like me could start getting anonymous calls about past conduct, maybe alleging criminal activity. And, especially now, with election time approaching, Bronson needs to look like a good old boy. He's got to stand by his man."

"I'm going to have to digest all this before I can discuss it intelligently. I'm sure I'll have more questions then. Will you be willing to get together again?"

"Certainly. I'll cooperate any way I can, within reason."

"Well, thanks for coming, Jim. You've been very helpful."

Both men stood up. Grant walked Doyle to the exit. "Thanks again, Jim. I'll be in touch," Grant said, extending his hand.

"Thank you, John. I'm glad you're in this. I wish you luck. You're going to need it."

CHAPTER FIVE

Grant arrived in front of 813 Hobart Street at 9:30 Saturday morning. Week-end traffic had been light. Although it was chilly, the appearance in the sky of a bright late winter sun had made the drive pleasant.

The building housing Forensic Investigations was a two story house, gray with burgundy trim. The bottom floor had been converted to office space, the upper floor was an apartment. Grant stopped at the door and checked his reflection in the window glass. He was wearing a navy blue sport jacket, white shirt, with dark blue slacks and tie, no overcoat. He had a pen and some business cards in his inside jacket pocket. He carried no briefcase or writing pad.

Satisfied with his appearance, he followed the "Please Walk In" instructions stenciled on the door. Inside, he found himself in a large room with three desks, a computer table and file cabinets. The two desks nearest him were unoccupied. Sitting at the desk against the opposite wall, phone to his ear, was the rooms only other occupant. This was presumably Pat Murphy.

Grant didn't advance any further, waiting for an acknowledgment from Murphy. He received only a stare as Murphy continued his phone conversation.

While waiting, Grant looked around the room. The desks and file cabinets were definitely not new. The walls were bare except for a large calendar and a framed PI license. There were no plants or flowers, no decorations. No sign of a woman's touch. Grant surmised that Murphy was either unmarried or had a wife who wasn't involved with the business. He also suspected that Murphy was struggling to get his new business off the ground.

He turned his gaze back toward Murphy. He found Murphy's eyes still on him. While he had been sizing up the room, he himself was being analyzed.

A few seconds later Murphy hung up the phone, got out of his chair and headed toward Grant. Murphy was five feet nine with an average build. Forty-six years old, his hair was dark brown with no evidence of gray. He was wearing a red flannel shirt and blue jeans. About half way across the room his face broke into a wide grin. "I'll bet you're John Grant," he said, extending his hand. "I'm Pat Murphy. Welcome to my humble establishment."

Grant liked him instantly. His smile was so warm and friendly it required a smile in response. Grant took a couple of steps forward to meet him. "Pleased to meet you, Pat," Grant said as they shook hands. He then handed Murphy his business card.

"Could you stand a cup of coffee, John?" Grant smiled his appreciation and nodded. "Good. Follow me," Pat said. He locked the door and led Grant across the room, past his desk and down a hallway. In a few feet they reached a room that had been a kitchen during days gone by. It still had a stove, refrigerator, sink and table. But a file cabinet and storage boxes on the floor eliminated a completely home like atmosphere. The smell of recently brewed coffee stirred Grant's taste buds. Murphy motioned Grant to a chair at the table. He then poured two cups and took a seat opposite Grant.

"Before we get started I'd like to tell you a couple of things about me and then ask you a question or two, okay?" Pat asked.

"Absolutely," Grant answered. "Shoot."

"As you know, I've spoken with Jim Doyle about you. He suggested that I meet with you to provide some background information and leads for your investigation. Jim thinks you're serious about this, and that we should take advantage of someone, other than the county, finally taking an interest in the morgue. I respect his judgment, and I know you're concerned about my motivation. I believe that Dr. Franz has done things that are not ethical or legal. In fact, I helped him by my own acts and omissions. Other than wanting the truth to come out, and maybe cleanse my own soul, I have no agenda. Now, and I realize it's early on and what you say will be speculation, do you have an investigative plan and how broad is your authority?"

"Before we get into that, Pat, I'd like to clarify something. You said you'll provide me with background and leads. Quite candidly, from what you and Jim have said, you have direct personal knowledge of events at the morgue. It's very probable that at some point I'll ask you for a sworn written statement. And, depending how things work out, you might have to testify at a hearing. Are you prepared to go that far?"

"I'm sorry for the misunderstanding, John, I thought Jim had told you. You see, after I was canned, I sued the county for improper dismissal. We reached an out of court settlement. As part of the deal I'm prohibited from talking publicly about Dr. Franz and the morgue. I think they call it a gag order. If I violate it, I could have to pay back the financial settlement plus a penalty. Franz could sue me on top of that. I can't take that chance, as much as I'd like to. That money is all that's keeping me afloat right now, and keeping my ex wife off my back. I'm sorry."

"I see," Grant said dejectedly. "I can appreciate the position you're in, but it's certainly a set back for my investigation."

"I assume DOH has a legal department. If they can figure a way around this, I'll go the whole route."

Grant's spirits brightened a little. "Yes, we have a Division of Legal Affairs, known as DLA. I'll mention this to them. I'll ask one of the attorneys to give you a call, maybe they'll be able to come up with something, okay?"

"Fine with me, John. I'll keep my fingers crossed."

"Now, Pat, the answer to your first question will depend a great deal on what you have to tell me today. We can talk about that before I leave. As for the second question, I have very broad powers, including subpoena power, under the authority of the commissioner. The department does administrative actions only, and I have no police powers, however."

"What if your investigation uncovers evidence of a crime?"

"We'd refer the information to a prosecutor, the attorney general or the local DA. Usually they go to the DA."

"Even if the target is a county official and the DA has already come out publicly in support of him?"

"I've never run into this situation before, Pat. I can't answer you," Grant said, shrugging his shoulders.

"I guess that's clear enough. Okay, John, let's get started. What do you want to know?"

"I'd like you to give me a little bit of your personal background, then I have some specific questions I want to ask."

"Let's see, I'm a native of this area, born in Syracuse. I've lived around here all my life, except from 1972 to '83. I was in Illinois during that period. I went to school there, got married and opened my own business, Murphy Funeral Home. My marriage failed and so did my business. I moved back here and worked for a couple of funeral homes. In early '86 I heard that the new ME, Dr. Franz, was very aggressive and planned to expand the morgue operation. That appealed to me. I put in an application, hoping to get in on the ground floor. Franz apparently liked what he saw and what I had to say. Within a few weeks after my first interview I was hired for a brand new position, Director of Operations. Franz and I were a great team for the first couple of years. Then he started to change, gradually at first. He still wanted to expand, but it became clear to me he was building his own empire, and he didn't care how he did it. We began to have major disagreements over the way he chose to do things. I had less and less input, less involvement, until my job was finally abolished in '91. That about covers it."

"Thanks, Pat. I think that's sufficient for now. Next I'd like to ask you some questions based on the articles that Jim Doyle has written about the morgue over the past three and a half years. There are six of them I believe. Jim indicated that you will have a good deal of knowledge regarding the things he reported. As we discuss them we can talk about whether the various activities were common occurrences or isolated incidents. Does that sound reasonable to you?"

"That makes perfect sense, but before we do that I've got another question for you. May I?"

"Be my guest," Grant invited.

"Jim told me that the only thing that concerned him about his meeting with you yesterday, was that you didn't take a note, not one note. Now you're here today, on what you said is an important interview, and I don't see any writing materials. You want to ask me questions about old newspaper stories, but you apparently didn't bring them to refer to. What gives?"

Grant gave a nervous laugh. "I took all kinds of notes yesterday, mental notes. I read the articles last night and I know what each one says. I'm not saying I can recite them verbatim, but I know their content sufficiently to ask you questions about them. As far as this morning, I'll be able to leave here and write a comprehensive report of this interview. I've been blessed with an excellent memory."

Pat gave a low whistle. "Wow! I envy you. I can't accurately remember what I did yesterday." One look at the concern on Grant's face told him he'd hit a home run. "I'm only kidding, John, only kidding," he said, raising his hands in the air, palms out. "I'm satisfied, please continue."

"That was a gotcha," Grant admitted with a smile. "Okay, Pat, the first story was from September of 1989. It had to do with anonymous allegations of the illegal removal of body parts. Franz was supposedly taking tissues and organs from dead bodies and providing them for research projects, without the knowledge or consent of the next of kin. The Dalton B. Crowne Memorial Hospital and Research Center, right here in Utica, was named as recipient. Franz and the county denied the allegations, so did Crowne. Is it true?"

"One hundred percent accurate. But there was more, he was providing tissue to one or two pharmaceutical companies too. They may not have been in the picture when this story appeared, though. Anyway, Crowne was first and foremost. Do you want to hear more?"

"Yes, all of it," Grant answered. "You're an investigator, Pat, a good one, I'm sure. You know the kind of details that I'll need to build my case. Please tell me anything you think is important."

"I hope you've got some time, I have a feeling we're going to be here a while," Pat said as he got up to refill their coffee cups.

"I've got all the time it will take. I want to do this right, there's no need to hurry."

"Well, as I said earlier, Bob started to change around the first part of '89, it may have been around March or April, I can't be exact. He had always disagreed with the laws relating to the requirements for obtaining research tissue. He feels that a dead body should be used to benefit the living. If a new drug can be developed, new ways to treat diseases, then the state should be able to take what it wants from the body without the consent of the deceased or family. He was very candid about his feelings, but he had never acted on them before. At any rate, around that time he became more bold. He went beyond talking and started doing."

"Excuse me, Pat," Grant cut in. "I had intended to just let you talk until you were finished and then ask questions. I don't think that will work, my curiosity has already gotten the best of me. Is it all right with you if I butt in once in a while, I'll try to keep the interruptions to a minimum?"

"Please do, John. I agree with you that this has to be done right. If you have questions, ask them anytime. I won't mind a bit."

"I'll do that, Pat, thanks. How did you first become aware that he was taking tissue for research? How did you know it was without consent?"

"I received a handwritten note from Dr. Franz stating that he was to be notified whenever we had a deceased, eighteen years old or under. I didn't understand the reason for that so I talked with him about it. He told me that he was assisting someone with a project that required testicles, bladders, urethras, prostates and vaginas from that age group. I didn't like the sounds of it, so I questioned him about it. He got very defensive, then mad. He told me not to worry about it, there would be no extra work for morgue staff, he'd do everything himself. My only responsibility was to make sure he was contacted when someone meeting that criteria was brought in. The consent issue was more of a suspicion at that point. I didn't know for sure until I started investigating, but that was much later."

"What about the other pathologists, Johnson and Samuels, were they involved in the tissue removal?"

"No, Franz did everything personally. If one of the others was handling the case, he'd do the removal between the time they had finished and when the body was released. They probably heard rumors about what he was doing but, as far as I know, they weren't involved. Something else you should know, is that Samuels and Johnson were new at that time. They'd only been on since the first of the year. Prior to that Franz did it all himself. He'd call in someone from another county if he got in a bind temporarily, other than that he was a one man show."

"But the morgue is an around the clock operation, Pat. Are you saying that he didn't take any time off, no vacations?"

"The morgue is Bob Franz's life. You could find him there at all hours. When he's there he's in his element, outside he's like a fish out of water. It's important that you understand that."

"What about his personal life? He must have a wife or girlfriend, right?"

"Yes, both. He's married, very unhappily, and he's been banging one of the morgue case investigators since a couple of months after he was hired. But, I'd suggest we save that for later. I don't want to lose my train of thought."

"Certainly, Pat. Go ahead."

"Franz did as he said. He came in whenever necessary and did what he had to do. Other than calling or paging him, there was no extra work involved for the rest of us. Let me correct myself, we sometimes had to call a guy from Crowne to pick the stuff up. Franz had the specimens preserved in gross jars, enclosed in brown paper bags. The donors were identified by a piece of paper containing the autopsy number, date of birth and date and cause of death. No names were used. Because that age group comprised a small percentage of our total cases, there weren't pick-ups on a daily basis. There might be three in a week, or none for a couple of weeks."

"I've got two questions, Pat. Did you happen to save the handwritten note from Franz, or any other related memos, and do you remember who the courier from Crowne was?"

"I didn't save the note, I saw no reason to at the time. There weren't any other memos that I know of. The guy from Crowne was a Lewis Marner. I think he had the title of research assistant."

"And you're positive that he was from Crowne?"

"Sure, we had two numbers for him. One was at Crowne, the other was a pager. I personally called or paged him many times. I used to look in the bags before he picked them up. There is no doubt as to who he was or what he was after."

"Did any of the other morgue workers ever call Marner?"

"Yes, Bill Maxwell, he was the morgue superintendent, and Steve Thompson, case investigator. And I'm sure Franz called him on his own sometimes."

"How long did this relationship with Crowne last?"

"It was still going on when I left in '91."

"Are you on good terms with Maxwell and Thompson? Can you call them to find out what's going on now?"

"I'm on good terms with them, but they're no longer there either. If you questioned Bob Franz, or disagreed with him, your career prospects were not good."

"I see," Grant said. "You mentioned pharmaceutical companies, what do you remember about them?"

"I believe there was an outfit called Acme Pharmaceuticals, out of Pennsylvania. There may have been another one, but I'm not sure. Franz handled this Acme guy personally."

"Then how do you know about Acme?"

"The door to the morgue is always locked at night and on week-ends. I was in doing some work on a Sunday, Franz was in too. The buzzer rang and I answered the door. There was a guy there who wanted to see Franz. I made him give me his name and affiliation before I'd call Franz. While he waited for Franz to come and get him he complained about the construction work on Rte. 81 coming up from Pennsylvania. Another funny thing was the visitors log. There is a shelf attached to the wall just inside the door. A visitors log book is kept on that shelf, and all visitors have to sign in. That's a morgue policy. When Franz showed up to get the guy, I told him the fella hadn't signed in yet. Those two looked at each other for a second, then Franz said he didn't have to sign in. Then Franz and he took off toward the autopsy room. The guy left about ten minutes later carrying a good size plastic bag that looked about half full."

"Was it a plastic trash bag? How do you know there was tissue in it?" Grant wanted to know.

"I think it was a trash bag. Not the real big ones, a kitchen size, one of those thirteen gallon capacity jobs. I don't know for sure that there was tissue in it. But what else makes sense? The guy's from a pharmaceutical company, very reluctantly identifies himself, doesn't have to sign in, goes in the autopsy room and leaves with this plastic bag. I can't think of anything else that could have been going on." "You certainly make a convincing argument," Grant conceded. "Can you be more precise as to when this went on and how long it lasted? And do you think this stuff came from kids also?"

"It was in '89, but as I think back it was later in the year, probably around late summer. As far as I know, it stopped just before I left in '91. This couldn't have been from kids, there was too much of it. There is apparently a market for research tissue from donors of all ages."

"What was in this for Franz? Do you think he was selling the stuff?"

"I honestly don't know, John. I don't believe that Bob Franz is driven by the need for money. He has a large ego that is fed by

49

recognition. He requires respect and admiration from his peers. And a lot of these scientific types think like he does, laws and regulations are for other people. But I can't rule out a financial incentive."

"When did you start checking into the consent matter?"

"Around the same time as he began taking the tissue he started demanding that staff get signed donation forms from next of kin in every case. And this was a hot item, believe me. He personally instructed everyone on how to get the forms signed. You couldn't take no for an answer, at least not the first no. He demanded that you ask at least three times. Heaven help you if you didn't. And it worked, grieving people can be manipulated. You tell them that their loved one, even in death, can help others, maybe save someone's life. It gets them, it really does. The trouble was, we had the people sign forms from the

Red Cross and the Eye Bank. They thought that's who was getting the tissue, they didn't know it was going to Crowne or Acme. They didn't know that at some point someone might turn a handsome profit based on research done on that tissue. And, as you pointed out, they didn't know that the tissue itself might possibly be sold."

Grant was beginning to feel slightly nauseated. "Can we take a little break, Pat, I'd like to stretch my legs. When we resume let's move on to the next story. We can talk more about this later."

"Sure thing, John," Pat said with a knowing smile. "I've got a couple of calls to make anyway. Go out and stretch and get some air. We'll start again when you're ready."

CHAPTER SIX

Grant stood outside of Pat's office for five minutes collecting his thoughts. He didn't like the way he was reacting to what Pat was telling him, and he was trying to understand why. It had to be because of Kim, he concluded. Kim was his step daughter, she had been killed in a car accident in 1986 at the age of eighteen. The accident had occurred in Franklin County, in the northern part of the state. But suppose Franz had been in business in Franklin County back then? She would have met his "criteria". Yes, that was it. Franz's attraction to dead kids had hit close to home.

After coming to grips with the problem he felt much better. The cool air had also helped to invigorate him. He took another deep breath of that fresh air and went back inside. It was time to ask about the cremation that didn't happen.

Grant asked that question as soon as he and Pat had settled back in at the break room table. Pat didn't seem anxious to answer. "I made some fresh coffee while you were out, join me?" he asked instead. After the coffee was poured and Pat was back in his chair, Grant tried a different approach.

"Look, Pat, we've got to have a great deal of trust in each other in order for this to work. You've got to know that I won't disclose your cooperation. I've got to know that you won't let anything I tell you get back to Franz, either directly or indirectly. I'm prepared to move forward with that trust, are you?"

"You've got it wrong, John. It isn't that I don't trust you, it's my involvement in this particular thing that is tough for me to talk about."

Grant leaned forward slightly, looking into Pat's eyes, "I was uncomfortable discussing some of the tissue stuff, and I know you sensed that." Grant briefly explained about Kim. "I've already come to the conclusion that there will be a lot of things

51

I'm going to hear that I won't like, but I can't, I won't, let that stop me. I'm sure you feel the same way, right?"

"Yes, I do. Right now I guess I'm concerned about your opinion of me. I'm not proud of what I'm going to tell you. I hope you won't be too harsh in your judgment."

Grant sat back in his chair, laughing. "I'm sorry, Pat. It's just that the thought of me judging you strikes me funny. God knows that I've made my share of mistakes in my life, done a number of things I'm not proud of either. So, please, you have nothing to be concerned about."

Pat smiled his thanks. "You missed your calling, John. You should be a politician. You seem to have a talent for saying the right thing at the right time. Okay, let's get back to Mr. Chambers."

"This story ran in August of '90. It said that an unidentified body that should have been cremated, was actually defleshed by scalpel and boiling, and the skeleton kept at the morgue. You say that this did happen and it was a guy named Chambers?"

"Yes, it did happen, and I set it up."

"Go on, Pat," Grant urged gently. "I need to know exactly what happened."

"It was early in '90, February, I think. We got a call that a man had been found dead in his apartment by the manager. The deceased was sixty-eight years old and had been in poor health. Because it was an unattended death it became an ME case. Franz and I went out to pick up the body, the cops were there too. But there was absolutely no indication of foul play. From what we found in the apartment, and interviews with the manager and neighbors, we learned a lot about Mr. Lyle B. Chambers.

"He was originally from Arkansas. He had moved up here in the early eighties, after his wife left him. He was collecting a veteran's pension and social security, he never held a job here. He was a recluse and an alcoholic, smoked three packs a day. He had serious liver problems, but wouldn't accept treatment. He apparently had a death wish. His closest relative was a sister,

Willa Mae MacPhearson, living in Paragould, Arkansas. I'll never forget her, or her wonderful accent."

"Did you meet her in person?" Grant asked.

"No, we spoke by phone. Franz assigned me to do the notification. Her brother had been dead for a few days and it would have to be a closed casket wake. Franz told me to make sure I told her that. If she expressed any concern over funeral expenses, I was to offer a cremation at county expense. She'd just have to send us a notarized letter of authorization.

"I reached her on the first try. She was a very nice lady. She was obviously deeply saddened by the news, but didn't break down. She reflected for a few moments on her brother, his qualities and his problems, then we got down to business. She confirmed that she was the next of kin. I told her about the condition of the body and asked what arrangements she planned to make. She told me right up front that her brother didn't have any life insurance, he'd always told her to have him thrown in a manure pile. She said that she and her husband were on a fixed income and didn't have any room in their budget for an extra bill. She asked what I thought it would cost to have Mr. Chambers shipped back for burial. I told her that funerals were expensive, but she'd have to discuss prices with her local undertaker. Then I hit her with Franz's cremation offer.

"Now, you've got to remember, John, at that time I thought Franz was just being compassionate. I felt good about what I was doing. Mrs. MacPhearson went for the deal like a drowning person would grab a lifeline. She said that as long as she received his ashes, she'd be comfortable with her decision. I told her we'd need the notarized authorization. She wanted to know how to word it. Since I'd never done this before, I told her I'd get the wording and call her right back.

"I went to the autopsy room to tell Franz and find out what he wanted in the authorization. He and Bill Maxwell were just finishing up with Chambers. I'll never forget his reaction when I gave him the news. He waved his arm toward Chambers, 'Gentlemen, we have a keeper', he said with a big smile. That's when I first realized this was a scam and I was right in the middle of it. I couldn't have been any more stunned if Rocky Marciano had hit me with a roundhouse punch. I looked at Bill, he was in shock too. It took me a few seconds to regain my senses. I told him that he couldn't be serious. He said he was completely serious. As soon as we received the authorization from Mrs. MacPhearson he was going to order Bill to deflesh the skeleton and boil the bones clean. I told him that Mrs. MacPhearson was giving us permission to cremate her brother, not keep the body. Bill started to argue too, but Franz cut us off. He said he'd word the authorization to suit his purposes. He couldn't believe we were upset. We had been given a golden opportunity, he said, and he wasn't going to let it slip through his fingers."

Pat paused when Grant stood up. "It's getting warm in here," Grant explained. He removed his jacket and placed it over the back of his chair. His shirt was soaked. He sat back down, loosening his tie.

"Did he say why this was so important, what he was going to do with the skeleton?" Grant asked.

"Not right then. Things got pretty heated. He said that we weren't doing anything wrong, not to worry. But the bottom line was that he was the boss, and we'd do what he said. He told us later that he wanted skeletons from every race and gender. That maybe someday they'd be needed for study by someone, and he'd be in a position to supply them. I don't know if he really believed that. I do know that he visited a big ME's office one time, it might have been in the City or Los Angeles, I don't remember, and they had some kind of a bone collection. Franz was impressed and mentioned it when he got back. He referred to the collection as having 'toys'. Franz had big plans and I think he wanted his own toys, just like the big guys."

"So, how was this authorization worded?" Grant asked next.

"I don't remember it word for word, but it was directed to Dr. Franz. The key thing was that he put in a tissue donation consent. I do remember that part. It went like this, 'to remove any tissue for research that he deems appropriate'. In his opinion that included the whole body. She did it just the way he wanted and faxed it in within a couple of hours."

"But you promised her that she'd receive her brother's ashes. How did you handle that if nothing was cremated?"

"But something was cremated. I wasn't personally involved with that, so I can only make an educated guess. Mrs. MacPhearson may very well have the ashes of a stray dog we called Spot sitting on her mantel."

Grant studied Pat's face closely, looking for a sign that he was joking, there was none.

"You see, John, cops and conservation officers used to drop off dead animals, road kill, from time to time for incineration. Franz kept some of the smaller ones, cats, raccoons and dogs, and put them in the freezer. I believe that as Franz built his 'collection', these animals ended up going to the crematorium.

"Now, before you say that couldn't happen, listen to me," Pat said, holding up his right hand. "You've got to understand that when the funeral director picks up a cremation from the morgue, they grab the box, load it in the wagon and take it to the crematorium. They don't look inside and neither do the crematory people. If you put something in the box, a little weight, the container will go through the oven with no questions asked. Spot was a stray mutt that hung around there for a while. He disappeared around the same time we got Chambers. That may have just been coincidence. But I'd bet that some animal went to the oven in his place."

Grant just stared, trying to rationalize what he had been told. Could this be possible? According to Pat, it could, and it was. He found the very thought to be obscene.

"John! Talk to me," Pat said, snapping him out of his stupor.

"I've got to tell you, Pat, you've worked at the morgue, you've owned a funeral parlor and worked at others. You have dealt with death on a regular basis, I haven't. I hope you can appreciate how repulsive this is to me. It isn't that I don't believe you, I simply find this kind of thing hard to accept."

"I can understand how you feel, John. But what I'm telling you now is just the tip of the iceberg. If you plan to see this through, you had better get a thick skin, quick."

"What do you mean 'the tip of the iceberg'? How much worse can it get?"

"I mean that I'm guessing that there are hundreds of these tissue incidents, and a lot more bodies that didn't make it to the furnace or grave."

"How many are there, tissue cases and bodies?"

"I don't know the numbers. I'm not even sure Franz knows himself. When Franz realized that I didn't agree with him, he shut me out of those operations. The same with Bill. He surrounded himself with lackeys who did whatever they were told. The tissues, of course, left the morgue, but the skeletons are somewhere in that building."

Grant was silent for several seconds. Then he said, "I'd like to move on now, but first, it seems to me that you were operating under the direct orders of Dr. Franz. I don't know as you need to feel as bad about Chambers as you seem to."

"Good try, John, thanks. But after I realized what was going on I made the second call to Mrs. MacPhearson. The one that generated the authorization, without which, Franz may not have dared to keep Chambers. No, I knew what was going on and I made the call anyway. I can't blame that on Franz."

Grant couldn't think of anything to say, so he changed the subject. "I said Doyle had given me six stories. One of them was a follow-up to the tissue story, another related to complaints about the stench from bodies being boiled. Franz explained the boiling business away by saying that sometimes certain bones had to be saved in unsolved homicide cases. I believe that he said a rib may contain evidence of the knife used in a murder, for example. It would have to be saved to ID the murder weapon sometime in the future. You're saying that instead of a bone or two being boiled for evidentiary purposes, whole bodies were boiled for Franz's collection, right?"

"I'm not saying he never kept a bone for evidence, he did. That's part of running an MEs' office. I am saying that he was building a skeletal collection. The complaints about the stench arose from those activities."

"Then I think we've covered those subjects sufficiently for right now. Let's talk about the last two stories. One of which may not have any bearing on my investigation. First for the one that does, June Miller. Tell me about her, Pat."

Grant thought he saw Pat's eyes harden. "Not my favorite subject," Pat said, keeping his emotions out of his voice. "June Miller is a dream come true to a man like Franz. Loyal, dedicated and will do whatever it takes to protect her boss. Bill Maxwell and I used to call her the 'Iron Maiden', behind her back of course. I did a little checking on June when I heard she was being hired for a new position, Morgue Administrator. I knew right then that I was expendable. She came on in July, 1991, four months before my job was abolished. I think she was fifty-six at the time. She retired from the Marine Corps as a lieutenant colonel, an administrator. She enlisted and came up through the ranks, that's a tough road. She's tall, around five feet ten, silver gray hair and cold, slate gray eyes. She stands and walks ramrod stiff. I never saw her laugh, or even crack a smile.

"Anyway, she had been the chief administrator at Crowne for four years before Franz recruited her. She'd built a reputation for being ruthless and was very adept at dealing with troublemakers. Franz was having his troubles then with anonymous sourced stories making the newspaper, obviously with inside information. He needed someone exactly like her to clean house. Crowne agreed to let her waive giving them notice if she'd be allowed to work half time for them and half time for the county while they hired and trained a replacement. I think that took a couple of months. The county also agreed to let her remain on the books at Crowne as a 'special consultant'. This was an on call deal. They use her once in a while if they run into problems, like discrimination or sexual harassment complaints. I think she was involved in contract negotiations too.

"She showed up on the job like an avenging angel, she called a staff meeting the first day. She introduced herself and said that she was going to get to the bottom of the problems at the morgue one way or another. She said that anyone who wanted to confess something to her would have five business days to ask for a meeting. Under those circumstances a 'counseling session' might be sufficient to avoid stronger disciplinary action, namely dismissal. If she had to track down the culprit, or culprits, there would be no mercy. Four months later I was let go, Steve Thompson got it four months after me, and Bill Maxwell three months after Steve. June is very efficient, watch out for her."

"I will," Grant assured him, "I will. Now for the last story. This one is from November of '92. It said that a former morgue technician named Rodney Flowers, pleaded guilty to sodomy and sexual abuse charges in satisfaction of a twenty-six count indictment. All the charges involved sexual activity with young boys. Is there any reason for me to pursue this?"

"Not because he was a pedophile. But he was one of Franz's trusted people, he worked on the special projects. He's in state prison now, though. He won't be much good to you, I'm afraid."

Grant leaned forward, thinking, rubbing the tips of his fingers on his temples. "I guess we've covered about enough for one day. I'm going to have to visit the morgue at some point, I'd like you to tell me where I'll find the records of the tissue donations and the easiest way to locate the Chambers file."

Pat shook his head slowly. "I'm afraid there are no records of the tissue donations. Franz didn't keep a record of that stuff, at least not in the official files or logs. You'll need the morgue case number to get the Chambers file, and I don't know it, damn it!"

Grant was now shaking his head. "Pat, I have to prove specific incidents of this illegal tissue removal, I can't just allege that from '89 to '93 he took X number of tissues from X number of unnamed donors. DLA would laugh me out of the building. Help me!"

"I'm sorry, I'm only telling you the way it is."

"Wait a minute," Grant said, hope in his voice. "You said that Franz included ID information with the stuff Marner picked up. He apparently needed that information, why?"

Pat snapped his right thumb and index finger. "By God, John, you might be on to something. A researcher has to be able to substantiate his results. He'd have needed that data to justify his findings!"

"So I'll have to work backward. Start with Marner and match his records up with the morgue's. Is that the way you see it?"

"It's the only way I can think of, and it just might work."

Grant looked at his watch, quarter after twelve. "Pat, I know you were going to tell me about Franz's love life, but I'd just as soon save that for another time, I need to rest my brain right now. Do you mind?"

"I'm with you, let's pack it in."

They exchanged home phone numbers. Before leaving, Grant promised to call Pat on Monday, after he talked with DLA about the gag order.

Grant got in his car and headed for home. He had never been one to bring his work home with him, but this case was different. It was time that he told his wife about it, he was sure he'd need her support before this was over.

The Grant's lived in a three bedroom ranch on an acre of land in Verona. The kids were all gone now and Faith Grant had converted one of the bedrooms to a craft room. The original white aluminum siding had been replaced with tan vinyl last summer. Purchased in 1976, seven years of payments remained.

Grant parked in the driveway and went in the house. Faith was standing at the kitchen counter, cutting up vegetables for a salad. He grabbed a beer as he passed the refrigerator, walked up behind her and wrapped his left arm around her waist. "Hi," he said, nipping the back of her neck. Faith was five one, and cuddly. She also worked for the state, taking care of the mentally retarded at the developmental center in nearby Rome.

"Hi," she said laughing, tilting her head back to hide her exposed neck.

"I want to talk with you about the case I'm working on, got time now?"

"Sure, but before that, you've got to return a phone call. A guy named Pat Murphy called a couple of minutes ago, it sounded important. He's at his office."

Grant grabbed the handset from the kitchen wall phone and dialed. "Glad you called, John," Pat said. "I don't know why I didn't think of this while you were here. You can get the Chambers autopsy number off his death certificate. Just go to the Vital Statistics office in the basement of the county building. Tell them you need the death certificate for Lyle B. Chambers, died in 1990. They'll be able to find it for you. If you show your ID it probably won't cost you anything."

"That's great, Pat, thanks. Did you happen to think of anything else to help identify the tissue or body donors?"

"No, but I do have some other news. Dr. Johnson has gone out on disability. Said he hurt his back and neck lifting a body yesterday."

"Do you think he's really hurt, or was it a little too uncomfortable having to face Franz?"

"Could be either, or a combination, I don't know. Speaking of facing Franz, I'll tell you what happens when he gets really mad at someone he's speaking with."

"Go ahead, Pat."

"His face turns a deep red, almost purple. He gets right in his victims face, inches away. While he's hollering, his saliva sprays on the other person's face."

"Gross!" Grant exclaimed. "Why do people tolerate that? Why not just walk away, screw him?"

"Have you ever seen him, John?"

"Only from a distance."

"Well, he's got red hair and green eyes, and when he's mad the eyes take on a life of their own. They say a snakes eyes can hypnotize it's prey, so can Franz's."

60

Grant didn't believe that, but he kept his thoughts to himself. "Thanks again, Pat. I'll give you a ring on Monday."

Grant hung up and turned to find Faith staring at him. "Yes," he said, knowing what she was thinking, "I'm investigating the ME's office. There are allegations that the ME, Dr. Robert Franz, has taken research tissue illegally, and maybe some bodies too. It seems that he took most of the tissue from kids."

Faith studied his face for a moment. "Does it bother you, the kid thing I mean?" she asked.

"It did this morning when I heard about it. I'm under control now, though. But I may need to talk things over with you once in a while. There may be some media coverage, depending on how things go. Any problem?"

"I don't think so. But tell me about this research tissue, why is what he did illegal?"

"He took it without the permission of the next of kin. In this state, that permission is required."

"Let's leave the legal aspect for a minute. How about morally? Research leads to the development of drugs that save lives, or improve the quality of life for people. Does this Franz have a good enough reason to do what he's doing?"

Grant pondered her question for a few seconds. "I really don't know enough about it yet to answer you. But there is some possibility that he sold some of the tissue. If that's true, then moral justification is out the window. As far as research itself, you made a good point. Certainly it's necessary, but I don't buy into the idea that the next of kin should be excluded from deciding what happens to a loved ones body. And, agree or not, the law is the law."

"Well, it should be interesting. You can talk with me anytime you need too, I can handle it."

"Thanks," he said, giving her a hug. Maybe this wasn't going to be as bad as he had thought.

At 8:30 that Saturday night, Melvin Kemp was at work. He was sitting on a step stool in the middle stall of the morgue garage. As soon as he had come to work at three o'clock, he moved the station wagon out of the bay and set up a fifty-five gallon drum over a propane torch in its place. He used a hose to fill the drum three quarters full of water, then turned on the torch. He next went to the autopsy room and took the badly decomposed body of Mr. Willie Brown from the cooler. Kemp grabbed a scalpel and went to work.

By six o'clock he had incinerated the visceral material and put the remains of Mr. Brown in the caldron and started the new ventilation system. The exhaust fans roared, sucking out most of the unpleasant odors. The smell that remained was tolerable. A guy from Price Funeral Home had stopped by earlier and picked up Brown's cremation container. Unless some business came in, Kemp was looking forward to an easy night.

He barely heard Franz's voice on the speaker over the noise of the fans. "It's Dr. Franz, Melvin, I'm in the building." It was policy that anyone entering the building during off hours announce their presence.

In a few minutes Franz entered the garage and stood next to Kemp, both of them staring at the barrel. As if on cue, a skeletal hand rose from the froth, seemed to hang suspended for a moment, then slowly settled back into the drum.

Franz took this as a good sign. Acting as though the hand had appeared to greet him, he waved back. "See that, Melvin," he said with a laugh, "I sense that Mr. Brown is happy that we are going to keep him with us." Still laughing, he headed back into the building.

CHAPTER SEVEN

"This is incredible, absolutely incredible!" Linda Ludwig said. It was a few minutes past nine on Monday morning, Grant had just finished briefing her on his interview with Pat Murphy.

Grant was tilted back in his office chair, sipping on his second cup of coffee. He was pleased. There was no doubt that Linda was hooked on this case, just as he was.

"When are you going to find out about his love life?" she asked mischievously.

"This is a serious investigation, Linda, not a soap opera," he chided back.

"Oh, all right," she said in mock dejection. "Seriously, though, what are you going to do next?"

"As soon as I hear back from you about DLA, I'll call Murphy. I'm going to ask him for some background on the morgue staff, and that might include the sleazy sex you'd like to hear about. I'm also going to ask him to help me get an interview with Bill Maxwell. I'd like to talk with him before we do our morgue visit. Oh, and I've got to get the Chambers death certificate."

"Okay, I'll go up to DLA right now. I'm glad this gag order thing came up. I think we should have DLA involved early on anyway. This is a perfect excuse to get them in. I'll call you back as soon as I can."

As Grant hung up his phone, Dr. Robert Franz was escorting June Miller into his morgue office. He shut the door and motioned her to take a chair. He walked around his desk and sat facing her. "June, we need to decide how we're going to get rid of our remaining personnel problems. As far as I'm concerned, if we can find a way to rid ourselves of Johnson and Samuels we'll be home free. Do you agree?"

"As far as you've gone, yes. But I think we may have one more problem beside them."

"What! Another one? Who?"

"Please don't get overly upset, Robert," Miller said, in a tone one would use to counsel a child. "I don't know for sure that there is another problem. It's just a feeling I have, that's all."

"Tell me who you think it is," Franz ordered.

"I'd rather not say anything more right now. If I mention a name it may effect how you treat this person, and it's possible that I'm wrong. I just wanted you to be aware that there is that possibility."

Franz backed off on his demand for the name. "Well, keep on top of your suspicions. If there is an additional problem, I want it taken care of right away, clear?"

"Yes, doctor. Now, about Samuels and Johnson. I think that Samuels is the most dangerous."

"Why?" Franz asked. "Johnson is the ring leader. He arranged that press conference. He's after me with a vengeance."

"That's all true, but Johnson's very venom will work against him. People will get tired of hearing him make these same accusations whenever he can get access to a microphone or camera. They'll start to think he's a nut, a disgruntled employee, just like you've said. He'll lose his credibility with the public and the media."

"Even with my friend Doyle? He's made me his pet project."

"Maybe not with him personally, but Mr. Doyle has editors. They won't continue to print stuff the readers have lost interest in. We can get rid of Johnson after he's been on disability for a while, but we can't shut him up. He'll end up discrediting himself, trust me. I'm more concerned with Dr. Samuels. I think he has a different motivation," she hesitated, waiting to see if she had captured Franz's interest.

"Well, what is it?" he asked, obviously agitated.

Miller smiled to herself in satisfaction. "I'm afraid Dr. Samuels wants your job. He's walking a fine line right now, he needs you gone, yet he can't incur the wrath of the county in
trying to get rid of you."

"He already has!" Franz hollered, pounding his right fist on the top of his desk. "Don't you think his appearance at that press conference took care of that?"

"Possibly," she said calmly. "But I found out that he sent a letter of apology to Ronald Bronson the day after the conference. He said he may have acted without thinking of the possible embarrassment to the county. He claimed that his motives were honorable, however. His only concern is that the morgue is operated in a manner above reproach. He sent a copy to Dr. Massey."

"He did?" Franz asked, obviously surprised. "I hadn't heard. Do you think that will work?"

"I don't know. He had to take the chance, though. I think he went along with Johnson to get the ball rolling, I bet we won't hear any more out of him, at least not directly. My concern is that he's still working here in this building. He can see and hear things. He can pass that information on to others, Johnson and Doyle, for example."

Franz's face darkened as Miller talked. He was now in a full blown rage. "I want that son of a bitch out of here!" he said, again pounding his desk. "Do you hear me? Do you understand me, June?"

"Yes, doctor," she said, "I'm working on it. In fact, I was reviewing his personnel file when I found a copy of that letter. We've got to be very careful though. Dr. Samuels has never run his own office, he's sixty-one, this will probably be his last opportunity. Our reason for terminating him will have to be solid, because he will challenge us on it. For that reason, this may take some time. You'll have to be patient."

Franz had regained his composure. "Okay, June, I'll be patient, but not too patient. I want these trouble makers gone."

Linda called Grant just before noon. "We've got an attorney assigned to us. Do you know George Epstein?"

"Never heard of him," Grant replied.

"I've never worked with him," Linda said, "but I have heard some good things about him. He's been around for a few years, he knows the law and, just as important, what you have to do to satisfy department politics."

"I don't like that word," Grant interrupted. "I'm probably going to have to deal with 'politics' here in Utica. Are you saying that politics will be a factor in Albany too?"

"I'm talking about office politics," Linda explained. "You know that the department tends to be pretty liberal in enforcement matters. I only meant that George will know what buttons need to be pushed, the 'hot buttons', if you will."

"Good, I feel better," Grant said. Linda didn't say anything, the silence made him uncomfortable. "Is there something else?"

"Well," Linda said hesitantly, "George did express a concern about Dr. McAree. Do you know who he is?"

"No, should I?"

"He's a deputy commissioner. He was hired the first part of last year to be the liaison with the parties the department regulates. There had been complaints from time to time that the deck was stacked against them. The commissioner thought that having a neutral person to handle grievances would allay those concerns. George seems to think that Dr. McAree is not really neutral, he is biased against us, especially when the complainant is an MD. George thinks that this is the kind of case that McAree may end up involved in, at the request of Oneida County."

"Great!" Grant said, disgust in his voice.

"Now don't get all worked up yet," Linda said, in a soothing voice. "Let's wait and see what happens. If he becomes a problem, we'll deal with it then."

"I'd just as soon you wouldn't have told me about this," Grant said.

"Do you really mean that?" Linda asked.

Grant thought about it for a few seconds. "No, I guess not. I suppose I'd rather know now, than have McAree pop up half way through the investigation."

"Good," Linda said, relieved. "That's what I figured too. As I said, don't worry about that now. We'll cross that bridge if we come to it."

"Okay, Linda. Let's get back to Epstein, is he going to call Murphy?"

"He's going to call you first to introduce himself and get Murphy's number. He wants to meet in person after you've been to the morgue. He's really interested in this case."

"All right, I'll call Murphy. Talk with you later."

As soon as Grant hung up he dialed Pat's office. A pleasant female voice answered. She said Pat was in, but busy. He left a message.

Grant had barely returned the handset to the cradle, when the phone rang. It was George Epstein. "It's a pleasure to speak with you, John, I've heard a lot of very flattering things about you."

"I guess Linda does like my work," Grant said modestly.

"It's not just Linda, You've earned a reputation in DLA as being a top notch investigator. The lawyers who have handled your cases really like your work."

"Well, thank you,", Grant said, embarrassed. "I've heard good things about you too. But I suppose you called to talk about Pat Murphy's problem?"

"Yes. This kind of thing will actually be handled by the AG, not us. I'll get the basic info and pass it on to them in an official referral. After that, I'll stay involved as kind of a middle man, to make sure everything gets done in a timely manner."

"What kind of time are we talking about?"

"Oh, probably three or four months," Epstein answered, matter of factly.

"Three or four months?" Grant groaned. "This case will be over by then. I'd like to be able to get Murphy on record during the investigation."

"Sorry, John. That's the way these things go. Papers have to be prepared and filed, the other side has to be given an opportunity to respond and a hearing has to be scheduled.

Allowing for a couple of adjournments, you're talking about that kind of time."

"Wonderful," Grant muttered. "So I had better only figure on Murphy as a source for leads, with no on the record involvement?"

"That's what I suggest. If things go more quickly, it will be a bonus for us. Look at it that way."

"Okay, George. Do you have any other uplifting news?"

Epstein laughed. "No. Give me Murphy's number and I'll give him a call."

Grant provided the number. "Give me a chance to talk with him first, will you? I'd like to tell him you'll be contacting him."

"Sure. How long do you want me to wait?"

"I'm expecting to hear from him any time now. Give me an hour, okay?"

"No problem, John. I'll be in touch."

Pat called twenty minutes later. Grant advised him to expect a call from Epstein, he didn't tell him how long it might take to get the gag order lifted. "While I've got you on the line, Pat, I'd like to ask you a favor."

"What is it?"

"I'd like to talk with Bill Maxwell. You said you're on friendly terms with him, will you call him and grease it for me?"

"I'd be glad to. But I'll tell you right up front, Bill is real sour on these investigations of Franz. He's been interviewed by the county attorney's office a couple of times in the past. Nothing has ever happened as a result of it. The last time we talked about it, he said he was washing his hands of it. But I will call him and see what he says."

"I appreciate that, Pat. While we're on that subject, what was your impression of the county investigations?"

"Shams! No question about it. The attorneys and investigators involved were probably capable enough. I think they were on a short leash, though. They just went through the motions."

"Any idea why?"

"That's the sixty-four dollar question, and I don't know the answer."

"Maybe we'll find out before this is over. Before I let you go, I'd like you to give me some background on the morgue employees, where their loyalties are, who might or might not be cooperative. Have you got time?"

"Yes, I do. Where would you like to start?"

"Well, I guess it's pretty obvious where Johnson, Samuels and Porter are coming from. You've already told me about Miller. Let's start with this woman Franz is having an affair with."

"Fine," Pat said. "But first I want to mention what I think of Samuels, Johnson and Porter. Johnson is just about what he seems, a crusader. If he believes in a cause, he'll go to the wall with it, do whatever it takes. That makes him a little dangerous. His desire to get Franz may effect his truthfulness. I don't know Porter very well, he actually works in the lab, on the fourth floor of the county building. I think he's a bit like Johnson, but not a leader. I don't know about his veracity. Samuels is kind of the opposite. He is definitely not a Franz man. But I think he's much more calculating, less emotional, than the other two. His cooperation will be based on what's best for him, not what's worst for Franz."

"I see," Grant said. "I'll keep that in mind if, and when, I interview them, thanks"

"Now remember, I'm not saying they don't have valuable information, I'm sure they do. I'm only suggesting that you corroborate what they tell you, especially Johnson."

"I understand, Pat."

"Now, for the others. Other than clerical help, there is one full time female employee. Her name is Marcia Longo, she's in her early thirties, and a good looker. Medium length dark brown hair, pretty face, and bumps in all the right places. She's never been married that I know of. She had worked part time under the previous regime. Franz hired her full time in February of '85, right after Bill Maxwell. According to what I heard around the office Franz started to bed her around the same time. I know they were certainly an item when I came on the scene in '86. Her relationship with Franz caused a certain amount of animosity among some of the guys. Marcia got the best schedule, went on field trips with Franz, was sent to seminars, stuff like that. But nobody dared bitch too loud. You can guess what kind of cooperation you'll get from her."

"What about Franz's wife, does she know what's going on?"

"Yes, she's known almost since it began. Back when I first started, Franz and I were pretty close. Many times we sat around the break room at night and talked about our private lives, my ex, and his current. He admitted that he's always had a problem keeping it in his pants. He even said that it isn't a matter of sex. It's more of an ego thing, he needs the conquest.

"Anyway, Ione, that's his wife, is a real nice looking lady herself. I've seen her a few times. She's around Franz's age, but attractive. She caught him in several affairs when they lived in Florida. Each time he whined and cried, begged for another chance. He didn't really care that much about her, I think he's only capable of loving himself, but having a wife gave the impression of stability. That's important to a man looking to move up in the world."

"Any kids?" Grant asked.

"None, they'd have been a drag on his career. When they moved from Florida, Ione told him it was a fresh, and last, chance. The rest, as they say, is history. He didn't want a divorce for appearances sake. She agreed to continue their marriage, at least on paper, in return for a financial incentive. His paychecks go to her, she gives him a small allowance for spending money, twenty dollars a week, the last I heard. She pays all expenses, including buying Franz what he needs, personal items and clothes once in a while. The rest of the loot is hers, to do with as she pleases. He doesn't know and can't ask, that's the price he agreed to pay to keep a wife."

"After paying all the bills, is there that much left for her?" Grant asked.

"I think she makes out pretty well. Let's see, he gets seventy-two thousand a year now, they bought an old farm out in Deerfield, paid cash for it. He uses a county vehicle, they're both covered by health insurance through the county. She actually has to pay very few bills. I bet she's feathered a nice nest for herself."

"I guess she earned it," Grant ventured. "Let's get on to the others."

"Right. You have Melvin Kemp, in his late twenties, he also used to work part time, got hired full time the same day as Marcia. Michael Hargrove, I think he's around thirty-five, he came on part time when Longo and Kemp went full time. I think he moved into full time in August of '85. Dale Fisher is in his mid twenties, hired in the spring of '90. Dennis Drummond is around forty. He was the only full timer Franz kept on when he took over. He's been there since '84. He's a little slow and kind of lazy. He works the midnight shift and loves it. That's it for the full timers."

"What's left, part timers and clerical?"

"Yeah, two of each. The part timers are Scott Browne and Linda Chovan. They're both in their mid twenties, were both hired in the spring of '90. They'd like to get on full time at some point, but they aren't big fans of Franz. They and Maxwell should be able to tell you about things that have happened since I left, like the organ dicing and flushing."

"How do you know they still want full time, or that they don't care for Franz? Things may have changed since you've been out."

"They're good kids, we still keep in touch. Nothing has changed."

"Good," Grant said, relishing the thought of possibly having inside sources at the morgue. He decided not to pursue the matter any further just then, however.

"The two clericals," Pat continued, "are Dorothy Larkin and Belinda Bernal. Mrs. Larkin is in her early fifties, she's been working there since early '89. Belinda is twenty-seven. She started at the tail end of '89, as Franz's expansion plans gathered steam. I'm sure they both have opinions of Franz's management style, but they don't get involved in any of the other stuff."

"So, Franz runs the operation with two assistant pathologists, five full timers and two part timers?"

"That's it," Pat agreed.

"Isn't that a little thin, considering the increased business he's brought in, and his special projects?"

"Yes it is. But Franz prides himself on operating under budget. No unnecessary personnel on the payroll. He's willing to work around the clock, seven days a week if he has to. He expects everyone else to give the same effort if asked. And the crew he has there now seem willing to do it."

"But if he has to pay a lot of overtime, how does he stay below his budget?" Grant asked.

"He doesn't pay overtime, he hands out compensatory time like candy. I suspect that everyone has comp time accruals in triple digits."

"Do they ever get to use it? I don't see how they can."

"Sure, remember that he demands that everyone be fully committed to the morgue. If someone needs time off, the rest will take up the slack. Even right now, with Johnson out on disability, Franz will personally take the extra load. He sets the example for the rest."

"Would it be accurate to say he operates with a skeleton crew?" Grant asked, tongue in cheek.

Pat roared in laughter. "You're a sick man, my friend, but it would be accurate."

"I guess that's all I need for now, Pat. On second thought I have one more question. I need to satisfy my curiosity, I hope you won't be offended."

"I won't, go ahead."

"I'm curious as to how you figured you could feed information to Doyle and not end up getting bounced, or were you at a point where you didn't care anymore?"

Pat laughed again. "I never told Doyle a thing, at least not while I was still working."

"What?" Grant asked, surprised. "If it wasn't you, who was Doyle's anonymous source?"

"You reached the logical conclusion, John. So did Franz and Miller. But after they let me go, the leaks continued. That's when they realized Bill Maxwell was the one."

"And you still like Maxwell? It looks to me like his actions cost you your job."

"You're right. But I knew what he was doing. When it became obvious that I was the suspect, he came to me and offered to confess to Franz. I told him no. It was time that somebody did something to get the word out. And I was fed up to the point I really didn't give a damn. It wasn't dealing with Franz so much, it was June Miller. She can beat a man into submission."

"She sounds like quite a woman," Grant said, more appreciative of Linda. "Let me know about Maxwell, Pat. Talk to you later."

CHAPTER EIGHT

At eight-thirty Tuesday morning Grant headed for the county office building to get the Lyle Chambers death certificate. It was a crisp, overcast day. There had been a two inch snowfall the previous evening, but the city workers had cleared the sidewalks overnight.

He was in a very good mood. Pat had called him late Monday afternoon to tell him that Bill Maxwell had agreed to be interviewed. He would be in Grant's office at ten o'clock on Thursday. A week from Thursday he and Tom would visit the morgue, after that the investigation would get in full swing.

Grant entered the county building and walked down one floor to the Vital Statistics office. He entered the room and got in line at the service counter, he was number seven. About fifteen minutes later he was being waited on by a young male clerk. Grant showed his ID and explained that he needed a copy of a death certificate as part of an official investigation. This seemed to make the clerk nervous. He excused himself, saying he needed to talk with his supervisor. In a minute or so he was back. He opened a gate in the counter and asked Grant to enter. He led him past two rows of desks, stopping at a cubicle on the left. "This is my supervisor, Theresa Jackson. She'll be able to help you," he said, and walked away.

The woman sitting behind the desk looked up at him and smiled. "I'm Terry Jackson," she said, rising to shake hands. She was in her mid forties, with a pleasant and attractive face. When she stood up, Grant realized how short she was. Not much over five feet, if that. They shook hands and Grant gave her one of his business cards. She motioned him to a chair next to her desk.

"I'm afraid you scared Walter a little bit. He's new, your badge and talk about an official investigation upset him," she explained.

"I'm very sorry, Mrs. Jackson," Grant apologized. "I certainly didn't intend that."

She smiled again. "Please, call me Terry. Now, what can I do for you?"

"Well, I am actually conducting an investigation, and as a part of it I need a copy of a death certificate. I know the persons name and year of death, but not the specific date. Do you think you can help me?"

"If he died in this county, we'll have a certificate on him," Terry promised. "What's the name and year of death?"

"Lyle B. Chambers, died in 1990. First part of the year, I think," Grant said, as Terry wrote the information on a note pad.

"Wait here please, Mr. Grant. I'll be right back."

"John, please call me John," Grant said. Terry smiled at him and disappeared toward a row of file cabinets.

She returned in five minutes and handed him a sheet of paper. "Here's a copy of the death certificate. Yours at no charge as a representative of another government agency."

"Thank you very much," Grant said. "Do you mind if I look this over while I'm here? I don't deal with these on a regular basis and I may have some questions you can help me with."

"No problem, John. I'll be glad to help, take your time."

Grant scanned the document. He found the ME's portion. It stated that Mr. Chambers had died as a result of natural causes related to heart disease. The date of death was listed as the date the body was found, February 27. The morgue case number was 02-90-0089. Franz signed as having performed the autopsy.

Grant next reviewed the personal data section. It showed that Chambers had been sixty-eight, born in Arkansas and a veteran. Willa Mae MacPhearson, sister, was next of kin.

Last, he looked at the information regarding the disposition of the body. Mr. Chambers had supposedly been cremated at the Evergreen Cemetery and Crematory on March 1, 1990. His ashes had been shipped to Paragould, Arkansas on the same date. This part of the certificate had been signed by Whitney Price, Funeral Director.

"I guess this information is more clear than I thought," Grant said. "I only have one question, does the signature of Mr. Price mean that he personally took Mr. Chambers to Evergreen for cremation?"

"Not necessarily," Terry answered. "Someone from his funeral home would have done the transport, but more than likely it wouldn't have been Mr. Price himself."

"A hired hand, not the boss," Grant grinned. "Just like the state."

"And the county," Terry chimed in.

"Could the morgue have taken Mr. Chambers to the crematorium, and just had Mr. Price fill out the form?"

Terry shook her head. "Not in New York, John. Other than a removal by an ME or coroner, a body can only be transported by a licensed funeral director, with a burial or transport permit."

"I see," Grant said, his eyes back on the certificate. "Oops, I just came up with another question. I see that a Marcia Longo signed as issuing the burial permit to Mr. Price. I was under the impression that she worked at the morgue, doesn't your office have to issue these permits?"

Terry laughed. "You're very observant, and you're right. But the morgue is a sub registrars office. A few years ago, Dr. Franz asked to be made a sub registrar. His office is open around the clock, undertakers can get permits at all hours now. They love it, and it's worked out well for everybody."

"So the entire morgue staff can issue these permits, or just Dr. Franz and Ms. Longo?"

Terry stopped smiling. Her eyes dropped to the blotter on her desk, her face flushed. After a few seconds she looked up at Grant. "I'm very embarrassed, John. A mistake was apparently made in this case. Only Dr. Franz is a sub registrar. Marcia had no business to sign as having issued this permit. I'll call Dr. Franz right now and point this out to him. Will that be satisfactory to you?"

Grant kept a poker face, but his stomach had just done a flip. The last thing he needed was Terry telling Franz that he had been in asking questions about the Chambers death certificate. "As you can tell, Terry, death certificates aren't my area of

77

expertise. I'm certainly not here to cause you any grief and, quite frankly, this doesn't seem like a big deal. Is it?"

"Not really," Terry said, looking more at ease. "I think there was just a lack of communication between her and Dr. Franz. No harm was done."

"That's what I thought," Grant smiled. "I stopped in here looking for help. I'd never forgive myself if someone got in trouble for such a minor thing. Let's just forget about it." He extended his hand. "Deal?"

"Deal," she said, smiling.

Grant thanked her and high tailed it out of Vital Statistics.

Bill Maxwell arrived at Grant's office at five minutes of ten Thursday morning. Grant met him in the reception area. He was impressed with Maxwell's appearance and demeanor. He fit into the Murphy mold, straight forward and sincere. After fixing their coffee cups, Grant led the way to his office. Ron Burrows had been in when he had left to meet Maxwell, hopefully he had left by now.

On the contrary, Burrows had not left, in fact he had been joined by Sue Keller. "I'm not stupid, Ron," she was saying as Grant and Maxwell entered the room. "I know when I smell cigarette smoke and I know where it's coming from. I'm not going to warn you again."

She noticed the new arrivals. "Hi, John. And who is this?" she asked, nodding toward Maxwell. Sue was fifty and not quite as cute as she thought she was.

"This is someone I need to meet with, in private. If this room is tied up, we'll find someplace else," Grant said curtly.

Sue ignored him and spoke directly to Maxwell. "Do I know you? Did you ever work at the Ford dealership on Commercial Drive? A mechanic, maybe?"

Maxwell looked to Grant for guidance. "Excuse me, Sue," Grant said, "but...."

"I need to make a pit stop before we get started," the quick thinking Maxwell said to Grant. "Can you direct me to the men's room?"

78

"I'll show you," Sue offered. "I have to go right by it on the way back to my office, come on."

Grant took Maxwell's coffee cup and watched as he and Sue disappeared down the hallway. He set the coffees down on his desk and turned toward Burrows. "Damn it, Ron, I've asked you several times not to smoke in here because of her. Your stubborn streak almost screwed up my interview!"

Burrows was retirement age. He was hanging around for some extra money, but made it known that if things didn't go to his liking, he'd quit. Because of that, he didn't particularly care what he said, or to who. "Listen big man, apparently the management here doesn't realize how important you are. If you tell them, I'm sure they'll assign you to a private office."

Grant started toward Burrows, stopping half way. He wondered if the satisfaction of getting his hands around Burrows' neck would be worth the consequences.

Burrows must have read something in Grant's eyes. "I've got to get going," he said quickly. He brushed by Grant and went out the door.

Maxwell returned a few seconds later. "I'm sorry about this, Bill. I usually have the place to myself."

"Don't mention it," Maxwell laughed. "This was the first time I've ever had a woman follow me in the men's room. She was so concerned about trying to find out my name, she followed me right in the door. Didn't realize where she was until she bumped into the urinal."

"Was she embarrassed?" Grant asked.

"Her face was as red as a beet," Maxwell answered.

With that image in his mind, Grant joined Maxwell in laughter. Perhaps this experience would dampen Ms. Keller's enthusiasm for sticking her nose in where it didn't belong.

A few moments later, with the door closed and locked, Grant opened the interview. "Bill, Pat told me that you're not real excited about these investigations of Dr. Franz. Your frustration is understandable. I don't want to mislead you now. I can't promise you what the outcome of this investigation will be. I can only assure you that I will pursue every relevant lead, dig for every bit of information. If the evidence warrants, I'll refer the case to our legal people for action. Once I do that, it's pretty much out of my hands. So, I can guarantee you my effort, not the final results. With that understanding, I'd like to have your cooperation."

"That's fair enough, John. Pat said he thought you were a square shooter. You've done nothing to contradict that. I'll be glad to tell what I know. And, unlike Pat, I can say it here or in court. There's no gag on me."

"I'm glad you mentioned that, Bill, because that's where this could end up. It's good that you recognize that."

"What do you need to know?" Bill asked.

Grant spent a few minutes getting some personal background information. "I guess we can get into the meat of this now, Bill. I'd like you to tell me about three areas; illegally taking research tissue, improper disposal of medical waste and keeping bodies that should have been cremated or buried."

"I'll start with the organ flushing. In January of '92, Dr. Franz ordered that the specimens we had stored in the autopsy room be diced and flushed down the commode. There were so many of them that the drain clogged and we couldn't get them all done at one time. We finished them up in March."

"Why were there so many of these specimens, where did they come from?"

"They were taken during autopsies and preserved in gross jars. The trouble was, Franz is like a pack rat. He doesn't like to get rid of anything. It got to the point that we didn't have room in the cabinets for anything else. I like to keep a neat and orderly work area. After I mentioned the situation to him a couple of times, he gave the order."

"Was the order verbal or written?"

"Verbal. He gave it to me directly."

"Was anybody else present?"

"No, just me."

"Who did the dicing?"

"Me, Linda Chovan, Scott Browne and Mike Hargrove."

"Did Franz participate at all?"

"No, but he was in the autopsy room on and off when we were doing it. There's no doubt he knew what we were doing, the others can verify that."

"What did you use, scalpels?"

"Yes."

"Were Samuels and Johnson involved?"

"No. They heard about it, but weren't involved personally."

"You said the drain clogged, how did you clear it?"

"We didn't. They had to call a plumber. He put a snake down it. The next day June Miller had us in for a lecture. She said we had to use better judgment in the future."

"I assume these things should have been incinerated?"

"Yes, definitely."

"Any idea why he went this route?"

"Bob has an odd sense of humor. He likes to shock people. It didn't bother Hargrove or me, but Scott and Linda weren't particularly happy about the assignment. And they were nothing compared to the plumber."

"How about the tissue?"

Maxwell confirmed what Grant had learned from Pat, but could add little. He remembered an altercation he had with Franz over removing the testicles and bladder of a young boy. But he couldn't remember the boys name or the date of the incident. After that, he too, had gradually fallen from grace. Eventually his involvement decreased to almost nothing.

It was the same story with the bodies. He corroborated the Chambers story. But after that, Melvin Kemp, Dale Fisher and Rodney Flowers had handled those projects. He felt sure that more bodies had been kept, many more. He didn't know how many or where the skeletons were kept. "You're going to have to get one of those guys to talk, or search the place," Maxwell suggested.

Grant knew that might be easier said than done.

Before leaving, Maxwell made a four page written statement, which Grant notarized. The next major development would be to meet Dr. Franz.

The following Saturday night, Bob Franz was laying on Marcia Longo's bed. The room was dark and he was alone in the bed. After a round of love making, Marcia had gone to the bathroom to shower. Naked, he was staring at the ceiling, thinking.

He suddenly sat up, swinging his legs over the side of the bed. He leaned forward toward the nightstand next to the bed, and opened the bottom drawer. He had kept a few clothes and personal items at her apartment since shortly after their affair had begun. In addition to some shirts and slacks in the closet, this drawer contained his socks, underwear and shaving kit.

Franz groped in the drawer beneath his underwear until he felt the envelope. He removed it, reached up and turned on the light on the top of the nightstand. He turned his head to check the bathroom door, it was still closed. The envelope was a standard white, business size envelope. There was nothing unique about it. He held the envelope up even with his eyes and closely examined the seal. There was no evidence of tampering. Satisfied, he started to bend forward to put the envelope back in its place. Sensing someone staring at him, he quickly swung around. Marcia Longo, wrapped in a towel, was standing in the bathroom doorway, watching him.

Franz had a very short fuse, it burned quickly. "Are you spying on me?" he shouted. "Can't I have any privacy?" He put the envelope in the bottom of the drawer and closed it, then turned his attention back to her.

Longo spoke before he could renew his attack. "This happens to be my apartment and my bedroom. If anybody is entitled to privacy here, it's me. If you've got something in there that you're so worried about, get it out of here! I refuse to have to get permission to walk into my own bedroom!"

Franz calmed quickly. He knew she was right. Storing something here had been a mistake. But he certainly didn't want it in his own house, around Ione. His office had been out of the question, that was county property and could be accessed by too many people. This apartment had been the best of his options at the time. It had been his intention to get a safe deposit box eventually. But, as time passed, that move seemed less urgent.

"I'm sorry, honey," he said softly. "It's just that I'm kind of like a man without a country. I don't have anyplace that's just for me. Not even a place to keep a personal document, like my will," he nodded toward the drawer.

"That's okay," she said. "I suppose it is difficult living the way you do. Let's forget it."

Franz smiled. "That's my girl. Would you like to go out for a bite to eat?"

"No. I'm a little tired, you wore me out," she smiled. "I think I'll go to bed and read for a while. You go ahead if you want."

"I'm not really hungry either. I guess I'll go over to the office for a few minutes," he said, starting to dress.

"Are you coming back tonight?"

"No. Ione has a couple of projects around the house she wants me to do tomorrow. I'll see you Monday," he said. Dressed now, he headed for the door.

Marcia followed him, kissing him lightly on the lips as he stepped into the hallway. As soon as he disappeared down the stairs, she closed the door and locked it. Almost at a jog, she went into the bedroom and opened the nightstand drawer.

CHAPTER NINE

John Grant was slowly pacing back and forth the length of the break room, deep in thought. It was quarter after eight on Thursday, March 18. Tom Fargo was due to arrive in fifteen minutes.

Although he would admit it only to himself, Grant was having second thoughts about how smooth this was going to go. Perhaps what he had learned about Franz over the last couple of weeks had intimidated him. Or, more likely, the fact that he was actually investigating a public official was finally hitting home.

He ran over possible scenarios in his mind. Would Franz be there? Would he accept Grant as a trainee? Would the request for the Chambers file go unnoticed? Grant thought of a lot of "woulds" and "what ifs". He didn't know the answers now, he would in a couple of hours. But he did know one thing for sure, he had to conceal his concerns from Tom Fargo. It wouldn't take much to spook him. No matter what the potential pitfalls, he had to exude confidence.

Tom arrived promptly at eight-thirty. He was thirty-seven, five feet five, slightly built with receding brown hair. Today he was wearing glasses rather than contacts.

Grant greeted him warmly. They took their coffees back to Grant's office. Grant was surprised to find that Velma had come in while he was in the break room. He hadn't seen Burrows since their altercation, which was all right with him.

Grant introduced Tom to Velma. Exercising common courtesy, she offered to leave if Grant needed privacy. He assured her that he didn't. "Not unless you plan to invite Sue in," he said with a grin.

Velma laughed, she was in her late fifties and sharp as a tack. "She's been keeping a very low profile since people saw her coming out of the men's room. I don't anticipate seeing her in here."

After a little more small talk, Tom and Grant turned to business. "How long do you think your inspection will take?" Grant asked.

"If everything I need to see exists, and is readily accessible, probably three hours. How much time will your stuff take?" he asked back.

"Well, actually, I've only come up with one specific file I need to see. I assume you'll be asking to review some files, either specific or random. How about if I give you the file number and you slip it in with the ones you're going to ask for?"

Grant could sense Tom's relief that there was only one file involved. "I don't see any problem with that," he said. "But what year is this file from? The reg has only been in effect since June of '91."

"This one is from February, 1990. Can't you ask to see files from prior to the regulation, to check on his record keeping habits?"

Tom's sense of relief had vanished. "I suppose," he said reluctantly. "But it would be too obvious if I only ask for one file, we'll have to look at a dozen or so. You realize that Franz can't be charged for anything we find that occurred prior to the effective date, don't you?"

"Yes," Grant said. He didn't tell Tom that there were other statutes that might apply, including criminal violations.

"How will looking at this file help, anyway? I understand from Dr. Lynch, that Dr. Franz supposedly didn't keep any records of the tissue he took without consent. In that case, you won't find anything in the files that will be of use to you."

"Not necessarily, Tom. He may have falsified records to cover his actions. That can include omissions. Remember, he's supposedly an arrogant son of a gun. Sometimes arrogance can lead to mistakes. Even if he is slick, other people would have worked on these files. Maybe they aren't as adept at covering up as he is. At any rate, I won't know until I look."

"I see," Tom said. "But it sounds like a waste of time to me."

"That may be, Tom, but Dr. Lynch wants it done, and I plan to do it. Just to see how the files are made up, what information they contain, will be worth something. Besides, this file is about a body that he kept, not research tissue. I've seen the death certificate, now I want to see the rest of the information."

Tom shrugged in submission. "Suit yourself," he said.

"I intend to," Grant responded.

Tom took a legal pad from his briefcase and wrote down the Chambers autopsy number. They randomly made up ten more case numbers from prior to the regulation, to accompany it. It was time to go, they agreed to take separate cars so that Tom could head straight for Albany upon completing the inspection. They walked to the parking lot. Grant waited for Tom to pull up behind him, then headed for the morgue.

The morgue was located on Blandina Street, twelve blocks from the state office building. Not being familiar with the location, Grant had done a drive by the previous afternoon. The building itself was about twenty years old, one story, brick and concrete block construction. The main entrance was on the side of the building facing the parking area. There were three windows to the left of the entrance door. Pat had told him that the two windows closest to the door were in the main office. The third window was in the office of June Miller. According to Pat, Miller had demanded that office so she would be able to watch who came and went, including employees. The far end of the building was a three stall garage with overhead doors.

Grant pulled into an empty parking space across from the entrance. He got out of his car and stood next to it, waiting for Tom to join him. As he waited, he couldn't help glancing at that third window. He was mildly shocked to see someone at the window, looking back at him. He quickly diverted his eyes. As Tom neared him they headed toward the entrance.

Upon entering the building, they found themselves in a vestibule containing the visitor log that Pat had mentioned. The main office was just to the left of the vestibule. A radio played softly, a display was visible on a computer screen, but the room was unoccupied. They filled in the required information for the log and stepped into the office.

A few seconds later, two women entered through a door in the left wall, both carried coffee cups. Grant knew immediately that they were Dorothy Larkin and Belinda Bernal. "Good morning, gentlemen," Mrs. Larkin said, identifying herself. "We were just getting our coffee when Mrs. Miller said we had company. How can we help you?" Tom stepped closer to Mrs. Larkin and gave her his business card. He then started to explain the purpose of the visit. While Tom was busy with her, Grant stepped further into the room. Belinda was a very pretty girl, long, light brown hair, and shapely. As he got closer, he noticed that she appeared a little bit pale. Maybe the flu bug, he thought.

As that thought was in his mind, Belinda caught him looking at her. "St. Patricks Day," she said in explanation. "I'm not an

Irishman, but I celebrate like one." Grant smiled back in understanding.

"I'll get Dr. Franz for you right away," Mrs. Larkin was telling Tom. She stopped part way to the door, "Oh, by the way, this is my co-worker, Belinda Bernal. I'm sure she'd be glad to get you some coffee if you'd like." She turned and disappeared out the door.

Declining coffee, they stood waiting while Belinda went to work on the computer. After a very short wait, Mrs. Larkin returned with Dr. Franz and June Miller.

Franz, dressed in a dark green suit with a white shirt and light green tie, was indeed impressive close up. His tie seemed to match his eyes. The suit contrasted the red hair. There was an aura of superiority about him that was keenly felt.

June Miller was impressive in her own right. Pat had accurately described her, as far as words could go. But she was more stern looking, more imposing, than Grant had imagined. He looked closely at her face, there were no signs of what he called "laugh lines" around the eyes or mouth. A formidable adversary, he concluded.

Tom introduced himself and his "assistant". During the handshakes and pleasantries, Franz smiled and acted sincerely pleased that his morgue was going to be inspected. Miller was stone faced, sizing Fargo and Grant up as though she considered them to be a threat.

"I can give you a tour of the facility if you'd like, or we can skip that and get right into the inspection," Franz offered. "What do you prefer?"

"The focus of my inspection will be primarily on policy, procedure and record keeping, not the physical plant," Tom said. "If you don't mind, doctor, I'd just as soon get started on the inspection."

"No problem at all," Franz said, smiling. "I know that a scenic view of a morgue doesn't appeal to everyone. If you'll follow me to the conference room, we'll get started."

Franz dismissed Miller, then led the way to the conference and break room. Fargo and Grant took seats at the conference table facing the door, backs to a wall. Franz sat opposite them.

For the next hour, Franz answered questions as Tom went through his inspection checklist. Grant did his best to appear interested. Franz responded promptly and with authority. Any documents Tom asked to see were produced without delay. Grant was impressed at how well things were organized, Tom seemed to be also.

Franz laughed easily and often. Grant had become almost totally relaxed, his earlier doubts forgotten. He was beginning to question whether this amiable man, could be the monster that had been described to him.

Finally, Tom said that the interview portion of the inspection was over, the rest would consist of reviewing randomly selected files. It would not be necessary for Dr. Franz to sit through that, as long as he, or someone would be available to answer any questions upon completion of the review. Franz said that he'd make himself available, meanwhile, he had business in the autopsy room. He promised to send June Miller in to coordinate pulling the requested files.

Rather than leaving right away, Franz hung around while Tom was busy reviewing his checklist. "How long have you been assisting Mr. Fargo?" he asked Grant.

"Not long enough," Grant answered. "He's very knowledgeable and I've learned a lot from him, but I'm afraid I still have a long way to go."

"What did you do before you became an inspector?" Franz followed up.

Grant was becoming uncomfortable with the conversation. He glanced at Tom, looking for help. Tom was lost in his own world, there'd be no assistance from him.

"Well, I've tried a lot of things in my time, but this is certainly the most interesting field I've ever been involved in," Grant said, avoiding a direct answer. Before Franz could ask anything else, Grant took a page from Bill Maxwell's play book. "Can you direct me to the rest room, doctor? I'm afraid I've had one too many coffees this morning."

Franz sent him down the hall to the men's room. Grant waited ten minutes before returning. When he got back, Franz had been replaced by June Miller. Tom asked for twenty files from cases listed in the required tissue bank log. The log showed donations to legitimate research facilities, the case files should contain matching documentation, including a signed consent form. Miller summoned Belinda Bernal and instructed her to pull the files. "Belinda, make sure you keep a list of all the files these people look at, and put it on my desk." She then turned to Tom and Grant, "We must show the proper custody of all morgue files, you understand," she explained. "Now, if you'll excuse me...," she turned on her heel and walked out, followed by Belinda.

After they had gone, Tom said, "I hope they're all as organized as this place. Everything we require is in place, and he knew just where to find it. I'm pleasantly surprised."

"What do you think of Franz and Miller?" Grant asked.

"I like Dr. Franz. It's obvious that he's proud of this place. I don't think he could have been nicer. I don't particularly care for Mrs. Miller, but I'm sure she's efficient."

Grant agreed. "If the files you have to look at are in as good shape as everything else, we'll be out of here soon. I should be able to go through the Chambers file in a few minutes. The extra ones we're requesting for show, will just be quick scan jobs."

Tom checked his watch, it was a few minutes before eleven. "I would think that another hour should do it. Maybe we can do lunch before I start back," he suggested.

"That would be nice," Grant said. "Remember how worked up you were when we first talked about this? I told you it would be a piece of cake."

Belinda was back in about ten minutes, arms full of files. She put them down on top of the table. "When you're finished with these, or if you need anything else, I'll be at my desk," she said, and left.

Tom grabbed the first file. They had decided to look at the first one together. Tom flipped the folder open, the first document was the "Case Data sheet". This was a fill in the blanks deal. The top portion showed the morgue case number, date and time the call was received, and by who. Next was the name and address of the deceased, who responded to the scene, the name of the investigating police officer and agency, and the name of the assigned pathologist.

The next section provided information about the deceased. Name, age, date of birth, place of birth, social security number, next of kin, the funeral home handling the body, and the date and time the body was released.

The bottom of the front, and the entire back of the sheet was lined for note writing. In this case, there were entries for attempts to contact the next of kin, contact with the funeral director and tissue donation request and consent. The latter showed the heart was donated to the American Heart Association for research.

The next few pages were copies of the deceased persons drivers license, social security card, and health insurance card. These were followed by copies of a police report, death certificate and burial/removal permit. Last were the autopsy protocol, the tissue donation consent, two fingerprint cards, and an envelope containing two pictures of the deceased on the autopsy table.

The tissue donation was on an American Heart Association Form. It included the name, date of birth and social security number of the donor, tissue to be donated, the name, signature and relationship of the person authorizing the donation. The signature was witnessed by Melvin Kemp. The document was dated the same day the person died.

Grant turned to Tom. "What do you think?"

"Everything is here that is supposed to be."

Grant and Tom then examined folders separately. Since they were now only concentrating on the donations, the process went quickly. As soon as they were finished, Tom gathered up the files and headed out for the main office. He gave the files back to Belinda, along with the list for the next batch. These were the older cases, including Chambers.

In about fifteen minutes Belinda entered carrying additional files. She again set them on the table. But this time she looked uncomfortable. She didn't look directly at them or offer any additional assistance. This attitude had nothing to do with a hangover, Grant surmised. He was already beginning to feel uneasy, when Belinda said, "These are all the files but one, Dr. Franz will be bringing that one in himself," she hurriedly left the room.

Grant shot a glance at Tom. The color was quickly draining from his face. He didn't look in Grant's direction, keeping his eyes on his legal pad instead.

A few seconds later Dr. Franz entered, with June Miller close behind. Franz was now clad in surgical greens, his face was several shades darker than when Grant had last seen him. He carried a file in his right hand. He strode to the conference table and stopped directly opposite from Grant. He slammed the file down on the table top between them.

"Why do you want to see the Chambers file? Who in the hell are you anyway?" he demanded, almost screaming.

Grant knew there was no sense getting in any deeper. "As you already know, my name is John Grant, I'm with the Special Investigations Unit of DOH. I want to look at these files as part of an investigation I'm conducting. Now, if you'll excuse me, doctor, I'd like to continue."

Grant reached for the Chambers file. Franz leaned forward, placing his right palm on top of the folder, pinning it to the table top. He continued to lean forward across the table, stopping when his face, now almost purple, was a foot from Grant's. His green eyes were shooting sparks, veins pulsed in his temples and throat.

Grant wanted to get out of there, but he couldn't take his eyes off Franz's face. He had never seen such rage, he sat still, unable to move.

"You're here under false pretenses!" Franz hollered. "You lied to me! This is my fucking morgue! Do you hear me? My fucking morgue! Get the fuck out of here now, and don't ever come back!"

As Franz raved, drops of saliva formed on his lips. With each word he shouted, the saliva sprayed on Grant's face like a fine mist. This unwelcome shower pulled Grant out of his trance. He pushed his chair back until it hit the wall behind him, out of range.

Grant was now convinced that Franz was a lunatic. He stood up and glanced at Tom. Tom's face was covered with perspiration, his glasses had slid half way down his nose. "I think it's best if I leave now, Tom. Are you coming?" Fargo didn't answer, but began cramming his paperwork into his briefcase.

Franz broke into another tirade. "I'll have your job for this! Who do you think you are? Do you realize who you're fucking with?"

Grant ignored him and walked around the table, toward the door. He kept well clear of Franz, but kept a sideways glance on him. As he walked, he heard Franz's footsteps and voice behind him.

Passing through the main office he felt Belinda and Mrs. Larkin looking at him. He kept his eyes fixed on the exit door and kept walking. He heard Franz yell, "Don't ever let that son of a bitch in here again! Never again!"

After what seemed an eternity, Grant was through the door and nearing his car. He thought he could feel Miller's eyes on him, watching from her office window. He didn't check. He got into his car, pulled out of the parking lot and didn't look back.

CHAPTER TEN

Grant stopped at an outside phone booth three blocks from the morgue. He sat in the car for several seconds before getting out. He felt angry and humiliated. He had dealt with people who resented his investigating them. Sometimes tempers were short on both sides, but he had never encountered anything like Franz. And, he had never been thrown out of a facility under investigation. If Franz had been rational, that wouldn't have happened this time either. In Franz's state, however, there had been no point in arguing. That would have only fueled the fire. He had done the right thing by keeping his mouth shut and leaving. He knew it then, and he knew it now. But doing the right thing wasn't always easy, and this was a classic example.

Grant loosened his grip on the steering wheel, his knuckles began to regain their color. He didn't know whether or not Franz's threats were idle. He needed to call Linda right away and tell her what had happened. Satisfied that he could keep his voice calm, he went to the phone and dialed, using his state issued calling card. A secretary told him that Linda was temporarily away from her desk. Grant left the number of the phone booth, along with the message that his call was urgent.

As Grant was hanging up, Tom Fargo arrived. "Piece of cake, piece of cake," he muttered as he approached.

"Listen, Tom," Grant said, "if there's any heat over this, I'll take it. You have nothing to worry about."

Tom's face flushed. "I wasn't thinking about myself," he said quickly. "I don't want either of us to be in trouble. What do you think will happen?"

"I can't say right now. It'll depend on what Franz does, whether or not he complains to his superiors, and what their reaction will be. It could be anything from just Franz and I having a bad day, to the shit really hitting the fan. I've got a call in for Linda right now so I can prepare her. My biggest concern is that if the county squawks loud enough, I could be taken off the investigation."

"Do you think Linda would do that?" "It's not Linda I'm worried about. But if Franz complains to someone above her, I just don't know what will happen."

Grant pounced on the handset on the first ring. "I'm sorry about the delay, John," Linda said. "I was just getting ready to call you when I received a call from Dr. McAree. He received a complaint from Dr. Massey and he wants some answers. I've got to report to his office as soon as I finish talking with you. Now, what can you tell me?"

Grant gave her the full story, he left nothing out. "Whew," she said. "Sounds like quite a scene. You don't sound very upset, considering. How come?"

"Don't kid yourself. I'm as teed off as I've been in a long, long time. The speed with which they contacted McAree, I haven't been out of the morgue over twenty minutes, leads me to believe things may get worse."

"Well, we'll have to see. I was told by Dr. McAree to suspend the investigation until he has a chance to talk with me. So, cool your jets until I get back to you."

"How are you going to handle McAree?" Grant asked.

"I'm not sure yet. I'm going to try to get George to go with me. There's strength in numbers, you know."

"You don't think he'll shut us down permanently, do you?"

"He can't, there are too many serious allegations. But I'm sure he'll question our methods, and maybe try to control the investigation himself. We certainly don't want that to happen."

"What about me?" Grant asked. "Do you think he'll want me out?"

"To be perfectly honest, the county will probably insist on it."

"Linda, I want to work this case real, real bad. Don't let them take me off it, please."

"Do you want to get even, John?"

"I want to get the truth. I think that matches my job description."

"I'll take care of it, John," she said gently. "Go back to your office and try to relax. I'll call you as soon as I know something."

Grant hung up the phone and turned to find Tom looking at him questioningly. "The county did file a complaint with the fourteenth floor. Linda is going up for a meeting now. That's all I can tell you at the moment."

Tom didn't comment on Grant's statement. "Do you want to get some lunch?" he asked instead.

"No thanks, Tom, I'm not hungry right now."

They shook hands and returned to their vehicles. Tom headed toward Albany, Grant went back to his office to await news of his fate.

As soon as Grant entered the room, Velma waved her arm toward Burrows' desk. "Look. While you were out Ron cleared out his desk. He put in his retirement papers last week, he's packing it in."

His eyes followed her arm to the now empty desk. "Did this have anything to do with me?" he asked.

"I think it's safe to say you've been on his mind a lot the past several days," she said, smiling.

A smile played at the corners of Grant's mouth, but quickly disappeared. "I didn't necessarily want to see him leave, Velma. I'd have been just as happy if one of us could have switched offices. Especially him, I wouldn't want to be too far away from you," Grant leered at her.

Velma blushed. "You know how to make an old lady feel good," she said.

The ringing of Grant's phone broke up the conversation. It was Pat Murphy. "Having a nice day?" Pat asked. Grant had a suspicion that he already knew the answer.

"How did you find out already?" Grant demanded. "Franz threw me out less than an hour ago."

Pat laughed. "I have my ways. Besides, I'm not the only one who's heard about what happened. As soon as you were out the door Franz ordered the office girls to call all off duty personnel and tell them his new guidelines to admit state people to the building. You don't get in without the express permission of Franz or Massey. No other state employee gets in without the blessing of Franz or Miller, except a trooper investigating a death, of course."

"Any other changes?"

"Not yet. Franz gave that order, then went into his office and made a phone call, presumably to Massey. He came back out of his office and said he was going to the county building."

"I guess I really made him mad, didn't I?"

"From what I hear, you may have jumped ahead of Johnson, Samuels and Doyle on Franz's shit list. He was supposedly as pissed off today as he's been in a long time."

"Any idea who he's seeing at the county building?"

"Massey, no doubt, maybe Bronson too."

"Right to the top, huh?"

"That's just a guess, but I'm sure Franz wants to nip this investigation in the bud. He'll want to get The Man involved right away." Pat paused, then, "Will this have any effect on you?"

"That's certainly a possibility. I don't see how I can do much of an investigation if I can't get into the building. I'll need to look at records and do some interviewing. If they hold tight on not wanting me around, I could be out. I pray it doesn't come to that."

"I'll let you know if I hear anything more. I'm keeping my fingers crossed for you."

"Thanks, Pat," Grant said, and hung up.

While Grant was talking with Pat, Dr. Robert McAree was in his Corning Tower office, awaiting the arrival of Linda Ludwig. He was irate at the way this Grant character had treated Dr. Franz. Using trickery and deception! That was the way real cops dealt with real criminals, but Franz was an MD for God sake! And Grant was just a glorified hot dog stand inspector, he probably didn't even have a degree. Ludwig was Grant's boss, she was responsible for his actions! In a few minutes he'd make that very clear to her.

On the other hand, this incident was a blessing. He had never met Franz, but he did know Massey. If he made a sufficient show of support for a colleague under attack, Massey would spread the word to their brethren in the state association. And very few of them were fans of DOH.

McAree walked to his office window and looked down at the street, fourteen floors below. His eyes then went to his reflection in the glass. He liked what he saw. Six feet-two, and two hundred forty well distributed pounds. Sixty years old with wavy gray hair. He was.....distinguished, no question about it.

Yes, there was an opportunity here. A chance to further prove that he was a champion of the regulated parties. He wondered if there was a state association presidency in his future?

Twenty minutes after his call from Murphy, Grant's phone rang again. "What kind of day are you having?" Jim Doyle wanted to know.

Grant thought of an obscene reply, but didn't say it. Maybe Doyle wasn't busting his chops, maybe he didn't know what had happened earlier. "Things can always be better, Jim. How goes it with you?"

"I hear that Franz and Massey have asked for an audience with Bronson, kind of an emergency thing. Does that have anything to do with your investigation?"

"Probably," Grant said. He gave Doyle the highlights of his encounter with Franz.

"John," Doyle said gravely, "I know how these people operate. If they want to go on the offensive, they'll probably issue a press release that won't be very flattering to you. You'll be portrayed as the bad guy right off the bat."

"What will be, will be, Jim. I have no control over that. My biggest concern right now is what will happen to me, whether

I'll be pulled off the investigation. Unfortunately, I don't have much control over that either."

"I want you to understand something, John. If the county does release something I'll have to use it. It won't be anything personal, okay?"

"I understand, Jim. Do what you have to do. There'll be no hard feelings."

"If something does come down, I'll let you know and give you a chance to respond if you'd like."

"I appreciate that, Jim. But I think I'm going to keep a low profile. My boss might take you up on your offer though." Grant told Doyle how to contact Linda.

"Okay, John, I'll let you know what develops. See ya."

For Grant, the next two hours dragged by. Finally, Linda called. "If I had a choice, I'd take a root canal over a meeting with Dr. McAree," she said. "He's one of the most arrogant bastards I've ever met. If you don't have an MD after your name, you're automatically several rungs beneath him. He even treated George with disdain."

Grant let her finish venting, then cut in. "All right, lay it on me," he said.

She got directly to the point. "You're still the lead investigator, but you will not go to the morgue, or speak with Dr. Franz without the approval of Dr. Massey. That approval will be coordinated by Dr. McAree."

Grant's heart sank, but Linda seemed fairly upbeat. "I don't understand how I'm going to be able to go much further if I can't have access to the morgue records. If this is going to be a sham, I don't want any part of it!"

"It's not going to be a sham, John. You'll get everything you need to do your investigation," Linda responded, almost bubbly.

"I give, Linda. What have you got up your sleeve?"

"You see, McAree ticked me off, and George too. He thinks McAree is very close to misconduct in trying to limit the investigation. We talked for quite a while after we left Dr. McAree's office. Any morgue records you need to see and any

100

morgue employee you have to interview, except Franz, will be subpoenaed to your office. You won't have to go to the morgue. We'll only have to get McAree and Massey involved if you want to talk with Dr. Franz. Pretty good, huh?"

Grant pondered the news for a few seconds, his face breaking into a grin. "This is a cute deal, no doubt about it. My compliments to both you and George. I must assume that the good Dr. McAree doesn't know anything about this, does he?"

"Of course not," Linda giggled. "What he doesn't know won't hurt him."

"I give George credit, it sounds like he's got a set of brass ones. But aren't you guys playing a dangerous game? You both might end up cleaning toilets after the first subpoena hits."

"That's true," Linda said, her voice now serious. "Dr. McAree will have to be dealt with at some point. But we're putting the cart before the horse. Right now, we don't know what records to ask for. You'd better concentrate on Crowne or that Acme Pharmaceutical Company. We need something beyond rumor and innuendo. Get it for me!"

"I will, Linda," Grant promised, "I will."

CHAPTER ELEVEN

Grant arrived at the state office building at seven-thirty Friday morning. He stopped at the first floor news stand and bought a copy of the Observer. He tucked the paper under his left arm without looking at it, and headed toward the elevator. He already had a pretty good idea what he'd find in the paper. Doyle had called him at home the previous evening and advised him that Massey and Bronson had unleashed a scathing attack on his conduct, and the state DOH's failure to properly train or supervise their employees. The only bright side, according to Doyle, was that Grant wasn't mentioned by name. The release simply referred to him as a "state investigator". Doyle said he had contacted Linda and she had given a brief response.

So, Grant went to his office with the bad news under his arm, not wanting to look at it, but knowing he'd have to.In the privacy of his room, door closed, he unfolded the paper and scanned the front page for the story. He didn't have to look far, the headline at the top of the page read, "State DOH Investigator Asked To Leave The Morgue." A sub headline said, "County accuses state of misconduct, as yet another investigation of ME's office begins." Doyle and his editors had been kind enough so far, Grant thought. But he knew it was the comments of Massey and Bronson that would bite. He read on.

"Dr. Robert Franz was forced to ask a state DOH investigator to leave the morgue Thursday morning, after it was discovered that this individual had not properly identified himself, gaining access to the building under false pretenses," Massey was quoted as saying. "While we want to cooperate fully with any inquiry, I have insisted, and Mr. Bronson has concurred, that this particular investigator will not be allowed future admittance to the morgue without the approval of both DOH and county officials. The state has agreed to that demand," Massey concluded.

Ronald Bronson stated, "I have no control over DOH personnel actions. But I can assure the people of this county, that if one of our employees engaged in this kind of conduct he, or she, would soon be seeking other employment. And, depending on the circumstances, the person responsible for supervising such an individual might be out of a job too. I also want to assure our residents, and especially county employees, that I won't allow our people to be bullied, intimidated, or otherwise taken advantage of, by rogue state employees."

Grant sat shaking his head. The next three paragraphs were more of the same, derogatory quotes from both Bronson and Massey, and expressions of support for Franz. The last paragraph of the story contained the brief statement from Linda. "The department is conducting an investigation into allegations of unauthorized tissue harvesting at the Oneida County Medical Examiner's Office. This investigation has been, and will continue to be, conducted in accord with state law and department guidelines."

Grant had just finished reading, when Velma walked in. "Good morning, John," she smiled. "You made quite a splash yesterday. Your escapade was on the evening TV news and I heard it again on the radio while I was driving in." She saw the startled expression on Grant's face. "They didn't use your name, don't worry about that. But it does appear that you annoyed some people."

Grant nodded and handed Velma the paper. She briefly scanned the article and gave him the paper back. "Yes," she said, "when I was walking through the main office, three of the guys from the air monitoring unit were standing around looking at the paper. When I passed by they wanted to know if my roommate was the 'rogue investigator'. I told them I didn't know."

"What in the hell do they care?" Grant asked. "My problems have nothing to do with them. None of those bastards have even spoken to me since I've been here."

"You know how offices like this are, John. When somebody has a rough time it's big news. Most of these people will work for the state twenty or thirty years, and never have anything they do be noted by the department, much less the media. On the one

104

hand they're probably jealous, on the other, they're damn glad it's about you, and not them. Well, I'm off to the wars," she said, grabbing some papers from her desk and heading for the door. She stopped in the doorway and turned to Grant. "Don't let it get you down," she advised him. "If your visit to the morgue generated this kind of response, you must be getting into something that they don't want you snooping around. Think of it that way."

After she left, Grant closed the door and sat back down, mulling over her words. They were probably only said to make him feel better, but she may be right. In the great scheme of things, his encounter with Franz should have been a minor matter. Yet it was reported on radio, TV and in the press. And the impetus was by the county. Even if they felt they had a legitimate complaint, they could have made their grievance to the department and stopped there. Instead, they went to the media, why?

The ringing phone interrupted his thoughts. "What do you think of the story?" Jim Doyle wanted to know.

"I thought the Observer was fair. I certainly don't see myself as the incompetent rogue Masssey and Bronson tried to portray. That leads me to a question, why did the county launch such a strong attack? They brought additional attention to an ongoing problem that they've been trying to put behind them."

"Do you want my educated opinion?"

"That's why I asked."

"Think back to our conversation about county politics. Who do you think Bronson was directing his comments to? I'll answer that for you. He was talking to the voters, especially the county employees and their labor unions. Mr. Bronson isn't going to let big brother misuse this county. I think he made that very clear. Your visit to the morgue was one of the best things that could have happened to Bronson, and he's going to take advantage of it. The second thing, in my opinion, is the obvious attempt to muster public support for a possible battle with the state over Dr. Franz. If a county investigation found something on Franz, the public would probably support any action the county took. But now, we have an outside agency sticking it's nose in. Bronson very smoothly put DOH in the role of the bad guy. I'd bet that they think roughing you up a little bit will cause you guys to back off. Will it?"

"Not as far as I'm concerned," Grant said, not mentioning his fears about Dr. McAree.

"How about as far as anybody else is concerned?" Doyle asked.

"I can only speak for myself," Grant answered.

"Okay, John, I can read between the lines. I've got to run, catch you later."

Doyle's opinions made sense. Bronson was facing an up hill political battle with Anthony Barone, he needed to strengthen his support. Along comes John Grant and opens up an issue that Bronson can use as a rallying point. Pretty slick, Grant had to admit.

Grant put the story out of his mind, and concentrated on a more important matter, how he was going to find evidence of the illegal tissue harvesting. That evidence would have to come from Lewis Marner and Crowne, or Acme Pharmaceutical. He decided to start with Marner.

A check of the county residential white pages revealed twelve Marner's, but no Lewis. He flipped to the business listings, looked up Crowne and dialed the main number. "Crowne Memorial Hospital and Research Center," a sexy female voice answered. Grant explained that he was trying to reach a research assistant named Lewis Marner. "One moment please," the woman said.

After a few seconds a male voice came on the line, "Dr. Rudolph, may I help you?"

"Yes, doctor," Grant said. "I'm trying to locate Lew Marner. I know he works at Crowne, but I don't know the best number or time to reach him, can you help me?"

"May I ask who you are, sir?"

"Certainly," Grant said. "My name is Don Fey, I went to school with Lew. I've been out west for a while, I'm back here now and trying to touch base with some of my old friends. Can you tell me when and where to reach Lew?"

"I'm afraid I can't, Mr. Fey. Lewis used to work for me, but he left a few months ago. I haven't heard from him since, sorry."

"I understand, doctor. Thanks for your time," Grant said and hung up.

Grant sat thinking for several seconds, drumming his fingers on the top of his desk. His decision made, he got up and left the office for Crowne.

Crowne Memorial was located on South Champlin Avenue, about six miles from his office. It was just inside the Utica city limits. The facility consisted of two brick buildings. The largest, seven floors, was the hospital, the smaller, five floor, building was the research center.

Grant parked his car and entered the research building lobby. Just inside the door he encountered a reception desk. He asked to see Dr. Rudolph. The receptionist had him fill in the visitor log, then dialed a number and told someone that a John Grant, state DOH, was waiting in the lobby to see Dr. Rudolph. He was issued a stick on visitor pass and told that someone would be down to get him shortly.

While he was waiting, Grant roamed around the lobby. He found a directory listing the scientific staff. There was only one Rudolph on the list, Joseph Rudolph, Ph.D.

The receptionist called his name, he turned to find an attractive woman, probably in her forties, wearing a white lab coat, standing next to the reception desk. "This is Skip Robinson, Dr. Rudolph's assistant. She'll take you to see Dr. Rudolph," the receptionist said.

Grant walked over, smiled and extended his hand. Skip returned the smile along with a firm handshake. "Nice to meet you, Mr. Grant," Skip said. "Is this your first time here?" Grant said it was. "Well, welcome. Whatever the reason you're here, I'm sure you'll find it a pleasant experience."

Grant followed Skip to an elevator that took them to the fourth floor. He didn't discuss the information he was seeking, not wanting to put her in an awkward position. He'd only involve her if things didn't work out with Dr. Rudolph.

They exited the elevator and Skip headed down the hallway to the left. The door to every room they passed was closed, no one was visible in the corridor, the only sound was their feet falling on the tile floor. Grant had anticipated an antiseptic, hospital type odor, there was none. If he didn't know better, he'd have thought the building was unoccupied.

Skip stopped in front of the door to room 417. "I'll introduce you to Dr. Rudolph, then I have some errands to run. If I don't see you before you leave, it's been a pleasure to meet you." With that, she opened the door and entered the room, Grant followed. Once inside the door she stepped aside, providing him with an opportunity to survey the interior.

The room was large, the walls painted a light green, the ceiling was white, and the floor was a dark green tile. There were two oversize desks, a computer on each, in the middle of the room. Bookshelves and file cabinets lined the walls. The sole occupant of the room was a man seated at the desk furthest from the door. He appeared to be in his late thirties and was also wearing a white lab coat. His hair was jet black, and he sported a full beard and pony tail.

"Mr. Grant, this is Dr. Rudolph," Skip said, nodding toward the man at the desk. She stepped out and gently closed the door.

Grant walked to Rudolph's desk, smiling, right hand extended. Rudolph remained seated, face expressionless. He reluctantly reached out to accept Grant's hand, but didn't grip it. Grant clasped Rudolph's hand and pumped it several times. After he released it, he produced a business card from his inside jacket pocket and handed it to Rudolph. "I'm sorry to pop in on you unannounced, doctor, but I found myself in the area and thought I'd stop in to see if you can help me with an investigation I'm conducting."

As Grant spoke, Rudolph's face seemed to harden. "I'm very busy and, as you admitted, I wasn't expecting you. I can give you a couple of minutes, if this is going to take any longer than that you'll have to make an appointment and come back. Well?"

"I'll try to be brief, doctor. I'm interested in research that is, or was, being conducted here using human tissue. I believe that a Mr. Lewis Marner was involved with it."

Rudolph stared at him for several seconds before answering.

Grant thought he saw a flicker of concern, anger, or both, cross his face.

"Do you know a guy named Don Fey?" Rudolph asked.

Grant's brow creased in thought. "I don't believe so, doctor, sorry. Can you tell me where I might know him from?"

"Never mind, I'm sure it's just a coincidence, but Fey called earlier today asking for Marner. His voice was very similar to yours. I told Fey, and I'll tell you, that Lewis no longer works here," Rudolph said sarcastically. Grant didn't respond.

Rudolph studied Grant's business card, still held in his right hand. He put the card down on his desk and looked back up at Grant. He snapped his right thumb and index finger, "I've got it, you're the guy who was at the morgue yesterday, aren't you? How does it feel to get tossed out of a county building?" he sneered.

Grant smiled at him without answering. He turned, grabbed the empty chair from the other desk, placed it as close as he could get to Rudolph, and sat down, invading his space. "Right now, we're going to talk about the research I'm interested in. If you don't care to answer my questions, give me the name of your supervisor. I don't really care who gives me the information. Now, you said you only had a few minutes, I suggest you decide whether you're going to cooperate, or if you want me to talk to your boss. What's it going to be?"

Rudolph's poker face began to crumble. It was obvious that he didn't want Grant to involve his superiors. "I certainly want to cooperate," Rudolph said with an insincere smile. "I'm sorry if I gave you the wrong impression. What would you like to know?"

Grant moved his chair back a few inches. "As I said, doctor, I'd like to know about a research project using human tissue. What the project was, or is, and the source of the tissue."

Rudolph was slow to answer, looking at his hands, his desk top, everywhere but at Grant. "Well, I'm afraid I can't help you very much," he said finally. "You see, Lewis was doing a private project, bladder research, I believe. Crowne wasn't involved."

"Are you saying that researchers here can run their own private research projects on premises, and that Crowne doesn't know anything about the nature of the research?" Grant wanted to know.

"Look, Mr. Grant, Lewis came to me one day and asked if he could do some private bladder research. He said that it wouldn't interfere with his regular duties. Crowne has never discouraged research. I told Lewis to go ahead, provided that he kept up with his official assignments."

"When was this?"

"I think it was in the spring of '89."

"How long did this research last?"

"I believe he worked on it off and on until he left, that was the first of the year."

"Was the project finished? Did Marner generate any paper or report of the research?"

"Nothing was written that I'm aware of. As far as I know, the research was ongoing."

"It's your statement then, that you gave Marner permission to conduct private bladder research here at Crowne. This research lasted around three and a half years. You weren't aware of the particulars of the project, you don't know if it was completed, and you don't know where Marner is now. Is that accurate?"Rudolph stroked his beard for several seconds, apparently thinking over Grant's assessment of what he had said. "Yes," he said, "that sums it up."

"Did you give Marner permission to use human tissue in his private research?" Grant asked.

Rudolph stared at Grant, appearing confused. "What..what do you mean?" Rudolph stammered. "I never said anything about human tissue."

"I told you that I was interested in research using human tissue, possibly involving Marner. You immediately referred to Marner's private project. Apparently you were aware of what was going on."

Beads of perspiration formed on Rudolph's forehead. The fingers of his right hand played with the beard again. "I...I only said that because Crowne seldom uses human tissue, I've never used human tissue in my research. You said you were investigating something Lewis was involved in, so I naturally assumed it was his private project."

"I see," Grant said. "You're saying that you have no knowledge that human tissue was being used by Marner, and you have never used human tissue in your projects."

"That's what I'm saying," Rudolph answered, his composure back.

"What tissue do you use for research, doctor?"

"Animal, primarily from rabbits."

"Why not use human? Wouldn't that be the best?"

Rudolph smiled. "Human would be better, you're right. We don't use it thanks in large part to DOH. You have put so many regulations on the use of human tissue that it's almost impossible to meet the criteria. Most scientists won't pursue a request unless they determine that their research can't be done any other way. And that is rare."

"In those rare cases, what is the procedure that has to be followed?"

"Well, the researcher has to submit a written request to our Research Oversight Committee, giving the nature of the project, the reason that animal tissue would not be satisfactory, the estimated amount of tissue needed and length of the project."

"Then what?"

111

"If the request gets approved by the Committee, which can take several weeks, it is forwarded to the Scientific Research Approval Program at DOH. There is never enough information for them on the initial application, you always have to submit more. To get a final answer from DOH takes months, and then it may well go against you."

Grant gave a sympathetic smile. "Let's assume the request is ultimately approved, how is the tissue obtained?"

"We have a Tissue Procurement Coordinator, Lorraine Banks, who handles that. I don't know the details, but she finds a source and gets what is needed. She knows her job and everything is done legally."

"It sounds like you're well aware that the use of human tissue is closely regulated, and that if it is not properly procured it is against the law, right?"

Rudolph glared at Grant. "I've told you that I was not involved in using human tissue. I resent your continuous attempts to have me admit that I had knowledge of it and that I knew it was a problem. You're inferring that I'm a liar, sir, and I don't like it!"

Grant ignored Rudolph's statement. "Did you make your superiors aware of Marner's private project?" he asked.

"No, since it didn't directly involve Crowne I saw no reason to."

"Who is your supervisor, by the way?"

"I report to the Director of Research. That position is currently vacant. The Oversight Committee is handling things until a new Director is appointed."

"Who was the Director and when did he, or she, leave?"

"Dr. Morris Slater retired last month."

"Are you in contention for his job?" Grant asked.

"What can that possibly have to do with why you're here?"

"Nothing, actually," Grant smiled. "Just my natural curiosity at work. Can you give me any help in trying to locate Mr. Marner?"

"No."

112

"Surely you must have his address and phone number around someplace. Even if he's moved, that information will be a good starting point."

"I don't have that information here. All that kind of stuff will be in his personnel file at Human Resources."

"Where is that office?"

"The first floor of the hospital. I suggest you go and talk to them, please shut the door on your way out."

"But I'm not finished here yet, doctor. Can I call over and see if they'll be able to help me?"

"I suppose so," Ruldoph said reluctantly. He picked up the phone and dialed a number. "Good morning, Anne, this is Dr. Rudolph. Is Dave Pelton in?" After a brief delay, "Good morning Dave. I've got a guy here from state DOH looking for personal information on Lewis Marner. He wants to talk with you." Rudolph passed the handset to Grant.

Grant identified himself and explained what he wanted. "I'm sorry, Mr. Grant," Pelton said. "But all information in our files is considered confidential. I suggest you have your legal department contact ours and work something out, otherwise I won't be able to help you." Grant thanked him and reached across the desk to hang the phone up.

"What was your relationship with Marner when he left?" Grant asked.

"You'll have to get the particulars of Lewis's departure from Mr. Pelton."

"I didn't ask you for any particulars, I asked what your relationship was."

"I'm not going to discuss anything involving Mr. Marner."

At that point the door opened. Skip Robinson came in, arms full of pages of computer printouts. She smiled, but didn't speak, as she walked to the other desk and put the printouts down.

Grant turned his attention back to Rudolph. "You say you weren't involved in Marner's research, did he leave anything here when he left? Any paperwork relating to his project?"

"No, he cleaned his office out."

"What about the file cabinet?" Skip asked.

Grant followed Rudolph's eyes as they fired daggers at Skip. Her face flushed, but she didn't back down. "Don't you remember his file cabinet? The one we moved to the storage closet across the hall?"

"I do now," Rudolph said icily. He swung his head from Skip and found Grant staring at him, eyebrows arched questioningly. "There was a file cabinet in Lewis's office with some junk in it. We put it in the storage room. I forgot about it," Rudolph explained.

"Did you go through it?"

"No."

"Then how do you know it contains junk?"

"I assumed, okay?" Rudolph said disgustedly.

"Let's go look at it now," Grant suggested.

Rudolph hesitated. "If you don't want to make the decision, I'll go to someone who will. I'm sure your legal department will cooperate," Grant said with much more certainty than he felt.

Rudolph stared at Grant for a moment. "That won't be necessary, follow me." He said and got up from his chair.

Grant followed him out the door and in another door across the corridor. This was an unused office containing a dust covered desk and telephone, and several empty bookshelves against the walls. Rudolph opened a door in the right wall, reached in and flipped on a light switch. "In here," he said, stepping aside.

Grant walked past him and entered a small room containing more empty bookshelves and a beaten up four drawer wooden file cabinet. "That was his," Rudolph said, pointing at the file cabinet. "Now, if you'll excuse me, I have work to do."

As soon as Rudolph left Grant opened the top drawer of the cabinet. It contained several loose sheets of paper. He just started to go through them when he sensed a presence behind him. He turned to find Skip in the doorway. "Dr. Rudolph sent me over to make sure you don't take anything," she explained.

Grant shrugged and smiled. "That's fine with me. In fact, it's probably a good idea." He returned to his examination of the drawer. To his disappointment, the documents seemed to be various memos relating to general policies and guidelines, nothing regarding Marner's research. He closed that drawer and opened the next one.

"Mr. Grant," Skip said, "I don't know what's going on here, but I don't think Dr. Rudolph really wanted me to watch you. I think he wanted me out of the office. I don't want you to think that I'm not loyal to Crowne, I am. I love my job here, but what's right is right. I don't like the vibes I'm getting from Dr. Rudolph. He seems very upset. He's usually very pleasant."

"I appreciate your position, Skip. And I'm thankful that you remembered this file cabinet. It remains to be seen if it contains anything helpful to me, but at least I've got the opportunity to look," Grant said, and returned to his task.

The second drawer held a dozen technical magazines, the mailing labels all removed. Grant closed that drawer and turned to Skip. "I don't want to ask you anything that will make you feel uncomfortable, or get you in any trouble, but I think you can help me with a couple of things. Do you mind if I ask you a couple of questions?"

"No, I guess not. I won't answer if I don't think it's appropriate. Go ahead."

"Do you know anything about Mr. Marner's private research project?"

"I not only don't know anything about it, I wasn't aware there was one. In spite of this lab coat, I'm not a scientist, I'm really a clerk, a 'girl Friday', if you will. So while I never actually worked with Lew, I am in a position to know what went on. I never had an inkling that Lew was doing anything on his own. That surprises me."

"Marner was supposedly doing private bladder research from '89 until he left. How long have you been here?"

"Since '90, and I find your scenario hard to believe. I know that there was some kind of bladder research going on, and it

115

may have been what you call 'private'. But if it was, it wasn't Lew's project alone. He and Dr. Rudolph discussed it regularly. Dr. Rudolph told Lew what he wanted done."

"Did you ever hear anything mentioned about them using human tissue?"

Skip shook her head. "Sorry, but I don't remember anything like that. Why is that important?"

"I'm investigating allegations that the ME's office was illegally harvesting research tissue. I have reason to believe that some of it made its way to Mr. Marner."

"Oh yes, I've seen that in the paper, but I didn't connect it to Lewis." Skip thought for a moment. "I don't know if this means anything, but Lew used to get calls from the morgue quite often."

Grant smiled. "That means a lot, Skip, thanks. Were you friendly with Lew? I'm trying to find out where he is now. I'll find out eventually, but if you know it would save me a lot of time."

"We got along well. I didn't agree with his lifestyle, but he was always nice to me."

"What about his lifestyle?" Grant interrupted.

"He's gay. I don't agree with that, but I try to judge everyone individually. Lew was okay. Anyway, just before he left, he told me that he had enrolled in a mortuary school, he's going to become a funeral director. I don't know the name of the school, but I think it was south of here."

"You're great, Skip, thanks again." He turned back to the cabinet and opened the third drawer.

As soon as he peeked inside he sensed that he may have found something of interest. The drawer held four manila folders, each had a year handwritten in ink across the tab. They covered 1989 thru 1992. He opened the file marked 1989. It contained several loose sheets of paper, forms of some kind. He examined the first one. Typed across the top were the words "Tissue Source Log". The top half of the page contained donor information. It included the sex, age, date of birth and date and

116

cause of death. There was no name, but there was an autopsy number, the same numbering system used at the morgue. He quickly scanned the other forms in that file, then the other three folders. They all contained the same forms. This had to be what he had been looking for. There was only one other thing to check. He turned and headed out the door. "I have to talk with Dr. Rudolph," he said as he passed Skip. "I'll be right back."

"Whatever you found must be good, you're sweating," she said.

Reflexively, Grant's right hand wiped his forehead. He was surprised when it came away damp. "It may be what I hoped to find," he admitted. "I'll know in a minute." He went out the door and back to Rudolph's office. He opened the door without knocking. Rudolph was at his desk, staring at a blank computer monitor.

"Does Crowne Memorial do autopsies, doctor," Grant asked, bringing Rudolph back to the present.

Grant saw concern in his eyes. "Yes. Why?" Rudolph asked.

"What is their autopsy numbering system," Grant wanted to know.

"The last two digits of the year, followed by a three digit sequential number. Why?"

"They don't use an eight digit numbering system?"

"No. Why?"

"Are you sure?"

"Yes, God damn it, I'm sure!" Rudolph shouted, obviously frustrated. "Why? Why are you asking? What's going on?"

Grant smiled at him. "Just curious," he said, turning his back and walking out the door. He was elated, the pressure to find evidence of the tissue donations to Crowne was off. Thanks to Skip, he had been successful. If she had returned to the office a few minutes later he may have been gone, and Marner's records would have continued to collect dust in the storage room.

In spite of his good mood, he knew he wasn't out of the woods yet. If Skip was right about Rudolph wanting her out of the room, it may have been so he could call someone for advice.

117

Dave Pelton, or someone from Crowne's legal department could still show up to dispute his right to access the file cabinet.

"Do you think this phone works?" Grant asked Skip, nodding at the desk in the unused office.

"It should. Just dial nine to get an outside line," she said.

Grant called Albany for Linda. He wanted to brief her on what he had found and tell her he planned to ask for copies of the contents of the four files. Linda was on another line, he left the number listed on the phone and said to tell Linda it was an emergency.

Grant had barely gotten back to the file cabinet when Dr. Rudolph poked his head in. "Call for you on my phone," he said.

Grant followed Rudolph back across the hall, wondering how Linda had ended up calling Rudolph's number. He took the handset from Rudolph. "Hello."

"Mr. Grant?" an icy voice asked.

"Yes, Mrs. Miller," Grant answered, a knot forming in his stomach.

"In case you didn't know, I'm an administrative consultant for Crowne. I'm speaking to you now in that capacity. As soon as the administrator became aware of the nature of your visit, she contacted me immediately. I'm in the administrative office on the first floor of the hospital building. I want you to stop and see me on your way out."

"Certainly, Mrs. Miller, I shouldn't be much longer. I'll stop and see you before I leave."

"No, Mr. Grant, you'll see me now. Your visit here today is over. I'll be waiting for you."

Rudolph took the handset back from Grant, flashing a wide grin. "Good news, I hope," he said.

Grant fought to keep a neutral expression. "Couldn't be better," he said.

He returned to the office across the hall just as the desk phone started to ring. "Hello," he said again, this time somewhat tentatively.

118

"What's the matter, John? You sound as though you were expecting the devil to be on the line," Linda said.

"I've already talked with her," Grant responded, turning to glance at Skip. She smiled understandingly, then walked out and closed the door.

Grant told Linda about his conversation with Rudolph, Marner's records and the call from Miller. Linda's excitement was obvious in her voice. "I'm going to call George. One of us will call you back. In the meantime, stall Miller the best you can. But don't leave that place without copies of those records, okay?"

"I'm with you, but I don't think I have any legal standing to demand those copies, or to even be in the building if they ask me to leave."

"You're probably right, that's why I'm going to call George. He'll be able to figure something out. Hang in there. Bye."

Grant replaced the handset. He looked at the closed door, hoping the phone would ring before it was opened. That wasn't to be.

Ten minutes later the door swung open. June Miller entered the room, followed by two uniformed Crowne security guards and a still grinning Dr. Rudolph. Miller walked directly up to Grant, the others waited just inside the door.

"Mr. Grant, you are trespassing. I asked you to leave this complex several minutes ago, you haven't complied with my orders," Miller said. Her voice was cold, but unemotional. "If you don't leave now, I'll instruct my security officers to escort you to their office and hold you there until the police arrive. I hope it doesn't come to that, but I will have you arrested if you don't leave voluntarily."

Grant looked at the security guards. They appeared uncomfortable, but they were employed by Crowne, and would follow Miller's orders.

"Mrs. Miller," Grant said, addressing himself to the guards as well as her. "I'm awaiting a call from my boss in Albany. She

119

should be calling on this phone momentarily. I'd appreciate the courtesy of being allowed to wait here until I hear from her."

As Miller was digesting his request, the phone rang. Grant grabbed the handset. "John," George Epstein said. "We're on a conference call with Mr. Thomas Sullivan, Chief Counsel for Crowne. I've explained the situation to him, I'll let him tell you what we're going to do."

"Hi, Mr. Grant, I'm Tom Sullivan."

"Excuse me," Grant cut in. "I want to make sure I have this right. You are Mr. Thomas Sullivan, Chief Counsel for Crowne?" he asked for the benefit of his audience. Their expressions indicated that Sullivan's name had an impact.

"Go ahead, Mr. Sullivan," Grant invited, "sorry for the interruption."

"What George has told me disturbs me greatly," Sullivan said. "If you have found what you think you've found, that may contradict previous statements we've made to the press. That would be in addition to any violation of law, of course. Quite frankly, I hope you're mistaken. But, regardless of how favorable or unfavorable the information is, we will cooperate with your investigation in any way possible. What do you need from us?"

"Right now, I'd like to obtain copies of all the documents in the files I found. I suspect there are several hundred of them. Then I'd ask that the originals be secured in your office. Is that okay?"

"That sounds reasonable. Anything else?"

"Not right now. That could change after we examine the records, of course."

"Understood. If there's nothing else, I'll try to track down Mrs. Miller. I understand she was called in to facilitate your visit. I'll instruct her to arrange for your copies."

Grant nearly choked at Sullivan's description of Miller being called in to 'facilitate' his visit. "I can save you some time in that regard," he said pleasantly. "It just so happens that Mrs.

Miller was here chatting with me when you called. Would you like me to put her on the line?"

"Yes, please," Sullivan said.

Grant handed the phone to Miller, not quite able to conceal a smile.

CHAPTER TWELVE

That same Friday morning, Dr. Robert Franz began his day at his dentist's office for his semi-annual teeth cleaning. He followed that with a time consuming, but more pleasant, visit to the barber shop. He arrived at the morgue around eleven o'clock.

"Good morning," he said to Dorothy Larkin and Belinda Bernal, as he entered the main office. "I didn't notice June's car in the lot, has she been in, or called?"

"Good morning, doctor," both women said. "June was here, but she had to leave, she said to tell you that there was some kind of problem at Crowne. She'll be back, or call, later," Mrs. Larkin explained.

"Some intern probably pinched a nurse on the ass, and got turned in," Franz laughed. "Anything else going on?"

"Everything's quiet, doctor," Belinda answered. "Dr. Samuels is in his office, Marcia and Mike are doing some cleaning in the back," she continued, nodding toward the autopsy room.

"Sounds good," Franz said. "I'll be in my office," he disappeared out the doorway.

Franz poured himself a cup of coffee in the breakroom, then went to his office and closed the door. He had read the morning paper, and was very pleased with the statements by Massey and Bronson. The people at his dentist's office and the barber shop had made favorable comments about the way he had handled Grant. "Don't let them push you around, Bob," the dentist had said. The strategy was working, he concluded. DOH was the bad guy. He was sure he had heard the last of Grant. His desk phone rang a few minutes later. "Dr. Franz," he answered.

"Bob, this is Joe Rudolph, how are you?"

"Fine, just fine, Joe. I had to kick a little ass yesterday, did you hear about it?"

"Yes, that's why I'm calling. We've got a problem."

Franz sat straight upright in his chair. "What kind of problem?" he asked slowly.

"A state DOH investigator showed up here this morning, a guy named John Grant. He said he's investigating a project here at Crowne that used human tissue, and involved Lew Marner. He's trying to locate Marner to ask him some questions."

"What did you tell him, Joe?"

"Well, it was obvious that he had some basis for his questions, somebody's already talked to him. I told him that if Marner was using any human tissue, it was for some private research he was doing. It didn't involve Crowne or me."

"Did he believe you?"

"I doubt it. But Slater was the only one who knew that we were doing the bladder stuff, and he's retired and moved to Phoenix. If Grant doesn't really pursue this, doesn't contact Slater, it will just be my word against Marner's. A Ph.D. against a fag. That'll be no contest."

"Okay, I understand your logic. You're assuming that Grant will find Marner, but that he won't be believed. You're banking on Grant not contacting Slater. I don't want to discourage you, but Grant was the guy who was here yesterday. I didn't think I'd ever hear from him again, but here he is, a day after being humiliated. I wouldn't count on him going away. If I'm right, then we've got big trouble." Franz hesitated briefly, then, "Did Grant ask about me or the morgue?"

"No, I laid everything on Marner and denied any knowledge of what he was talking about. But there's more," Rudolph said. He had a lump in his throat, and his stomach was rolling from Franz's pesimistic assessment, and what he had to tell him next.

"What?" Franz asked warily, beginning to connect June Miller's absence to Rudolph's call.

"Grant asked to look in an old file cabinet that Marner had used. He found Marner's 'Tissue Source Logs', all of them."

Franz couldn't believe what Rudolph was saying, it was inconceivable to him that those logs were still laying around months after Marner had left. "You stupid son of a bitch!" he shouted, throwing his coffee cup across the room. "Why in the fuck didn't you get rid of that shit when Marner left? Why did you let Grant search that cabinet? Where in the hell was your head?"

Rudolph sat in his chair quivering for several seconds before answering. "Bob, the guy came in here without warning. I had to make some fast decisions. I did what I thought was right. I didn't tell him about the file cabinet, my clerk let it slip. I didn't want to let him rummage around, but he threatened to go over my head. I can't afford that. I've got a good shot at the Director position, I can't let the big wheels get wind that I might be under investigation. Anyway, as soon as Grant went to look in the file cabinet I called my administrator for help. She called June, she's here now."

"She stopped his search, I presume."

"She tried. She told him to leave, even threatened to have him arrested. But a DOH lawyer got hold of our Chief Counsel and worked out a deal to have the files copied. June and Grant are doing that now. When they're finished, the files have to be turned over to our counsel's office for safe keeping. As far as the files still being here, I have to take responsibility for that. But that's history now, Bob. We need to figure out what to do next."

"You're right," Franz agreed, grudgingly. "I'll need to think this over, make some calls. Don't talk to Grant again unless you absolutely have to. I'll get back to you. Oh, by the way, do you have a personal attorney?" Rudolph said he did. "Good," Franz said, "you may very well need him."

Dr. Morton Massey sat in the chair behind his office desk. The office was huge, covering the south side of the fourth floor of the county building. In addition to his desk, the room contained a conference table, with a couch, four overstuffed chairs and a coffee table in a sitting area. It was the envy of all the other county department heads.

Massey's door was closed. It was twelve-thirty, most of the employees were in the cafeteria, or elsewhere, for lunch. Massey swiveled his chair around so he could see the left corner of the office behind him, containing a small coffee pot on a table. His eyes settled on the buttocks of his private secretary, Gloria Daniels. She had just finished preparing the pot to produce it's third strong dose of the day. She was leaning slightly forward to turn the pot on, her back to Massey.

The view caused a smile to creep over Massey's face. Gloria was twenty-six. She had long, chestnut hair, and an hour glass figure. The thought of her naked began to arouse him. Gloria straightened up and walked to Massey's desk. "Anything else I can do for you?" she asked with a smile.

Massey smiled back, a twinkle in his eye. His left hand reached down and stroked the back of her right knee. The hand started to crawl up the back of her leg, under her skirt.

Gloria looked at her watch. "Do you think we have time?" she asked.

Before Massey could answer, his office door burst open and a red faced Bob Franz walked in. Massey quickly moved his hand and straightened up in his chair. Gloria's hands reflexively reached down and smoothed her skirt. Both of their faces were flushed. Gloria walked past Franz and out the door without a word.

As soon as the door had closed behind her, an irate Massey screamed at Franz, "Who in the hell do you think you are? What gives you the right to barge into my office without knocking?"

"Come down off your high horse, Mort," Franz said, unimpressed by Massey's outburst. "I need to talk to you about something more important than your afternoon delight."

Massey's anger quickly left him. Franz's expression and tone convinced him that this was a matter of importance. "What is it, Bob?"

"I'd like you to call your buddy in Albany again, I want Grant reined in," Franz said.

Massey looked surprised. "I thought this was already taken care of. That guy can't talk to you, or visit the morgue, without our knowledge and approval. What more do you want?"

"You're right, and that was great as far as it went. But Grant is over at Crowne as we speak, ransacking file cabinets and refusing to leave when ordered. June was called over there and was going to have him arrested. Unfortunately, the Crowne and DOH lawyers reached some kind of agreement. It looks to me like Grant is running amok, and I bet your friend doesn't know about it."

"My God, Bob, the county has nothing to do with Crowne. I can't call and complain because Grant is over there. It's up to Crowne to make that complaint."

Franz, still standing, walked over and sat on the couch. "They won't do that now. Not after the lawyers made their deal," he said, shaking his head. "What's that deputy commissioners name, McAree?"

"Yes, Dr. Robert McAree."

"You told me yesterday that he was upset over Grant's conduct, he said he'd take care of it. I bet he'd be pissed off if he knew what Grant was doing today. All I'm saying, is that he should be tipped off."

"I see," Massey said. "But I wouldn't dare call McAree without consulting Bronson. He's using this situation for his own political purposes. He made it clear to me that he wants input on any contact we have with DOH."

Franz jumped to his feet and walked to Massey's desk, his face darkening. "I don't give a fuck about politics. I want Grant stopped and I want you to do something!"

"I'll have to think this over, Bob. It could be rough on me if I go behind Bronson's back."

Franz leaned forward, his palms on Massey's desk. "It could be a hell of a lot rougher on you if you don't do as I ask, screw Bronson!" Franz hissed.

"Is that a threat, Bob?" Massey asked, hurt and anger in his voice.

Franz straightened up, a smile on his scarlet face. "No, Mort, not a threat. Let's call it a statement of fact. You rely on me to help you with all major decisions. I doubt that you're capable of picking out a tie to wear by yourself. You've got a sweet deal here, big salary, big office and me making the decisions for you.

And remember, you're only in this position because I don't want it!" Franz paused for Massey to comprehend what he had said. "And you've got your little playmate here as a fringe benefit," Franz concluded.

"You've got a lot of balls talking about my indiscretion," Massey protested. "You've been doing the Longo broad for years!"

"There's one big difference," Franz said. "My wife knows, does yours?"

Massey looked as though he had been kicked in the stomach. His face was white with fear, he was having trouble catching his breath. He recognized that he was in a losing argument. When he was able to speak, he looked up at Franz. "I'll see what I can do, Bob," he said.

Grant arrived back at his office at two o'clock. He immediately called Linda. "It's been a good day, hasn't it?" she asked.

"Absolutely great!" Grant answered. "Especially after yesterday. But, I have to admit that it had its moments."

Linda laughed. "I didn't envy you having Miller on your neck. Thank heaven everything worked out. How many forms do you think you've got, and are you sure they are what we need to go further?"

"The clicker on the Crowne copier read 432. I'm confident that the autopsy numbers on these forms are morgue numbers. When we look at those files, the other data should match. I'm suspecting they won't contain donation consent forms."

"Good. I'd like you to bring the forms here to Albany on Monday morning. I'll have George down here, and we'll review the stuff and make an extra copy for here. Can you be here by ten?"

"Sure. Did you have any luck on Marner?"

"I talked with the Bureau of Funeral Directing right after I talked with George this morning. They said that if Marner enrolled in a mortuary school, they can find him. We'll have the answer on Monday."

"Beautiful!" Grant said. "I'll see you Monday, then."

"Hold on a second, John. I almost forgot, you'll be meeting somebody else on Monday. Lieutenant Eric Woods of the state Department of Environmental Conservation called me. He's been assigned to investigate the morgue dumping medical waste down the sewer. He learned that we were involved and asked to meet with us. I invited him to be here on Monday, okay?"

"Fine with me," Grant said. "As long as DEC doesn't try to take over."

"He won't. We have two entirely separate areas of jurisdiction. We agreed on that."

"I'll be looking forward to meeting him, then," Grant said. "See you Monday."

CHAPTER THIRTEEN

Grant arrived at the Corning Tower a few minutes before ten Monday morning. He carried a large folder containing the Marner files, clipped together by year. At the reception desk he was told that Linda was waiting for him in the conference room opposite her office.

When Grant poked his nose into the conference room, he found Linda in conversation with a tall, balding man, presumably George Epstein. "Good morning," Grant said, walking to the table and depositing the folder.

"Good morning, yourself," Linda beamed. "This is George Epstein," she said, waving an arm at George.

Grant met George halfway, accepting his hand. "A pleasure to meet you in person, George," he said. "I really appreciate your efforts on Friday. I was in a bit of a spot for a while there at Crowne, thanks."

Epstein was forty-one years old, around six feet tall and a hundred ninety pounds. He had been with DOH for ten years. "Luck was on our side," he smiled. "Not only was I able to reach Mr. Sullivan right away, he was reasonable besides. I wouldn't want to have to count on that on a regular basis.'

Linda grabbed the folder off the table. "I'll get these copied," she said. "I've got coffee coming. And Lieutenant Woods called, he'll be a little late."

Linda was back in a few seconds, carrying three cups of coffee in a cardboard tray. With the cups handed out and everyone seated around the conference table, Linda opened the meeting. "We should use this time to talk about anything that we don't necessarily want to discuss in front of DEC. George, do you have anything?"

"No. In fact, I'd just as soon have Woods know what my plans are. That way he can give an accurate briefing to the DEC lawyers."

"John?" Linda asked.

"A couple of things. What exactly are we going to discuss with Lt. Woods, and is there anything new on the Dr. McAree front?"

"We're going to see if we can reach a level of cooperation with DEC. We clearly have different responsibilities, but we may have some common ground. Neither DEC nor us are over staffed. If we can share resources it will benefit both of us. As far as Dr. McAree goes," she continued, raising her eyes toward the ceiling, hands in front of her face, palms together as if in prayer, "He flew off to Atlanta on Friday. He had to attend a conference at the Center for Disease Control, he won't be back to work until next Monday."

Grant and George laughed. "Are you keeping tabs on the good deputy commissioner?" George asked Linda.

"Not really," she said, "but I do pay attention to the 'powder puff grapevine' whenever his name is mentioned."

"If the plan is still to subpoena the morgue for these tissue records, then you'll want to get that done while Dr. McAree is out of town, won't you?" Grant asked George.

"I want the subpoena served by the end of this week, but not because McAree is out of town. I want the subpoena served quickly to get the ball rolling. The county might fight it, there will probably be delays. The sooner we get started, the better. I wish McAree was here, actually. Remember, he only put restrictions on your activities, John. I'm under no obligation to clear my activities with him. I'm concerned it will appear that the subpoena was generated to coincide with his absence, and that isn't true."

"I see," Grant said. "Do you share my opinion that the county will complain to McAree after the subpoena is served?"

"No doubt in my mind," George said.

"What will you do if he goes on the warpath?"

"There is also no doubt in my mind that we'll have to have a showdown with McAree at some point. I'm developing some ideas on how to handle that. But that's nothing to concern yourself with, John. Linda and I will deal with that issue."

"Anything else?" Linda asked.

"Have you heard back from Funeral Directing about where we can find Marner?" Grant asked her.

"Yes, I have," she said, pulling a piece of paper from her blouse pocket. "Mr. Marner is currently doing an internship at the Malloy Funeral Home in Waterville."

Grant looked at George. "I'll prepare a subpoena for him too," George said. "When do you want to see him?"

"As soon as possible," Grant answered. "I'll feel better when he identifies these forms as being his and that the tissue was obtained from the morgue."

"Okay, I'll make it returnable next week," George said, removing a notebook from his inside jacket pocket. "Let's see, how about a week from Wednesday, that will be the thirty-first?"

"That's fine, George. Will you send me copies of the subpoenas?" Grant asked.

"Sure. I'll have them handled by an outside server. I'll fax you copies as soon as I know they've been served. We'll serve the county attorney for the morgue records and Marner personally, of course."

"Anything new on getting the Murphy gag order lifted?"

"I'm afraid that I'm not very optimistic about that, John," George said. "The AG confirmed what I told you earlier, it can take months to get something like this through. If I were you, I wouldn't count on having Murphy on the record in time to do you much good. I think you'll have to use him only for leads."

"That's unfortunate," Grant said. "Pat knows a lot about what has gone on in the morgue, and I think he'd make a good witness."

"I agree," George said. "but we'll just have to work around it."

At that point the receptionist appeared in the doorway. "Lieutenant Woods is here," she said to Linda. She turned away and Woods entered the room. He was in his mid thirties, just over six feet and a hundred eighty pounds. He had light brown hair, worn short. He was dressed casually, in tan sport shirt and slacks.

Linda rose from her chair and met him in the doorway. "Nice to meet you, lieutenant," she said, shaking his hand.

"Please call me Woody," he said, with an infectious smile.

Linda then introduced him to George and Grant. "Would you like coffee?" she asked Woody.

"No thanks. Please continue your conversation, it's bad enough that I'm late, I don't want to interrupt any further."

"As a matter of fact, I believe we were about finished," she said, glancing at Grant and George. "If you're ready we can start. Make yourself comfortable."

Woody took a seat at the table next to Grant. Linda closed the door and returned to her chair. "I explained our phone conversation to George and John," she said. "But it may be best to have you tell them what's on your mind in your own words."

"Sure," Woody said. "I've been assigned to investigate the allegations that the Oneida County Morgue improperly disposed of medical waste by dumping it into the sewer rather than incinerating it." Woody turned toward Grant and smiled, "I read in the paper that DOH was also investigating the morgue. I thought that there might be some areas that we can work together on. I eventually got in touch with Linda, and here we are."

"Anything specific that you think we can cooperate on?" Linda asked.

"Before we get into that, I'd like to give you a little background about me and my previous dealings with Dr. Franz. I'm a resident of Oneida County, I live just east of Utica. When I started with DEC in '86, I was assigned to Oneida and Herkimer counties. When we had deaths on state land in Oneida County, mostly hikers and hunters, Franz's office handled the autopsies. I met him several times, always at the morgue. I must tell you that I was very impressed. There were subsequent newspaper stories and rumors about Franz doing funny things, but Franz always said he was being attacked by disgruntled employees. I believed him. I got promoted a couple of years ago and assigned to Albany, I haven't dealt with Franz since.

"When the latest accusations were made a few weeks ago, I was asked to look into them. I accepted the assignment with a total lack of enthusiasm. I figured that this was more of the same old stuff. But apparently Franz's accusers threatened to bring on some heat if we didn't investigate. That's why I'm here today."

"We had similar threats from Dr. Johnson and his associates," Linda said. "That got us started, too."

"Well, as I said," Woody continued, "I wasn't very happy about this case. But I've changed my opinion since then. I've interviewed some people, I started with those who are not currently working at the morgue. I haven't found them to be what I had expected, I believe them. Even Dr. Johnson is credible, in my opinion." He turned to Grant again, "I spoke with a guy you've talked with, Bill Maxwell, he holds you in high regard, John."

Grant nodded. "I appreciate that, thanks," he said.

"The people that I've talked with so far have told me things that go way beyond my area of responsibility, the medical waste. If they're telling the truth, Franz needs to be held accountable. I believe that a thorough investigation of the morgue is called for. Most of what needs to be looked at is beyond my jurisdiction. I can help, but I can't carry the torch. I'm here to see what your plans are, whether we can be allies."

"Do your superiors and legal people share your feelings?" George asked.

Grant knew that George was trying to find out if Woody was a rogue or acting with the knowledge of his superiors. He was relieved when Woody said that he came to the meeting with the approval of DEC.

"Good," George said. "Let me tell you where I see this thing going from a DOH perspective. We're an administrative agency. If we find that Dr. Franz has been taking this tissue illegally, we can take action against the county, the county, not Franz. If we're successful, we can ask for a substantial fine. As part of any settlement we could ask that Franz surrender his Laboratory Director's license. If we can't get it that way, we'd have to go after Franz directly. The Medical Conduct people could go after his medical license, but that would be a separate action. This is presuming that the allegations are true, and the evidence is there to prove it."

"Why not charge Franz and the county?" Grant asked.

"That's a can of worms I don't want to open unless I have to," George said. "As long as we charge the county we deal with their attorneys and their interests. The state gives a lot of money to the counties, you know. If we ask for Franz's license as part of a settlement, the county will have to negotiate with him, not us. If we tackle Franz directly, he'll have a private attorney with only one concern, saving Franz's ass. No, we'll name Franz only if all else fails."

"We can go civil or make a criminal referral," Woody said.

"Quite frankly, it looks like all DEC will have here is the medical waste. I'm sure that will be handled as a civil matter."

"If we all understand where we're coming from, let's discuss a strategy and define areas where we can work together,' Linda said. She looked around the table, everyone nodded.

"As I see it," she continued. "our primary interest is the tissue harvesting at the morgue. As an extension of that, the recipients of the tissue, Crowne and one or two pharmaceutical companies, may have violated our regulations also. It looks to me as though John will have to investigate those matters, and you, Woody, will have to do the medical waste stuff. It seems to me that we don't really have any areas of joint investigation. We might be better off to coordinate the filing of charges and exert additional pressure on the county during settlement negotiations."

"I agree with you about the filing of charges," Woody said. "But I also think that we have at least one area that we can investigate together, that is Franz's skeletal collection. I know that this doesn't sound directly like a DEC problem, but when I heard that Franz has allegedly kept one or more bodies, I became

136

curious. I was told that he boiled the bones clean. That led me to wonder how he disposed of the contents of the boiling drum when he was finished. In at least the one case, a Mr. Chambers, the 'broth' was just dumped down a drain in the floor of the morgue garage. That liquid contained human tissue, and shouldn't have been released in the sewer any more than the tissue that was diced and flushed. So, this has become part of my investigation. It seems to me that DOH would be even more interested in this angle. Mr. Chambers, and any others that Franz has kept, aren't where their death certificates say they are. Now you have falsification of records, now you have felonies."

George, Linda and Grant exchanged glances. "We are looking at the tissue donations first because they seem the easiest to pursue, especially since we would have a very difficult time getting into the morgue to search for this alleged collection," George said. "We don't have police powers, Woody. We'd have to make arrangements for a morgue visit through the county attorney, we'd have to tell them what we're looking for. If the county is interested in covering for Franz, as has been alleged, that morgue would be clean as a whistle before we were let in. My plan is to investigate the tissue donations first. Depending on how we make out with that, and John has come up with information to make me think we've got a shot, we'll go after the skeletal collection. In the meantime, I don't want John to pursue it and tip our hand."

Woody seemed to ponder George's words for several seconds. "Are you asking me not to investigate this now?" he asked George.

"No. I'm telling you what our plans are and why. Hopefully you'll agree," George smiled at him.

"Since you put it that way, I see no reason why that has to be investigated right now," Woody smiled back. "But I do feel that this could be a major issue, and only a small piece of it is mine. Do you agree?"

"Yes," George said, "I agree. And you have my word that we'll be on board after the tissue business is fully developed."

"Okay," Woody said, satisfied. "But I will be doing a little background on this while I wait. You don't have to worry, though, I'll be discreet."

"Fine," Linda said. "Now, let's get a strategy in place based on what we've discussed so far."

"Let me give the DOH strategy first," George said, "then we can talk about any disagreements."

Everyone nodded. "Go ahead, George," Linda said.

"We're going to issue subpoenas for the morgue files that correspond to the numbers on the records John found at Crowne, and for Mr. Marner to identify those records and explain his arrangement with Dr. Franz. If the data matches, as we suspect, and there are no donation consents, we'll interview the families and get statements. If things go well, we'll join Woody in the skeletal collection investigation. John will also follow-up on any violations that may have been committed by the recipients of the tissue. We'll have to be able to adjust according to events, of course. Questions?"

"Do you want me to try to track down the pharmaceutical companies now? I've got the one name, Acme," Grant asked.

"No," George said. "For right now, for our purposes, the number of cases you found at Crowne are more than enough."

"Good," Grant responded. "They'll keep me busy for a while."

"How long do you think this part of the investigation will take?" Woody wanted to know.

"With luck, three to four weeks," George answered.

There were no more questions or comments. Grant and Woody exchanged business cards and home phone numbers. Grant picked up his copies of the Marner records and headed back to Utica.

That afternoon, James Doyle received an anymous phone call, suggesting that he file a Freedom Of Information Law request with DOH. Doyle followed that suggestion. He made the request very broad, and included "any subpoenas that have been, or are issued to Oneida County". He faxed the request to the DOH Public Information Office, and mailed the original.

CHAPTER FOURTEEN

"The subpoena for the morgue records has been served," George Epstein told Grant. It was three o'clock Thursday afternoon, George was obviously proud of himself for getting the subpoena finished and served, in less than three days. "I'll be faxing your copy in a few minutes."

"That's great, George," Grant complimented him. "You ended up with 433 files? The 432 from Crowne plus Chambers?"

"Don't worry, John. I asked for everything."

"When is it returnable?"

"April first, subject to change if the county fights it."

"Do they have any real grounds to stall?"

"Their reasons don't have to be legitimate," George explained. "If you're looking to buy time, a lawyer can always come up with a reason for a delay."

"And you expect that here, don't you?"

"Let's say I wouldn't be surprised."

"How about Marner, when will he be served?"

"By tomorrow, I'll let you know as soon as I hear. Oh, by the way, I'm a little disturbed about something. I'd better let you in on it. That reporter there, James Doyle, filed a FOIL request for anything related to the morgue investigation. He seems to be pretty sharp and, I suspect, persistent. The PIO will be faxing him the morgue subpoena this afternoon, Doyle will likely have an article in tomorrows paper."

"Why does that disturb you, George? Isn't it possible that if the public is informed about what's going on, they'll be more supportive of wanting to get to the truth?"

"Yes, that's possible," George admitted. "But I don't necessarily trust reporters. I don't like him knowing what we're up to almost as soon as we do it. But, we don't have to give him the Marner subpoena right away. I don't know the details, but

139

the PIO tells me that we can hold off on releasing subpoenas of individuals until after they appear and give testimony, maybe even longer than that."

"Well, I'll keep my fingers crossed that Mr. Doyle is an honorable and ethical man. If there's nothing else, I'll get back to preparing questions for Mr. Marner."

"No, nothing else, John. Keep an eye out for that fax, I'll send it right now."

"Thanks, George," Grant said and hung up.

"Sit down, Pam," Oneida County Attorney Charles Allen said to Pamela Ashley. She was an assistant county attorney, one of his most competent and personable lawyers. Allen had just summoned her to his office. "We've just been served with this subpoena," Allen said when Ashley was seated. He passed the document to her across his desk. "I'd like you to handle it."

Ashley quickly read the cover page and scanned the attached list. She was thirty-four, and had worked for Allen for eight years. Slim and attractive, she was a tenacious defender of county interests.

"Wow!" she said, when she had finished reading. "What's all this about?"

"I suspect it has something to do with these latest allegations about the morgue," Allen said, stating the obvious. "And there's undoubtedly a connection to that state investigator Franz had the run in with."

"I can understand that they're investigating, but why the subpoena, returnable to their office? Why not just work through us and do the review at the morgue?"

"You might not be aware of this, but Mr. Bronson and Dr. Massey worked out a deal with the state that their investigator can't get back in the morgue without an act of God. It looks like DOH wants that guy to handle this file review, ergo, the records go to his office."

"That doesn't add up, boss. If the state already agreed to keep that investigator on a short leash, why not assign somebody else to go to the morgue and look at the records?"

140

"Very perceptive, Ms. Ashley," Allen smiled at her. "I think it's safe to say that not all of DOH is marching in step."

"So it would seem," Ashley agreed. "Where did they come up with these case numbers, certainly not out of thin air?"

"I'm not sure, but I've heard that this investigator, a guy named John Grant, was at Crowne last Friday. He supposedly found some records there with these morgue numbers on them."

"Well, whatever," Ashley shrugged. "What do you want me to do?"

"Call the morgue and talk with Dr. Franz or June Miller. Tell them about the subpoena and fax a copy to them. Find out if they can have these files pulled by the first. I don't see any reason why they can't. The main thing, I suppose, is whether there are any reasons why some of these shouldn't be shown to the state, open homicides, for example. Short of something like that, we'll have to comply. Make that clear to them, if not, I expect they'll ask you to fight it."

"I see no problem in stalling this for a while, if anyone wants," Ashley offered.

"I'm sure you could come up with several reasons that would delay things, Pam. But I don't think that would be a smart move here. If we were being sued by John Q. Public, it might be different. Most plaintiffs get impatient and can't afford the extra legal bills involved with hearings and motions. In this case, the state has deep pockets, and they're well within their rights. To stall them without good cause would probably just antagonize them. Let's play this straight. We'll fight when, and if, we have a chance to win. Keep me up to speed on this, Pam."

"I sense that you don't think this subpoena will be the last of this, am I right?"

Allen smiled, "I again compliment you on being so perceptive. No, I don't think this is the end, I'm afraid it may be the first of many."

"You believe there is something to these allegations, then?"

"I'll reserve comment on that. I will say that this is starting out unlike any investigation I've ever seen by a state regulatory agency. You've been around for a while, Pam, when was the last time a state agency issued a subpoena to us? I'll answer that for you, never. I'm not saying they'll find anything, but it's apparent they're going to make a serious effort to try."

As soon as Ashley left his office, Allen called in his secretary. "Take that copy of the DOH subpoena back out of the file and fax it to Mr. Bronson's office," he ordered. When the secretary reached the door, Allen called to her. "Oh, and you'd better fax it to Reggie Whitehurst too. Just put 'FYI' on the transmittal sheet."

Twenty minutes later, June Miller walked into Dr. Franz's office. She placed a copy of the subpoena on his desk in front of him. "This just came in from the county attorney's office," she said. "It was preceded by a phone call from one of the lawyers, a Pam Ashley. She said that unless we have a very good reason for not showing these to the state, we'll have to comply. She asked me to talk it over with you and get back to her."

Franz glanced at the subpoena and smiled. "I'm glad this finally arrived. We've been expecting this since Grant found those records at Crowne, haven't we? Now we at least know what files are involved and we'll be able to review them ourselves and make sure they contain appropriate consents."

The color drained from Miller's face. "I'm not sure what you're suggesting, doctor, but I'll tell you right now that I draw the line at tampering with the documentation that's in those files, including adding things. I'm not a lawyer, but I do know that you can end up in jail for that kind of thing. I hope that wasn't what you had in mind."

"Certainly not, June, certainly not," Franz said quickly. He had apparently over estimated her loyalty. "I only meant that we'd have an opportunity to look at the files and see what they contain. As you know, we've been very active here in getting consents. I bet we'll find that most, if not all, of the folders will contain signed donation forms. I'm sorry if you thought I meant anything other than that."

Miller's color returned to normal. "I appreciate hearing your clarification, Bob," she said. "When do you want to start pulling the files, and who do you want involved?"

"Have Belinda, Mike and Marcia pull them. You, Marcia, Mike and I will review them. Let's get started today."

"I'll get things moving." Miller said, heading for the door. She stopped in the hallway and turned around. "You seem to be taking this very well, if I may say so. How come?"

"I told you, June, I'm sure the files will prove of no use to the state. Besides, I have a feeling that this investigation will come to a halt before much longer. There's nothing to worry about."

Buoyed by Franz's confidence, June Miller went to round up her troops and begin the assignment.

Reginald Whitehurst read the lead story in the Friday edition of the Observer a second time. He had learned about the subpoena the previous afternoon via fax from the county attorney's office. He was uncomfortable with the direction the state investigation seemed to be heading. When he had joined Franz at his rebuttal press conference weeks earlier, he hadn't counted on this. Had he said too much, too soon? He was beginning to think he had. The fact that James Doyle had gotten the story almost concurrent with the subpoena being served, compounded his concern.

Whitehurst put the paper down on his desk and dialed the private number of Ronald Bronson. "Have you seen this mornings paper?" he asked when Bronson answered.

"Yes," Bronson replied. "What's your take on it?"

"I don't like it. I've got to believe DOH is on to something here. I've never heard of them serving a subpoena on a county government, here or anywhere else. Have you talked with Chuck Allen about this?"

"Yes. He sent me the subpoena yesterday afternoon. I got back to him right away."

"And? How does he plan to handle it?"

143

"He feels that we aren't in a very strong position to fight the subpoena. In fact, he plans to comply fully, with the exception of any files that may involve open police investigations. He doesn't anticipate many of those. His idea is that to try to quash the subpoena without good cause will serve to antagonize DOH, and will make it appear that we have something to hide. He's as concerned about public opinion as I am. We scored a public relations coup last week over this. Chuck feels we could lose that edge quickly if we appear to be obstructing, I agree. I told him to go ahead and comply."

"Have you heard anything from our friend, Dr. Franz?"

"Surprisingly, no. I expected him to be in here jumping up and down. Quite frankly, his silence is as upseting as the subpoena itself."

"Isn't it," Whitehurst agreed.

"By the way, Reggie, what has you so interested in this?

Your office never investigated the morgue. Barone and I have been accused of protecting Franz, not you."

"True, but I jumped on his bandwagon after these last allegations. Publicly, no less. I'm sure I've done more stupid things in my political life, but I can't recall any right at the moment."

"Cheer up, pal. This will blow over in a while, well before the next elections. I don't really think either of us has much to be concerned about."

"I appreciate your optimism, Ron, but I'm not so sure you're right. Can I be completely candid with you?"

"Certainly! I regret you felt you had to ask. What's on your mind?"

"I've been thinking this thing over ever since that altercation between Franz and the state investigator at the morgue. You've had Franz and the morgue investigated several times, in one way or another. I must ask you now, were those investigations for real, and were they conclusive in their findings? Is there any chance that these allegations are true?"

144

After a long hesitation, Bronson responded. "Well," he said cautiously, "we did rely to a great deal on Franz's explanations. After all, he is one of our officials. We certainly should be able to trust his veracity."

"Were the county attorney's, or others who investigated the morgue, instructed not to delve too deeply? Were these various investigations restricted?"

"They were told to rely primarily on Franz's explanations," Bronson said testily. "I find that perfectly acceptable under the circumstances. Do you disagree with that?"

This was the answer Whitehurst had feared, but he decided against pursuing the matter any further at the moment. "Have you thought about what you're going to do if the state comes up with a solid case against him?" he asked.

Another hesitation. "What exactly are you saying, Reggie?"

"I'll be blunt. I'm saying that you should consider the possibility that Franz has done some things he shouldn't have. Since the morgue is a county operation, and the county is ultimately responsible, you should develop a damage control strategy. That may include throwing Franz over."

"Do you really believe this is that serious? I think you're over reacting."

"Maybe, but a plan now, even if never needed, is better than having to operate under the gun. I'm only suggesting that it is prudent to be prepared."

"I guess that does make some sense. I'll consider it. I still think you're more nervous about this than your involvement warrants. Why?"

"Some of the things that Franz has been accused of may be crimes. If the state comes up with any proof, I may have to do my own investigation. I wouldn't want to, but it could be forced on me. If that happens, I won't cover for Franz, or anybody else. So, I'd like it not to come to that."

"I think I understand your position, now," Bronson said. Suddenly perspiring, he loosened his tie.

"Good," Whitehurst said. "Now, I'm sure that Doyle will call you for a comment. What will you tell him?"

"Publicly, the county position has been that we support Bob Franz one hundred percent. That will continue to be our position, at least for now."

Whitehurst smiled. He hung up feeling he had made headway.

At 1:45 that Friday afternoon, Lewis Marner was standing in front of the mirror in the men's lounge at the Malloy Funeral Home. Visitors would begin to arrive soon to pay their final respects to Mable Duffy. Marner was checking his appearance one last time before meeting the public.

Marner was forty-eight, with average height and build. He wore his dark brown hair in a crewcut. He knew he was not handsome. His nose was a little too large. His poor eyesight required glasses with "coke bottle" lenses. He had tried contacts, but found them to be too uncomfortable.

Satisfied, he had just turned away from the mirror when the door opened. His boss, Harold Malloy, entered. "Lew, there's some guy here to see you. He's waiting in the office."

"Any idea who it is," Marner asked, slightly nervous.

"No. He asked to see you. He's well dressed, thirty or so. Try to make it short, we'll have visitors in a few minutes."

After Malloy left, Marner waited a few seconds, trying to figure out who his visitor could be. A cop! he concluded. Bad thoughts raced through his mind. Had that young man he picked up last night been under age? Had he reported the liaison to the police? Feeling dizzy, Marner headed toward the office.

He found the man Malloy had described sitting in a chair near the receptionist's desk. "Are you Lewis Marner?" the man asked, standing up.

"Yes," Marner squeaked.

The man pulled a folded document from his inside jacket pocket and handed it to Marner. "Have a nice day," he said and walked out the door.

Marner slumped into the chair that the man had vacated. With trembling fingers he unfolded the paper. "In the matter of the investigation of the Oneida County Morgue", the caption said. "Greetings, You are hereby commanded......" Marner sat the paper down in his lap and reached for his nitro pills.

Dr. Robert McAree arrived in his Corning Tower office at 2:30. Just off the plane from Atlanta, he had decided to stop by the office and check his mail and messages before starting his week-end. His third message, coupled with the last, sent him into a rage.

Grant! Making more waves. A subpoena served on Oneida County without his knowledge or approval! He had thought this thing had been resolved. There was no way that Ludwig and Epstein could have misunderstood his intention to manage this investigation. As soon as he was away they ran amok! He started to reach for the phone, he wanted Ludwig and Epstein in those chairs across from him. He gripped the handset, but hesitated before lifting it from the cradle. No, this wasn't the time to confront them. He was too angry now. He might do something stupid. He'd think about it over the week-end and deal with them on Monday.

This time he did pick up the handset and dialed the number for Dr. Massey. "Mort, this is Bob McAree. I just got back from Atlanta and got your messages. I want to assure you that I didn't know anything about this. When I left here, I thought these people knew what I wanted. Obviously, I misjudged the situation."

"No need to explain, Bob," Massey said. "I figured that your people hadn't gotten the message you intended. I have my share of incompetent people here too."

"I appreciate your understanding, Mort. You can rest assured that there will be no further misunderstandings. I'll get with these clowns next week and straighten things out."

"I'm relieved, Bob. I'll pass this on to Bob Franz. This will certainly make him feel better. Have a nice week-end."

147

Grant's desk phone rang at quarter of four. "You're going to receive a call from Mr. Marner in five minutes," George Epstein said.

"He's been served, I take it," Grant said.

"Oh, yes," George chuckled. "It had quite an impact apparently. My name and number were on the subpoena, so he called me. Either he has a speach impediment or he's very nervous. His voice cracked so that I could hardly understand him."

"What did he want?"

"He said he can't understand why we want to talk to him. He claims to know nothing about the morgue, there must be some mistake."

"What do you want me to tell him?" Grant asked.

"Whatever you think is appropriate, John. This is going to be your show, I didn't want to tell him anything that you may not agree with."

"What if he asks for a postponement?"

"That's your decision, John. You don't want to delay this do you?"

"Absolutely not!"

"Okay, then, tell him to be there as scheduled."

"What if he says he has a lawyer, or has his lawyer call me?"

"If there's a lawyer involved, refer him to me."

"Fair enough," Grant said. "I'll let you know if anything important happens."

Grant's phone rang again two minutes later. "My name is Lewis Marner," the shaky voice said. "A Mr. Epstein referred me to you. I received a subpoena today ordering me to appear before you on the thirty-first. There must be some mistake, I never worked at the morgue, I hardly know Dr. Franz."

Grant broke the bad news to Marner. "There is no mistake. I'll expect you to be here as ordered."

Marner, obviously disappointed, went on. "Can you at least tell me what this is all about, Mr. Grant? I've got to know!"

"I'm sorry, Mr. Marner, I really am. But this is a very sensitive matter. I won't discuss it over the phone. Especially when I can't be positive that you're really Lewis Marner. I have only your word for that. I'm sure you appreciate my position."

"I hadn't thought of that," Marner admitted. "I'll see you next week, then. Should I bring anything with me?"

"Yes," Grant said, "a good memory."

CHAPTER FIFTEEN

Dr. Franz arrived at the morgue at 8:30 Saturday morning. He hadn't left there until ten o'clock the previous night. By that time all the subpoenaed files had been pulled and the review had been started. When Franz entered the large conference room he found Marcia Longo, Mike Hargrove and June Miller already at work. Longo and Hargrove were going through the files while Miller sat at the table with a copy of the subpoena in front of her. As each folder was searched, Miller would mark the presence, or absence, of a donation consent next to the file number on the subpoena.

Since the sole focus of the search was on the consent forms, they were proceding rapidly. In their haste, they were not reviewing the comments contained on the Case Data Sheets.

"Good morning," Franz said pleasantly. "You even beat the boss in, what a team!"

"This is going more quickly than I had imagined," Miller said. "We should be done by early afternoon."

"Wonderful!" Franz grinned. "Then we can all enjoy what's left of the week-end. Have you found everything to be in order so far?"

Miller looked at her worksheet. "Let's see, we've gone through eighty-one files. That's a little under one fifth of the total. They've all had either an ARC of Eye Bank donation form except two, they didn't contain a consent. If you project that out, we should end up with ten or so that don't have donations."

"Great!" Franz said, clapping his hands together. "Ten out of four hundred and something. The state won't be able to make much hay on that. Have you found any open cases yet, any that we can hold back?"

"No, we haven't," Miller answered. "I'm sorry."

"Don't be sorry, I didn't really expect to find any," Franz said, then changed the subject. "You know, this Grant must be a glutton for punishment. He had to be embarrassed about getting thrown out of here, then he jumps into this subpoena thing and will be red faced again. My friend Doyle may end up with a little egg on his face too before this is over. I detected a little gloating in his article yesterday. Wait until he finds out what the results are!"

Everyone smiled at Franz's glee. "You know, all this good news has made me hungry," Franz said. "Michael, why don't you take some money out of the petty cash drawer and go get us some donuts. June, you go with him and make sure he gets something good. Marcia and I will keep plodding along here."

Everyone knew that Franz's suggestions were actually orders. Miller and Hargrove headed out for the bakery a couple of blocks away.

As soon as they were gone, Franz walked up behind Marcia, who was standing next to the table, leaning over to examine a file. He grabbed her buttocks, firmly encased in her tight jeans. She reached behind her and pushed his hands away, then went back to her task.

"What's wrong with you lately?" Franz demanded, his feelings hurt. "I've seen more of Ione the past few weeks than I have of you. You've suddenly come up with a million and one excuses why we can't get together. Care to tell me what the problem is?"

Marcia turned around to face him. "Nothing is wrong. A lot of things have been happening, that's all. I've told you my mother hasn't been feeling well, I'm going to ceramics two nights a week, I've just been very busy. Things will get back to normal after a while."

Franz stared into her eyes. "Are you sure that's all?" he asked.

"What else could there be?" Before he could answer she changed the subject. "Will you please explain to me why you're so upbeat. None of these donation forms are for Crowne. I don't see how they help you very much."

Franz's grin returned. "Ambiguity, my dear. These consents will muddy the waters. In order to be found guilty of any wrongdoing, the state will have to prove that I knowingly and intentionally violated the rules. The regulations themselves are ambiguous to begin with. Add the fact that we'll have signed authorizations in about ninety-eight percent of the cases, and they'll play hell convincing a review board that I did anything intentional. I'll just say that my concern was in getting the consent, not the name on the letterhead. Let them try to prove any different! The most I'll get is a warning. They might not even bring any charges when they realize how well documented these donations actually are."

Marcia considered his words. She could see why he was optimistic. It wasn't a matter of his guilt or innocence, it was what the state could prove. "I'm impressed," she said. "It looks like you've got it all figured out."

"I have," Franz said flatly. "I've even got an ace in the hole. Massey has a friend at DOH, a deputy commissioner, who is going to keep a lid on this. Mr. Grant's rein of terror is about over. I'm sure he won't see it this way, but he's so inept that this will actually benefit him. Keep him from making a fool out of himself over and over."

"Maybe we should finish these files before you start to celebrate," Marcia cautioned.

"Yes, you're right," Franz said. "You look and I'll write", he said, assuming Miller's place at the table. "I want to show some progress before June gets back."

Marcia turned back to the files. "Okay," she said, "number 01-90-0032, ARC donation." Franz made a note on the worksheet.

When Pamela Ashley arrived at her office on Monday morning, she found Dr. Franz waiting for her. She had met Franz a few times at county functions but, other than that, knew very little about him. She had heard the allegations made against him over the years. Although she hadn't been directly involved in any of the morgue investigations, she had believed the findings of no wrong doing. In fact, she had felt sorry for Franz, a man apparently surrounded by disloyal employees.

"This is an unexpected pleasure, doctor," Ashley said, leading the way from the reception area to her office.

Franz gave her one of his warmest smiles. "You're very kind, Mrs. Ashley. I was afraid that you people wouldn't be very glad to see me, with this subpoena business, the investigation, and all."

"Please, doctor, we're all on the same team here. We'll all get through this just fine, don't worry about that." Arriving in her office, she motioned Franz to a chair. She closed the door and sat in the visitors chair next to him, so that there were no obstacles between them. She believed this atmosphere promoted a smooth flow of dialog. "What brings you here this morning, doctor?"

"I wanted to discuss the terms of the subpoena. There are a couple of things I'm not comfortable with."

Ashley tensed slightly, "Oh? What problems have you found?"

"Well, I don't think we should let those files out of county custody. We didn't find any open cases, but the content of all of our files is highly confidential. We're responsible for the security of that information. I feel very strongly that the state's review should be done at the morgue. If that's not possible, then they should at least remain on county property, here, for example. And I want one of my people present at all times while the files are being examined, regardless of the location."

Ashley pondered Franz's concerns for a few seconds. "I think you have some valid points, doctor. Before I commit on those issues, however, I need to know if there are any problems with the content of the files. You know what documentation they'll be looking for. Is it there?"

Franz smiled sheepishly. "I can't answer that, Mrs. Ashley. We've had our noses to the grindstone just to get everything pulled and confirm there were no open cases. We didn't have time to look through every document. But," he added in a hurt voice, "you must understand that I've done nothing wrong in my running the morgue. For that reason, I'm confident that no irregularities will be found."

"I'm sorry if I offended you, doctor," Ashley said quickly. "I certainly didn't mean to imply that I expected anything to be wrong. Now, getting back to where the files will be looked at, I see no reason why we can't ask for that to be done on county property. I'll call the DOH attorney this morning and try to work something out."

"Good, that will make me feel much better. Do you think they'll go along?"

"They may not be completely happy about it, but they almost have to agree. If not, we'll have to let a judge decide the matter. That could take weeks and might be resolved in our favor anyway. DOH won't want to delay this for such a relatively unimportant issue. I'll get back to you as soon as I can get this worked out," she said, standing up. "Is there anything else, doctor?"

"No," Franz said, also rising. "I feel much better having you handling this. Thank you."

Ashley accepted Franz's outstretched hand. Instead of a shake, Franz raised their hands and leaned forward, kissing her hand lightly just behind the knuckles. She blushed and withdrew her hand.

"I'm sorry," Franz said. "I only intended that as a sign of respect and appreciation. I hope you didn't take it the wrong way."

Ashley recovered quickly. "I'm flattered, doctor. I'll be in touch later," she said, opening the door.

She watched Franz walk down the corridor toward the exit. She was feeling better about things. Franz had seemed sincere. She was sure that her boss was worried over nothing.

George Epstein answered her call on the first ring. After exchanging pleasantries, she explained the reason for her call. Epstein gave in easily as soon as he was assured the files would be ready for inspection on April first. She prepared a brief memo, stating that the files would be examined at the county attorney's office starting at ten o'clock on the first. The state had also agreed to have a morgue representative present. She faxed the memo to Dr. Franz.

George Epstein hung up from his conversation with Pamela Ashley and sat reflecting on what had happened. All the files would be made available on the date requested. In return, they would be examined at the county attorney's office, and Franz could have an employee present. A fair exchange, he thought. Keeping the investigation moving along was paramount. Giving up a little privacy was a small price to pay to avoid a delay. Pleased with events, Epstein decided to visit Linda and give her the good news. He was almost out the door when his phone rang. It was Linda.

"Dr. McAree just called me," she said. "He wants us in his office. Now!"

"He's not happy, I suppose," George guessed.

"He called me himself, not his secretary, and there's no doubt in my mind that he's pissed. Sounded like he had a full head of steam. How long before you'll be ready to face the music?"

"Hold on just a second," George said. He put the handset down on the top of his desk and left his office. He was back on the line within a minute.

"I'm going to talk with Kate before I see him," George said. Linda knew he was referring to his boss, Kate Harris. "I just checked, she's free right now. I should be ready to see McAree in fifteen minutes or so."

"What are you going to tell her? Are you going to ask her to intervene?"

"No. I talked with her about McAree after our first go around, she asked me to keep her informed. As feisty as she is, she'll probably want to go with us. In fact, that is the protocol McAree should be following. If he's got a gripe he should address it to my supervisor. But I don't want Kate directly involved right now. I want to hear what McAree has to say first.

Right now, I just want to tell her what's going on and get a little guidance."

"I don't know much about her, do you think she'll be supportive of you, or intimidated by Dr. McAree?"

"Kate is very fair. She believes in equal enforcement. I'm sure she won't be happy if it looks like he's trying to limit our investigation. If he tries to go too far, she'll be on our side."

"Okay, what if I meet you next to the elevators on the fourteenth floor in fifteen minutes? I don't really want to go in there alone."

George chuckled. "That makes two of us. I'll see you in fifteen minutes."

Twenty minutes later, Dr. McAree's secretary ushered George and Linda into his office. She walked out and closed the door behind her. McAree waved them to the chairs across from his desk without speaking. After they were seated, McAree glared first at George, then at Linda. After several more seconds of icy silence, he spoke.

"What in the hell do you two think you're doing? Who do you think you are? Who do you think you're fooling with here?" he demanded, his voice just below a shout. For emphasis, he pounded the top of his desk after each question.

George and Linda stared at him without attempting to answer. They were both shocked by his tirade, expecting better of a man in his position.

"I'll tell you the answers to those questions," McAree went on. "You're trying to make names for yourselves by going on a witch hunt against a highly respected forensic pathologist! You're a couple of mid level employees who are making decisions beyond your authority! And I'm the man who is going to get you back under control! How do you like that?"

Again George and Linda didn't respond.

McAree took their silence as submission. His face broke into a triumphant smile. His voice became normal, but his tone was patronizing. "Now, I'm going to lay down some ground rules that will be strictly adhered to. First, no subpoenas, no letters, no

157

reports, no nothing, regarding this investigation will leave this department without my knowledge." He fixed his gaze on Linda, "I want a written investigative plan submitted by your Mr. Grant. I want him to justify his actions, what he hopes to accomplish and why. Until I have received that plan, and approved it, this investigation will be suspended. Questions?"

Linda couldn't believe her ears. She wanted to argue back, but her brain wasn't in full gear. Not able to think of what to say, she remained silent.

"Doctor," George said, "the county attorney's office is expecting us to start reviewing the subpoeaned records on the first of April, that's this Thursday. Are you saying that we won't procede with that if this plan isn't submitted and approved by then? If we don't show up after issuing the subpoena, the department will be a laughing stock. I can't imagine that would make the commissioner very happy."

The word "commissioner" got McAree's attention. "Well, I certainly wouldn't do anything to embarrass the department," he said, backing off slightly. "You can go ahead with that, even if I haven't approved any other actions by then. But nothing else, understand?"

"Yes," Linda mumbled. George nodded.

"Good," McAree said, the gloating smile back. "Before you leave," he went on, lowering his voice, "if either of you cross me again, I'll see to it that you'll be emptying trash cans until you retire." He again glared at George and Linda, wanting to make sure he had made his point.

"I take it that I've made myself clear, then. If you behave yourselves, we'll be able to get this thing over with quickly, without harming anyones career or reputation unnecessarily. I see no reason why we can't have a good working relationship, now that this initial misunderstanding has been resolved. That's all."

"That pompous bastard!" Linda fumed. They had just gotten behind the door in George's office. "I'd like to slap the shit right out of him!"

"I agree with you, Linda, but this is a time for cool heads. We've got a big problem here and we've got to figure out how to deal with it."

Linda and George sat in silence for a couple of minutes, each going through a mental replay of their meeting with McAree. "We've got to be careful here," George said, finishing his reflection first. "I've been thinking over what McAree said. We need to concentrate on the content, not the manner. If we complain to anyone because we didn't like the way he talked to us, they'd laugh us out of their office. So, the question is, did McAree say anything that suggests some type of misconduct?"

"And the answer is?" Linda prompted.

"In my opoinion, no. Now don't give me that look, Linda," George laughed, noticing her glare. "I think the closest he came was saying that we could get this over 'without harming anyones career or reputation unnecessarily'. In my mind, that sounds like a suggestion that we proceed with the investigation with that as our goal. An investigation should be aimed at finding the truth and let the chips fall where they may, not tempered by a desire to protect someones reputation. In McAree's defense, he did use the qualifier 'unnecessarily'. I think that makes his statement open to interpretation. I think his intent is to control the investigation to Franz's benefit, and that would be wrong. But I don't think he's done anything in that direction yet that is sufficient to accuse him. In short, right now we have suspicions and opinions, we need more."

Linda seemed to accept the reality of George's argument. "Assuming we're right, what will he be violating? Just department policy?"

"Depending what he does, if anything, he could be in violation of department policy, Ethics Law, Public Officer's Law, and possibly the Penal Law. If he takes an overt act to protect Franz, and gets caught, he'll be in a lot of trouble."

"What do we do now?"

"Let me worry about how to deal with Dr. McAree. In the meantime, we need to get this investigative plan prepared and submitted to McAree."

"Okay, I'll call John and we'll get started. I know he's going to be enraged when I tell him what's going on."

"I don't see any reason to upset him with this, Linda. In fact, I thought you and I could put something together right here, right now. What do you say?"

Linda didn't answer right away, trying to figure out what George was up to. "Sure," she said finally, "good idea. We'll keep John right out of this for now. What if McAree wants to know how we got this done so fast?"

"Tell him you did it by phone, just like you would have done it." Linda nodded. "Okay," George said, removing a legal pad from his desk drawer. "Let's get started."

CHAPTER SIXTEEN

"Well, what do you think?" Grant asked Pat Murphy. It was 9:30 Tuesday morning. Grant had stopped by Murphy's office for a review of the questions he planned to ask Marner. They were in Grant's favorite spot, at the kitchen table.

Murphy looked up from the paper containing the questions. "They look good to me, John. You're going to ask how the tissue arrangement was set up, by who, who else knew about it, if any money was paid, I can't think of anything you forgot."

"Good," Grant said. "The answers to those questions could lead to others, of course. But, pending that, I can't think of anything else either. By the way, if he tries to deny making the pick-ups, I plan to tell him that I have several witnesses who contradict his denial. At the moment those several witnesses are you and Maxwell. As I see it, if push comes to shove, you could give a sworn statement to that without being in violation of the gag order. What do you think?"

"Probably. But it won't come to that, Marner will tell you the truth. I think he's been set up as a fall guy. Yes, he'll tell the truth. The question is, will you be able to prove it?"

"I'm going to get to the truth, whatever it takes. The deeper I get into this, the more convinced I am that this investigation must be conclusive. If I do a half assed job, the suspicions and allegations will continue. Then, a year or two from now, somebody else will be in the same position as I am today. No, I've made up my mind that I'm not going to let that happen. The department is behind me and we drew a good attorney. I'm going to do a thorough job and get to the truth, whatever that truth might be."

"Great speech," Pat said, clapping his hands. "All kidding aside, though, I think you just might do it."

"We'll do it, Pat, believe me. You, me, Bill Maxwell, and who knows how many more. If the cooperation I've received so

161

far continues, excluding the county, naturally, we'll be able to force Franz to answer an awful lot of questions. That's what I'm looking forward to."

Pat walked Grant to the door. "Good luck tomorrow, John. Let me know how you make out."

"Thanks, Pat," Grant said earnestly. "I'll keep in touch."

When Grant arrived at his office he found a message from Linda. He poured himself a coffee and returned her call. "We're on for doing the morgue records on Thursday, the first," she said. "There were two points that we agreed with the county on in order to avoid a potential delay. First, we'll review the files at the county attorney's office, and second, a morgue employee will be present during our review. George felt that these weren't unreasonable requests on the part of the county. Better to give a little than to risk not getting access to the files for weeks, or maybe longer."

Grant smiled to himself. The way Linda had rushed through her explanation, without giving him a chance to respond, was a clear indication that she expected him to object to the deal that had been made. "That's great news!" he said, much to her surprise. "As long as the 'morgue employee' isn't Franz or Miller."

"It won't be. And I've decided to come to Utica myself to help you with the review. I had thought about sending one of the other investigators, but I decided it wouldn't be fair to throw someone into this thing cold."

"I'm honored, Ms. Ludwig. I agree with your logic. When and where will we meet?"

"The files will be available at ten o'clock. How about I meet you at your office at 9:30?"

"Fine. I hope you're allowing more than one day for this, are you?"

"Yes. I'm booked in at the Hotel Utica for that night. If we can't finish by Friday afternoon I'll come back again on Monday."

"I hope that we can finish that quickly. Since we're only interested in the consents we should be able to move right along. Anything else I should know?"

"Not that I can think of. Just that George and I will be waiting anxiously to hear about the Marner interview. Will you promise to call as soon as you finish with him?"

"Certainly," Grant promised. "I stopped to see Pat Murphy this morning. He predicts total honesty and cooperation from Marner. Quite frankly, I think it will be very difficult for him to deny everything. The records are his, I'm confident of that. He'll have to explain them."

"Okay, John. Give us a call tomorrow." After Linda hung up, her thoughts went to George Epstein. She hoped he was holding his own with Dr. McAree.

On the fourteenth floor, Dr. Robert McAree finished reading the copy of the investigative plan Epstein had brought him. He sat the document down on the top of his desk and looked at Epstein. "You just don't get it, do you?" he snarled. "I thought sure that I made my wishes very clear at our last session, then you spring this on me! Another subpoena! What does it take to penetrate your skull, a two by four? Who is this Marner, anyway. Why was he subpoenaed?"

"Doctor, that subpoena was served before we talked. You knew about the others, I assumed you knew about that one too. There was no intent to 'spring' anything on you. As you can see, that interview is scheduled for tomorrow. You agreed that we have to procede with the records subpoena in order to avoid looking foolish. Certainly this one falls into the same category."

"Okay, let's say this was another example of a failure to communicate, which you seem to specialize in. I repeat, who is this guy and what is his role?"

"Lewis Marner was a former research assistant at Crowne. We have witnesses that he visited the morgue on numerous occasions to pick-up tissue. The tissue that we believe was harvested illegally. We found records at Crowne that were supposedly created by Marner, and seem to corroborate his dealings with the morgue. We need to hear his explanation of events."

McAree made notes on a legal pad as Epstein talked. "Was it necessary to subpoena him? Wouldn't he have come in voluntarily?"

"Mr. Marner proved to be somewhat difficult to locate. We still don't know his home address. We found out that he's currently doing an internship at the Malloy Funeral Home in Waterville, south of Utica. I determined that under the circumstances a subpoena was appropriate. Marner was served at·the funeral home. He has contacted both Grant and me, he plans to appear at Grant's office tomorrow."

McAree was deep in thought before speaking again. "Okay," he said reluctantly. "Grant can go ahead with the interview tomorrow." McAree picked up the investigative plan and shook it in the air. "But all these other plans of his are on hold. There will be no contacting these families, no interviewing morgue employees, nothing further until I say so! Understand?"

"Completely, doctor," George answered and arose to leave.

"Before you go, Mr. Epstein, I won't accept any further excuses of innocent misunderstandings, remember that!"

"There will be no more misunderstandings, doctor, I can assure you of that. From now on everything will be crystal clear."

"I'll hold you to that. Please shut the door on your way out."

As soon as Epstein was gone, McAree called Dr. Massey. "Mort, I just wanted to let you know that I've straightened out my rebels here. Grant's investigation is on hold after the subpoenaed files are looked at. I want to impress upon you that I had no control over that. Speaking of subpoenas, were you aware that they also had a witness served while I was away?"

"No, I wasn't," Massey answered, concerned. "Who is it?"

"A guy named Lewis Marner. He supposedly used to work at Crowne and picked tissue up at the morgue. You might want to pass that along to Dr. Franz, in case he doesn't already know about it. He may want to review Marner's testimony with him before Grant sees him tomorrow," McAree laughed.

"Can you tell me where we can reach Marner, just in case?"

"Let's see," McAree said, scanning his notes. "Yes, he's working at the Malloy Funeral Home in Waterville."

"I can't begin to tell you how much I appreciate this, Bob. Will you let me know what you decide about how much further this will go?"

"You'll know as soon as I do. You might want to keep in mind though, that if Grant does come up with anything, we'll likely have to work out some sort of a resolution. I mean, if he can make a case that your Dr. Franz has done something wrong, we'll have to get a mea culpa from the county and a little fine or something. I can assure you it will be something easy to live with."

"Do you think it will come to that?"

"It may very well not. Grant could come up empty. I just wanted to mention it now. They're exerting a lot of effort on this. If there is any evidence of misconduct, I wouldn't be able to sweep it under the rug completely. But I can certainly control the damage."

"I understand, Bob. Thanks again, and keep in touch."

Lewis Marner arrived at the state office building at 9:50 Wednesday morning. Grant greeted him in the reception area. Marner was impeccably dressed in a dark blue suit with a dazzling white shirt and blue tie. His black shoes were buffed to a high gloss. Grant was impressed with Marner's appearance and the accuracy of Murphy's description. Grant introduced himself and handed Marner his business card. His manner was pleasant, but formal. With no offer of coffee, he escorted Marner to the main conference room.

Grant had reserved the room for this interview. He had spent twenty minutes prior to Marner's arrival arranging the room to his liking. Two of the rooms three large tables were now pushed against the walls, chairs next to them. The remaining table was in the center of the room, a single chair on either side of it. The

165

room was located in the interior of the building, there were no windows, no distractions.

Grant let Marner enter the room ahead of him. He followed, closing the door behind him. He motioned Marner to one of the chairs, then took the one opposite. Grant was pleased at Marner's obvious nervousness. He was sure Marner would be a relatively easy target.

Before Grant could begin his attack, however, Marner took the offensive. "I want to tell you that I don't think much of your methods, Mr. Grant. You subpoena me here and refuse to provide any explanation of why. Then you turn around and tell Dr. Franz about it, and where he can reach me. I don't know what I'm going to do about this yet, but I'm not happy!"

Grant was taken totally by surprise. He hoped his face didn't betray his feelings. He tried to keep the concern out of his voice. "Mr. Marner, I can assure you that I haven't spoken to Dr. Franz recently. And, let me ask you this, does it make any sense at all that I'd want to see you as a potential witness against him, then tell him what I plan to do? I think you'll have to admit that your assumption borders on the ridiculous."

While Marner thought that over, Grant regained his mental composure. He couldn't let Marner put him on the defensive or the success of the interview could be in jeopardy.

"I suppose you're right, Mr. Grant. But why would Dr. Franz call me on the eve of our appointment? How did he know where I was?"

"Let's not make this any more of a mystery than it is, Lewis. Is it okay if I call you Lewis?"

Marner nodded. "Actually, I prefer to be called Lew."

"Okay, Lew. I know that I had nothing to do with this call from Dr. Franz, but I would be interested in the answers to the questions you've raised. Let's take a few minutes for you to tell me exactly what happened, then we'll try to come up with some kind of an explanation."

"I appreciate your sharing my concerns, Mr. Grant. I must admit that hearing from Dr. Franz unnerved me."

"Understandable, Lew. Now, tell me exactly what happened."

"I left the funeral home at around 4:30 yesterday afternoon and came back about six for evening calling hours. When I arrived I was told that someone had called for me, a man, who refused to leave his name or a message. A few minutes later I was called to the phone. Dr. Franz identified himself immediately and I recognized his voice. 'I understand you're going to be interviewed by a state DOH investigator tomorrow. I think we should talk before you see him,' he said."

"What did you say, Lew?"

"Nothing. I hung up on him. That call shook me up. I have nothing to hide, I saw no reason to discuss what I planned to say with him. I just hung up and, thankfully, he didn't call back."

"So, he never actually tried to tell you what you should say to me, he gave you no instructions?"

"I hung up before it got that far I tell you. Did I do the right thing?"

Grant wished Marner had carried the conversation out for a little longer, found out exactly what Franz wanted. But he couldn't fault him for what he had done. "You did just what you should have done, and for the right reasons. You came here to tell the truth, right? As long as that was your intention there was no reason to discuss your testimony with Dr. Franz or anybody else."

"Yes, Mr. Grant, I am here to answer your questions honestly. I'm relieved that you agree with how I handled the situation, thank you. But how did he know about me coming here today? How did he know where I was?"

"I don't know the answer to your first question right now," Grant admitted. "I sense that you feel your whereabouts are some kind of a secret, why is that?"

"I'm not in hiding or anything like that," Marner explained. "But when I left Crowne there were some hard feelings. It seemed to me that I had wasted ten years of my life. I wanted to get a fresh start. I moved out of my apartment in Utica and left no forwarding address. I had been a morgue technician at Crowne from when I was hired in '83 until I got involved in research in '89. I liked being a morgue tech. As part of my fresh start I decided to get into funeral directing and enrolled in mortuary school. I'm single, never been married and have no family here. I only told one person, a girl I worked with at Crowne, about what I might do. And those plans were tentative at the time. I haven't seen or heard from anybody from Crowne since then. I have an apartment now in Waterville near the funeral home. My phone is unlisted. You apparently don't even know my home address or phone number. You find me at Malloy's and so does Dr. Franz. What would you think?"

"You have reached a logical conclusion," Grant conceded. "Wrong, but logical. This has raised my curiosity, Lew, no question about that. I'll give it some more thought later. There has got to be a simple explanation. We'll get to the bottom of it, don't worry. Now, let's get to the reason you're here. I know you've been very anxious to find that out. Starting in the early part of 1989 you became involved with a research project using human tissue. I want to know the details of how the human tissue was obtained, all the details."

Marner gave a nervous laugh. "I have been trying to figure out why you wanted to see me, of course. This tissue thing was the only reason I could think of that involved me and the morgue. Do you want to know anything about the research itself?"

"No, Lew, I don't. I'm not a scientist. If you got into that you'd be talking way over my head, about things that I don't need to know. If it becomes necessary to get into the technical stuff, we'll have someone from the department talk with you on your level. My only focus is the human tissue. Please confine yourself to that for today."

"Okay, Mr. Grant, where do you want me to start?"

"Start at what you consider to be the beginning. Go ahead."

"Well, let's see," Marner began. "As I already told you, I was working in the hospital morgue until the middle of January

168

of 1989. At that time a Dr. Joseph Rudolph approached me. He said that he would be starting multiple research projects and needed an assistant to help him manage them. He told me that I had an excellent reputation as an organizer. He painted a nice picture about challenge, chance for advancement and stuff like that. I liked the morgue job, but I thought maybe it was time for a change. I accepted his offer on the spot. The necessary paperwork was completed and I started working for Dr. Rudolph the first week of February."

"Did you know Dr. Rudolph prior to that?"

"I knew who he was, but that was about it."

"You must have been flattered that he wanted you for such an important position. Can you briefly tell me what your new duties consisted of?"

"There were actually three projects running concurrently. He wanted me to develop a system for tracking the progress of each project. I developed forms and computer programs we'd need to use to keep everything running smoothly."

"You're a computer man?" Grant asked.

"No," Marner smiled. "I knew what was needed to record and track the projects. I told our computer people and they handled the programs."

"Did you actually participate in the research?"

"Yes, but only in one project, the bladders."

"Why only that one?"

Marner shrugged. "I don't know, at least I didn't until the last few days. I think I know now."

"Go ahead, tell me, Lew."

"The bladder project was the one using the human tissue. Based on what's happened, I believe now that Dr. Rudolph knew he was doing something wrong and didn't want direct involvement in the tissue procurement. He wanted a buffer in his dealings with the morgue, I was it. I believe that he recruited me solely for that reason. The rest was just smoke."

"You're saying that knowing what you know now, you were set up?"

"That's the way it appears to me," Marner answered.

"Tell me about the tissue. How did Dr. Rudolph present that to you? What did he say?"

"He was very matter of fact about it, I'll tell you that. He just said that we'd be using human tissue in the bladder research. He'd already arranged to obtain the tissue from the morgue. I would pick it up from Dr. Franz, or his people, bring it back to Crowne for processing and testing."

"What types of tissue are we talking about?"

"Testicles, bladders, vaginas, uteruses and prostates mostly. Nearly all of the tissue came from young donors, usually under eighteen."

"So this was already set up between Rudolph and Franz before you got involved?"

"Yes, it happened just the way I've told you."

"Did you think anything was wrong with that arrangement? Did you wonder why the tissue wasn't being taken care of by the Crowne Tissue Procurement Coordinator?"

"At that time, no. My current opinions have only come about since I received your subpoena. Back then, I didn't question what Dr. Rudolph told me. He was a rising star at Crowne, and Dr. Franz was a county official. I had no reason to think that either of them, much less both, would be involved in anything shady."

"Were Rudolph and Franz close friends?"

"Not that I know of. But Franz was a friend to the scientific community in general. When he first got hired he made the rounds of all the hospitals and schools. He let everyone know where he stood."

"Tell me about the tissue pick-ups. How were they handled?"

"I'd get a call at Crowne, or on my pager, when a pick-up was ready. I'd go to the morgue and get it. Very, very simple."

"How was the tissue packaged? Was there anything to identify the donor?"

170

"It was in gross jars in a brown paper bag. There'd be a slip of paper in the bag with the donors age, date of birth, date and cause of death and autopsy number."

"Did you deal with Dr. Franz directly?"

"Sometimes. I dealt with most everybody over time."

"But there is no doubt that Franz knew what was going on?"

"Absolutely not! I must have gotten hundreds of tissues from the morgue. A great many of them were received right from Franz and he personally made a number of phone calls to me. He knew what was going on!"

"Did you ever bring anything to Franz? Maybe a check or sealed envelope?"

"My God, Mr. Grant! Are you suggesting that Dr. Franz was selling the tissue?"

"I'm only trying to be thorough. I have no reason to believe that is the case, as of right now. Did you deliver anything to Franz?"

"No! As naive as I may have been, I'd have been suspicious of that."

"You say that you kept records of the projects. Did you keep any records specific to the tissue you got from the morgue?"

"Yes. I devised a 'Tissue Source Log' that contained the donor information and had room for test results."

"Where are those forms now?"

"I don't know. When I left Crowne they were in an old file cabinet I used. That's the best I can tell you."

Grant got up from his chair and walked to one of the tables against the wall. He picked up a stack of file folders from the table top and returned to his chair. He pushed the files across to Marner. "Would you mind looking through these. They're copies, but they are quite legible."

Marner opened the first folder and started leafing through the pages. A smile spread across his face. "These are the forms, just like I told you."

"Please go through the rest of the folders," Grant instructed. "A cursory look will be fine."

171

Marner finished his review quickly and looked at Grant. "Are these the forms devised and maintained by you, that reflect the human tissue you received from the morgue?"

Grant's tone had become so formal that Marner became nervous again. "Should I answer that?" he asked. "You make it sound as though you're accusing me of something."

"These forms are very important to this investigation, Lew. I'm treating the importance of their identification with the seriousness it deserves. Please answer my question."

"Yes. These are reproductions of documents devised and maintained by me in conjunction with research tissue received from the morgue," a somber Lewis Marner said.

"Good," Grant said. "Now, let me recap what you've told me. You were recruited by Dr. Rudolph in January of 1989 to manage three research projects. You were responsible for developing a system for tracking progress for each project. But your primary involvement was in bladder research, which involved the use of human tissue. At the time of your recruitment, an arrangement already existed between Rudolph and Franz to obtain the tissue from the morgue. You dealt with various morgue employees, including Franz himself on several occasions. You created and maintained the 'Tissue Source Log' that reflected the receipt of that tissue. Am I right so far?"

"Yes, I think that's accurate."

"Okay, now tell me about why you left and the status of the bladder research at that time."

"Dr. Rudolph and I got along very well at the start. But by the summer of '92 I was getting frustrated about the lack of progress with the bladder research. I thought that we had learned enough to generate an interim report, at the least. I approached Dr. Rudolph and he said he disagreed. He made it clear that he was in charge and nothing would be written until he was ready. That was the start of my downfall. Rudolph began to find fault with everything I did. He started to ride me unmercifully, pick, pick, pick! It got to the point where I hated to come to work. I asked to meet with Dr. Rudolph a couple of times to try to resolve things. His answer was that he had no problem. The problems were all on my end. By the fall, I'd had enough. I asked Rudolph if he'd like me to resign. He said it was obvious that things weren't working out. He'd like me gone, either by resignation or transfer. I dismissed the idea of a transfer. In a place like Crowne, once you get the reputation of being a problem your life is hell. I'd seen others go through that and decided it wasn't for me. Rudolph negotiated a deal for me with Human Resources so that I could sell back my unused time and leave with a good record. I left the first of the year. As far as I know, the bladder research was still going on."

"You said that you felt the bladder research had yielded sufficient results to put something down on paper. Do you have an opinion as to why Dr. Rudolph felt different?"

"At the time I thought he was just being overly cautious. That opinion has also changed recently."

"What do you think today?"

"Let me preface my answer this way, different things drive different people. I believe that most scientists seek the recognition of their peers. I thought that Dr. Rudolph fit into that majority. Now, I think I was wrong."

Grant waited for Marner to finish his thought. Marner squirmed in his chair, but said nothing more. "Go ahead, Lew. What's the matter?"

"I'm not sure I should tell you what I'm thinking. I don't want to get sued."

"You've made it clear that we're discussing an opinion. This is America, you're entitled to your opinion. I'm asking you to tell me what that opinion is. I don't act on anything without sufficient evidence, believe me. You know Rudolph, I don't. I'm trying to get some idea of what makes him tick. Your thoughts will just be another piece of information I'll use to make my own decision. Please tell me what your thoughts are today."

"All right, Mr. Grant, I accept your assurance. I think now that Dr. Rudolph was not motivated by ego. I think he may have been more interested in money."

"Money?" Grant asked, leaning forward.

"You asked me not to get into details of the research, and I won't. But the results of that research could have been used to develop new treatment and drugs for certain medical problems. Drugs that could make someone a lot of money, tons of it. I think Dr. Rudolph may have been passing our results on to someone else for financial gain."

Grant leaned back in his chair, eyes still fixed on Marner, but not seeing him. He had finally heard a theory that made sense to him. Money!

"You're staring at me. Did I say something wrong, Mr. Grant?"

"I'm sorry, Lew. I was thinking, I didn't realize I was staring."

"You don't think I'm a crackpot then?"

"No, not at all. Let's move on, did you receive any written instructions from Dr. Rudolph regarding the tissue procurement? Do you have any documentation at all to support your story that you were acting under Rudolph's orders?"

The color drained from Marner's face. "Why, no! Why would I need that type of documentation? What are you saying?"

"I'll give it to you straight, Lew. I've talked with Dr. Rudolph. He claims that this bladder thing was your private project, including the use of the human tissue. He gave you permission to do your private research at Crowne as long as it didn't interfere with your duties. Can you prove he's lying?"

Marner leaned forward, elbows on the table, head buried in his hands. "I can't believe this," he said, voice breaking.

"I know this is upsetting, Lew, but don't go to pieces on me. Let's try to figure out where we stand here."

Marner slowly raised his head. "Help me. Mr. Grant," he pleaded. "Don't let him do this to me."

"Do you think we can prove that the bladder research itself was a Crowne project? That would be a good start."

"There's got to be some proof of that. In fact, Dr. Slater,

the Director of Research, knew about it. He mentioned it a couple of times in passing. Get hold of him right away!"

"He's retired now, Lew. I'll have to track him down. Anyone else, anything else, you can think of?"

"The paperwork they did when I transferred from the morgue to Rudolph's section may show something," Marner said hopefully.

"Maybe," Grant agreed. "But I'm afraid it will take an act of God to get a look at any of Crowne's records. I was hoping you'd have something in your possession. If you don't, you don't."

"I'm sorry, Mr. Grant. I can't think of anything else to help you."

"Help 'us', Lew, not just me. If your story can be proved, it will help both of us. I think we've done enough for now. I'd like you to make a written statement before you leave today. I want you to include all factual information. No opinions, such as that Rudolph may have sold research results. Okay?"

"I guess so. Do I need a lawyer? It sounds like I may be facing some legal problems here."

"I want to make it perfectly clear that you can have an attorney with you whenever we meet. Do you need one? I can't answer that, it's a decision you have to make. As far as today, as long as you have told me the truth, and your written statement is the truth, you have nothing to fear from me. That's all I can tell you."

"Okay, I'll trust you, Mr. Grant. What do I write on?"

Grant got up and retrieved another folder from the other table. He handed Marner a stack of statement forms. "Use all you need, Lew. I want accuracy, not brevity."

Forty-five minutes later Marner finished a six page statement, which Grant notarized. "I'll be contacting you again, I'm sure," Grant said, as he walked Marner to the exit door.

Marner grabbed Grant's left arm firmly. "Please, Mr. Grant, please help me get through this."

175

"I'm going to get the truth, Lew," Grant promised. "You can take that to the bank."

As soon as Marner was gone, Grant returned to his office and called Linda. She answered on the first ring. "How'd it go?" she asked.

"Before we get into that, we've got trouble," Grant responded. "Franz called Marner at the funeral home last night and wanted to discuss his testimony. I don't know how Franz knew about the interview, or where Marner is working, but Marner initially accused me of blabbing it! We need to get to the bottom of this, now!"

Linda glanced across her desk. George was slouched in one of the chairs, his legs raised, resting on the corner of the desk. She smiled at him and gave a "thumbs up" with her right hand. George lowered his legs and straightened in his chair with an ear to ear grin.

"It looks like we do indeed have a problem." Linda said seriously. "We'll talk about that in a minute. How did the interview go?"

Grant briefed her on what Marner had said, including his opinions. "Do you believe him? Even after he talked with Franz?"

"Yes, I believe him. As far as Franz goes, if Marner had tailored his story based on that call, he almost certainly wouldn't have mentioned it."

"That makes sense. Good job, John. George is here and wants to talk with you. I'll see you at your office at 9:30 tomorrow morning." Linda passed the handset to George.

"I heard Linda mention something about a problem, what happened?"

Grant gave him the details. "Yes, this is serious. Send me an e-mail about this right away, will you? I want to get on this asap."

After he hung up George gave Linda another big smile. "I think we now have what is known as 'probable cause to believe'.

As soon as I get John's e-mail I'm going to see Kate. I'm not worried about getting laughed out of her office now."

"When are we going to let John in on this?" Linda asked.

"Sometimes ignorance is bliss, let's keep it that way."

CHAPTER SEVENTEEN

Linda and Grant arrived at the county attorney's office at ten o'clock sharp on Thursday morning. At the reception desk, Linda identified herself and asked for Pamela Ashley. After a short wait Ashley arrived in the reception area. Greetings were pleasant and business cards were exchanged.

"I think you'll find that everything you wanted to see is here," Ashley said, leading the way down a corridor. "You'll be using our large conference room. That will give you ample work space."

Linda nodded and smiled. "We appreciate your consideration, Mrs. Ashley."

"I know it can be difficult working in a strange office. We'll make it as convenient for you as possible," Ashley smiled back.

They turned into a room on the right. As Ashley had promised, this was a spacious room. A large conference table in the center, smaller tables and extra chairs against the walls. Those tables were covered with file folders. The walls were decorated with pictures of the outdoors, pleasant and colorful. The atmosphere was cheerful.

In stark contrast to that was the man seated at the conference table. A dour looking character who it seemed would rather be elsewhere. "This is Michael Hargrove," Ashley announced, waving in the seated mans direction. "Michael works for Dr. Franz. As I explained to Mr. Epstein, he is here to ensure the security of the files. Since he's an expert on the documentation used by the morgue, I suggest you utilize him to answer any questions."

Grant sat his briefcase down and walked over to Hargrove, extending his hand and flashing a big smile. "I'm John Grant, Mr. Hargrove. Pleasure to meet you." Hargrove accepted Grant's hand without enthusiasm. Grant's smile went unreturned.

"Oh, I'm so sorry," Ashley blushed. "Michael, you've already met Mr. Grant, and this is Ms. Ludwig, both with state DOH." Linda smiled at Hargrove. He nodded back.

179

Ashley pointed to the tables containing the files. "These are the files you'll be looking at. They are arranged by year in sequential file numbers. Can you think of anything else you'll need right now?"

"Not at the moment. You've been very efficient," Linda replied. "What about a phone, though? Is there somewhere we can make and receive calls?"

"Yes, of course. Come with me," Ashley said. Linda followed her out the door and down the hallway.

Grant picked Linda's briefcase, and his own, from the floor and placed them on the top of the large table. When he glanced at Hargrove their eyes met. There was no doubting the hostility in Hargrove's stare. Well, Grant thought, Hargrove was an avid Franz supporter. He supposedly was happy with the way Franz ran things. Then along comes Grant, rocking the boat.

Whether Hargrove's attitude was justified or not, Grant didn't feel any sympathy toward him. In his mind, Hargrove was part of the problem. And, although Grant didn't want to admit it, he was still smarting from his treatment at the morgue. In his mind Hargrove was part of that also.

Michael Hargrove stared straight ahead. He was thirty-five and had been working for Franz since August of 1985. He did, in fact, like the way Franz ran the morgue. He believed that Franz's aggressiveness would lead to additional expansion and career opportunities. He liked Franz letting him rub elbows with the cops. It was great to have some clout if you got pulled over for going a little fast, or not stopping for a stop sign or red light. He knew too, that Franz took some tissue he may not have been entitled to. Maybe he had a skeleton or two that he shouldn't have. So what? These people were dead, what difference did it make? June Miller had ordered him to be here this morning. She said he should remember what the state people asked, what they said. He had to report to her when they left for the day.

Grudgingly he had obeyed, but he didn't like it. And he definetly didn't like Grant! On the bright side, he had confidence that Franz and Miller would see to it that Grant got his. That thought brightened his spirits ever so slightly.

Grant finished removing a legal pad, pencil and the folders containing Marners records from his briefcase. He couldn't resist having a little fun with Hargrove. "So how long have you been with Dr. Franz?" Grant asked pleasantly, smiling.

Hargrove glared at him. He wanted to knock that smile off Grant's face, but kept his temper under control. "Is that question part of your investigation?" he asked.

"No, not at all. I'm just trying to make conversation. You look a little down in the dumps to me, I thought some light chat might cheer you up."

"I'm here to keep an eye on our files, not to entertain you. If I want to talk, I will. Otherwise, unless you have a question about the files, leave me alone!"

"I'm sorry you're so miserable, Michael," Grant said soothingly. "If you change your mind, I'm a good listener."

At that point Linda returned to the room. "Okay, John," she said, "we've got a phone we can use. I called Albany and gave them the number. Let's get started."

Grant grabbed the 1989 files from the side table and sat them on the big table opposite Hargrove. He then opened his briefcase and placed it in the middle of tha table between him and Hargrove. Linda followed suit. Hargrove was now effectively blocked from seeing what Grant and Linda were doing. His expression darkened further.

Without speaking, Linda and Grant opened the first file. Linda checked the number off on her copy of the subpoena. They leafed through the file until they found the death certificate and compared the information with that on Marner's log. It matched exactly. On her legal pad Linda wrote the file number and the word "match" next to it. They next located the "Case Data Sheet". There was a notation reading, "agreed to tissue donation". A few pages later they found an American Red Cross donation consent form. The form seemed to be properly signed.

In the space where the specific organ to be donated should have been listed were the words, "any tissue necessary for research".

They went through several more files with similar results. Grant was beginning to feel as blue as Hargrove looked. The fact that the personal data matched was great. They had the right files, little doubt about that. But the consent forms, even though not directed to Crowne, did indicate that the next of kin had agreed to tissue removal, in very broad terms at that. Grant feared that these forms created the kind of "gray area" that Franz and the county could hang their hat on. Certainly they could make it difficult to prove willful intent to violate the law. Without that, major sanctions would not be levied. A slap on the wrist would be the best that could be hoped for.

After twenty more files Linda suggested a break. They stuffed their paperwork into their briefcases. "Is there a coffee shop in the building?" Linda asked Hargrove.

"Basement," he answered.

A few minutes later, Linda and Grant were seated at a secluded table in the cafeteria, coffee cups in front of them. "I think we've got troubles," Grant said.

"Why do you say that, John?"

"These consents are going to put us dead in the water I'm afraid. I don't mean that we don't have a case at all, we do. But I think it's going to be watered down. I don't see us getting substantial penalties without being able to show intent. It seems to me that these forms take that away from us."

"You may be right, but that's something for George to figure out. It looks like we're getting past the big hurdle, we're getting all matches with Marner's stuff. And we've got a lot more files to look at. Don't give up quite yet."

"I know. I was hoping for something more conclusive, that's all," Grant said, then changed the subject. "Do you have the feeling that Mr. Hargrove would like to slit our throats?"

Linda laughed. "If looks could kill, huh? You're right, I don't think we're his favorite people. Keeping our briefcases open between us was a good move, though. It teed him off even more."

"What are we going to do when we go back up?"

"We'll have to work separately or we'll never get done. Why don't you finish the '89's and I'll start '90. I'll continue to log the files and whether they match. But we'll search for the documentation on our own."

"I'm ready when you are," Grant said.

"Let's go," Linda said, getting up. "We'll plan to talk again at lunch time unless something comes up before hand. If that happens just give me a sign and we'll step into the hall or something, okay?"

Grant nodded and they headed for the elevator.

By noon Grant was more frustrated, more down. He had encountered a steady diet of donation forms. All either ARC or the Central New York Eye Bank. He didn't see how the eye bank could use testicles and bladders, but where the tissue went wasn't the problem. The signatures of the next of kin were the problem. They agreed to the harvesting.

"Will you lighten up?" Linda said when they were back in the cafeteria. "I don't see anything to be sad about."

"Sorry," Grant said. "I was so sure that this would be productive. I wanted to find a smoking gun and so far I'm not even close."

"I guess this is my lucky day then. I've got two with clear declinations. The Case Data Sheets state that donations were asked for and refused. There are no consents of any kind in those files. We're going to have multiple smoking guns, John"

Grant was ecstatic. "Thank the Lord," he said.

Linda laughed. "Now you can enjoy your lunch," she said. "Before we start again I'll call George and update him. I'm sure he will be happy too. We're going to get it done, don't worry."

By four o'clock that afternoon Linda and Grant had gone through one hundred eighty files. Linda had found three cases with tissue donation declinations, Grant had found two. "Let's get some air," Linda said.

"I've got an idea," she said when they were in the hallway. "These files seem to contain only three documents that we are interested in right now, death certificate, Case Data Sheet and donation form, if any. I'm going to ask Mrs. Ashley to copy those documents from all the files, those we've already looked at and those we haven't. We can take the copies to Albany and finish looking at them there. We'll be away from our friend Hargrove and able to talk freely. What do you think?"

"I'm sold. Do you think Ashley will go along?"

"George said that the county agreed to provide reasonable copying services as part of our deal with them. Besides, they would probably just as soon have us out of here. If not, we'll have to be here at least part of Monday."

"Let's go for it," Grant said. Linda headed for Ashley's office while he went back to the conference room.

A couple of minutes later Linda entered the room with Ashley behind her. "Mrs. Ashley agrees with my suggestion," Linda announced.

"Yes," Ashley said. "As long as you know what you need to look at, I see no reason why we can't cooperate. It will certainly speed things up."

"What's going on?" Hargrove asked, a puzzled expression on his face.

"I'm sorry, Michael," Ashley said. "They've decided that they only need to see certain documents from each file. They have asked me to have those particular documents copied and they can finish their examination in Albany." She looked back at Linda. "We have a couple of interns working in the office. I'll have them get started right now."

"How long do you think this will take?" Linda asked.

"We should be finished by late tomorrow morning, early afternoon at the latest. Will you be coming back in the morning, or do you want me to call when the copies are ready?"

"What documents do they want?" Hargrove asked.

"Death certificates, donation forms and Case Data Sheets," Ashley answered.

"Why? Why those?" Hargrove demanded.

"That's our business, Mr. Hargrove," Grant answered firmly.

Hargrove glared at Grant, then looked to Ashley for help.

"They are entitled to look at all the files. They don't have to explain to us what their interest in certain documents is," she explained.

"Mrs. Ashley," Grant said, "please instruct your interns that we want the entire Case Data Sheet copied, front and back, not just the front."

Ashley looked to Linda for confirmation. "That's right," Linda said.

Ashley nodded. "What about tomorrow morning, will you be coming in?"

"Can we have a minute, Mrs. Ashley?" Grant asked.

"Certainly. Come on, Michael," Ashley said, nodding toward the door.

Hargrove didn't budge. "I was ordered to stay with these files," he declared flatly.

Ashley's face turned red. "Never mind," Grant said. "Linda and I will step out."

"We should come back here in the morning," Grant said, out of earshot. "We can scan the copies and make sure we've gotten everything. You know the only proof we have of the declinations is in the Case Data Sheets. Right now we have five, I'm sure there are more. If anything happens to those documents we've got nothing."

"What are you suggesting, John?"

"If I was Franz, and didn't realize what those forms contain, I'd want to get at those files tonight. Even if he didn't actually tamper with them, he'd at least know what we know. I'd prefer to try to get a little advantage on him."

Linda thought that over briefly. "Okay, now what?"

"I want Ashley to assure us that the files will be secured in that conference room tonight, except for the copying, of course.

And I think we should be here tomorrow morning to check on things."

"Let's go talk to her," Linda said.

Back in the conference room, Linda made her request to Ashley. "Are you saying that you think we would tamper with subpoenaed documents?" Ashley asked angrily.

"Certainly not!" Linda answered. "We're simply trying to make sure that we have an understanding on how these files will be handled. I think that's prudent, not unreasonable."

Ashley shrugged, still upset. "Okay, Ms. Ludwig, we have an understanding. The files will be secured in this room. They will only be accessed by the interns for copying. Does that satisfy you?"

"But these are morgue records," Hargrove protested. "What do you mean we can't have access to them?"

"These files have been presented pursuant to a subpoena, Michael," Ashley explained patiently. "They were originally to have been surrendered to the state building. We worked out a compromise to have them looked at here. They do have a right to expect that the records will be secure until they are finished."

"To answer your question, Mrs. Ashley, we are satisfied with your response. Right, John?" Linda asked.

Grant nodded. "One more thing," he said. "There is one file that I want copied in its entirety. That is number 02-90-0089."

"Why? How come that one is different?" Hargrove asked, getting up and walking toward Grant.

"Michael! Please!" Ashley said, annoyed. "Sit down, please. I've already told you that they don't have to explain their reasons to us." Hargrove returned to his chair.

Ashley grabbed a piece of paper from one of the small tables. "What was that number again?"

"It's 02-90-0089," Grant repeated.

Ashley wrote the number on the paper. She looked at Grant's empty hands, then looked questioningly at his face.

Grant knew what she was thinking. He touched his right temple with his right index finger. "Good memory," he explained.

Ashley left the room. She returned in a minute with the key to the conference room door. "Okay, everybody out," she ordered.

As soon as the room was clear, she locked the door. "See you in the morning. You know your way out," she said, turning on her heel and heading back toward her office.

Grant and Linda went toward the exit. Hargrove walked briskly past them, apparently in a hurry to get somewhere. "Michael," Grant called after him. Hargrove stopped and turned around. "I just wanted to say what a pleasure it was to work with you today", Grant said. "We'll see you tomorrow?"

Hargrove turned away without answering, his fists clenching and unclenching at his sides.

Grant dropped Linda off at her car. He agreed to pick her up at her hotel at 9:45 the next morning.

June Miller knocked on Dr. Franz's office door at a couple of minutes after five. "Come in," he hollered.

"Michael is in my office," she told him. "You had better come over and hear what he has to say."

Hargrove gave his account of what had transpired during the day. "Did we check what was on the Case Data Sheets in those files?" Franz asked.

"I don't believe so, doctor," Miller said. "I think we were concentrating on the donation forms."

"That's what I remember too, doctor," Hargrove chimed.

"Those forms shouldn't contain anything of interest to them, should they?" Franz asked.

Miller and Hargrove shrugged.

"What do you suppose they found?" Franz wondered. "We need to get at those files. June, call Mrs. Ashley and see what we can do."

"I don't know, doctor. The state made a big issue out of this. Mrs. Ashley gave them her word that no one will have access to those files until the state is finished with them," Hargrove said.

"Call her anyway, June," Franz ordered. "If we can't go over there and look, see if we can hold up the copying until I can figure something out."

"I'll see what I can do, doctor," Miller said obediently.

Franz turned to Hargrove. "Michael, unless you hear different, be back at the county attorney's office tomorrow morning, understand?"

"Yes, doctor, I'll be there," Hargrove promised. "This Grant guy is going out of his way to antagonize me. Do I have to put up with his crap?"

Franz got up from his chair and walked over to stand next to Hargrove. He reached out with his right hand and clasped Hargrove's shoulder. "Just for now, Michael. Just for now."

Linda and Grant were back at the county attorney's office at ten o'clock Friday morning. The receptionist ushered them to the conference room and promised to tell Mrs. Ashley they were there. The still sullen Hargrove was seated in the same chair he had used the previous day. He gave a barely perceptible nod to acknowledge their presence.

Ashley showed up a few minutes later. "You'll be pleased to know that I found everything secure when I arrived this morning," she said with a cool smile. She pointed to a new pile of documents on one of the small tables. "There are the copies you wanted from the files you looked at yesterday. They include the entire file that you asked for, Mr. Grant."

"Thank you," Grant said.

"It happened to fall within the sequence of numbers you had already looked at," Ashley explained. "No thanks are necessary for that."

"We'll browse through those while the rest of the copies are being made," Linda said. "Do you still anticipate being finished by early afternoon?"

"That depends on how fast you review the files and how much you want copied from each one," Ashley answered.

Grant didn't like the way things were going. He peeked at Hargrove. The smirk on his face confirmed Grant's suspicion that all was not well.

Linda seemed confused. "I don't understand. When we left yesterday afternoon I thought everything was settled. We asked for the death certificate, Case Data Sheet and donation form from each file and you agreed. Right?"

"Yes," Ashley said. "But I spoke with Mrs. Miller yesterday evening. She pointed out, correctly I believe, that there is no way you could know in advance which documents you'll need from every file. My agreement with Mr. Epstein called for reasonable copying of necessary documents. You can't possibly know that until you've looked at the particular file. Therefore, I had the interns stop copying after they completed those files you had already reviewed."

Linda and Ashley stared at each other for several seconds.

Linda then turned to Grant, "Come on, John. Let's talk."

Briefcases in hand, they left the room and went several feet down the hall.

"Bitch!" Linda said. "What do you think they're trying to pull?"

"Buying time, I suspect," Grant answered. "But they haven't bought much, an extra day at most."

"But why? What good is this little ploy going to do them?" Linda's questions hung in the air, unanswered.

"Well, Franz must be nervous about what's in some of these documents, the Case Data Sheets, no doubt. He wants to hold them back a little longer. But I can't answer why. I don't see any long term benefit in what they're doing."

They stood in silence, each deep in thought.

"Wait a minute," Grant said. "This is Friday. This building will be unoccupied over the weekend. Franz is going to demand that the files go back to the morgue until Monday. The morgue is a twenty-four hour operation, the files will be secure there, he'll argue. And he'll have a point."

"But that's where they'll be the least secure, as far as we're concerned," Linda said.

"You and I know that, yes. But how are you going to argue that to Ashley? Can you accuse Franz of having the intent to monkey with the files? I don't think that would go over very well," Grant said.

"You're right about that. But maybe you're wrong about the scenario. Maybe they just want to put us through our paces."

"Maybe," Grant shrugged.

"Okay, I'll call George and see what he thinks. Unless he has a solution we'll have to look at them all. As far as moving the files back to the morgue, we'll cross that bridge if we get to it. In the meantime let's not worry about it."

"Fine," Grant said.

"You don't sound convinced, John."

"Hargrove has the look of the cat who swallowed the canary. I think we're being had."

"You worry too much," Linda said, again full of confidence. "Let's go."

Back in the conference room Linda excused herself to use the phone. She was almost out the door when Ashley called her. "If you're going to talk with Mr. Epstein, tell him that we'll be moving the files back to the morgue for the weekend, assuming you won't finish today. They'll be brought back Monday."

Linda was back in five minutes. She stopped in the doorway and motioned Grant to the hall. "George is pissed. He's going to see Kate Harris right now. While we wait for him to get back to us we'll start looking at the rest of the files, okay?"

"Sure," Grant said. "Let's get started."

"Yes?" Charles Allen answered his intercom.

"There's a Kate Harris from DOH on line one for you," his secretary announced.

Allen pressed the blinking button. "Kate, how nice to hear from you, long time no see, huh?" Allen was anticipating a 'thank you' for the cooperation his office was providing her people.

"What the fuck are you trying to do to us, Chuck?" Kate demanded without pleasantries. Allen nearly dropped the phone. Not because of the language. He had known Harris for years, they had attended countless state association conferences and seminars together. He had learned that she could hold her booze, play poker and swear as good as the men. In spite of looking like a typical grandmother, with gray hair and wire rimmed glasses, she was one tough cookie. No it wasn't the language that bothered him. He was stunned because he had absolutely no idea what she was talking about. "You have me at a loss, Kate. Would you mind explaining what has you all riled up?"

Kate gave him all the details. "I didn't know a thing about this, Kate, believe me. Based on what you're telling me, I can understand how you feel. Let me talk with my attorney who is handling this. I'll call you back shortly."

"Okay, Chuck. But I want to make something clear. Those files aren't going to leave your office until we're through with them. If you try it you'll have one hell of a fight on your hands!"

"Now, now Kate. You don't have to get nasty with me," Allen said lightly.

"I'll take you to the mat on this one if I have to, Chuck. And I'll get just as nasty as I have to get, make no mistake about it."

Allen hung up the phone, his palms and forehead were damp with perspiration. He called his secretary on the intercom. "Tell Mrs. Ashley I want to see her, now!"

"Who in the hell told you to try this maneuver, Pamela?" Allen demanded.

"Well, June Miller felt very strongly that the state should have to review the files. It's their subpoena, after all. I didn't see anything wrong in making them do their work," Ashley explained, surprised at Allen's anger.

"For your information, June Miller doesn't run this office, I do! All you've accomplished is to get a tiger like Kate Harris on my neck. Now, go out there and tell DOH that the copy job is back on. Get the interns started right now. I want those files copied before you or the interns leave tonight. When that is done, ship the files back to the morgue."

"You mean tonight? You want the files out of here tonight?" Ashley asked.

"That's exactly what I mean! I want this mess over with and the files out of here tonight. Tell Mrs. Miller that it will be her job to arrange for their return. Work something out with DOH to get the copies to them tonight. Meet them somewhere if you have to. Just get it done! Clear?"

"Yes, Mr. Allen," a chastened Pamela Ashley said.

As soon as Ashley left, Allen picked up the phone and called Kate Harris. This time they had a more pleasant conversation.

CHAPTER EIGHTEEN

Grant arrived home a little after seven Friday evening. He entered the house carrying a large cardboard box containing the copies of the morgue files. He deposited the box on the dining room table. "I'm home," he said in a loud voice.

"Hi, hon," Faith hollered back, her voice coming from the living room.

Grant found her sitting in her favorite recliner watching television. He gave her a kiss, then spent a few minutes chatting about their respective days.

"So, you think you've found something?" she asked.

"I certainly hope so. Linda is quite sure we'll find more than the five cases we've already located. It's likely she's right. I'll know before Monday. All the copies are on the table waiting for me to finish looking them over."

"You said there were over four hundred files and you only found five problem cases so far? Isn't that a very low number?"

"Well, yes. I guess it is when you put it that way. But I'm only counting the cases with specific declinations of tissue donation. We're not sure about the others. They've all had consent forms, but nothing authorizing donation to Crowne. I'm afraid they may fall into the dreaded 'gray area', something Franz can explain away. That will be for the lawyers to figure out."

"Oh, I almost forgot. A guy named Woody called for you about an hour ago. He said you'd know what it's about. His number is on the kitchen counter. Do you want to call him now, then I'll warm up your supper?"

"Sure. But don't wait on the supper, I'm starved. I'll use the phone in the bedroom so I'll be out of your way."

Grant grabbed the phone number on his way to the bedroom. Woody answered on the third ring. They exchanged small talk for a minute, then Woody got to the point. "I've been continuing my investigation, John. I'm getting quite a bit of disturbing news about Franz's skeletal collection. I don't want to down play the tissue angle, but I think this skeleton thing is bigger than we thought."

"What kind of information have you developed?" Grant asked.

"How much do you know about the crime scene courses Franz has been running for the past three years?"

"Not much, actually. Murphy and Maxwell mentioned that he's been teaching a course like that for law enforcement types. How to process crime scenes involving skeletal remains, I believe. As of now that doesn't seem to be of interest to us."

"Unfortunately, that may not be entirely true. Have you got the time to talk now? If you'd rather I can stop in your office on Monday and go over this in person."

"I'd like that better, Woody. Only Monday is out. I've got to be in Albany Monday to review what we found in the morgue files."

"What did you find?" Woody asked. Grant gave him the details.

"It sounds like you did well. Can we get together Tuesday, then? We can talk about the bones and you can tell me what you guys plan to do next."

They agreed to meet at Grant's office at nine o'clock on Tuesday.

Four hours later, Dr. Franz, June Miller, Marcia Longo and Michael Hargrove had just finished reviewing the files Hargrove had brought back to the morgue. "Thirteen," Miller said, looking at her notes and slowly shaking her head. "Thirteen files with declinations of tissue donation. Every one of them documented in the file's Case Data Sheet, an official record."

"Will you two excuse us for a few minutes? I need to speak with June," Franz said to Hargrove and Longo. They quickly left the conference room.

"I can't believe that Melvin made these entries!" Franz said dejectedly. "Why would he do that?"

"First of all, doctor, it wasn't just Melvin. Linda Chovan, Scott Browne and even Dennis Drummond did it. Did you ever tell them not to? Did you ever say 'I don't want anything in writing' if someone refuses to sign a donation form?"

"Of course not! How would that have looked?"

"Well then, we really shouldn't be surprised. Everybody here knows how you feel about getting these forms signed, and that you don't accept excuses. Because of that, they felt the need to document their efforts, even when they weren't successful."

"You're saying that this is my fault?" Franz asked, offended.

"This isn't the time for blame or finger pointing, doctor. We thought the state might find a few of these files that simply didn't have donation forms. We could have gotten around that fairly easily. We didn't anticipate that the declinations would be documented. The question now isn't who is at fault. The question is what are we going to do about it?"

"Is thirteen out of four hundred thirty-two that big a deal?" Franz asked hopefully.

"One will be a big deal to Grant," Miller said, dashing his optimism. "We had best not underestimate Grant any further. No matter what we think of him personally, he's determined. We've got to give him that. And there's something you may have forgotten, there were four hundred thirty-three files. He's got Chambers too. Grant didn't ask for that one on a whim. He's going to follow up on those stories Doyle did about you keeping bodies here, mark my words."

Franz got up from his chair and started to pace. "Do you think my skeletons pose a bigger problem than the tissue, June?"

"I'm not a lawyer, I can't answer that question from a legal perspective. But I can imagine the public reaction if word about your collection gets out. At least the tissues went for research, and the actual bodies were disposed of as the families wanted. Neither situation is good, but I think the public would be more enraged about the skeletons."

Franz continued to pace. "I'm afraid you are right, June. We need to get a damage control plan in place. Do you have any suggestions?"

"The best thing, of course, is to get this investigation stopped. Short of that, I think you may have to make some admissions about the tissues. The skeletons are another matter. I have no idea what you can say or do about them."

Franz stared at Miller in disbelief. "Admit I've done something wrong? You can't be serious!"

"I know that doesn't sit well with you, Bob. You don't believe that you have done anything wrong. Unfortunately, the state disagrees and it's their laws. I think the biggest fear we have is public reaction. Just the word 'morgue' makes most people uncomfortable. They associate us with death and misery. Some think you have to be a ghoul to work here. But we're a necessary evil. As long as we behave we'll be ignored. But if stories start to come out that things have been done to dead bodies here that shouldn't have been done, we'll get no sympathy. And Doyle is probably licking his chops waiting for such stories to develop."

Franz's pacing slowed as he considered his options. Again he had to admit that Miller was probably right. "I have to agree with you, June. The farther this goes the worse it will look to people. I'm going to try to get this thing stopped right now. If I have to swallow my pride and concede some sloppy practices I will. Hopefully the state will be satisfied with only a couple of ounces of my flesh. What do you think?"

"When you say 'sloppy practices' I assume you're talking about these thirteen tissue cases. Lack of communication, you thought the people had agreed and your subordinates failed to tell you any different, right?"

"Sure. I think that would sell, don't you?"

"Probably. As long as the people who made those entries in the Case Sheets don't contradict you."

"If the investigation ends, Grant won't even talk to them. But you can control them in any event, can't you?"

In her mind, Miller did a quick analysis of Kemp, Chovan, Browne and Drummond. "Yes, that should be no problem. But what about the skeletons? I still think they're potentially our biggest problem. How many of them do you have?"

"I don't know," Franz answered.

"You don't know?" Miller asked, surprised.

"That's right, June, I don't know!" Franz said, irritated by her tone. "Look," he said, quickly calming down, "let's get an inventory of those bones. Have Melvin start on it right away. Tell him to do it on the weekend when we don't have many visitors. I want him to start tomorrow and finish by next weekend. Tell him I also want the body parts in the back freezer incinerated. Okay?"

"I think that's a good start. But why not just dispose of the skeletons?"

"I've been building that collection for three years, June. I'm not just going to throw them away."

"What are you going to do with them? I don't think it's a good idea to have them around."

"Once we've found out how many we're talking about, we'll see if our friend Whitney Price can find a place to store them until things blow over."

Miller thought for a moment, then nodded. "Yes, I think that will work. I feel better about things now."

"Me too," Franz said. "One other thing, June. At our weekly staff meeting next Friday, I'd like you to give a little pep talk about loyalty, being one big family, that kind of thing. In case the heat does get turned up, I'd like everyone to be in the proper frame of mind."

Miller smiled. "That's my strong suit, doctor. The troops will be properly motivated."

Franz smiled back. "I'm sure they will, June. Okay, I think we've done everything we can for now. Get hold of Melvin and give him his instructions. Then go home and enjoy your weekend."

"You too, doctor," she said as she headed for her office.

Melvin Kemp arrived at the morgue at seven o'clock Saturday evening to begin his assignment. He knew from Mrs. Miller's tone when she had called him that this was an important mission. He was to inventory all skeletons and miscellaneous bones in storage, and the body parts in the freezer. He was then to incinerate the freezer items. Miller wanted him to submit a written report containing the case number and what they had. For the skeletons and bones that would be simple. The freezer stuff might be a problem. If the identification tags had fallen off any of the items he'd have to guess what went with what case number. But since it was all going to be incinerated, it probably didn't make much difference.

After letting himself in, Kemp went to the break room to get a cup of coffee. As he approached the door he saw Scott Browne, the part timer, sitting at the conference table, back to the doorway, doing a crossword puzzle. Kemp approached him stealthily. When he got within a foot of Browne's back he yelled, "Hey!"

Browne shot out of his chair and about two feet in the air. He swung around to face Kemp, his face white. "You crazy bastard!" Browne hollered. "You know you're supposed to let people know when you let yourself in. You scared the hell out of me!"

Kemp doubled over in laughter. "You should have seen the look on your face," he said after catching his breath. "Did you think one of our guests in the other room was after you?" He went into another fit of laughter.

The twenty-five year old Browne waited in silence for Kemp to recover. He didn't like Kemp. He thought he was an obnoxious jerk. But Kemp seemed to be in tight with Dr. Franz. And Browne wanted to get on full time someday. He didn't want anyone talking against him, so he took the abuse and kept his mouth shut.

Kemp finally tired of his joke and poured himself a cup of coffee. He started out the door without another word. "Melvin!" Browne called after him.

Kemp swung around to face him. "What do you want?"

"What are you doing here tonight, anyway?" Browne wanted to know.

"None of your business, lad," Kemp answered in a surly tone. "I'm here doing a special assignment for Mrs. Miller and Dr. Franz. That's all you need to know."

Browne realized further inquiry would be futile. "Okay," he said. "Let me know when you leave, will you?"

"Why? Are you going to keep track of my hours?" Kemp asked accusingly.

"I wouldn't do that, Melvin," Browne protested. "I just like to know who's in the building, that's all."

Kemp turned back toward the hallway without responding. "And don't even think about spying on me!" he said over his shoulder.

After Kemp disappeared, Browne resumed his position at the table and tried to concentrate on the crossword. It took several minutes for his anger to subside, and his hand stop trembling.

At 10:30 Monday morning Grant, George and Linda were in George's office. They had just completed discussing what Grant had found in his examination of the morgue records. Thirteen files had specific declinations. The rest had signed donations, but none of the forms designated the tissue to go to Crowne. George had browsed through the declinations and a sampling of the consent forms.

"Well, what's the verdict, counselor?" Grant asked.

"These refusals are potential dynamite!" George said. "The others give Dr. Franz wiggle room. They certainly aren't as valuable to us as those thirteen."

"So, we won't use them all, then?" Grant inquired.

"Not necessarily. When Linda called me last Friday she told me what you were finding. I've had a chance to do a little research and talk with Kate Harris. Assuming we end up in a hearing, and that's the way I'm going to procede with this, we can't expect to score a knockout with the cases containing the authorizations. But they certainly aren't the informed consents the law intended. I think we can score some points with them, but the declinations are what we'll be counting on."

"Then you're going to use everything?" Linda asked.

"Yes," George said. "We're going to rely on the declinations and use the rest as add-ons, or throw aways if you prefer. By using everything, the number of violations will be awesome. And, if we negotiate a settlement we can throw the ambiguous stuff out in return for admissions to the more serious charges, the documented refusals."

Grant and Linda smiled in satisfaction. "That's great, George," Grant said. "I'm glad to know we didn't waste our time."

"Let's not count our chickens just yet." George cautioned. "These declinations look good on paper, but they still need to be verified. These people are going to have to be interviewed. When can you get to that, John?"

"I can start contacting them and asking for interviews right away," Grant said. "But some of these are several years old. I might not be able to find them all."

"I understand that," George said. "But since we have so few to begin with we can't afford too many misses."

"Agreed," Grant said, nodding. "By the way, how do you want me to approach these families? What if they ask about suing the county?"

"I'd just identify myself and ask to meet. Tell them you don't want to discuss details over the phone. When you actually meet with them, don't encourage them to take any legal action. That wouldn't play well at a hearing. If they ask, tell them that you can't advise them. Tell them they should consult their own attorney."

"Okay," Grant said. "What else do you want me to do regarding the tissue?"

"We need to do something about Crowne. If we file charges over the handling of the tissue I want to cite everybody involved at the same time. I want you to develop conclusive evidence of what happened at Crowne. Who's telling the truth, Marner or Rudolph? If Rudolph is lying, and if Crowne was aware of the bladder research, then they can be held accountable for his actions. If Marner or Rudolph were operating totally on their own, then we'll probably go after them individually. Can you fit that in along with the other things?"

"Sure," Grant answered, smiling. "I was kind of hoping for another chance to talk with Dr. Rudolph. Do you think Mr. Sullivan, the Crowne attorney, would cooperate in setting up an interview with Rudolph? Also, I'm sure he could get me the current address for Dr. Slater a lot faster than going through normal channels."

"Slater is the former Director of Research?" George asked. "The same," Grant confirmed. "I'm sure he can clarify who knew what."

"I'll call Sullivan and see what I can do," George promised. "But remember, we could end up as adversaries. That could dampen his enthusiasm to cooperate."

Grant shrugged. "Well, whatever you can do, George."

"What about Acme Pharmaceuticals?" Linda asked. "They were supposedly receiving tissue from the morgue too. Are we going to follow-up on that?"

"No, John has enough on his plate for now," George said. "If we can prove the Crowne stuff we'll have all we need. If anything comes up during the investigation about Acme or anyone else, we'll pass it along to an appropriate agency. Let's not spend any time pursuing it now."

"All right," Grant said. "One more thing before we move on. Do you want me to go to the Eye Bank and ARC to confirm they didn't receive tissue from these people?"

"Good idea," George said. "We're assuming they didn't, but we should confirm it. No sense in leaving a loose end like that."

"Can you have an extra set of these copies made for me Linda?" Grant asked. "I'll need them to work from back in Utica."

"I'll have them done this afternoon. We'll send them to you with the mail courier tomorrow," she said.

"Thanks. Can we move on to Mr. Chambers now?" Grant wanted to know. "Oh, and I talked with Woody. He's been looking into the skeleton collection allegations and he said he's come up with 'disturbing news'. We're going to get together tomorrow morning to talk about it".

George scowled. "I want to finish the tissue piece before we get into anything else."

"You don't want me to meet with him?" Grant asked.

"I didn't say that, John. Go ahead and talk. Just don't get side tracked on that until you finish the other stuff. Now, what about Chambers?"

There is a tissue donation authorization from Chambers' sister in the file. But there is no mention that the whole body was kept. On the contrary, the death certificate and burial permit show a cremation. So, if Chambers wasn't cremated and is on a shelf in the morgue, has anyone done anything wrong?"

"It would certainly seem as though," George said. "Some pretty serious things I think."

"But we need to get into the morgue to find Mr. Chambers and any more of the alleged collection. We're still in the catch twenty-two, though," Grant said. "We can't just walk in unannounced and look around. If we ask the county for permission to search, chances are nothing will be there by the time we can make the arrangements. And we can't get an inspection warrant unless we've been denied admission. What do we do?"

"I don't know," George admitted. "That's one of the reasons I didn't want to tackle this right now. Let me give it some thought while you finish up the tissue investigation. We'll discuss it then."

"Okay," Grant said, getting up. "I guess I'll have lunch and head back to Utica."

Linda got up also. "Can you stay a minute, Linda?" George asked. "I need to talk with you about something."

Grant went out and closed the door behind him. Linda sat back down. "What's on your mind, George?" she asked.

"Dr. McAree," he answered bluntly. "In case you might have forgotten, we're under orders to clear any action with him. In fact, he ordered the investigation on hold after we looked at the morgue records."

"You're right, George. I did put that out of my mind."

"I didn't. We're going to have to come up with an updated investigative plan and submit it to him."

"But we've already given John his instructions. He's going to be doing things before Dr. McAree has a chance to approve them."

George waved his right hand in dismissal and smiled: "That's right Linda, and we may well end up emptying waste baskets because of it. But that's a chance I'm willing to take to get to the bottom of the information leaks we've been experiencing. How about you?"

"I'm with you, George. What are we going to do?"

"As I said, prepare an investigative plan and submit it to Dr. McAree."

"That's it? Are we going to have to lie?"

"Far from it. We're going to tell the absolute truth. How's that?"

"It sounds too good to be true, and I'm sure it is. But go ahead, I'm ready."

"Good," George said. "Listen carefully, because what I'm going to tell you can make or break us."

CHAPTER NINETEEN

By two o'clock Monday afternoon George and Linda had finished the document to submit to Dr. McAree. "Let's go over it one more time," George suggested.

"Yes, let's," Linda agreed.

"First, John is going to contact and interview the families who declined tissue donation," George began. "Next, he's going to visit the Eye Bank and ARC. Third, he's going to follow-up at Crowne. And last, we're going to subpoena the morgue employees to John's office for interviews, right?"

Linda looked up from her copy of the draft. "That's what it says, George. We've rewritten this twice and argued about it for two hours, and you still insist on having this business about the subpoena in here. The first three things are the truth. In fact, John is probably working on setting up the interviews now, or he will be when he gets his copies of the records tomorrow. You said we were going to tell the truth. Why are you so hung up on having that last thing in here?"

"But I've told you, that's the truth too," George said patiently. "This is an investigative plan. What kind of a half assed job would we be doing if we didn't talk with the employees? Since John isn't welcome in the morgue, it has to be done elsewhere. It's that simple."

"Why didn't you tell John, then?" Linda asked.

"I'll tell him, don't worry. Let him get caught up on the other things first."

Linda was not convinced. "You told me to listen to you carefully, you were going to tell me something that could make or break us. I haven't heard anything like that yet. We're keeping John in the dark, and you're holding out on me, George."

George leaned forward across his desk. "Linda, I have told you," he said, speaking very slowly and softly. "You're a smart woman. You have to read between the lines a little bit."

"So you can't just tell me? We've got to talk in code?"

George reversed his position, tilting back in his chair. "You're tough, smart, but tough," he said. "Let me put it this way, there is no sense involving John in the problems we're having here in Albany. By doing it this way we're protecting him. If things don't go right, he's got clean hands. John is an investigator, he'll understand why he was kept out of this. And, to be blunt, there are times when the less that is known by the least number of people is the best. This is one of those times.

We're dealing with a deputy commissioner, a powerful man. There are no guarantees. I'm sure you have already figured out what I'm trying to do. You just want to hear me say it, and I can't. Now, are you still with me?"

Linda smiled. "You're tough too, George. I have a suspicion that I'd like your plan. But I understand where you're coming from. What do you want me to do now?"

George returned her smile. "Atta girl. Right now, don't do anything about this. Go back to your office and do whatever else requires your attention. I want to check on a couple of things, then I'll have this plan typed up. I'll be in touch with you by five o'clock. I'll let you know then what comes next."

"Okay, George. How far are we sticking our necks out?"

"We're like a couple of giraffes," George laughed. "But don't worry too much. I really believe we're doing the right thing. You've got to realize that this case has the potential to be one of the biggest the department has ever handled. I mean think of the issues involved. A government official using dead bodies entrusted to his care as his personal property. Maybe even keeping entire bodies for some kind of collection. Falsifying official records to cover his misconduct. Does a person lose all rights at death? Does a dead body belong to the person in possession of it, to do with it as they will? There are all kinds of issues here. And the public will be able to relate to this. Every adult has had a relative or friend die. If this stuff hits the papers a lot of people are going to wonder what happened to that person at the funeral parlor or morgue."

Linda's face had turned pale. "I hadn't thought of it that way, George. Kind of scary isn't it?"

"Very. That's why I feel very strongly that we can't let this case fold up before we find out just how bad it really is. That's why I'm willing to risk my career here," George explained.

"I'll be in my office, let me know when you're ready," Linda said as she walked out the door.

At three o'clock that same afternoon Dr. Franz, Peter Gorsky and Dr. Massey were shown into Ronald Bronson's spacious office in the county office building. They took their places in the three over stuffed chairs facing Bronson's desk. Bronson looked at Massey, "Well, Mort, you indicated this was some sort of emergency. What is it?"

Massey blushed slightly. "I didn't mean to make this sound that serious, Ron. I'm sorry if I did. But it is rather important that we discuss something."

Bronson glanced at Peter Gorsky, then back to Massey. "Obviously," he said. "Let's hear it."

"Well, it seems the state is taking itself very seriously with this investigation of the morgue. It appears they are going to make big issues of things that Bob has done that were totally innocent. Our fear is that the public might not understand the necessity for doing certain things and reach conclusions that are based on emotion rather than reality. And certainly none of us want the public upset."

Bronson's expression hardened. "I've already received calls from the public after the subpoena story ran. Not a lot, but enough," he said, looking at Franz. "Let's just say that the callers feel that maybe Bob isn't the right man for the job."

Franz bristled, his face coloring. Gorsky saw what was happening and began speaking before Franz could get started. "There are always a few people around looking for an opportunity to bash a public official. I'm sure your callers represent a miniscule percentage of the population."

"My thoughts exactly, Peter," Bronson said. "That's why I haven't mentioned it before." He turned back to Massey. "So, we all agree that it's not good to have the public mad at you. Now what?"

"Well, I have a contact in Albany, a deputy commissioner at DOH. I've spoken with him about this investigation a couple of times. He seems to share our opinion that the whole thing is a lot of bullshit. He indicated that he may be able to get the investigation shut down. But we may have to be willing to admit to some minor violation to satisfy the investigator and the attorney involved." Massey switched his eyes to Franz and announced, "Bob is prepared to accept responsibility for such an infraction."

Bronson also turned his attention toward Franz. "You're

willing to admit that you did something wrong?" he asked, a trace of disbelief in his voice.

Gorsky again leaped into action. "You must understand that Bob honestly believes that he has done nothing wrong. In spite of that, he's willing to accept an amount of blame in order to avoid any major embarrassment to the county. We should praise him for that."

"If your minds are already made up, why are you here?" Bronson asked.

"Because," Gorsky answered, "any charges the state files will be against the county, not Bob. The county will have to agree to any settlement and Chuck Allen's office will have to handle the negotiations and paperwork."

Bronson nodded in understanding. "No offense, Peter, but if Chuck is going to have to handle this, why are you here?"

"I'm simply protecting Bob's interests," Gorsky answered. "I want to make sure he knows what he's admitting to, and if there will be any exposure to him personally."

"Exposure?" Bronson repeated. "What kind of exposure?"

"I want to make sure he doesn't do anything that will open him up to civil liability," Gorsky explained.

"Okay, Peter. I acknowledge your interest in this," Bronson said. "I have a couple of points I'd like clarified, though. It seems to me that the county would be admitting guilt, not Bob.

And if there is any monetary penalty the county would pay it, not Bob. Is that right?"

"Exactly," Gorsky said. "But as far as public relations, you can spin this that Bob admitted to you that he may have been a little careless on occasion. Nothing intentional, just a lapse or two. You got on top of things right away and got everthing settled quickly, and fairly painlessly. You could even end up looking like a hero, Ron."

Gorsky was smooth. He knew about Bronson's political woes, what buttons to push. Bronson's expression told him he had hit home with his "hero" comment.

Bronson smiled. "You make sense, Peter," he said. "I'll need to run this by Chuck Allen, of course. But your plan sounds good to me."

Massey took the ball now. "Wonderful, Ron. Let's get this all behind us. I have meetings the rest of the afternoon. I'll call my contact tomorrow morning to get the ball rolling."

"Okay," Bronson said. "And I'll call Chuck. Let me know as soon as you have an idea of what the state will be willing to accept to settle this. Good day, gentlemen."

As soon as the room was clear Bronson called Reggie Whitehurst. "I think the state is getting close to something with this morgue investigation," he said.

"What's happened to make you say that?" Whitehurst asked, concerned.

"Massey, Franz and Gorsky requested an emergency meeting with me. They just left. Massey knows a deputy commissioner of DOH in Albany. They want to call him and offer a deal if he can get the investigation stopped."

"Deal! What kind of deal? I don't like the sounds of that!"

"Relax, Reggie. It's nothing like that. They said Franz is willing to admit to some minor wrong doing if the state will call off the dogs."

The tension left Whitehurst's voice. "That sounds like the most sensible thing Franz has done in a while. But I never thought I'd hear him offer to admit that he's mortal. That surprises me."

"It bothers the hell out of me! What's he afraid they might find?"

"I don't want to know," Whitehurst said. "I say that if this scheme works, we'll all be better off. What does Chuck Allen think about it?"

"I don't know yet. He's my next call."

"I'm sure Chuck will see it the same way I do. He and I both know that if anyone is investigated for long enough, something will be found."

"I agree," Bronson laughed. "But the state has only been on this for a few weeks. Either they're awful good, or there's a lot of damning stuff out there."

Whitehurst chuckled. "No comment, Ron. Give me a call any time you need a sounding board."

Bronson clicked down the receiver, then released it and called his county attorney.

Dr. Franz waltzed into the morgue's main office. He was elated, his feet barely touching the ground. June Miller, Belinda Bernal, Dorothy Larkin and Michael Hargrove were gathered around Bernal's desk, talking. "What in the world are you grinning about?" Miller asked.

Franz glanced around, "Where is Samuels?" he asked.

"Dr. Samuels is out. He's at the lab," Larkin answered.

"Good. Then I can say that everyone here will be glad to hear my news. The wheels are going to be put in motion to settle our differences with the state and send Mr. Grant off to greener pastures. It will take a few days, but it's in the works."

"How?" Miller asked.

"Dr. Massey and his friend at DOH, the deputy commissioner, are handling it," Franz crowed. "Things will be back to normal soon."

The small group broke into smiles. "Great news, doctor," Hargrove said.

"Congratulations," a familiar voice said from behind them. All heads turned toward the main doorway. Dr. Harrison Samuels walked toward them.

"How long have you been standing there?" Franz demanded.

"Long enough to hear your good news. Congratulations again, Bob," Samuels said, heading down the hallway toward his office.

George Epstein entered Linda's office at ten minutes of five. "Are you ready?" he asked, handing her the typed investigative plan.

"Yes. Tell me what you want me to do."

"Make a copy of the plan for yourself, then put the original in an envelope addressed to Dr. McAree. Stamp it 'Personal and Confidential'. Wait until about five-thirty, he'll be gone by then, and hand carry it to his office. If his private office is open, leave it on his desk. If not, put it on his secretary's desk. After you do that, I want you to send McAree an e-mail. Make sure you request an electronic acknowledgement that it was opened. If you want to grab a piece of paper you can write down what I want you to say."

Linda reached for her legal pad. "Shoot," she said.

"Say that you hand delivered an updated investigative plan to his office for his review. Tell him that the information contained in the plan is highly confidential. Stress that if our intentions are divulged prematurely the investigation will be in jeopardy. Use your own words, but make those points very clear. Finish with a request to meet as soon as possible. Have this ready to go but don't actually send it until after you're back from delivering the envelope."

Linda put her pencil down and looked up at George. "Sounds simple enough. What happens when we meet with him? Suppose he doesn't go along with our ideas and John is already out there following our instructions?"

"When we meet with McAree we're going to have to stand firm on the necessity for following that," George said, pointing at the investigative plan on Linda's desk. "If he doesn't agree

211

we've got to make him put his own plan on the table. We'll play it by ear from there."

"Okay, George. I'll get this ready to go," Linda said, nodding at her notes, "and I'll send it after I drop off the envelope."

"Good. And try to keep a flexible schedule for tomorrow. Things should start popping."

"I'll be ready whenever you need me," Linda promised.

Woody and Grant were seated in Grant's office a few minutes after nine on Tuesday morning. "So they still don't want you to get involved with the skeletons?" Woody asked.

"That's what they said," Grant responded. "I suppose you could tell me something today to change that, but George was quite firm on that point."

"Let me make sure you understand the problem I've got, John. My only reason to investigate the skeletal collection, is that when the bodies were boiled down they may have improperly disposed of the juice containing human tissue. I know that some of it went in the sewer and more went into the ground out in the country. That endangered the wells supplying several homes out there. I can make a case against the county for that on my own. That's a DEC matter from start to finish. But where the bodies came from, where they are supposed to be, and where they are now is none of DEC's business. I have absolutely no legal standing to investigate that. And, quite frankly, the dumping is the mole hill. The bodies themselves are the mountain. A mountain I can't touch. You've got to do it, John. I'll help all I can, but DOH has to do it!"

Grant thought Woody's words over for a moment, then grinned. "The pressure builds, huh?"

Woody grinned back. "You said it. Right now there are only two people in the world looking into this thing, you and me. You're going to have to take the lead if we want to do this right. And I know that's what we both want."

212

"Okay, Woody. Tell me what you've found and I'll see what I can do to convince George and Linda that we've got to expand our investigation now, rather than later."

"I've been sniffing around for information about Franz's crime scene courses," Woody began. "I had to be very low key because I promised Epstein not to make any waves. Under those conditions, information hasn't been easy in coming. But I got lucky. I found out that one of the investigators from our Buffalo office actually attended the course in July of '91. I called him and then met with him in person. The guy is sharp. He kept his notes from the class and some still pictures he took. In addition, he still had the course schedule and lists of the instructors and students."

"Do these lists include addresses?" Grant asked.

"Not individual home addresses," Woody answered. "But they do give the agency or institution the instructors and students are affiliated with. These people will be easy to find if need be."

Grant nodded in approval. "Don't make this sound too easy, Woody. I know how those deals usually work out."

Woody chuckled. "We've got a good starting point, but I'm sure it won't be easy. Before I tell you what our investigator had to say, let me tell you about the instructors and students.

Those lists were very impressive. One of the instructors was from the FBI. Two others were department heads at universities in Georgia and Louisiana. The students represented everything from coroners offices to the Royal Canadian Mounted Police."

Grant tried to whistle, without success. "These courses were apparently no joke, then," he said.

"Absolutely not! The investigator I spoke with, Mike Durant, thought it was the greatest training he'd ever attended. He couldn't believe there might have been something wrong with it."

"You've got me hooked, Woody. What was wrong with it?"

"In short, they used human remains. Franz supplied skeletons and body parts for the course. Where do you suppose he got them?"

"Don't all these ME and coroner's offices have a skeleton available for training? You know, the kind they use in medical school."

"Yes. But that's not what Mike saw. These were skeletons that had been autopsied, the tops of the skulls removed. And the body parts had flesh on them."

"How many skeletons are we talking about? How many body parts?" Grant asked.

"Mike says there were six whole skeletons, two partially decomposed bodies, and dozens of body parts."

Grant rubbed his chin, thinking. "How were these things used? In a classroom? The woods? Where and how?"

"Let me back up and explain how the course was structured," Woody suggested. "It was a five day deal, Monday thru Friday.

The first two days were classroom lectures at the Hotel Utica. The next two and a half days were in the field. The final afternoon was back in the classroom for a critique and issuing of certificates. The skeletons and body parts were used in the field."

"Where was 'the field' and what did they do there?" Grant questioned.

"In this case the field was the farm of Mr. Rodney Flowers, one of Franz's morgue workers, and the Evergreen Cemetery. On Wednesday morning they exhumed a 'John Doe' from Evergreen. From Wednesday afternoon until Friday noon they were at Flowers' place processing crime scenes with human remains. The skeletons had been placed around the property, some on top of the ground, others partially buried. The body parts were strewn about above ground. The class split up in teams, each with an instructor, and did mock investigations of the various scenes."

"How many students were in the class?"

"There were twenty-eight in Mike's group."

"Then what?"

"Starting Thursday afternoon they boiled down the 'John Doe' and the body parts containing flesh. They finished up Friday morning and cleaned up their work area. The skeletons and bones were packed up and loaded in the morgue wagon. Presumably they were taken to the morgue. They took a long lunch break to eat and get cleaned up. Then they met back in the hotel for the final session. A well run program, no doubt about it."

"So, if your information is accurate, Mr. Chambers has some company on the morgue shelves, or wherever he is," Grant speculated.

"Franz has been putting on these courses for three years," Woody said. "He could use the same skeletons each time, I suppose. But the fleshy body parts are boiled down at the end of the class. If he uses dozens of them each time he must have quite an inventory built up."

"So it would seem," Grant agreed. "Anything else?"

"Yes. I believe the John Doe was exhumed illegally. Franz told Mike's class that he had obtained a court order for the exhumation. According to our attorney's, you can only get an exhumation order to determine the cause of death or identify the deceased. As soon as that purpose is accomplished the body has to be put back. Mike said Doe had already been autopsied. That means the cause of death was not an issue. Nothing was done in the way of identification, such as doing a facial reconstruction. Doe was used as part of the course on Flowers' farm, then boiled down and taken to the morgue. I'd like to take a look at the application Franz submitted to the court, and the wording of the order. Until I can do that, it's my suspicion that Franz lied to the court on the application. And it certainly doesn't look as though he returned Doe to his grave. I'll bet we find that he's done an exhumation as part of each course. Exhumations based on false submissions to the court."

215

Grant pondered that information for several seconds. "What do you want me to do?" he asked.

"Have you people thought any more about trying to get into the morgue to look around?"

"Not really. As I said, George is hung up on doing the tissue first. He agrees it's a problem for us, though. He told me yesterday that we'd talk about it when I get my other assignments finished."

"In that case, you need to change George's mind. I've already decided that I'm going to try to get an interview with Rodney Flowers. This one course was held on his farm. He'll be able to tell me where the boiling tub was emptied. That's about all I can talk to him about. If I can get his lawyer to agree to make him available, would you like to go along? Maybe you can learn enough to press George to see things our way."

"Where is Flowers now?" Grant asked.

"He's still at the state prison reception center in Watertown, waiting to be placed."

"This would only be a day trip, right?" Grant asked. Woody nodded. "Yes, I'd like to go. I'll figure some way to get Linda's blessing. When will you know if you can set it up?"

"I'll try to contact his lawyer this afternoon."

"Okay. I've got a couple of more questions about the course. Can we get a copy of the check DEC sent to the county for Mike's registration?"

"With the shape of our budget DEC is only paying for mandatory training. Mike took time off and went at his own expense. He paid five hundred bucks. He's getting me a copy of the check."

"Good," Grant said. "Let's see. If my math is correct, this course brought in fourteen grand, minus expenses. I wonder what he had to pay the instructors."

"Mike said the FBI guy told him their time was free. The county paid for lodging and meals. Transportation costs were picked up by their employers for public relations purposes. So the county got away cheap on them. The county had to pay for the conference room at the hotel. And they provided lunch every day and coffee and soft drinks. The students took care of their own accomodations and other meals."

"All in all, the expenses probably weren't that bad," Grant surmised. "Do you think Flowers got anything for the use of his farm?"

"I don't know, but that's certainly something we can ask him."

"No wonder the county supports Franz," Grant said. "He operates under budget and brings them in a few extra bucks on the side."

"He's a shrewd operator," Woody agreed. "You said you had another question?"

"Yeah, next time you talk with Mike, ask him if a funeral director was involved with moving Doe around or transporting the skeletons and bones to the morgue. It's my understanding that only a licensed funeral director can do the transporting."

Woody reached into his shirt pocket and withdrew a small spiral note book. He leafed through a few pages until he found what he was looking for. "The Price Funeral Home took Doe from the cemetery to Flowers' place in a hearse. On the trip from the farm to the morgue they used a morgue wagon, but one of Price's people rode along."

"You're very efficient, Woody," Grant complimented.

"Thanks," Woody said, standing up. "I've got to get going.

I'll call you as soon as I talk with Flowers' attorney. Sit still, John, I'll find my own way out."

After Woody left, Grant sat staring at the wall, trying to figure out how he was going to bring George around to his and Woody's way of thinking.

CHAPTER TWENTY

Dr. Robert McAree started his work day on Tuesday finding an envelope on his desk marked "Personal and Confidential". He didn't know who it was from, but he liked the implied secrecy. He enjoyed having information that others didn't. He decided to delay opening the envelope right away to let the excitement build. He put the envelope back down on the desk top and swiveled around to his computer terminal. He flipped the "on" buttons and waited during the brief warm-up period. He then signed on and went straight to his e-mail screen. He had four messages. The first two were meeting notices, the next was from Commissioner Bowers, and the last was from Linda Ludwig. He opened hers first.

As he read, his left hand went back to the envelope. He held it in his finger tips. This had to be what Ludwig was referring to in her note. Plans that could jeopardize the investigation if made known prematurely? What the hell was she talking about?

He turned from the computer and opened the envelope. He read the document three times. It was obvious that Ludwig and Epstein had no intention of wrapping the investigation up. They wanted to go deeper, in fact. And another fucking subpoena!

McAree put the paper down. He had to do some serious thinking. How much could he limit the investigation and not get his ass in a sling? He owed Franz nothing, he'd never even met the man. It certainly seemed that Grant was gathering information indicating that Franz's activities were more than the innocent mistakes he had been led to believe. But he'd shot his mouth off to Massey, built himself up. Could he get this mess straightened out without damaging his reputation?

After twenty minutes of running through possible options he settled on a plan. He'd summon Epstein and Ludwig, find out how firm they were about implementing their plan. If they were determined, he'd have to tread lightly. He couldn't risk pushing them to complain to their superiors, maybe even have someone go over his head, right to the commissioner.

He now saw Massey's desire to stop the investigation as a sign of desperation. Fear over what Grant might find, rather than simply an effort to spare Franz or the county any embarrassment. Those thoughts comforted him. If he was right, Massey would be willing to accept a little bit more severe punitive action to reach a settlement.

Feeling better now, he was confident that he could broker a deal acceptable to both the county and the department. He called to his secretary and asked her to call Epstein and Ludwig.

At 10:30 George and Linda got off the elevator at the fourteenth floor. Linda had received the electronic confirmation that her note to Dr. McAree had been opened. "Now remember, let me do most of the talking," George said as they neared McAree's office. "With pleasure," Linda answered. A few seconds later they were seated in the all too familiar chairs across from Dr. McAree.

"Good morning you two," McAree said pleasantly. "I've had a chance to look over your investigative plan. I wanted to take a few minutes to review it with you, okay?"

"Certainly, doctor. That's why we're here," George said agreeably.

McAree picked the paper up and held it in the air. "It sounds as though you plan to procede full tilt with this. Complete with interviews and another subpoena. Before I make a decision, please tell me where you think all this will lead."

"My answer is going to be based on facts that we've already developed, and speculation based on those facts," George explained. "I believe that we have established that Dr. Franz used his position as ME to illegally harvest and provide tissue to research facilities. The primary recipient was Crowne, but we're quite sure there was at least one other. This tissue was taken without the informed consent required or, in several cases, over the specific refusals of the next of kin."

"You say that you have proof of this?" McAree asked.

"We have hard evidence to support that the tissue was harvested and passed on to Crowne. Mr. Grant will have to do the interviews of the families to verify that they did in fact object to tissue donation. Those interviews are obviously a critical part of our case."

"Obviously," McAree concurred. "And you're reasonably sure that Dr. Franz acted with knowledge that what he was doing was wrong?"

"Yes," George said bluntly.

"There is no chance that Dr. Franz simply didn't understand the law?" McAree asked hopefully.

"In my opinion, no. Not a chance," George answered.

"I see," McAree said. "Why do you want to interview all of Franz's people. Why the subpoena? Don't you think they'd be cooperative on their own?"

"We want to be fair and thorough. We realize that most of those employees are loyal to Dr. Franz, but we want to give them a chance to get their information on the record, regardless of who it favors," George said. "As far as the use of subpoenas, everyone will be compelled to give testimony. That will help to avoid recriminations should anyone provide information harmful to Dr. Franz. That is my main reason, but I also see no reason to leave their cooperation to chance. Subpoena power is a tool available to us, there is no reason not to use it."

"What do you feel would be an appropriate penalty for violations of this sort?" McAree wanted to know.

"If we can prove my scenario, I'd be inclined to seek revocation of Dr. Franz's lab director licenses with a referral for action against his medical license. Our action will actually be against the county. But we'd ask that Franz surrender his lab licenses as part of any resolution. The Medical Conduct people would go after Franz directly of course."

"Loss of his licenses? That's a bit severe isn't it?" McAree suggested.

"Almost all of the donors of this tissue were children, doctor," George explained. "If, as one of those parents, you found that Dr. Franz had ignored your wishes and removed tissue from your dead child, what action would you expect the

221

department to take? I doubt if they will be satisfied with a slap on the wrist. I think they'll demand more than that. I would!"

McAree was silent for a few seconds, contemplating his next move. Epstein had taken a firm stance. He had made a good argument, and he had done it with conviction. Under these circumstances McAree didn't want to force a confrontation.

"I must say that I agree with you, George," McAree finally said. "Your plan is approved. Go ahead and give Mr. Grant his instructions. Continue to keep me fully informed as to your progress and future plans."

"Do you mean that you only want to be kept informed and that we can run the investigation?" George asked, nodding toward Linda.

"I'll settle for being informed in a timely manner," McAree said. "But I would appreciate it if you touch base with me ahead of time on anything major, issuing subpoenas for example."

"We will, doctor," George said. "If there's nothing else, we'll get started."

"Nothing else," McAree said. "Thanks for coming."

Alone in the hallway, Linda turned to George, "What the hell? He did a one eighty. Do you suppose we're wrong about him?" she asked.

"I'm more convinced than ever that he's been playing ball with the county. The difference now is that he knows he stuck his nose into this without knowing the details. He's dug himself into a hole and now he's trying to get out of it. He's scared. I could almost smell the fear, couldn't you?"

"I don't know as I can call it fear. But there is no mistaking his change in attitude," Linda said.

"It was fear, trust me," George said as they waited for an elevator car. "The bastard is scared now, and he doesn't even realize what he's in for."

"You're looking forward to this, aren't you?" Linda asked.

"People like McAree use their positions to benefit themselves and their friends. They care nothing about the people they are supposed to serve. He can't be allowed to succeed. To answer your question, yes, I'm looking forward to what's coming."

"So, his being so nice today did nothing to warm your heart, George?"

"Absolutely not! We were holding the cards today. If he had the pat hand he'd squash us as if we were a couple of bugs."

The mail courier delivered the box containing Grant's copies of the morgue records at one o'clock. He removed the thirteen declinations and placed the box on the floor next to his desk. When he had been reviewing the files at the county attorney's office he had been focusing only on Case Data Sheet entries relating to tissue donation. Now he wanted to learn about the people he planned to interview. In addition to their names, addresses and phone numbers, he hoped to find some personal background information.

Even before looking at the copies he had made one decision. He knew that these interviews would be the most difficult part of the investigation for him. If at all possible he planned to do all the interviews in one day and get them over with. He knew he couldn't do all thirteen, but he didn't expect to be able to reach them all. And there may be some who wouldn't agree to talk with him. He felt that with good luck he would be able to schedule eight appointments. And he could fit that number into one long day.

As he browsed through the records he was pleased with the information he found. The "fill in the blank" entries contained the basic stuff, including name, address, phone and employment information for the next of kin. In addition, some of the morgue employees made entries giving additional family members to be used as alternate contacts. In these cases they were mostly the grandparents of the deceased.

The name on the fourth file jumped out at him. Two year old William Clinton had died in 1991. His grandfather was also William Clinton, the man who had sat next to Grant at Franz's news conference. The man who had felt Franz's accusers should be crucified. It now appeared that his hero had taken his grandson's testicles, bladder and prostate without permission. Grant shook his head sadly and moved on.

He finished the rest of the files without finding anymore familiar names. Now it was time to start trying to contact them. With little enthusiasm, Grant grabbed the first file and reached for the phone.

Dr. Robert McAree didn't return Massey's call until a little after three o'clock. "Mort, I think your man may have done a bit more than make a few innocent mistakes. The attorney handling this investigation is very confident that he's already got a strong case, and that more things will be coming."

"What do they have now? What else do they expect to get?" Massey demanded.

"There is some pretty solid evidence that Dr. Franz was taking these tissues without informed consent. That's bad enough, but they've found cases where tissue was taken over specific objections of the families. The attorney pointed out that this is the type of thing that will not set well with the public," McAree said. "And get this, they are going to have Grant interview all these people and tell them what happened. They're also going to subpoena all of Franz's employees and have them give sworn statements."

"Can't you do anything? Aren't you in charge down there?" Massey asked, voice shaking.

"Quite frankly, they're finding too much. If I order them to stop and they complain over my head, I don't have a leg to stand on. I could never justify halting the investigation at this stage of the game."

"Are you saying that you're throwing us over?" Massey asked accusingly.

"No, that's not what I'm saying at all, Mort. I can't stop the investigation, but I can still broker a settlement that can save Franz's career."

"Save his career? What in the hell are you talking about, Bob?"

"Here's what I'm talking about," McAree answered. "Right now they're intention is to go after his licenses, lab director and medical. For an administrative action, that's a death sentence. I still think I can save his licenses and avoid his having to resign."

"Resign! Are you fucking crazy, Bob?" Massey said, losing his cool completely. "Bob Franz will never resign! If you're thinking that he will, you'd better think again!"

"You aren't listening, Mort. I said I can still do something to avoid things coming to that. But it may take a little more sacrifice on Franz's part than we originally thought."

"I'll talk to Dr. Franz and get back to you," Massey said.

Dr. McAree hung up, sorry he had ever heard of Bob Franz.

Utilizing the numbers and names on the Case Data Sheets, the phone book and directory assistance, Grant had made contact with six of the thirteen families by five o'clock. He had tried to arrange the interviews without providing much detail as to the reason. As he had expected, nobody would commit without additional information. He went as far as to say he wanted to discuss the death of their child, or a grandchild in one case.

Four had subsequently agreed to meet with him on April 16th, including the Clinton's. One family had declined his request, stating that the incident was too painful to talk about. In the remaining case he had been able to reach the grandparents. He was told their daughter and son-in-law had moved out of state. While they would provide no contact information, they did promise to pass on Grant's request to speak with them.

In another four cases the numbers on the morgue records were no longer valid and no information was available from the phone book or directory assistance. To pursue them further would require field work. It could be as simple as a visit to the last known address, the post office, or a former employer. Or it could end up being very time consuming. He wanted to check with George before doing anything further on those.

The numbers for the remaining three families seemed to be valid. They rang through without a problem. They were simply not answered. Grant decided to try them from his home later in the evening. The next morning he planned to go to the Eye Bank and ARC. Then he'd have to see if George had been successful in enlisting Mr. Sullivan's help in the Crowne piece of the investigation. Grant left for home feeling pretty good about the way things were developing.

"Resign! Are you fucking crazy? I'll never resign!" Dr. Franz screamed at Morton Massey. They were in Massey's office along with Peter Gorsky. It was a little after six o'clock.

Franz was pacing like a caged animal. His face was the deep scarlet that Massey and Gorsky were becoming used to. Massey came out from behind his desk and approached Franz. "You've got to calm down, Bob. You've got to remember who your friends are," he advised.

"Easy for you to say! Nobody is talking about taking your license!" Franz snarled.

Massey turned toward Gorsky, seated in one of the chairs in front of Massey's desk. "Talk to him, Peter. Please," he begged.

"Mort is right, Bob," Gorsky said. "But I have something to say that is more important, at least to me. I've heard you both make comments about having this deputy commissioner in Albany somehow exert influence in this investigation to Bob's benefit. I want to advise both of you to be very cautious about what you ask this man to do. You may very well be dancing around the edge of legality. It's one thing to negotiate a legitimate settlement, it's quite another to conspire to limit or compromise an investigation for the purpose of benefiting the target of that investigation. In the early stages, that kind of contact might have been appropriate. You were simply explaining that you felt the DOH probe was without merit and could unfairly harm an innocent person. You asked that DOH use good judgement. Now, things have changed. Be damn careful what you ask this guy to do. It could come back to haunt you!"

"Peter, let me assure you....," Massey began.

Gorsky raised his hand, palm out, toward him. "I don't want to hear it, Mort. You just got some free legal advice. Take it for what it's worth."

"Okay, okay," Massey said, getting flustered. "Let's come to some decision. It's getting late."

"Is your secretary waiting for you at some motel?" Franz sneered. "My situation is a little more important than you getting your pipes cleaned. We'll stay here as long as it takes to resolve this."

A red faced Massey glanced at Gorsky. He found that he was the subject of the lawyer's penetrating gaze. "You bastard!" Massey said to Franz.

"Gentlemen," Gorsky said calmly. "Let's save our arguing for the state. That's where we need to direct our energies. Now, if you two will take your seats let's conduct this as a business meeting. That way we can accomplish something. Agreed?"

Franz and Massey glared at each other for a few more seconds, then did as Gorsky had asked.

When they were seated Gorsky began. "Based on what this Dr. McAree told you today, Mort, I think I have an idea that will get done what we want, be acceptable to the county, and be legal."

"What's your idea?" Franz and Massey asked in unison.

"First let me repeat something," Gorsky said. "My proposal involves a legitimate attempt to resolve a pending matter with the state. The person we will be dealing with has the authority to entertain our proposal, right, Mort?"

"Full authority," Massey said, hoping he was right.

"Good. And our proposal will only be made in that context, honest discussion with an appropriate member of DOH, right?"

"Yes, yes, yes!" Massey said, frustrated. "What are you driving at, Peter?"

Gorsky leaned forward, resting his forearms on Massey's desk. "I don't want you guys to back door me! I won't be a part of anything that's not above board. The proposal we come up with tonight will be the only one presented to this Dr. McAree. No secret deals, understood?"

Massey nodded. "Certainly not, Peter. I'm somewhat offended that you'd think such a thing."

Gorsky didn't respond. He sat back in his chair and turned his head to look at Franz. "What about you, Bob?"

"I just want out from under this! It's turning into a nightmare!" Franz said, still agitated.

"Okay. But I'm afraid that this won't be as pain free as you might like," Gorsky said, still looking at Franz.

Franz stared straight ahead and remained silent.

"All right, then," Gorsky continued. "I think we should be prepared to admit that Bob did take this small number of tissue without appropriate permission. We can soft pedal it as some kind of misunderstanding, nothing intentional. This admission would be in full satisfaction of any and all charges. That's the easy part, more or less standard operation in the business. The penalty will be a little more diffucult." Gorsky paused, watching Franz's expression. Still red faced, he continued to stare ahead in silence.

"Remember, we have to offer something that both the state and county will agree to," Gorsky went on. "Bob will consent to attending any training the state may offer regarding the proper handling of tissue donations. The state will be allowed to closely monitor morgue operations for a period of twelve months. This will include unannounced visits and inspection of records and policy and procedure. A fine of...let's say ten thousand dollars, will be levied, but suspended for the same twelve month period. If the state's inspections find no continuing problems, the fine is forgotten. This will actually cost the county nothing, assuming Bob behaves himself. We're offering enough to let the state attorney feel that he's gotten something. And the biggest selling point is that there won't be a hearing. The state doesn't like hearings. If we give them something they can live with, they'll take it. And, this kind of settlement will avoid all this stuff coming out in public."

Franz popped out of his chair. "The state train me? What a fucking joke that is! What you're saying is that I'd be on probation. That asshole Grant will be able to show up and bust my balls whenever he feels like it! No dice, Peter! You're going to have to do better than that!" Franz shut up and began to pace back and forth again.

Gorsky had anticipated this reaction, although he had hoped against it. "Listen, Bob," he said, turning in his chair so that he could look at Franz as he walked, "this may not be exactly what you'd like, but it beats the hell out of losing your licenses or getting fired."

Franz stopped dead in his tracks and swung around to face Gorsky. "That's bullshit! Those bastards will never get my licenses! You had better remember that I haven't done anything wrong. At least nothing to lose my licenses over. And what's this business about getting fired? Where did that come from?"

"A little dose of reality, Bob," Gorsky said. "Now, if you'll calm down and sit down, I'll explain it to you." Reluctantly, Franz returned to his chair.

Satisfied, Gorsky went on. "It's obvious that you and I see the situation differently, Bob. I think the state has a pretty good case right now, and I believe it will only get stronger with time. And Ronald Bronson has his own agenda. As long as he can get out of this at little or no cost to the county, and may even be helped politically, he'll be on your side. But as soon as you become a liability, if the public catches on to what you've been doing with the tissue, for instance, he'll drop you like a bad habit! My idea may not be a panacea from your point of view, but it will work. What do you say?"

Franz sat in thought for several seconds with Gorsky and Massey watching him closely. They were relieved to see the red begin to drain from his face. "I suppose you're right, Peter," he said finally, with just the trace of a grin. "When you put it in those terms, I guess your idea is the lesser of two evils. Now what?"

"I'll contact Chuck Allen and ask for a meeting with him and Bronson," Gorsky answered. "While I'm doing that, Mort, I'd like you to call McAree. Tell him what we're thinking about. Impress upon him that we're just in the talking stages, the county has got to be consulted. But he'll probably give you some indication of whether or not he thinks this will fly. Will you do that?"

"Sure, Peter," Massey promised. "I'll call him tomorrow. I think he's just as anxious to get this over with as we are."

"Fine," Gorsky said, getting to his feet. "Give me a call after you talk with him. I want to know how he reacts." Massey nodded. Gorsky started toward the door, "Are you coming Bob?" he asked.

"I need to talk with Mort for a minute," Franz said, still seated.

Gorsky eyed him suspiciously. "Don't worry, Peter," Franz said, smiling now. "There's more to my job than this state crap. I need to speak with Mort about a couple of unrelated matters."

Gorsky shrugged. "Sure. I'll be talking with you tomorrow then. Good night, gentlemen," he said and left the room.

"What's this other business?" Massey asked, looking at his watch.

"When you call McAree don't mention this probation thing. I won't have the state snooping around my morgue at their whim!"

"God damn it, Bob," Massey hollered. "I thought we had this settled. What are you trying to pull now?"

"I'm not pulling anything!" Franz bellowed back. "I'm only telling you that I won't tolerate the state looking over my shoulder for a year!"

Massey stared at Franz. "Do you simply resent their presence or are you hiding something? What is in that place that you're so afraid might be found?"

"Nothing!" Franz snapped back. "And don't question me again!"

"Question you? I'm your boss! It's my job to know what is going on over there!"

Franz was again on his feet. He placed his palms on the top of Massey's desk, leaning forward. His face was again scarlet, his eyes glowing. "You were never concerned about what I did until now! Forget it!" Franz raved, spittle forming on his lips. "You'd better get something through your head. I'm fighting for my professional life here! I don't give a fuck about you, or Gorsky, or Bronson! My only concern is me! If I have to call your wife and tell her a few things to get your attention, I will. Don't make the mistake of doubting me! Now, are you going to make that call tomorrow?"

Massey's hand wiped his face. "I'll do as you say, Bob."

CHAPTER TWENTY - ONE

Grant got to his office at quarter of eleven Wednesday morning. As soon as he got settled in at his desk he placed a call to George Epstein. "Here's the scoop," he said when he had George on the line.

"Before you get started," George interrupted, "I heard from the AG. They finally filed the paperwork on the Murphy gag order. Next time you talk with Murphy tell him that, will you?"

"Sure, but we already know nothing will get done in time to help us now. I think Pat knows it too. But I'll tell him anyway. The reason I called is to tell you about how I made out with my efforts to contact these thirteen families."

"Yes?"

"Things could have gone better," Grant admitted. "Out of the thirteen, I've got six appointments, all for next Friday, the sixteenth. Two families refused to meet with me. The other five have apparently moved from the area. I did make contact with the relatives of one of those. They promised to pass on a message for me, but they wouldn't give me any other information."

There was silence for a moment. "Only six, huh? That's less than half, not very good is it?" George said.

"I'll be happy to give you the phone numbers and let you try your luck," Grant said testily. "Maybe you can do better."

"I'm sure that you did all that could be done, John. I was just expecting a little better results, that's all. But if people have moved it's certainly not our fault."

"Would you like me to put some more effort in trying to trace these people? I might be able to come up with locations for a few of them," Grant offered.

George pondered that suggestion briefly. "No," he said. "At least not now. Let's see how we make out with the six you're going to talk with. What were their reactions to your call?"

"Curiosity, certainly. Fear, in some cases. Anger. A little bit of everything," Grant answered.

"How much did you tell them?" George asked.

"The most I said was that I wanted to talk with them about the death of their child. These people aren't stupid. They read the paper, I guess. I didn't go into any detail, but they know, I'm sure."

"Any questions about suing the county?"

"Yes, George, there were. I did just as you told me. I first said that the question was premature since we hadn't even met yet. But, as I said, they knew. I told them that if, after we talked, they felt some legal action might be appropriate they could consult their own attorney."

"Good, John. That's exactly the way we have to handle this. We can't leave the impression that we're encouraging people to sue the county."

"I understand, George. Now, I stopped at the Eye Bank and ARC this morning. The directors of both programs stated flatly that they don't receive research tissue from the morgue. Their only involvement is for the harvesting of organs for transplant. When the morgue receives an organ donor, or the next of kin expresses an interest in donating an organ for transplant, the morgue worker notifies the appropriate agency. They send a team to do the actual harvesting. The morgue provides the 'clean room' where the harvesting is done. After they finish, the body is put back in a condition to make it suitable for viewing. That means in as good a condition as when the harvesting team received it. Other than making the notification to them, the morgue people only wheel the body to and from the clean room."

"Do they know that the morgue has their donation forms and how they're using them?"

"Yes," Grant said. "They did say that sometimes they will ask the morgue staff to start the paperwork while they get their team together. Forms are left at the morgue for that purpose. But they had no idea they were being used for this research tissue stuff. They are not very happy about it. I made them promise not

234

to take any action until our investigation is over. I'll be receiving letters from each detailing what I've just told you.

"When do you anticipate receiving those letters?" George asked.

"They should be faxed to me by close of business today. Do you want copies for your file?"

"That's what I was going to ask for," George said. "I'd like you to send me an e-mail with the results of your contacts with the families of the tissue donors. Can you do that today too?"

"Sure thing, George. Have you had an opportunity to talk with Mr. Sullivan at Crowne about helping us out?"

"Yes. When you check your e-mail you'll find a note from me with Dr. Slater's address in Phoenix. Sullivan was even able to provide a phone number for him."

"Thanks, George. Did Sullivan say anything about any further cooperation, like setting up an interview with Dr. Rudolph for example?"

"He promised continued cooperation in general terms. I didn't get specific about Rudolph. I figured it would be better to wait until you were ready to talk with Rudolph before I asked for his help. No sense in giving him additional time to think it over, right?"

"Sounds right to me," Grant agreed. "I certainly don't want to see Rudolph until after I hear what Dr. Slater has to say. I'll give Slater a ring this morning and see if he's willing to answer a few questions."

"Okay, John, good luck. Let me know how it goes. And don't forget to send me that note. Talk to you later."

Grant hung up the phone and went to the computer to check his e-mail. He printed the note from George and returned to his desk. It was just after eleven o'clock local time. That would make it just after nine in Phoenix. Time for Dr. Slater to be up and about, he reasoned. He picked up the handset and dialed Dr. Slater's number.

His call was answered on the second ring. " The Slater's," a female voice announced. Grant identified himself and asked to speak with Dr. Slater. "I'm sorry, but my husband is at a conference in San Francisco until a week from Saturday. If this is something urgent I'll get a message to him for you. Otherwise, I'd rather that you call back after he returns."

"It's important, but not urgent, Mrs. Slater," Grant said. "I'll call back on Monday, the nineteenth, then?"

"That will be fine, Mr. Grant. Anytime after nine o'clock here. You'll find him more pleasant to talk with after he's had his breakfast and a couple of cups of coffee," she chuckled.

Grant thanked her and hung up. He returned to the computer and began preparing his report to George, including the results of his call to Phoenix.

Dr. McAree's first phone call that Wednesday morning was from Dr. Massey. "I've talked with Bob Franz. He said he would agree to admit that a small amount of research tissue was taken without sufficient consent, and that this happened on his watch," Massey said. "This admission will be in satisfaction of all charges the state plans to file against the county. The penalty will be a ten thousand dollar fine. The fine will be suspended pending compliance with DOH Tissue Bank regulations for a period of one year. There will be no action against his licenses, and DOH will not publicize the nature of the charges or terms of the stipulation. If you agree, we'll refer this to our county attorney for finalization."

"What?" McAree screamed. "I told you that he'd have to be willing to make a fairly substantial concession. This proposal is a joke. He's giving nothing! Our attorney may not be a Perry Mason, but he's not retarded. I can't approach him with something like this! I can't believe that you have the nerve to expect me to try it!"

"Now calm down, Bob. We're just talking. I just wanted to run this by you and see what you thought."

"That's not the impression I got. It sounded to me like you expected me to run with this half baked proposal. Does your boy realize that he's not in a very strong bargaining position? He's going to have to be a lot more realistic before I stick my nuts any further in the ringer!"

"How realistic?" Massey wanted to know.

"I don't know. But I'm sure it will take more than that."

"Bob, will you talk with your attorney? Feel him out for us. See what he'd accept as a reasonable settlement. Will you do that, please?"

The pleading in Massey's voice made McAree feel much better, much more in control. "Sure, Mort. I'll see him this morning. I'll call you back a little later, okay?"

"Thanks, Bob. Try not to get too impatient with me. I'm right in the middle of this and I'm under a lot of pressure."

"You're under a lot of pressure!" McAree roared. "If the department ever found out how I've been trying to help you I'd surely be fired, maybe even end up in jail! And you think you've got problems!"

"I'm sorry, Bob. I've been very selfish, only thinking of my own situation. Let me tell you now how much I appreciate your help. And I promise that I'll remember that when you need a little help with something. Just hang with me on this a little longer. I know that you don't even know Bob Franz. But it's not just him you're helping, it's me too. I'm his boss, I'm responsible for his conduct. That's why it's so important that we get this investigation stopped as soon as possible. None of us need to be embarrassed at this stage in our carreers."

"So, you're no longer claiming that Franz is an innocent victim of persecution. What in the hell is Franz hiding?" Before Massey could respond, McAree said, "Never mind! I don't want to know!"

"I don't know myself, Bob," Massey said. "And I don't want to know, either."

"Then I guess we're both in the same boat, Mort. We're both putting ourselves in harms way for Franz. For different reasons, no doubt, but the same bottom line. Is he worth it, Mort?"

"I don't know anymore, Bob. I honestly don't know."

"Good morning, George," Dr. McAree said as he walked into Epstein's office. His smile was broad and his tone friendly.

"Good morning, doctor," George replied. "What brings you to see me this morning?"

"I'll buy the coffee if you've got time to go to the cafeteria," McAree offered.

"No thanks, doctor, I'm bogged down here with paperwork," George said, waving at the several stacks of papers on his desk.

"What can I do for you?"

McAree sat down in one of the chairs opposite George. "Well, as you know, I originally got involved in this investigation of the morgue at the request of Dr. Massey, the Oneida County Commissioner of Health. He called me earlier this morning. After speaking with him, I think I may owe you an apology. I had taken his initial position at face value, that the department was not being objective in it's investigation of Dr. Franz. I believe now that Dr. Massey's story was not quite accurate."

"What's happened to change your mind?" George asked.

McAree smiled and chuckled. "Massey took a different position with me this morning. He expressed an interest in wanting to settle this thing. He asked me what it would take. I certainly didn't want to comment without talking with you first. This is your ballgame, after all."

"I appreciate that, doctor," George said, trying to sound like he believed what he had been told. "Did Dr. Massey give you any indication of what the county is prepared to admit? What penalties they'd be willing to pay?"

"Not really, George. He made it clear that they're just talking, trying to get some ideas. Preliminary stuff."

"Who is talking? Massey and who else?"

"Why, I don't know. He didn't say. The county attorney I imagine," McAree said, sounding surprised by the question.

"Wouldn't it be more appropriate for the county attorney to be dealing directly with me?" George asked.

McAree's discomfort was now obvious. "I only said I assumed that the county attorney was involved, Massey didn't say that. Look, George, I think his call was understandable. Apparently you people have found some evidence of wrong doing and, as Franz's boss, Dr. Massey wants to get things straightened out. I'd probably do the same thing in his shoes."

George shrugged. "Maybe so. Now what?"

"I promised to get back to him with a possible settlement scenario. You know the facts of the case, what would you consider a fair settlement?"

"Fair to who, doctor, the department or the county?"

"Both, naturally!" McAree said, voice rising. "Now listen to me Mr. Epstein. I don't like your attitude. I come to you and admit that I may have used poor judgement initially. I offer an olive branch and you respond with snide and sarcastic remarks! It sounds to me like you think this is pay back time. Let me assure you that I won't put up with any crap from the likes of you! Now answer my question!"

George was pleased with himself, he had pissed McAree off. Emotions sometimes led to mistakes, and right now McAree was emotional. But he couldn't let his pleasure show. "I'm sorry, doctor. I didn't intend any disrespect. As for what it would take to settle, I think a full admission to all charges, a hefty fine and close supervision of Dr. Franz for a couple of years would be a minimum. His director licenses would have to be surrendered if any serious problems are found at the morgue during the period of probation."

"Who would supervise Franz, Dr. Massey?"

"No. We would."

"Does that mean Franz would have to deal with Grant?"

"No. John is not an inspector. He'd probably only get involved if additional problems were found," George explained.

"Could the fine be suspended?" McAree asked.

"Wait a minute, doctor. This sounds more to me like you're negotiating. I'm just giving you some of my ideas. Anything I say would have to be approved by my boss, remember that. And besides, talk of settlement is way too early. We haven't even completed the investigation yet. I believe that we've only scratched the surface of Franz's activities so far."

"God damn it!" McAree hollered, leaning forward in his chair and pounding his fist on George's desk. "The investigation would be stopped if there's a settlement! Can't you understand that?"

"I see," George said calmly. "So that is the main impetus for Massey's interest in settlement, that the investigation be stopped?"

McAree's face turned beet red. He knew he had said more than he had wanted to. He was smart enough to realize that he needed to leave and gather his composure without saying anything more.

He got to his feet, gave George a final glare and stalked out of the room.

Dr. McAree returned to his office and closed the door. He sulked for a while, then forced himself to try to figure a way out of this mess he had gotten himself in. He didn't want to admit to Massey that he couldn't control the situation. Word of that would spread quickly to his colleagues, he was sure. What could he do to extricate himself without losing face? A half hour later he thought he had the answer. He picked up the phone and called Massey.

"Mort, I have some information for you. It will probably require some admissions of guilt, close scrutiny of the morgue by us for a couple of years and a substantial fine to settle this. And that's probably a minimum," McAree said.

Massey tried to sound disappointed, but he was really ecstatic. This sounded almost identical to what Gorsky had proposed. It would be much easier to sell to Franz coming from DOH. This "close scrutiny" by DOH would take him off the hook completely. If they didn't find any future problems, he could take credit for overseeing a good operation. If problems were found, DOH would have to deal with them, not him. "Who

240

would be monitoring the morgue, Grant? Can the fine be suspended?", he asked.

"I did find out that Grant wouldn't be involved. One of the technical people would do the site visits. I don't know about suspending the fine," McAree answered.

"I don't know if Dr. Franz will go along, but I'll talk with him about it," Massey said.

That was more than McAree could stand. "Fuck him!" he hollered. "I don't want to hear anymore about what that bastard wants or doesn't want! And you might as well know something else, the attorney is not at all receptive to talking settlement before the investigation is completed. He feels that there's a lot more dirt yet to come. I can't order him to settle now. In order to get what we both want, the investigation halted, we're going to have to try something different."

"What?" Massey asked, now legitimately concerned. "What do you mean you can't order him to settle? What do you mean we've got to 'try something different'?"

"Let's lay our cards on the table," McAree said. "This is no time to beat around the bush. You want to get this over with to protect your friend Franz, and who knows why else. I want it ended too, but for other reasons. If this thing continues and they find more, and I'm sure they will, my attempts to control the investigation will put me in deep trouble. So we have to get it stopped, but I need to get out of the middle. Your county attorney is going to have to get involved and initiate contact with our attorney. If his efforts are rejected, then he can ask for me to intervene on his behalf. That's what I'm supposed to do, that's part of my job. But we need to involve someone else. This can no longer be just between you and me. There has to be an official county request, a formal record that Oneida County wants me to assist in resolving the matter."

"So, if your attorney won't play ball with our attorney, we write you a letter asking for your help?" Massey asked.

Now that Massey was getting the message, McAree's usual asurance returned to his voice. "Not exactly. The request will have to be made in writing to Commissioner Bowers, with a copy to me. Once that is done our troubles will be over."

"How so? If we get the commissioner involved it will be totally out of your hands won't it?" Massey asked, sounding confused.

"Just the opposite, Mort. Once Bowers is contacted by your people, rather than via a complaint by our legal department, he'll turn it over to me. He'll tell me to handle it. When I can approach this attorney of ours with the blessing and support of the commissioner we're home free."

"I see," Massey said. "But what if your legal department opposes the settlement you propose? Will Bowers back your decision?"

"Let me explain something to you, Mort. Bowers has his head up his ass most of the time. He's really only interested in the department's scientific endeavors. Everything else gets handled by the deputies with Bowers staying at arms length. After he assigns the request for intervention to me he'll want to stay out of it. Because he's not interested in this kind of thing I can manipulate him fairly easily. But remember, I have to have some basis for recommending settlement. That's why it's critical that you people agree to these minimum conditions I mentioned. As long as I can show that the penalties are severe enough, the attorney probably won't bother to protest. Even if he does, I'll be on solid ground to defend my decision."

"And you think the sanctions we've discussed will be considered 'severe' enough to stand up to a challenge?" Massey wanted to know.

"Absolutely! Remember that this is a very liberal state and this is a very liberal department. Almost any action will be considered severe, trust me," McAree assured him.

Massey contemplated developments for a moment before answering. "As I see it, this is the perfect solution," he said finally.

McAree was elated with Massey's response. "Just remember. Mort, that I'm still going to save the bacon! I'm just going to do it in a little different manner than I first thought."

"I understand, Bob. I'll start getting my ducks on the pond right now."

"Good. But don't forget that the sanctions are absolutely necessary. Don't ask Franz, tell him," McAree advised.

"I will," Massey promised. "I'll get back to you soon."

Dr. Franz attended the monthly meeting of the Oneida County Medical Association on Wednesday. He arrived back at the morgue at three o'clock. "Hi, doctor," Belinda Bernal greeted him. "Dr. Massey called for you twice. He wants you to call him right away. He said it was urgent."

"I'll be in my office," Franz said, heading for the hallway. "I don't want to be disturbed."

"Why weren't you at the association meeting today?" Franz asked when he had Massey on the line.

"Because I was busy with the state, that's why!" Massey snapped. "I've got some news for you. Can you talk?"

"Yes. But before you start, Mort, I know that you're upset with me, and I can understand why. I only ask that you try to put yourself in my position, try to understand the pressure I'm under. I've come too far to be derailed by a couple of disloyal employees or DOH. I'll do whatever it takes to prevent that from happening. I've always been there when you needed help. I simply expect the same from you. I don't feel that I'm asking too much."

Massey wasn't surprised by Franz's comment. Disappointed, but not surprised. The man was blackmailing him, and expecting understanding at the same time! Worse, he undoubtedly believed he was right. He hadn't realized how arrogant Franz really was until the past few weeks. He had learned a lot about Franz during that time, and he didn't like any of it.

"Dr. McAree said that it will take something very similar to what Gorsky proposed to get this thing settled."

243

"God damn you!" Franz shouted. "I told you not to tell him about Gorsky's plan!"

"I didn't, Bob, I didn't. I did just what you wanted. But McAree told me that at the minimum it will take an admission of guilt, a fine, and a couple of years of probation to satisfy the DOH attorney. My comment to you is that this sounds just like what Peter proposed."

"I see," Franz said after a few seconds of silence. "What will this probation business consist of? Visits by my friend Grant I suppose?"

"No. That's one piece of good news. McAree said that they would have someone with a technical background stop around from time to time. He mentioned a period of two years. If they find any serious problems during that time you'd have to surrender your director licenses. When Chuck Allen gets involved he may be able to negotiate that down to one year and get the fine suspended."

"I don't give a shit about the fine, that's a county problem. But I don't like the idea of my licenses being held hostage for any amount of time, whether it's one year or two. And I still don't want the state snooping around in here. Grant or no Grant. No, call McAree back. Tell him he's going to have to do a little better. And make sure he agrees to limit publicity."

"Bob, you had better understand something. McAree isn't even sure their attorney will go for those concessions. He's intent on finishing the investigation before any settlement talks. It's entirely likely that we're going to have to write to Commissioner Bowers and ask him to intervene. McAree wants to get out of the middle of this. He said he's already done enough to be in serious trouble if word gets out. The bottom line, Bob, is that there is no more room for negotiations between us and McAree. We've got to be willing to go along with these things and then bring in Chuck Allen. If he can improve on things, fine. But I wouldn't count on it. If you won't concede, then the state investigation will continue. More subpoenas, interviews and newspaper articles. And we'll still have to deal

244

with them in the end. Those are the choices, Bob. What's it going to be?"

Franz didn't answer right away. "It's that bad, huh?" he asked finally.

"It's that bad," Massey answered.

"I guess I have no choice," Franz said after another pause. "Will you call Peter and tell him? As long as I don't seem to have any alternative, I want to get this done right away."

"Now you're being sensible," Massey said, the relief was evident in his voice. "I'll call Peter right away and tell him to get a meeting set up with Bronson and Chuck Allen. I know you're not very happy about this, but it's the only way out, believe me."

Massey hung up the phone and sat in his chair grinning. He had done it! He stood his ground and Franz had caved. And now Gorsky would never even know that he had made a different proposal to McAree. He would not be cowed by Franz again.

Woody called Grant at eight o'clock Thursday morning. "We're on for Flowers for next Friday, the twenty-third. Okay?" Woody asked.

"Sure, Woody. I haven't cleared this with Linda yet, but I don't anticipate any problem. Will Flowers' lawyer be there?"

"No, thankfully. But we do have some ground rules. We can only ask questions about his duties at the morgue. Nothing about his personal life, and specifically nothing about his sex life. And the lawyer may ask me for a letter stating that Flowers was cooperative during my investigation."

"What good will that do?"

"He's already appealed the conviction, and he's apparently also working on getting a sentence reduction. He feels the sentence was too stiff for a first offender. He wants to build a case showing his client isn't really such a bad guy. That's where the letter would come in."

"This letter will be contingent upon his being truthful won't it?" Grant asked.

"You bet! Mr. Flowers will have an incentive to be honest with us," Woody answered.

"That's a plus for our side, then. What time do you want to leave and who's driving?"

"We have to be there at ten. I'll pick you up at your office at seven-thirty. That will give us time for breakfast on the way."

"Okay, Woody. I'll be looking forward to it. See you then."

At nine o'clock that night Dr. Franz was sitting on the couch at Marcia Longo's apartment. She was sitting on the couch with him, but at the other end. This was the first time she had invited him over since he confronted her at the morgue about their strained relationship. She had told him then that things would soon be back to normal. They weren't. He had wined and dined her earlier in the evening, and she had seemed like her old self. Now that they were alone she didn't want anything to do with him.

"Come on over here," Franz said in a husky voice, patting the cushion between them. He flashed her an evil leer for effect.

Marcia shook her head. "Not tonight, Bob. I'm just not in the mood right now."

"Not tonight? Lately it's not any night. And what's this 'Bob' deal. It used to be 'honey'. We need to be honest. There's obviously a problem here. Tell me what's bothering you, and I don't want to hear that bullshit about your mother not feeling well! There's nothing wrong with her that a good stiff prick wouldn't cure. She's been a whiner ever since your father left her, don't use her as an excuse!"

Marcia jumped up from the couch and stared down at him, her face crimson with rage. "You son of a bitch! Don't you ever dare talk about my mother like that again! Now get the hell out of here! Right now I can't stand the sight of you!"

"Honey," Franz said softly as he got up. He reached out toward her. "I didn't mean to hurt you. It's just that I feel your mother is coming between us. I resent her for it, I'm just jealous I guess."

Marcia backed away from his outstretched arms. "I think you had better leave," she said. Her voice was calm now, and firm. "I need to get my emotions in check. Please."

246

Franz knew he had gone too far with his comments about Marcia's mother. This was not the time to pursue the matter of their relationship. "I understand, Marcia. I'll leave, but remember that my callous remarks were a result of my caring for you so deeply. Please don't judge me too harshly."

Franz turned away from her and walked to the door, grabbing his jacket on the way. Marcia said nothing and didn't follow him. As Franz opened the door and stepped into the hallway he turned back toward her. "Please forgive me," he said with a weak smile. He looked into her eyes for a second, then was gone.

Marcia sat back down on the couch. She had been so very close to breaking off their affair. For days she had been trying to get up the nerve to tell him. But these last few seconds tonight were causing her to have second thoughts. In her mind she saw him standing in the doorway. The pained look on his face. She convinced herself that she had even seen a tear on his cheek. That wasn't the arrogant Bob Franz that most people saw.

That was the human Bob Franz, the caring Bob Franz, the Bob Franz who loved her. Marcia buried her head in her hands and cried softly.

Franz got in the county station wagon and started it up.

He was frustrated and horny. He sat thinking, drumming his fingers on the steering wheel. Suddenly a smile crossed his face. He pulled away from the curb and headed for a bar called the Pink Cadillac, about ten miles outside of Utica. He'd never been there before, but the guys at the association meeting had talked about it. They said it was a hang out for nursing students. If you couldn't get laid there, you couldn't get laid anywhere. His smile broadened at the thought of getting some strange stuff. And right now he needed it.

CHAPTER TWENTY - TWO

Pat Murphy called Grant at eleven o'clock Friday morning. "The paperwork to lift the gag order has been filed," Pat announced.

"How do you know?" Grant asked.

"Because I was just served with a letter from Mr. Gorsky reminding me that the gag is in effect until such time as the court orders otherwise. He pointed out what could happen to me if I violate the order."

"A threat to keep you in line?"

"Let's just say he was very clear."

"I know it's easy for me to say this ,Pat, but I don't think you have anything to be concerned about. I haven't mentioned our conversations in my reports. Your name is included, but only as a potential witness who should be interviewed at some point. And this will be over, one way or another, before the order is lifted. It's likely that you'll never be asked to go on the record in this case."

"My concern is just the opposite, John. I'd like to be able to tell my story so the public can hear it. You don't see that happening, huh?"

"Doubtful, Pat. Things are moving fairly quickly. Let's see, this is April ninth. I predict we'll be finished by the middle of May. There's no way your case will be heard by then, especially if Gorsky doesn't want it to be."

"The middle of May? Aren't you being a little too optimistic?" Pat asked.

"I don't think so," Grant answered. "The interviews regarding the tissues will be done next week. Another four weeks to do the employee interviews and check into the skeleton collection. Then prepare the charges, if any. I think that's a reasonable estimate."

"What do you mean, 'if any'? Do you think you may not have enough evidence to take any action against Franz?"

"I'm confident that we'll have a strong case. But I always try to keep in mind that I don't make the final decision. I've learned that sometimes strange things happen, that's all.'

After a short hesitation Pat spoke again, changing the subject. "Apparently you're not the only one contemplating the matter of interviewing morgue employees. I found out that June Miller is getting her forces mentally prepared for such an event."

With new interest, Grant leaned forward in his chair, elbows on his desk. "Tell me about it, Pat," he prompted.

"Mrs. Miller gave a moving speech at the weekly staff meeting this morning," Pat answered. "She ordered that any contact by DOH be reported to her immediately. Prior to that she reminded everyone that they are a family, a family under attack by an outsider. Regardless of any minor personal differences they may have, it's time to pull together. The wagons were already circled, Miller is closing the circle even tighter."

"Does the entire staff attend these meetings?" Grant asked.

"Yes. They keep Drummond, the midnight man, over. Everybody else is either on duty or comes in, including the part timers. The two office girls, Larkin and Bernal, alternate attending. One at the meeting while the other handles the office."

"Did your source indicate whether Miller's words had any effect?"

"Most everybody there was already firmly behind Franz. The intent was apparently to motivate anyone who might waver. It was probably effective. The 'we're all in this together' business can solidify resistance. The exception is Dr. Samuels, of course. He has his own agenda, which is anti Franz. Miller can talk until she's blue in the face and not change his attitude."

"Let's talk about Samuels for a second," Grant said. "Based on our earlier conversations, he's anti Franz but pro Samuels. He won't do anything just to hurt Franz. His actions would have to benefit himself also. Am I right on that?"

"Precisely. And Dr. Johnson is just the reverse. I think he'd do anything to hurt Franz. Even if it meant stretching the truth a little. That makes them both somewhat unreliable."

"Do you think there will come a time when you'll feel comfortable in telling me who your source is, Pat? Before I start the employee interviews it might benefit me, and him or her, to know who it is. I certainly don't want to do anything to hurt this person. What do you think?"

"Let me sleep on it, John. You make sense, but I want to run it by my contact before I give you an answer."

"Okay, Pat, let me know. And thanks for the info."

At nine-thirty Saturday night Melvin Kemp was in the morgue office using Mrs. Larkin's typewriter. He had just completed his inventory of the skeletons and bones. He was now putting the information from his handwritten notes into a typed report for June Miller. Kemp was not a skilled typist. He pecked away using his right index finger. He wanted to make sure he did this right to impress Miller and Dr. Franz.

Absorbed in his work, Kemp didn't hear anyone approach him. He did, however, sense someone standing behind him, looking over his shoulder. He swung around in his chair, a snarl forming on his lips. "What the fuck do you think you're doing?" he hollered, anticipating finding Scott Browne. "I ought to....." Kemp didn't finish the sentence. The words caught in his throat as he found himself looking up into the face of Dr. Harrison Samuels.

The two men didn't like each other and both knew it. Samuels had to struggle to keep from laughing at the expression on Kemp's face. "You were saying, Melvin?" Samuels asked, straight faced.

"I'm sorry, doctor. I thought Scott was behind me," Kemp explained. "I didn't know you were in the building."

"I just got here," Samuels said. "But that kind of language and attitude isn't acceptable! It doesn't matter who you are talking to. Understand?"

"Yes, doctor. I'm sorry," Kemp said.

251

"You're not scheduled to be working tonight are you?" Samuels asked.

"No," Kemp said, turning back toward the desk, using his body to shield his paperwork from Samuels' eyes.

But Dr. Samuels wasn't satisfied with that answer. "Then what are you doing here?" he wanted to know.

Kemp turned back toward him. "I'm finishing up an assignment for Mrs. Miller," he said.

"What kind of assignment?" Samuels persisted.

Kemp hesitated a moment, trying to think up a suitable answer. Samuels didn't wait for a response. He stepped around Kemp and grabbed his notes from the desk. He scanned them for several seconds, then put them back down. "I believe I understand," Samuels said, smiling. "You say that Mrs. Miller asked you to do this?"

"Yes," Kemp answered, his eyes looking down at the floor.

"That's good, Melvin. It's nice to see that you're willing to give up part of your weekend for a good cause. I'll be in my office for a while. Have a pleasant evening," Samuels said, heading for the corridor.

Kemp sat for several minutes, stewing. He hoped that Dr. Samuels finding out about the inventory wouldn't cause any problems. He debated calling Mrs. Miller, but decided against it. He went back to his typing instead. When he finished he made a copy of the report. He put the copy and his notes in his pocket. He placed the original typed report in an envelope, sealed it, and put it in Miller's mail slot. He then hurried out of the building, before Samuels thought of any more questions.

John Grant went to bed right after the eleven o'clock news Saturday night. Faith had gone in earlier to read. He found her asleep with the light on, her book had fallen on the floor next to the bed. He picked up the book, put it on her night stand, and shut off the light. After undressing he walked around to his side of the bed and crawled in. In a few minutes he was fast asleep.

The ringing phone awakened him. He raised up on one elbow, trying to get his bearings. He was able to get an eye focused on the red numbers displayed on his digital alarm clock on the dresser. It read 2:27. The phone was now on its fourth ring. "Answer it!" Faith growled.

Grants experience with phone calls at this time of night was that they were either wrong numbers or bad news. With a sense of anxiety he reached for the phone on his night stand. "Hello," he mumbled.

"John Grant, please," an unfamiliar male voice said. So much for a wrong number, Grant thought.

"This is John Grant," he said, becoming more alert.

"The state investigator?" the man asked.

"Yes," Grant answered, trying to figure out what was wrong with the man's voice. It wasn't natural. It had an almost mechanical quality to it, as though it was being altered somehow.

"I want to know why you're dropping the investigation of Dr. Franz? Why are you letting him off the hook?"

Fully awake now, Grant swung his legs over the side of the bed, feet on the floor. "Why don't you introduce yourself and we'll talk about it?" Grant suggested.

"I have reliable information that the state is prepared to drop the investigation of Franz and let him off with a slap on the wrist. True?" the man said, ignoring Grant's request for an introduction.

It was apparent to Grant that the caller wasn't anxious to reveal his identity, and was somehow doctoring his voice to protect himself. He decided not to press the issue. What the man said had grabbed his attention. He wanted to hear more. "I'm interested in where you're getting your information, mister. This is all news to me."

"I'll only say that my sources are in a position to know what's going on. Now, is this true or not?"

"I just told you that this is the first I've heard about it. Did your sources tell you who at DOH is involved in this decision? And what is your interest in this?" Grant asked.

"Let's just say that I'm a concerned citizen," the caller said after a hesitation. "And I don't have a name to give you. Just that it's some big wheel in Albany."

"Do you know any of the details of this alleged deal?" Grant asked. "And give me something to call you. It's ridiculous to carry on a conversation with somebody without a name."

There was a longer hesitation this time, followed by what sounded like a chuckle. "I guess you're right. You can call me Paul. I told you what I've heard. I don't know any more than that."

"I gather that you wouldn't be happy if that happened, Paul. Why?" Grant asked.

"I think Franz has gotten away with a lot of things for too long. It wouldn't be right for him to get out of this with nothing," Paul said.

"Do you have any information that would help me, Paul? If you do, we should get together and talk. I might be able to work something out to protect your identity if that's a concern."

"I'm afraid I can't help you, Mr. Grant. But from what I hear you're doing fine on your own. You're a smart guy. Just keep an eye on your back. I think the biggest problem you have right now is sabotage from within. I've got to go now. I'll be following your progress in the paper, and in other ways. Good luck."

Grant heard the click as Paul disconnected. He replaced the handset and turned to find Faith sitting up in bed watching him. "About the morgue?" she asked.

"Yes," he answered. "And according to this guy I'm being sold out. The bad thing is that this man didn't sound drunk or high. In fact, he sounded intelligent, and knowledgeable. And as much as I hate to say it, I wouldn't be totally surprised if he was right."

"What are you going to do?" Faith asked.

"I think I'll call Linda and ask if there's anything to this," he answered, reaching for the phone.

"Now? Are you out of your mind?" Faith yelled. Then she noticed his grin. "Well, I wouldn't put it past you," she said.

"I have no particular desire to become unemployed at the moment," he said. "I'll let Linda enjoy her weekend, but rest assured that I'll be on her line when she gets to work Monday morning."

At eight-thirty Monday morning Charles Allen, Reginald Whitehurst and Peter Gorsky met in Ronald Bronson's office. After coffee was served and his guests were seated across from his desk, Bronson started the meeting. "Just for clarification purposes, we're here this morning to discuss the ongoing DOH investigation of Dr. Franz and the morgue. To be more exact, we're going to review and evaluate a possible settlement scenario as presented by Mr. Gorsky. Go ahead, Peter, tell us what you have in mind," Bronson invited, waving his hand toward Gorsky.

"I believe it is safe to say that this investigation has been on all of our minds to one degree or another, over the past several weeks," Gorsky began. "I'm here representing Bob Franz. In that capacity I want to present a proposal that I think will resolve this matter to everyones satisfaction." Gorsky paused and looked at the faces of the other three men. Satisfied that he had their attention he continued.

"This state inquiry is having an adverse effect on the operation of the morgue. Responding to subpoenas is time consuming, and the resultant publicity causes the public to lose confidence in their officials. We are all aware that no agency or individual can withstand an extended period of scrutiny without something derogatory being developed. This means that a minor oversight, or an isolated lapse in judgement, can be magnified to appear to be a major malfeasance. Certainly, none of us would like to be under a microscope as Bob Franz is now." Gorsky again surveyed his audience. He sensed that they were all imagining what a similar investigation into their activities would turn up.

255

"So, in order to bring the state investigation to a conclusion as soon as possible, thereby avoiding any unnecessary embarrassment to either the county or Dr. Franz, I have developed a proposal to present to DOH," Gorsky said. "Before I get into the details, are there any questions?"

"Yes," said Whitehurst. "What makes you think that DOH will be receptive to a settlement proposal before their investigation is completed?"

"Before I answer that," Gorsky said, smiling, "I'm not quite sure I understand why you're here to discuss a matter that doesn't involve your office. Are you here in an official capacity, Reggie?"

"Some of the allegations that have been made against your client would constitute crimes, if true. I want to make sure I know what's going on and what the county may be contemplating. I don't want to be surprised at what I find in the Observer some morning," Whitehurst explained.

"Is your office conducting a criminal investigation of Dr. Franz?" Gorsky asked.

"No, not at this time. There have been no complaints against Dr. Franz made to my office," Whitehurst answered.

"Are you hinting that a criminal investigation is likely?" Gorsky asked, eyebrows raised.

"I'm not hinting at anything," Whitehurst said, becoming annoyed. "I'm simply stating the facts."

"We're here to try to resolve problems, not create new ones," Bronson cautioned. "Let's be constructive, not combative."

"I plan to be," Gorsky said, directing his comments to Bronson. "But my first duty is to protect my clients rights. Now that the threat of a criminal probe has been introduced I'm not sure it's appropriate for the DA to be here."

"I have not made any threats!" Whitehurst said, his face darkening. "And I am well aware of my ethical requirements. If I sense a conflict developing I'll know when to leave. I damn sure won't need you to tell me!"

"Gentlemen! Please!" Bronson said, extending his arms, palms out, toward the two adversaries. "I trust that Reggie knows what he's doing, Peter. Now, please answer his question. Then let's move on to your proposal."

"As I'm sure you already know," Gorsky said, still talking to Bronson, but for the benefit of Allen, "there is a deputy commissioner at DOH, a Dr. McAree, who is a liaison between DOH and the parties they regulate. Since this investigation started Dr. Massey has been in contact with him several times. You may have even spoken with him, Mr. Bronson."

Bronson shook his head. "I've never spoken to him, but I am aware of him and his position. Go ahead."

"At any rate, during these conversations, Dr. McAree indicated that DOH had no desire to cause the county or Bob any undue hardship," Gorsky continued. "He conveyed to Mort Massey that if the county admits that mistakes may have been made, and expresses remorse, the matter could be resolved now with rather modest penalties. Dr. Franz has agreed to take responsibility for problems that the state feels occured on his watch, even though he may disagree with their conclusions. As his personal attorney I have discussed with him the ramifications of his taking blame. Although I feel the state will not be able to develop a provable case against him, he would prefer to end this now and is willing to make the necessary concessions."

"Very noble of him," Bronson said. "Chuck?"

"No matter how much responsibility Dr. Franz is willing to accept, the county is ultimately on the hook. Any findings will officially be against the county, not Franz. Any penalties will be levied against the county, not him. With that in mind, I'm in favor of an early resolution. But only if the terms are sufficiently beneficial to the county. Now I'd like to hear the details," Allen said.

"Certainly," Gorsky responded. "Bob would admit that tissue was taken and provided to a research facility without sufficient consent. This is the area that seems to be of primary interest to DOH. So the stipulation would involve one charge

257

and one admission. The penalty would be that Bob attend any training provided by DOH addressing tissue procurement. A monetary fine would be levied, but suspended pending future compliance with tissue bank regulations. DOH would closely monitor the tissue banking operations at the morgue, including unannounced site visits. The length of this probationary period and the amount of the fine will be determined by negotiation between Chuck's office and DOH."

Allen pondered the proposal for a few moments. "So this would actually cost the county nothing, at least concerning DOH. What about civil actions from the families of the people these tissues were taken from?"

"That's a possibility," Gorsky admitted. "But I've looked at the regulations that were in effect during the time period we're talking about. They were poorly written. Any first year law student could successfully defend an action based on those antiques."

"Then why are we talking about a settlement?" Allen wondered. "If they'll be that easy to beat DOH will know it and wouldn't be foolish enough to file charges. If we wait them out they'll just go away won't they?" Allen already knew the answer, but he wanted to hear how Gorsky would handle the question.

Would he admit that additional investigation might unearth more serious problems?

Gorsky was unflappable. "I certainly asked the same question when Bob said he wanted to explore settling this thing," he said without hesitation. "But that morgue is his life. He has a lot he wants to get done and this investigation is too distracting. He just wants to get DOH out of his hair so he can get on with his business."

"What do you think, Chuck?" Bronson asked.

"Well, since Peter's proposal wouldn't cost the county any money, and it would remove the uncertainty of a continuing investigation, I'm in favor of following up on it. But what about

DEC? Don't forget that they are investigating the disposal of medical waste."

All eyes turned toward Gorsky. "Sorry, gentlemen. DOH has control over Bob's licenses. That was my concern. DEC isn't my problem," he said.

"I have a question," Bronson said. "How can we present this to the public in a more positive light? Saying that tissue was taken 'without sufficient consent' doesn't sound like it will go over very well with the voters."

Gorsky stifled a grin. This was the truly important issue. Would Bronson be able to get any political mileage out of the situation? "First of all," he said, "I hope that Chuck can work something out with DOH to word the stipulation in the most favorable way possible. Second, Bob will issue a statement, or appear in any forum you suggest, to explain his side of the story. Remember, there was nothing intentional here. This unfortunate situation was the result of ambiguous regulations and a dedicated public servant who may not have given the matter the amount of attention he should have. Everybody in this county can relate to that. And, Mr. Bronson, the way you've handled this so far, coupled with a prompt resolution, will be a feather in your cap."

All eyes now went to Bronson. A smile formed on his face and slowly grew. "Let's do it," he said. "What's next, Chuck?"

Gorsky answered instead. "If I may, I can get you on the right track. The attorney handling the case for DOH will have to be contacted. Dr. McAree will only be involved if their attorney proves to be unreasonable. In that event a letter will have to be sent to Commissioner Bowers requesting assistance in the effort to reach a resolution, with a cc to Dr. McAree. It is my understanding that upon receipt of this letter Dr. McAree would be assigned to intervene."

Next the focus turned to Allen. "Okay. I'll get this proposal down on paper and then give the DOH lawyer a call. I'll also contact DEC. We might as well try to clean everything up at the same time."

"Very well, Chuck," Bronson said. "Keep me up to speed on this. Thank you for coming, gentlemen," he said to Gorsky and Whitehurst. "Chuck will handle things from here."

True to his word, Grant was on the line as Linda arrived in her office at nine o'clock on Monday. "Am I going to like this call, John?" she asked with a laugh. "I haven't even had a chance to hang up my coat yet."

"That depends," Grant answered, his voice pleasant, but serious. "I made a new friend over the weekend. Some guy who called himself Paul, called me at two-thirty Sunday morning. What he had to say has caused me some concern."

"I see," Linda said, now all business. "And just what is it that Paul said?"

"He claimed to have information from what he described as 'reliable sources', that the department is ready to cut a deal with Franz. This alleged deal would stop the investigation, and Franz would get off with a slap on the wrist. Have you heard about anything like this being discussed down there?"

"Do you have any idea who this Paul is? Did he say who in the department is involved?" Linda wanted to know.

"No, and no," Grant answered. "I think he was using something to alter his voice. I didn't recognize it anyway. And he didn't have the name of the person involved. Just that it was a 'big wheel' in Albany."

"You're in your office, John?"

"Yes. Why?" Grant asked.

"I want to get George on the line. He should hear this. Hang up and I'll set up a conference call."

"Okay, Linda, I'll be waiting," Grant said.

Linda hung up her coat and sent her secretary for coffee. Then she called George. "We've got a new player in the game," she told him. She related the gist of her conversation with Grant.

"And John doesn't have any idea who this caller is, huh?" George asked.

"No, but he must have been referring to whatever the county and Dr. McAree are up to. Do you agree, George?"

"I hope to hell that's what he's talking about!" George said.

"You do?" Linda asked. "Why would you be glad if some stranger knows what's going on here?"

"I'm not glad about that! But if he isn't talking about McAree, then somebody else from here is involved that we don't even know about. That would be worse yet," George explained.

"I see what you mean," Linda agreed. "I promised John a conference call. What are you going to tell him?"

"I guess it's time to tell him the truth," George said. "Go ahead and hook us up."

A few seconds later George began to brief Grant on the situation in Albany. He told of the efforts of a 'deputy commissioner' to limit and otherwise obstruct the investigation. He said that steps were being taken to correct the problem, but wasn't specific.

"So you've known about this for quite some time, haven't you? And that must account for how Franz located Marner, right?" Grant asked.

"Yes, we have known about the problem and been trying to deal with it," George said. "There's no doubt about that person being responsible for the Marner leak."

Linda held her breath, waiting for Grant to explode in rage for being left in the dark. After what seemed like an eternity Grant spoke. "It sounds like you guys have had your hands full down there. I appreciate your leaving me out of it. If I would have known all this crap was going on it would have driven me nuts. Thanks."

"I knew you'd understand, John," George said, as Linda slowly exhaled.

"You're in kind of a tough spot, aren't you?" Grant asked. "I mean if you accuse this guy, and it doesn't stick, where does that leave you?"

"That's too horrible to even consider," George laughed. "But you're right. We took a chance, Linda and I. But it's going to work out. I can't say any more right now, but the problem here will be settled no later than the first part of next week. Just go about your business, John. There's nothing to worry about."

"And my friend Paul? Just ignore him?" Grant asked.

"I don't see what else you can do," George said.

"Okay, then. I guess I'll get back to work. Thanks again, and good luck," Grant said and hung up.

Grant was at his desk late Tuesday morning when Pat Murphy called. "Got a minute?" Pat asked.

"For you, absolutely," Grant joked.

"I've got some news you might be interested in," Pat said. He was so nonchalant that Grant wasn't prepared for what came next. "It seems that there was a recent inventory of the skeletons, bones and body parts at the morgue. Everything was recorded by case number."

Grant was silent while the impact of what Pat had said hit home. "What? Did you say that there is a written inventory of Franz's collection?" Grant asked finally, unable to control his excitement.

"Yes. The collection and other stuff. All typed up in a report to June Miller," Pat said.

Grant was again silent as he finished digesting the information.

"Well, if you don't want to hear any more I guess I'll get going," Pat said, enjoying the moment.

"Damn you, Pat. Don't you dare hang up that phone," Grant hollered, playing into Pat's hands.

Murphy's laughter reached Grant's ear as a loud roar. He held the set away until Pat calmed down. "I've got my act together now, Pat," Grant said. "When you're composed, I'd like you to give me all the details about this inventory."

"Sorry, John. I guess I shouldn't tease about something as important to you as this must be."

"Quite all right, Pat," Grant said with a chuckle. "I'd have done the same thing to you. But I am anxious to hear the rest of the story."

"Okay, here it is," Pat said, serious now. "Over the last couple of weekends Melvin Kemp has done an inventory of all the skeletons and assorted bones in storage, and the body parts that were in the freezer. He was acting on the orders of June Miller and, presumably, Dr. Franz. When he finished last Saturday he typed a report for Miller. It supposedly lists every item, whole skeleton, type of bone or body part, by case number."

"So Miller has the inventory now?" Grant asked.

"As far as I know, yes. But Kemp kept a copy, plus his original handwritten notes. I assume he still has them," Pat answered.

"This could be the break that leads to Franz's downfall. You know that don't you?" Grant asked.

"That's the way I see it too," Pat said.

"I don't mean to be rude, but I want to call George Epstein right away. Is there anything else I should know, Pat?"

"Yes. The freezer stuff was inventoried and then went to the incinerator. The skeletons and bones are still in the building, at least for now."

"What do you mean 'at least for now'? Do you have information that they'll be moved?" Grant asked.

"Not information, no. But they incinerated the frozen body parts. I don't think Franz would get rid of the skeletons. He's worked too hard to get them. But he may have wanted them counted to see what he'd have to move. That's just a hunch, John."

"Yeah, but it makes sense," Grant agreed. "Before I call George, let me ask an obvious question. Did your source happen to tell you the numbers? How many skeletons are there?"

"I was wondering when you'd get around to that," Pat said. "Care to take a guess?"

"Sure. Don't laugh, but I'll say he got two per year from '89 to '92. That's four years, for a total of eight," Grant calculated.

Pat laughed. "Not even close. Are you ready?"

"Shoot," Grant said.

"Your good buddy Franz has amassed forty-eight full skeletons, sixty-two assorted bones, and he did have twenty-seven frozen limbs, torsos, etcetera," Pat announced.

Grant was shocked. "Forty-eight fucking bodies!" he mumbled. "This is incredible, Pat. I wonder who they were? Where their families think they are now?"

"Those are certainly questions that need to be answered," Pat said.

"Let me get going," Grant said. "Thanks, Pat. I owe you big time."

"You don't owe me anything, John. Just put the information to good use," Pat advised.

Fifteen minutes later Grant, George and Linda were on another conference call. Linda had been summoned from a meeting when Grant told her secretary that his call was urgent.

"Wow!" Was George's response to what Grant told them. Linda let out an awed whistle.

"That was my reaction too," Grant said. "Pat has a suspicion that Franz may intend to move these things out of the morgue. I think he's right. What are we going to do?"

"Give me a minute to think about it," George said. In about half that time he had made his decision. "We were going to interview the morgue employees at some point anyway. Let's get the subpoenas out now. But we'll issue a second subpoena to Kemp. One for his appearance, and a duces tecum for any notes, reports or records in his possession relating to the morgue. When can you do the interviews John?"

"I'm free this afternoon," Grant said.

"Come on, John. Give me a break." George groaned. "How about a week from today, the twentieth?"

"Can we afford to wait that long?" Grant asked.

"I'm not a superman," George said. "The subpoenas have to be prepared, and done right. Then they all have to be served. That means we'll have to come up with home addresses for everyone. This all takes time."

"Okay," Grant said, giving in. "I can save you some trouble on getting them served. The morgue has a weekly staff meeting every Friday morning. Everybody is there, including the part timers. You can get all the active employees at one time."

"Great!" George said. "Now who do you want to see beside Kemp?"

"Longo, Drummond, Hargrove, Fisher, Chovan and Browne," Grant said. "And the two pathologists, Samuels and Johnson."

"Johnson is out on disability, right? Do you have an address for him?" George asked.

"I've got his phone number," Linda said. "He wants to talk. I'll give him a call and get you his address, George."

"Good. How about Miller and the office girls?" George wanted to know.

"Let's let Miller go for now," Grant said. "The clericals too. I might want to talk with them later, though."

"Okay, I'll get on these right away," George promised. "Anything else?"

"Yeah," Grant said. "What about the inventory that Miller has? And what if they move the bones before we get the inventory?"

"My plan is to get Kemp's documents first. We'll use them to prepare another subpoena for all the case numbers listed in the inventory and ask for Miller's copy at the same time. As for the bones, if they're moved, they're moved. We can't do anything about it. If we have Kemp, an eyewitness that they were there, and his records, that will meet our needs."

Grant realized that there was no sense in discussing the matter any further. "While we're on the subject of the bones, Woody has invited me to accompany him when he interviews Rodney Flowers a week from Friday. I think I should go, especially now.

What do you think?"

"I agree," Linda said. "George?"

"I guess so," he answered reluctantly. "It looks like my plan to get the tissue stuff done first is falling apart."

"We have to respond to events," Grant said cheerfully. "Don't worry, George. I'll get that end wrapped up as soon as possible."

"Okay. Keep in touch," George said, and disconnected.

"Good boy, John," Linda said, and also hung up.

Bob Franz spent Wednesday morning at Dr. Massey's office working up a budget to submit to the county legislature on June first. This was the first of several sessions that would have to be devoted to budget preparation. It felt good to be able to spend time on something other than the state investigation.

Franz arrived at the morgue just before noon. "Anything important going on?" he asked Mrs. Larkin as he passed through the office.

"Nothing here," she said, looking up from her keyboard. "But Dr. Rudolph has called twice. He said it's very important. The messages are on your desk."

Franz nodded. "I'll be in my office," he said, leaving the room.

He reached Rudolph on the first try. "Hi, Joe. Bob Franz returning your calls. What's up?"

"Thanks for getting back to me," Rudolph began. "I've been dodging phone calls from Lew Marner since he had his meeting with Grant. This morning he caught up with me. He demanded that I tell Grant the truth about the bladder research. He was so upset he started to cry. I almost felt sorry for him."

"Don't!" Franz instructed. "This could come down to a him or you situation. Pity is a luxury you can't afford. What else did he say?"

"Not much, really. Oh, he did say that you called him just before he saw Grant. Was that wise?" Rudolph asked.

Franz felt his face getting warm. "It could have gone either way," he said. "If he had talked with me we might have been able to work something out. But he hung up on me. What does he plan to do if you don't confess to Grant?"

"He wasn't specific. I assume he'll sue me."

"Are you worried, Joe?" Franz asked.

"Sure, but not overly. As far as I know Grant didn't contact Slater. It will still be my word against Marner's. I can handle that."

"That's good, Joe," Franz said in a soothing voice. "And I'm doing everything I can on my end to get this over with. Just hang in there. Don't say anything to anybody, don't answer any questions. This will all blow over in a little while."

"Did you have to use the word 'hang'?" Rudolph laughed. "By the way, do you remember the last time we talked you asked me if I had a lawyer?"

"Yes," Franz answered. "And?"

"I met with him. I'm not to talk with anybody about this without his permission. Not Grant, not Crowne, nobody."

"How much did you tell him, Joe?" Franz asked.

"Everything. He told me to sit tight and not talk with anybody," Rudolph answered.

"You told him the whole story?" Franz asked, a knot forming in his stomach.

"He's my lawyer! You don't lie to your lawyer!" Rudolph stated firmly.

Franz didn't necessarily agree with that, but he didn't argue the point. "I see," he said simply.

"There's something else, Bob," Rudolph said. "I really shouldn't be talking with you either. He told me that there could come a time when our interests conflict. Nothing personal, Bob, but I'm going to keep my distance. I just wanted you to know."

When Franz replaced the handset he realized that his hand was trembling slightly.

At nine-thirty on Friday morning, the sixteenth, Grant left his office for the first of his interviews with the families of the children Franz had used as tissue donors. It was a dark, overcast day, complete with a light drizzle. In Grant's mind, the weather reflected his mission.

267

He pulled out of the parking lot and started the twenty minute drive to Oriskany. He was scheduled to be at the home of Fred and Joan Morris at ten o'clock.

Grant found the residence with no problem, pulling in the driveway at a few minutes before ten. The house was an older two story job. But it appeared to have had new siding recently and the property looked well maintained. Grant waited in the car for a couple of minutes, then went to the front porch and knocked on the door.

It was opened immediately by a man who introduced himself as Fred Morris. Grant guessed he was in his mid to late thirties. Average height and build, with a pleasant face. But there was no doubt that he was apprehensive about Grant's visit. Morris ushered Grant into a spacious, well furnished living room and took his coat. Grant detected the smell of freshly brewed coffee. That pleasant aroma served to improve his mood.

"My wife is in the kitchen. We thought it might be better to sit at the table, in case you have to write or something," Morris explained.

Grant followed Morris out of the living room and into a large, modern kitchen. Joan Morris was sitting at the kitchen table. Probably around her husbands age, she had an attractive face. Although she didn't stand, Grant had the impression she had a nice figure.

Fred Morris introduced Grant and had him sit opposite Joan. He then poured coffee for everyone. As soon as Fred joined them at the table he lost his composure. "What did that dirty bastard do to my son?" he demanded.

"Before we get into that, I need to get some background information," Grant said calmly, taking control.

"We've got questions!" Fred said, defiantly.

"They'll be answered," Grant said, "later."

"Take it easy, honey," Joan Morris said, reaching over to hold her husbands hand. "We must let Mr. Grant do his job."

Grant smiled his thanks. He then spent a few minutes getting the basic background information. He directed his questions to

Fred and tried to engage him in some unrelated conversation. When he felt the situation was under control, Grant turned to the purpose of his visit.

"On the day Timmy was killed you went to the morgue. While you were there did anyone ask you to donate your son's tissue, for research or any other purpose?" Grant asked.

"Yes," Fred answered. "Several times. I said no every time."

"Who asked you to make the donation?" Grant asked.

"A guy named Melvin Kemp. After I told him no on three or four occasions he left the room. Just left us sitting there," Fred said.

"What happened next?"

"Kemp finally came back and he brought Dr. Franz with him. Franz seemed nice enough at first. Concerned about Joan and all that. But it turned out he just came in to take another shot at me about the tissue donation. It reminds me of buying a car. The salesman works you as far as he can, then calls the manager in to close the deal. You know what I mean?"

Grant nodded. "Yes, Fred. I've had that experience. What did you tell Dr. Franz?"

"I told him to go to hell! I grabbed Joan by the arm and we got out of there!" Fred said, voice rising. His wife squeezed his hand tighter.

"So you never told Mr. Kemp, Dr. Franz, or anybody else that they had your permission to remove tissue from Timmy for research?" Grant asked.

"No, God damn it!" Fred shouted, his voice shaking with emotion. He got up from the table and walked into the living room. As Joan got up to follow him, Grant noticed the tears running down her cheeks.

Grant sat alone for several minutes listening to the murmur of the Morris's voices from the next room. When they returned to the kitchen, both appeared in control and ready to continue.

"Is what Fred said the way you remember things, Mrs. Morris?" Grant asked.

"To be honest with you, Mr. Grant, I was not myself. But I'm sure that what Fred remembers is accurate. We've talked about it several times since. That whole episode is etched in his mind, believe me. And I know that we would never have told them to take anything from Timmy."

"Now it's your turn, Mr. Grant," Fred said. "What did they do to Timmy?"

"We have developed evidence indicating that his testicles, prostate and bladder were removed and sent from the morgue to a research facility," Grant answered.

"What are you going to do about it?" Fred wanted to know.

"I'm gathering information to submit to our lawyers. They will decide what action to take," Grant explained.

Fred reached over and grabbed Grant's arm. "You tell your lawyers they had better do something," he said. "If they don't, I will."

"I understand your anger, Mr. Morris," Grant said. "But if you want to do anything yourself, do it through an attorney, please."

Morris let go of Grant's arm. "We're counting on you, Mr. Grant. Don't let us down."

A half hour later Grant left the Morris house with a three page sworn statement from Fred Morris and a one page statement from Joan. He walked back to his car with renewed dedication to his task.

Grant's next four interviews were similar to the first. Some anger, some tears and demands for action. He arrived at his last stop at six o'clock, the Clinton residence in Chadwicks. He had mixed emotions when he found William Clinton, the dead child's grandfather, at the house. Would he be a help or hindrance?

Clinton recognized Grant immediately. "I kind of thought it might be you," he said, shaking Grant's hand.

The elder Clinton sat silently while Grant transacted his

business with the man's son and daughter-in-law. When the interview was over and the statements obtained, Clinton walked Grant to his car. "The night I met you at that news conference,

I told you that the people accusing Dr. Franz of all those things should be crucified. Do you remember that, Mr. Grant?" Clinton asked.

"I remember," Grant said.

"I was a fool," Clinton said. "I thought Franz was a great man. I thought that I could trust a public official. After being alive all these years, I've finally lost my innocence. I hate Franz as much for that as what he's done to my kids and grandson.

Dr. Franz is going to burn in hell, Mr. Grant. He'll burn in hell."

As Grant drove home Clinton's words sent chills down his spine.

CHAPTER TWENTY - THREE

While Grant was at the Morris home Friday morning, George Epstein's process server was at the morgue. Dorothy Larkin called June Miller out of the staff meeting to tell her that a man was in the office asking to see all of the employees, but refusing to state his business.

Miller went to the office to investigate. After a few attempts, the server admitted why he was there. Miller returned to the conference room, summoned Dr. Franz into the hallway and explained the situation to him. "What do you want to do?" she asked when finished.

"Let that guy cool his heels while we get Chuck Allen on the line," Franz said. "You call him while I go back in there and make an excuse to leave the meeting for a while," he ordered, nodding toward the conference room door. "I'll meet you in your office. Put the call on speaker."

When Franz reached Miller's office a few minutes later, Allen was already on the line. Franz sat in one of the visitors chairs. "Good morning, Charles," he said.

"Good morning, doctor," Allen replied. "What's going on over there? June said a process server is asking to see your employees?"

"That seems to be the situation," Franz said. "I need your guidance on this. Do we have to let him serve his papers on county property?"

"I'm going to assume that his papers are for the employees individually. If they related to county records he'd be serving my office like the last time. To answer your question, no, you don't have to accomodate him. He has no right to disrupt your operation or harass your people at their place of employment. But that's a technical answer. The real question is whether it would be smart to throw the guy out."

"And the answer to that is?" Franz asked.

"The answer is that I'm not going to give you an answer," Allen said. "I'm going to call Mr. Bronson and let him decide. I will suggest, however, that we cooperate. The papers will get served anyway. Rest assured of that. The best we can do is delay the inevitable for a few hours. And if we give this man a hard time it will make news. You can rest assured of that, too."

"Damn it, Chuck!" Franz stormed. "When are we going to stand up to these people?"

"You fight when you can win. When the situation favors your side," Allen said. "Anyway, Mr. Bronson will call the shots on this. Sit tight and I'll get back to you in a few minutes."

"Okay. But don't leave us hanging too long," Franz instructed, motioning for Miller to disconnect.

Allen called back ten minutes later. "Mr. Bronson said to compromise. Let the server see who he wants at a time and location in the building convenient to you. He suggested that we use this to our advantage."

"How?" Franz demanded. "How can he think that my people being subpoenaed is to our advantage?"

"That's not what he thinks, Bob. But we will be able to look at the subpoenas right away, find out what they want and when. Plus, you'll be able to calm your people down if they get upset."

"I guess that does make sense", Franz agreed.

"Good," Allen said. "I want you to fax me copies of the papers as soon as you can. I'll be here if you need me. Good luck."

"Okay, June," Franz said after Allen hung up. "Arrange for this guy to serve his papers. Let's get it done right away and get him the hell out of here. Then I want you to call everyone in here, one at a time. Copy the subpoenas and get a feel for how they react. If they seem real scared, or real mad, calm them down. After we know exactly what's going on we'll decide what else to do."

"You're going to be with me when I talk to them aren't you?" Miller asked.

"No. I want to use you as a buffer. You get the lay of the land so we can plan a strategy before I have to address their concerns."

274

"How do you suggest I calm them down?" Miller asked.

"For right now, you can tell them that there is still a possibility that this thing will be settled in the next few days. They'll probably be able to throw the damn subpoenas out. Get with me as soon as you've finished."

Franz was almost out the door when Miller called his name. "What is it?" he asked, turning to face her.

"Please be honest with me, Bob. Do we have anything to worry about?" she asked.

"No, June, of course not," he answered and walked out of her office.

June Miller deftly handled her assignment. She went to the conference room and announced that the meeting was over. She then excused Belinda Bernal and asked the rest to stay. She next explained the situation and how it would be handled. The process server would set up shop in the back conference room. They would see him one at a time to get their subpoena. It would only take a few seconds. They would then return to the break room and wait for her to call them to her office individually. She issued her orders quickly, allowing no time for questions. Five minutes later the server was gone, and Miller began her interviews.

She called Dr. Samuels first. There was no sense in wasting much time with him. She made a copy of his subpoena and dismissed him. Fisher, Drummond, Chovan and Browne expressed some anxiety, but nothing major. Miller told them that she anticipated that there would be a resolution before they had to appear before Grant on the twentieth. Her comment made them feel better. Longo and Hargrove were defiant. They'd see Grant if they had to, but he'd be wasting his time if he expected them to say anything derogatory about Dr. Franz.

The last person she had to see was Melvin Kemp. On her way to the conference room to get him she stopped in Franz's office. "How's it going?" he asked.

"Better than I anticipated," she told him. "I'm on my way to get Melvin now. But the rest of them don't seem overly concerned. The subpoenas don't say much. Just that they all have to appear at the state building next Tuesday to give testimony. Do you really think the settlement can be finalized by then?"

"I don't know." Franz said. "I'll call Peter later and ask him what's going on."

"Is he handling that?" Miller asked. "I thought Chuck Allen was doing it."

"He is. But Peter doesn't want me discussing it directly with Allen. He thinks he's got to protect me, you know," Franz explained.

"I'll finish up with Melvin and fax the papers to Allen. Then we can talk, okay?" she asked.

"Certainly, June, certainly," Franz assured her. "Melvin can get quite emotional if he feels he's being picked on. You'll probably have to treat him with kid gloves."

"Don't worry, I can handle him. See you soon," she said.

Five minutes later Miller was back. One look at her face told Franz that something was wrong. "What is it?" he asked.

"Grant knows about the inventory that Melvin did," she answered.

"What?" Franz said, jumping to his feet and walking around his desk. He stopped just in front of Miller. "How do you know that, June? How do you know? How could that happen?"

Franz's reaction, a near panic, did little to settle Miller down. "Melvin was served with two subpoenas. One for his appearance, the other to produce any records or reports relating to the morgue. Nobody else got a second subpoena. They must know about it!" Miller explained.

Franz reached out, grabbing Miller's shoulders. "Melvin doesn't have any records, does he June?" Franz asked slowly, hopefully.

Miller lowered her eyes. "Yes. I'm afraid he kept his notes and a copy of the inventory he typed for me," she said.

Franz dropped his arms back to his sides. Miller watched his face. Instead of turning red with rage, it was chalk white. She was sure now, despite Franz's assurances and bravado, that the situation was very serious. "What do you want to do?" she asked.

"Does Melvin have any idea how the state learned about this?" Franz wanted to know.

"He's not sure, but Dr. Samuels came in while he was typing the inventory. He said Samuels looked at his notes and questioned him."

"Why in the hell didn't he say something about this earlier?" Franz exploded, fear giving way to anger. "Why would anyone in their right mind keep a copy of the God damn report?"

"Melvin couldn't explain it and I didn't press it. I don't think this is the time to alienate him, do you?" she asked.

Franz returned to his chair. "No, of course not," he said in an even voice. "How far do you think Melvin will go to help us?"

Miller shrugged. "He's always been very obedient. Why, what are you thinking?"

"If Grant gets his hands on that inventory there will be big trouble. What if Melvin denies that he has any reports? What if he denies doing the inventory at all?" Franz wondered.

"Do you realize what you're saying? These things are now under subpoena! If we even suggest that Melvin destroy them, or lie under oath, we'll end up behind bars! Besides, there's still my copy of the inventory. They must know about that, too."

"Yes, that would have to be addressed also," Franz admitted.

"Count me out!" Miller hollered. "If you want to go that route, you're going on your own!"

Franz glared at her for several seconds. "I thought I could count on you," he said in a hurt voice.

"I've always been loyal to you, Bob. But this is asking too much. Maybe the settlement will be in place before Melvin has to show up at Grant's office. Maybe it's not as bad as you think," she said hopefully.

"The way things are going I wouldn't count on that," he said. "These bastards are like sharks who have detected blood in the water!"

"Who are you talking about? Grant?" Miller asked.

"All of them! Grant, DOH, Samuels, Johnson, Doyle, all of them!" Franz spat the names.

"Maybe you'll just have to bite the bullet. Pay a little heftier fine or something," Miller suggested.

Franz shook his head dejectedly. "I'm afraid not, they're determined to bring me down, June. Those bastards won't rest until they drive me out!"

"I've got to get back to Melvin. What do you want me to tell him?" Miller asked.

"Tell him not to worry. Tell him everything will be over by next Tuesday, he won't have to see Grant. Tell him whatever it takes to keep him from going into a panic. I need some time to think."

"Okay, Bob, anything else?"

"Yes, call Whitney Price. Ask him if he can store some boxes for us. And I'd like to get them to him as soon as possible," Franz ordered.

Miller weighed these last instructions. She determined that following them couldn't get her in any trouble. "Certainly, I'll let you know what Whit has to say."

"I won't be here for a while," Franz stated.

"What if I need you? Where will you be?" Miller asked, annoyed that he was going to take off when things were happening.

Franz detected her annoyance. "I'm sorry, June, but I'm going to see Peter Gorsky. I've got some important decisions to make and I need his advice."

"I understand," Miller said. "I'll call you there if anything happens."

Franz stood up and headed out of his office, Miller following him into the hallway. "The more I think about this, something's bothering me," she said. "Why didn't they subpoena me, or my records?"

Franz mulled the question over for a moment. "I don't know, June. I'll ask Peter, maybe he'll have an answer."

Miller returned to her office and the very nervous Melvin Kemp. "I've just discussed this with Dr. Franz. You don't have a thing to worry about, Melvin," she lied.

In a few more minutes Miller escorted Kemp out of the room. She closed the door and went to her desk to call Whitney Price.

Bill Franchell was summoned to the office of Reginald Whitehurst at three o'clock Friday afternoon. Franchell was the Chief Investigator for the DA's office. He was five feet eight inches tall. His one hundred seventy pounds were solid and well distributed. At fifty-three years old, it was becoming ever more difficult to keep in that shape. He had been an Oneida County Sheriff's deputy for twenty years before deciding to transfer to the DA's office. He wore steel rimmed glasses, was well mannered and soft spoken. He could easily have passed for a school teacher instead of a cop. But his looks were deceiving. He was a top notch investigator, and could hold his own in any situation.

"What's the matter boss?" Franchell asked, noticing the troubled look on Whitehurst's face.

Whitehurst motioned him to a chair. "Have you been following the DOH investigation of Dr. Franz?" he asked.

"A little bit. I've seen the stuff in the papers and there's been the usual gossip. Should I be paying more attention?"

"I don't know, but I'd like to find out," Whitehurst said. "I've got my neck exposed a little bit on this. I opened my mouth in support of Franz when this started, and I'm beginning to wonder how big a mistake that was."

"I didn't think it was that serious," Franchell said. "Has something happened that I missed?"

"Yes, as a matter of fact, the morgue employees got served with appearance subpoenas today. They all have to appear before the DOH investigator next Tuesday."

"That must be this Grant character, right?" Whitehurst nodded. "Well, it stands to reason that he'd want to interview the employees before he finishes his investigation. He apparently isn't welcome at the morgue, so he's going this route. That doesn't seem like any big deal," Franchell said.

"There's a little more, Bill. One of the employees, a guy named Melvin Kemp, was also served with a subpoena for records or reports in his possession. Apparently the state has reason to believe that Kemp has some important documents. I think it's time that I find out where the state investigation stands, what they think they've got and where they're going with it. But it has got to be done unofficially. It can't appear that I'm trying to solicit a referral to get involved. I need your help for that."

Franchell was becoming interested. Perhaps this morgue thing wasn't just the bureaucratic bullshit he had thought. "Sure, what do you want me to do?" he asked.

"Make contact with Grant. Tell him you've been impressed by the way he's handling the investigation and you want to meet him. Or use an approach you're more comfortable with. The bottom line is that I want you to meet with him and pick his brain. Can you do it?"

"I can do it," Franchell replied. "And soon I imagine?"

"That's right. He's seeing Kemp Tuesday. Do it before then, even if it means over the weekend. Just get it done."

Dr. Franz didn't return to the morgue until 3:30 that afternoon. He was in a foul mood, after having to wait an hour and a half just to see Gorsky. When he finally talked with him and told him the truth, at least concerning the skeletons, Gorsky suggested he consider resigning if the settlement offer wasn't accepted by DOH. For what he was paying, he expected better.

When he saw June Miller he hoped to hear something more positive. He got a mixed bag.

"Is Melvin under control?" he asked, sitting in Miller's office.

"Yes, doctor," Miller smiled. "After I told him he probably wouldn't have to see Grant, he felt much better. He even got a little defiant, like Marcia and Michael."

"I don't suppose he offered to make those inventory records disappear?" Franz asked, mentally crossing his fingers.

Miller's smile faded. "No, he didn't. And I didn't ask him," she said, noticing Franz's face fall.

"What about Whitney? I hope you're not going to tell me that he is turning on me too," he said.

"Listen, Bob," Miller said, frustration in her voice. "I haven't turned on you. I've only said I won't do anything that I think is illegal. Other than that, I'm as supportive of you as ever. I resent you implying otherwise."

Franz nodded, but didn't believe her. "What about Whit?"

"His secretary said he left last night to visit his uncle on Long Island. She said he wouldn't be back until Tuesday."

"What?" Franz shouted. "You haven't even talked with Whit yet?"

Miller raised her arms, palms out. "Let me finish, Bob, please. The girl gave me the uncle's number. I reached Whit there."

"That's better," Franz said. "When can we move the boxes?"

"When Whit gets back Tuesday afternoon," she answered.

"Why not now?" Franz demanded. "We'll transport. All we need is somebody to let us in and tell us where to put them."

"Whit said that he doesn't want to involve any of his people in this. He wants to handle it himself," Miller explained. "Did you tell him I'm in a jam? Maybe he'd have come back early to help me out," Franz suggested.

"I didn't want to make it sound like the sky was falling, no," she answered. "Anyway, he was all excited about playing some early season golf. Apparently the snow has been gone there for a while and some of the courses are opening."

Franz shrugged in defeat. "Okay, Tuesday then. We'll move them as soon as Whit gets back."

"There's something I don't understand, Bob. If Grant gets his hands on the inventory, and gets Melvin in his office, what difference does it make whether these skeletons are here or not?

If they have the list and the person who prepared it, isn't that enough. Won't moving them make things look even worse?"

Franz stood up, a glimmer of his old confidence back. "From now on I will personally deal with Melvin on this issue. And I want you to bring that inventory, and any copies you may have to my office, understand?"

Their eyes locked for a few moments. "As you say, doctor," Miller said, breaking the silence.

Franz turned and started out the door. "Wait a minute!" Miller said. "Did Peter have any idea why they didn't subpoena me?"

Franz turned around to face her. "He thinks they want to put some pressure on you, soften you up a little. Waiting for something you fear is coming is difficult you know."

Miller's expression reflected her concern over Franz's statement. "What about you? What does Peter think of your situation?" she asked.

Franz glared at her, then walked out without answering.

When Grant pulled in his driveway Friday evening he determined to put the days interviews out of his mind and enjoy the weekend. As soon as he entered the house he stopped at the refrigerator and grabbed a can of beer. "I'm home," he hollered. In a moment Faith appeared in the kitchen. She looked frazzled. "What's wrong?" Grant asked.

"It's been a zoo here since I got home from work," she said.

"Go ahead," Grant said, "tell me".

"Well, there were messages on the answering machine from Pat Murphy, James Doyle and Ron Cole, a reporter from Channel 3. They all said they needed to talk to you right away. Then they all called back and gave me the same messages. Then Linda called, she wants you to call her at home. After that I watched the six o'clock news on 3 and, sure enough, this Ron Cole did a segment on subpoenas being served on morgue employees."

"What was the gist of Cole's story?" he asked, keeping his mounting nervousness from his voice.

"The only thing he reported as fact was that the subpoenas were served. Everything else was speculation. The morgue administrator, the county and DOH all refused comment. They did show some nice footage of the morgue and file tape of Franz for background, though."

"What did Cole speculate about?" Grant wanted to know.

"He said that 'a source close to the investigation' revealed that the state has developed new evidence indicating that Dr. Franz may have misappropriated several bodies. This information may have been the impetus for the subpoenas."

"Did Franz or Dr. Massey make any statement?" Grant asked.

"No. Cole explained that this was a late breaking story. He said he couldn't reach either of them," Faith said.

Grant stood leaning against the kitchen counter, holding the still unopened beer can. "I don't know what's going on," he said, shaking his head. "I certainly didn't expect any of this."

"What are you going to do?" Faith asked.

"The first thing I'm going to do is down this beer," he said, popping the tab. "Then I'm going to change clothes and start making phone calls."

Ten minutes later Grant was back in the kitchen. He was perched on the counter top next to the wall phone, a fresh can of beer next to him. The phone rang just as he was reaching for it to call Linda.

"I'd like to speak with John Grant, the DOH investigator, please," an unfamiliar male voice said. "This is Bill Franchell calling."

The name sounded vaguely familiar to Grant, but he couldn't quite place it. "This is Grant," he said. "Should I know you Mr. Franchell?"

"Not at all," Franchell responded. "I don't believe we've ever talked."

"I see. What can I do for you?" Grant asked.

"I'm an investigator with the DA's office," Franchell said, downplaying his position. "I've been following your investigation of Dr. Franz, both in the press and by word of mouth. As an investigator myself, I've kind of taken a personal interest in the case. I thought maybe we could get together for a beer. I'd really like to meet you and swap some war stories."

"I'm flattered," Grant said, not believing a word of it. "When would you like to get together?"

"I'm free all day tomorrow if you are," Franchell said.

Grant did some quick thinking. "I think I'll have some time in the afternoon," he said. "I'll have to make a couple of calls before I can make a final commitment though."

"I understand," Franchell laughed. "I know that schedules are always subject to change in our business. Let's make it tentative then," he suggested.

"Fine, Bill, where and when?"

"How about three o'clock at Griff's Pub on Columbia Street? You know where that is don't you?" Franchell asked.

Grant was familiar with the place. It was a cop bar. Owned by the Griffin brothers, Tony and Larry, both retired Utica cops. "Yes, I've been there a couple of times," he said.

"Okay, I'll see you there at three. If something comes up call my voice mail and leave a message," Franchell said, rattling off a number.

Before hanging up they exchanged physical descriptions, and agreed that whoever showed up first would wait by the jukebox for the other.

Next Grant called Linda. "I was bad today, John," she said gravely. It was seven-thirty, and Grant suspected that she may have had a few cocktails after she got home from work.

"You could never be bad, Linda," Grant said with a chuckle.

"Oh yes I was. In fact, I was worse than bad, I was anonymous," she said.

Grant was now sure that she was in her cups. But he was equally sure that his calls from Doyle and Cole were connected to her being 'anonymous'. "What did you do, young lady?" he asked, legitimately interested.

"I called Jim Doyle and your local TV station and told them about the subpoenas. I teased them with a little speculation, then I hung up. I bet I drove them crazy."

"I think your call had an effect," Grant observed. "They both called my house twice, and a Ron Cole with Channel 3 did a report about the subpoenas on the evening news."

"What did you tell them?" Linda asked.

"I haven't spoken with either of them yet. I'll probably call Doyle, but I don't think I'll bother with Cole unless you think I should," Grant explained.

"Is there something about Cole you don't like?"

"I don't know anything about him. That's why I don't want to talk with him under these circumstances. I know Doyle and I trust him. I can't say that for Mr. Cole as of yet," Grant answered.

"That makes sense," Linda agreed. "How was Cole's reporting?"

"I didn't see it myself. My wife did, and she said it referred to new evidence of Franz misappropriating bodies. That apparently got Cole's attention, and probably that of his listener's too," Grant said.

Grant next told Linda about the interviews and the call from Bill Franchell. "So, I think the interviews went very well," he summed up. "I got some good statements, and these people will make powerful witnesses if we need them. But this Franchell call bothers me a little."

"Why? Because Whitehurst wants to know what we've got? I'm sure he's getting a little nervous. I don't blame him, do you?"

"It's not that," Grant said. "Franchell played me cheap with that line about him taking a 'personal interest' in the investigation. That was kind of an insult."

285

"Don't be so sensitive," Linda admonished. "What else was he going to say?"

"You have a point," Grant admitted. "How do you want me to handle him?"

"You're a good bullshitter. Just keep in mind that you're really talking to Whitehurst. Tell him what you think he should know, but not everything. Save some ammunition, just in case."

"Will do," Grant promised. "I'll call you on Monday."

Grant's calls to Doyle and Murphy were informative. According to their respective sources, the subpoenas had caused a furor at the county building and the morgue. Charles Allen had spent much of the afternoon closeted in his office with Ronald Bronson. Franz had been absent from the morgue most of the day to visit his attorney.

Grant finished his calls and reflected on the days events. His interviews had been successful, and it sounded like Franz, and others, were worried. It had been a good day, he concluded.

Grant arrived at Griff's Pub at ten minutes of three on Saturday. The tavern boasted a large horseshoe shaped bar where most of the action took place. An open area to the left of the bar held several tables, all of which were empty at this time of the day. The walls on both sides of the main entrance were adorned with pictures of police officers who had gained notoriety for heroism in Oneida County. A large picture of "Dirty Harry", portrayed by Clint Eastwood, brandishing his .44 magnum was displayed above the door.

The several patrons at the bar were in groups of three or four, engaged in their own conversations. No one seemed interested in the baseball game being played on the TV, or paid any attention to Grant when he approached the bar and ordered a draft beer. He took up station next to the jukebox to wait for Franchell. Grant amused himself listening to some of the stories being told at the bar. As the off duty cops discussed their exploits, the words "scumbag" and "dirtball" were the most frequently used adjectives.

About five minutes later Franchell came in. Grant recognized him instantly from his self-description. Franchell headed right for him, with a big friendly smile and outstretched hand. "John Grant, right?" he asked.

Grant nodded, shaking his hand. "Nice to meet you, Bill."

"Let's get a couple of brews and go to a table where we can talk," Franchell suggested.

They adjourned to the table furthest from the bar. The feeling out process lasted about five minutes. They found that they had mutual acquaintances, and both had attended the police academy located in Utica. Grant found Franchell to be very likeable. He hoped they could be friends, but he was still concerned that Franchell held him in low esteem.

"Okay, John, let's get down to business," Franchell said. "You seem pretty sharp to me, so I'm sure you know why I really called you. I'd like our conversation to be candid, okay?"

"That's fine with me," Grant answered.

"I'll go first," Franchell said, looking Grant in the eye. "My boss asked me to meet with you, to 'pick your brain', I believe he said. He wants to know what you really have on Franz and what you plan to do with it."

Grant felt much better that Franchell was being honest with him. "No problem," Grant said. "But why is he so concerned? And why not just ask me to come over to his office and talk?"

"Good questions, John. The first answer is that he feels he may have shown too much support for Franz when this started. I think he really believed Franz's explanation, disgruntled employees and all that stuff. Now, if the papers and rumor mill are accurate, you supposedly have developed evidence that is contradictory to that. As for your second question, this is a political hot potato. Mr. Whitehurst is a lawyer, and a darn good one. But he's also a politician. He doesn't want it to appear like he's looking for an invitation to investigate another county official."

"Why does he want to know what I've found if he isn't interested in getting involved?" Grant asked.

"I didn't say he doesn't want to get involved. He didn't tell me this, but it's my supposition that if there is good solid evidence that Franz has committed crimes, he'll go after him. That's not to say that he'd enjoy it. I'm sure it would be an uncomfortable situation for him. Remember, Dr. Franz is a hell of a good forensic pathologist. He's helped us get a lot of convictions."

"If my investigation does come up with this solid evidence you're talking about, and he doesn't do anything, he'd be open to a lot of second guessing wouldn't he? Maybe some embarrassment?" Grant asked.

"That's true," Franchell conceeded. "Let's not spend all afternoon debating Whitehurst's motives. If you've got something and there's a prosecution, what difference does it make?"

"Okay," Grant said. "I'll tell you what I know, but your boss will have to talk with our attorney about where we're going with it. That's not my call."

Franchell let Grant talk, interrupting with a question on occasion. Fifteen minutes later Franchell knew almost everything about the DOH investigation that Grant did.

"Body stealing!" Franchell said, shaking his head in disbelief. "The tissue stuff sounds bad, but maybe it can be explained away. But the body stealing is hard to believe, especially when you're talking about that many."

"If I was in your chair I'd be saying the same thing, Bill. That seems to be the case, though. I should know for sure next week."

In another five minutes their meeting was over. They walked to the parking lot together. "I'll talk with the boss on Monday," Franchell said. "If he's got anymore questions I'll be in touch. Thanks for coming."

"My pleasure," Grant said, wishing he could be a fly on the wall when Franchell told Whitehurst the story.

At eleven o'clock Saturday night Marcia Longo, clad in a bathrobe, watched Dr. Franz's back as he walked down the

288

corridor away from her apartment. When he had disappeared down the stairs she closed and locked the door. She grabbed a diet Coke from the refrigerator and sat down on her couch.

She had made a decision on how to handle her relationship with Franz a few days ago. Her conclusion had been that Bob Franz was really a decent man. Oh, he had faults, and had made his share of mistakes, no question about it! But couldn't that be said about everyone? And how could she break off their affair at a time like this? He was the subject of a merciless attack by the state, and under tremendous pressure. She couldn't do that to him now, it just wouldn't be right! And the bottom line was that she was sure that he really cared about her.

So, despite her misgivings, she was determined to stand by her man. When this state investigation was over with, and he survived, he'd be stronger than ever. And then she'd pursue his earlier hints that he was planning to divorce Ione.

Having sufficiently justified her decision, she leaned back, closed her eyes, and was soon asleep. She dreamed about one day becoming Mrs. Robert Franz.

CHAPTER TWENTY - FOUR

Dr. Robert McAree arrived at his office at nine o'clock on Monday, April 21st. He had just hung up his coat and sat down at his desk, when his secretary stuck her head in the door. "Doctor, the commissioner called. He'd like you to come to his office right away," she announced.

"Did he say what this is about?" McAree asked.

"I'm sorry, doctor, he didn't."

"Okay," McAree said, getting up. "I'll head over there. If I find out I'm going to be long I'll call and let you know."

McAree walked down the hall to the commissioner's suite, stopping in front of the secretary. "He's expecting you, go right in," she said.

McAree entered the spacious private office of Edgar Bowers. Bowers was seated at his desk across the room, a large picture window behind him. He was still wearing his suit coat. McAree found that somewhat unusual, since the commissioner was known for disdaining formality, preferring to work in his shirt sleeves.

"Good morning, Ed," McAree said pleasantly.

"Shut the door," Bowers said cooly, without returning the greeting.

"Sit down," Bowers ordered next, nodding to the chair in front of his desk.

As McAree approached the chair, he realized that there were usually three chairs there, today only one. He sat down and looked at Bowers. "What do you want to see me about," he asked.

Bowers stared back at him without answering. Bowers was sixty-three years old, with steel gray hair and penetrating blue eyes. He was considered to be a nice guy and a good boss. He was also known to have a nasty temper when provoked.

McAree tried to meet Bowers' withering stare, but couldn't. He lowered his eyes to Bowers' desk. His stomach began to knot as he noticed another oddity, a tape recorder/player on the edge of the desk. McAree had been in this office numerous times and had never seen the machine before.

McAree sat there trying to make some sense out of all this. He could feel Bowers' eyes boring into him, but didn't look up. The silence was becoming unbearable.

The movement of Bowers' arm caught his attention. He glanced as Bowers made a "come here" motion toward the far right side of the room. His eyes followed in that direction. A tall, well dressed man, previously unnoticed, stepped from against the wall and walked toward the commissioner's desk. "This is investigator Tallman, New York State Police," Bowers said.

McAree looked at Tallman's face. It was an unreadable mask, conveying no emotion. Tallman nodded at McAree, but said nothing.

"Go ahead, investigator," Bowers said. Tallman stepped to the desk and turned on the tape player.

McAree cringed, knowing what was coming. He listened for several minutes, eyes glued to the floor, as his last several phone conversations with Massey were played back. It was all there, the promises he had made, how he would accomplish them, his description of Bowers, everything.

Mercifully, the tape finally ended. "Do you want to hear it again?" Bowers asked.

McAree simply shook his head, fighting to control the bile rising in his throat. "Would you excuse us for a moment?" Bowers said to Tallman. The trooper left the room, closing the door behind him.

"I want your resignation," Bowers said. "If you decline to give it, I'll terminate you and issue a press release containing all the reasons why. And I'll see to it that your name goes in bold print."

"What about the police?" McAree asked, his voice so low it was almost inaudible.

"My concern is the integrity of this department. Your problems with the law are just that, your problem," Bowers said without sympathy.

"When do I have to make a decision?" McAree asked.

"You've got thirty seconds," Bowers said.

"Okay, I'll resign if that will satisfy you," McAree said.

"I won't be satisfied until you and your stench are out of my office!" Bowers answered.

At eleven o'clock that morning Grant placed a call to Dr. Morris Slater in Phoenix. Dr. Slater answered the phone. Grant identified himself and the general reason for his call. "Oh yes, I've been expecting your call for the past hour," Slater said pleasantly. "You say this has something to do with a research project at Crowne. Ask away and I'll see if I can help you."

"I'm currently involved in the investigation of the Oneida County ME's Office," Grant explained. "I've developed evidence showing that tissue was taken from bodies at the morgue and sent to Crowne for research. I'd like to ask you some questions about the particular project and researcher who received this tissue."

"I'm sorry that you wasted your time waiting to talk with me, Mr. Grant. I'm afraid you could have gotten the information much sooner by talking with Mrs. Banks at Crowne. She is in charge of tissue procurement. She'd have all the information on any projects using human tissue. And there were damn few of them."

"Yes, I'm aware of Mrs. Banks, doctor. But the problem is that the project I'm interested in wasn't handled through the regular channels, Mrs. Banks wasn't involved. I've been told that although this research was done at Crowne, it was described as a 'private project', being run by a rogue employee."

Dr. Slater didn't respond immediately. "This is very troubling, Mr. Grant. And you think this happened during my term as Director of Research?" he said finally.

"The evidence shows it went on from 1989 until at least '92," Grant said.

"Okay, Mr. Grant, give me the name of the person involved and the type of research, if you know it."

"This was some sort of bladder research, conducted by a Lewis Marner. His supervisor, Dr. Joseph Rudolph, allegedly gave Marner permission to do this research on his own time."

"I don't know what's going on here, and I don't want to take sides. I'm simply going to tell you the truth," Slater said.

"I can't ask for any more than that, doctor. Please go ahead."

"Dr. Rudolph was in charge of a bladder research project that was ongoing during the period you stated. Marner was recruited by Rudolph to be the project manager. And there was never a request made for human tissue, and none was ever used that I'm aware of," Slater declared.

"So this was an official Crowne project then," Grant asked.

"Yes, under the direction of Dr. Rudolph," Slater replied.

"Did this research produce any results that were reported?"

"You know, now that I think about it, that effort seemed to be plagued by problems all the way through. There was always a setback of some kind, like it was jinxed. No, there were never any reports published," Slater said. "Wait a minute! How long did you say this tissue was being sent to Crowne?"

"At least thru 1992. Why?"

"The research was such a flop that I pulled the plug long before that. I don't know the exact date, but I think it was in '91."

"That's very interesting, doctor. I'm going to impose on you by asking that you prepare a letter to me reflecting what you've told me. I also want to let you know that it might be necessary to ask for something more formal down the road, an affidavit possibly. Are you willing to do that?"

"I'll do it this morning. Do you have a fax?"

Grant gave Slater his fax number, and the address to mail the original. "Before we hang up, I'd like to ask you another question. This is nothing that should go in your letter."

"Go ahead, Mr. Grant."

"What's your opinion of Marner and Rudolph?"

"Lew Marner is a very capable researcher. He's intelligent, dependable and efficient. Just as important, he's as honest as the day is long."

"And Rudolph?" Grant prompted.

"Are we off the record now?"

"This part of the conversation is just between us, doctor."

"That's good enough for me. Dr. Rudolph is a very smart man. He's got all the credentials. But I always had a bad feeling about him."

"What kind of feeling?"

"That I couldn't trust him," Slater said. "I thought of him as being sneaky. I hear that he's in contention for my old job. I certainly hope they don't pick him. In my opinion they'd be making a giant mistake."

"Did you ever actually catch him doing anything?"

"No, just suspicion. And his close relationship with his brother-in-law disturbed me. I didn't like that at all."

"I'm sorry, doctor, but this is new to me. Rudolph's brother-in-law worked for you too?"

"Forgive me Mr. Grant, let me start over. Rudolph's brother-in-law is a fellow by the name of Gordon Kirk. He works for a pharmaceutical company in Pennsylvania. As I recall the company is Acme. Anyway, Kirk seemed to be in Utica quite often. It seemed like he was always hanging around Crowne."

"You saw him there on a regular basis?"

"Not personally. But remember, in my position I had no shortage of people wanting to tell me things," Slater said.

"Is Kirk a scientist also?" Grant asked.

"No, a salesman. At any rate, I never found anything wrong. I was just uncomfortable, that's all."

They talked a few minutes more, then Grant thanked Slater again and hung up.

Slater finished his letter by late morning. He faxed one copy to Grant, and another to Thomas Sullivan, his close friend at Crowne.

At ten o'clock that morning Bill Franchell reported to Whitehurst to discuss his meeting with Grant. "So how did Grant impress you?" Whitehurst started off.

"He's no fool, not what we think of as the typical state worker," Franchell said.

Whitehurst nodded. "Were you able to find out where his investigation stands?"

"Yes, I think he told me most of it."

"You think he held something back?"

"Maybe a little, but not much. I had the feeling he was being pretty straight with me."

"Good," Whitehurst said. "What did he tell you?"

Franchell related the details of the conversation to Whitehurst. When he finished, Whitehurst stared at him, a perplexed expression on his face. "Jesus!" Whitehurst said. "Do you believe him?"

Franchell shrugged. "The story is hard to believe, I admit that. And Grant knows that too. But I've spent most of my adult life interviewing people, and I can usually tell when I'm being lied to. I'm sure that he believed what he said. On the other hand, I haven't seen the evidence. Grant could be misreading or over estimating it."

"Do you think that's the case?"

"No, I don't. I just wanted to mention the possibility."

"I've never been overly concerned about the tissue allegations, at least from a criminal standpoint," Whitehurst said. "In my opinion, it would be difficult to prove criminal intent. I think they're more of a public relations and civil problem. But if Franz does have over forty skeletons over there...., well...., that could be bad news."

"Can Franz come up with a valid reason for having them?"

"In a word, no. I've talked with Chuck Allen about this. There is no legal justification, period. And if this body stealing allegation is true, there would have to be a myriad of related crimes."

"So what do we do?" Franchell asked.

"Nothing overtly. But I want you to keep in touch with Grant. Encourage him to discuss his investigation with you. If you can help him with something, do it. Unofficially of course. I'm going to start doing some research to see what may be involved here. Now don't be insulted, but I want to state openly what we both already know. This has got to stay just between us. If word gets out it will be all over this building in a matter of minutes. Be careful."

After talking with Dr. Slater, Grant called Albany. Linda wasn't available, but he was able to reach George. Before they discussed Dr. Slater, George insisted on telling Grant about the sacking of Dr. McAree. "Justice!" was Grant's one word response.

There was no mistaking the delight in his voice. He changed the subject to Dr. Slater almost immediately, however.

"What's your take on this?" George asked, after listening to Grant's account of the conversation.

"It sounds to me like we've got Rudolph by the short hair, and Crowne too, right?"

"That's my reaction," George agreed. "But what about this Gordon Kirk? Wasn't Acme getting tissue from Franz too?"

"According to Pat Murphy, yes. I think this whole deal smells. I bet there's a lot more here than just Rudolph ignoring the rules. Can we go after this Acme connection?"

"This case is like an octopus," George complained. "It seems like everytime you talk with somebody another scenario opens up."

"I can't argue with that," Grant laughed. "I'm awaiting your decision, boss."

"Before we do anything I want to talk with Kate. This is all very intriguing, but I don't know if we should get involved in that angle. We might want to refer it to a criminal investigative agency."

"Okay," Grant said, disappointed. "Can we at least interview Rudolph about what went on at Crowne?"

"Yes, that's definitely our responsibility. I'll tell you what, do your interviews tomorrow and see if anything else comes up that you want to ask Rudolph. Then I'll call Mr. Sullivan and see if he'll help us set up the interview."

"Right. Melvin Kemp is due in at nine, that's what I'm looking forward to. Will you prepare a subpoena for the additional files as soon as we get the inventory?"

"You bet, John. We're on a roll and I plan to keep it going."

"You're a good man, George. We were lucky to have you assigned to work with us on this. I say that very seriously."

"Thank you, John," George said, sounding embarrassed. "Oh, and something else you'll be glad to know. The county attorney called me to see if we were interested in resolving this thing."

"And, what did you tell them?"

"That I was insulted with their offer, and that I wouldn't discuss any possible settlement until our investigation was over."

"As I said, George, you're a good man," Grant repeated.

Dr. Franz buzzed Belinda Bernal on the intercom shortly before ten. "Belinda, I want you to call Melvin, he's probably at home now. Tell him I want to see him here in my office as soon as he can come in."

"Certainly, doctor, I'll try him right away."

"Belinda?"

"Yes?"

"Make sure he understands he is to see me personally, okay?"

"I will, doctor," she promised.

Chuck Allen called Ronald Bronson at ten-thirty. "I just heard from Peter Gorsky," he said. "I told him that we struck out with the DOH attorney, and that I was drafting a letter to Commissioner Bowers. He told me he'd inform Dr. Franz. I just wanted to keep you updated."

"I appreciate it, Chuck," Bronson said. "Keep on it, I want this over with sooner rather than later."

Allen knew that in a few months, or sooner, Bronson would face the challenge from Barone that everyone knew was coming. He wanted time to crow if a satisfactory settlement was reached. Or time for people to forget, if it ended in embarrassment. "I'll get it done, don't worry," Allen assured.

Melvin Kemp got to the morgue just before noon. He went straight to Franz's office. Franz greeted him warmly, even going to get him a coffee. When he returned he handed Melvin the cup, then closed the door and took his chair.

"Melvin," Franz began, "you're probably my most loyal employee. You have never refused an order, and always gone out of your way to help. I just wanted to tell you how much that has meant to me."

Kemp groped for the right words to tell Franz how much he appreciated the praise. Franz held up his hand. "It isn't necessary to say anything, Melvin. When I told Belinda to ask you to come in, I was hoping to give you good news about your appearance before Mr. Grant. Unfortunately, I've just found out that it won't be possible to reach a final resolution by tomorrow. I want to apologize for you having to go through all this because of me."

"It isn't because of you, doctor!" Kemp said. "It's because of stupid laws and a misunderstanding of what we do here."

Franz smiled patiently. "That's part of it, but not all. You see, there are certain people out to destroy me. When you try to improve things, make changes for the better, you make enemies. That is what has happened to me. I'm so close now to getting things straightened out, I'm afraid that the existence of our skeletons will be taken completely out of context. If Grant and Doyle succeed in inflaming the public I'll probably be forced to leave. I just wanted you to know how serious things are, so you won't be surprised if I have to go."

"Do you think if Grant doesn't find out about the skeletons you'll be okay?"

"Yes, Melvin. If I can just have a little more time everything will be all right."

"What if I don't go to see Mr. Grant?" Kemp asked, impressed with himself at coming up with the idea. "If you only need a day or two, I just won't go to see him. Would that help?"

"Melvin, I can't tell you how much I appreciate your offer. But I can't ask you to do that," Franz said, affection oozing from his voice.

"You aren't asking me to do anything, doctor. It's my idea. I just want to know if it will help."

"It certainly would, Melvin. But this has to be entirely your decision. I'd never forgive myself if you suffered any additional grief because of me."

"If I have to see Grant, I will. I just won't go tomorrow. If things work out as you hope I won't have to go at all."

The more Kemp thought this over the better he liked it. Wait until the rest of the crew found out that he defied the state to help Dr. Franz! And he'd make damn sure they found out!

"That's it, doctor," Kemp said standing up. "I've made my decision. This is between me and Grant, you have nothing to do with it."

A few seconds later Kemp left Franz's office to start spreading the news.

CHAPTER TWENTY - FIVE

Dr. Franz got to his office at seven-thirty Tuesday morning. His desk phone was ringing as he walked in the door. He put the phone to his ear, but the caller began talking before he could say "hello". Franz wasn't sure he recognized the voice at first. "Who is this?" he demanded angrily.

"It's Mort, Mort Massey, damn it!" Massey said, frustrated by the interruption.

"Get hold of yourself, man," Franz directed. "You're talking so fast I can't understand you. Slow down and start over."

Massey followed those orders the best he could. "I got a call at home last night from Bob McAree. He was forced to resign yesterday morning. They know about him trying to help us. They had most of our phone conversations on tape. He spent the rest of yesterday talking with his lawyer. They've got to meet with the Albany County DA this afternoon."

"Are you in your office now?" Franz asked, suddenly lacking confidence in the security of the county phone system.

"God no! I'm at a pay phone. McAree called me from a pay phone last night too. He shouldn't have called me, but he wanted to tip me off."

Massey may have been at a pay phone, but Franz was well aware that he wasn't. He decided to play to any potential listeners. "I'm very, very sorry to hear about your problem, Mort. You should have listened to me when I told you it wasn't right to involve Dr. McAree."

"You rotten bastard!" Massey screamed.

"I'm not going to listen to any more of this," Franz said. "It's obvious that you're under a great deal of stress now and aren't yourself," Franz said calmly.

As he started to return the handset to the cradle, the voice of Morton Massey faded. But his final words stuck in Franz's mind. "Nothing can stop Grant now! Nothing!" Massey had screamed.

Grant also received a phone call as he walked into his office at quarter after eight. Pat Murphy was on the line.

"I've got some hot news for you," Pat began, bypassing the usual pleasantries.

"Go," Grant said, sensing the urgency in Pat's voice.

"Mr. Kemp won't be in to see you this morning. He thinks some kind of settlement is going to be reached any minute. He's going to stall his appearance for a day or two and buy Franz some time."

Grant's heart sank. Kemp, and the inventory, were the key. Even with McAree out of the way, he didn't want any delays. He knew very well that the unexpected could always happen. "Did Franz or Miller tell him not to see me?" Grant asked.

"Kemp's presenting this as being his own idea. But I've got to believe that one of them planted the seed. What are you going to do?"

"I'll call George, but I know he'll tell me that we'll have to take enforcement action through the court. That could take a long time, and at this stage anything is too long. But the first thing I've got to do is wait until nine o'clock comes and goes. Then I think I'll try to locate Kemp myself and see if I can talk him into coming in."

"I can help you there," Pat said. "Melvin is at the morgue right now. Apparently he wanted to be near Franz and Miller in case there's more trouble over this than he bargained for."

"I appreciate this, Pat," Grant said. "Not the message, of course, but it's nice to have the warning. I don't know what I'd do without you and your access to information."

"Good luck, John. I'll be in my office if you need to talk."

Grant tried unsuccessfully to reach George. It was too early to even try Linda. He sent both an e-mail explaining the situation. He then went to arrange the conference room for the days interviews.

At nine o'clock he was back at his desk, waiting. Velma had tried to engage him in conversation, but he was not in the mood to talk. His was as sullen as she had ever seen.

At ten after nine Grant called the morgue and asked to speak with Kemp. "I'll get him for you," Belinda Bernal promised. "Hold on a second."

She went to the break room where Kemp was sipping a coffee and reading the morning paper. "There's a John Grant for you on line one," she told him.

Kemp got up and followed Belinda back to the main office. He preferred to talk to Grant on her phone rather than the extension in the break room. He knew that he was taking a risk. While sitting alone at home last night, he wished he hadn't made such a rash decision. But what was done, was done. Other than serving Dr. Franz and June Miller, his top priority was to get in Belinda's pants. In his mind that would only happen if he sufficiently impressed her. He attempted to do that at every opportunity. So far his tactics hadn't paid off. But if she could hear him put Grant in his place, maybe she'd see him in a different light. Hopefully a bedroom light.

"This is Melvin Kemp," he said in a firm, loud voice. "What do you want?"

Grant knew from Kemp's tone that he was in trouble. "I just wanted to remind you that you were supposed to see me this morning. Apparently you forgot so I thought I'd give you a call," Grant said, keeping his voice pleasant.

"I didn't forget at all," Kemp said. "It just so happens that I have my own life. And your request to see me didn't fit into my schedule. So I won't be coming to see you today. I'll give you a call when I have the time to fit you in. Good-by."

Grant hung the phone up and sat staring at the wall in front of him. "Son of a bitch!" he finally said to himself.

Velma swung around in her chair toward him. "What did you say." she asked.

303

Still staring at the wall, Grant spoke without even realizing he was talking to anyone. "The dirty son of a bitch said he's not coming!"

Bill Franchell got Grant's call at nine-thirty. "I hate to impose on our new friendship, Bill, but I'm in a spot," Grant said.

"Tell me what's wrong and I'll see if I can help," Franchell offered.

Grant explained the situation. "I haven't heard back from my boss or the lawyer. If it was anybody but Kemp it wouldn't be so bad. But he and the inventory are crucial to my investigation."

"Let me talk with my boss and see what he says," Franchell suggested. "Fax me over copies of both of the Kemp subpoenas. I'll get right back to you."

"God damn it!" Whitchurst groaned. "Do you know this Kemp?"

"I know who he is," Franchell said. "I've spoken to him on occasion when I've been over there."

"Okay, here's what I want you to do. Go over to the morgue and try to convince him to comply with the subpoenas. Bluff him a little if you have to. Tell him if he doesn't comply you'll run him in front of the grand jury. Do what you have to do."

"Will do, boss," Franchell said, heading for the door.

"Bill!" Whitehurst hollered to him before Franchell could step into the hall.

"Yes?" Franchell said, spinning around.

"While you're there I want you to look at this so called skeleton collection. Don't leave there until you've seen every bone in the God damn place."

Franchell nodded and walked out of the room. He placed a quick call to Grant, then grabbed his jacket and headed for the morgue.

Melvin Kemp had stayed in the main office after talking with Grant. He was on a roll, and continued to tell Belinda and Mrs. Larkin that he was not a man to be pushed around. He would not roll over for anyone just because they had a badge or a little authority, he said.

Franchell parked the county car in front of the morgue and went in. He had been in the building countless times over his career and knew the layout well. He swooped into the office wearing his game face. He spotted Kemp standing next to Belinda's desk and went directly to him. He ignored the girls as though he and Kemp were the only ones in the room.

Kemp didn't immediately connect Franchell's appearance with his conversation with Grant. His smile was returned with a withering glare.

"You're Melvin Kemp aren't you?" Franchell demanded in a hiss.

"Yes," Kemp said, his voice already beginning to crack.

"Come with me," Franchell ordered. He grabbed Kemp by the elbow and propelled him out of the office and down the hall to the back conference room.

After Franchell hustled Kemp out of the room, the girls looked at each other in disbelief. "Do you think we should tell Dr. Franz or June?" Mrs. Larkin asked.

"Not right away. Let's give Melvin a little time to show Bill how tough he is to push around," Belinda suggested.

"Good idea," Mrs. Larkin said. Both women laughed and then went back to work.

Kemp didn't know exactly what was going on, but he knew it was terribly wrong. He went meekly, without resistance or protest.

Alone in the conference room, Franchell shoved Kemp into a chair and nudged the door shut with his toe. He rested his left hip on the conference table next to Kemp's chair and leaned toward the terrified face of his victim. "Were you supposed to be someplace this morning?" Franchell said. It was as much a statement as a question.

Now Kemp knew. "Yes, sir," he stammered. The telltale quiver was already in his lower lip.

"Where?" Franchell asked, trying not to feel sorry for the helpless Kemp.

"At Mr. Grant's office," Kemp answered.

"Then why in the fuck aren't you there?" Franchell said, leaning closer.

"I thought.....I just thought.....," Kemp said, struggling to explain.

"Shut up!" Franchell said, raising his voice slightly. "Now listen to me very carefully, Melvin. You have two choices. You can go to see Mr. Grant right now, ask him to forgive you for being an idiot, and answer all his questions."

"I'll go right now," Kemp said starting to get up.

Franchell's right palm flashed out to the center of Kemp's chest, knocking him back into the chair. "Sit down! I haven't given you your other choice yet," he said.

"If you decide not to see Mr. Grant, or tell him the truth, you can take a short ride with me. You can go right in front of the grand jury and explain to all those nice people why you're ignoring a subpoena from the state Commissioner of Health. What's your decision?"

"I'll go see Mr. Grant right now, honest Mr. Franchell. And anything he asks me I'll answer. I won't give him any trouble," Kemp promised, tears running down his cheeks.

Franchell stood up with Kemp following suit. "I think you're a good boy, Melvin," Franchell said, smiling now. "You must have just been a little confused."

"Yes," Kemp agreed. "I guess I didn't understand how important this is. I'll get going now, thanks Mr. Franchell."

Just as Kemp's hand touched the door handle Franchell hollered his name. "What?" he asked turning toward Franchell, new fear in his eyes.

"You're supposed to bring something to Mr. Grant. Do you have it?"

Kemp removed some folded papers from his pants pocket and waved them toward Franchell. "They're right here," he said proudly.

306

"Good for you, Melvin. Make sure you have them when you get to Mr. Grant's office," Franchell warned. "Now get going!"

Kemp almost ran out of the conference room and down the corridor. He went through the office without exchanging a word or glance with the girls. Ignoring the speed limit, he headed for the state office building.

After Kemp had gone, Franchell allowed himself a smile. He then used the conference room phone to call Grant. "Kemp is on his way," he told him, "and he's got what you want."

"Thanks, Bill," Grant said simply.

"Don't mention it," Franchell said. He hung up and went to find June Miller. It was time to look at the bones.

Grant's interviews of the morgue employees had been scheduled at one hour intervals. He had been talking with Dennis Drummond, his ten o'clock appointment, when Franchell had called.

He finished with Drummond quickly and waited in his office for Kemp to arrive. After Kemp, the next two interviews were Scott Browne and Linda Chovan. They were followed by Dale Fisher, Dr. Johnson, Dr. Samuels, Michael Hargrove and Marcia Longo. Kemp, Fisher, Johnson and Samuels were where Grant hoped to get the most information. He expected Hargrove and Longo to be the most contentious.

Kemp came in at twenty of eleven. Grant went to the main office to meet him. Kemp had the look of a man on his way to be executed. Franchell had done his work well, maybe too well. "Good morning, Melvin," Grant said with a warm smile. "It's so nice of you to come."

Kemp pumped Grant's hand vigorously. "I'm so sorry about the mixup," Kemp apologized. "I didn't...., I was going to.....,I.."

"That's fine, Melvin," Grant said, holding up his hand. "Let's go where we can talk, follow me."

When Grant closed the door to the conference room Kemp became very nervous. "Don't worry, Melvin, nobody is going to hurt you," Grant assured him. "I just want to ask you a few

307

questions and look at some documents you've brought for me. As long as you tell me the truth we'll get along fine."

"You don't have to worry about that," Kemp said, visions of Bill Franchell on his mind.

Forty-five minutes later Grant had the information he wanted. Kemp told all about his involvement in defleshing and boiling bodies. Others involved in these "projects" had been Dale Fisher and Rodney Flowers. He said he acted on the direct orders of Dr. Franz, and Franz had prepared the containers that were sent to the crematory. He also detailed how he conducted the inventory of the bones, and that he inventoried and incinerated the contents of the freezer. The latter activities were ordered by June Miller. Kemp even seemed relieved to hand over his inventory documents.

Grant left Kemp to write his statement while he placed a call to George. This time he was able to talk with him on the first try. Grant updated him on what had happened since the earlier e-mail. George asked that Grant fax him the inventory so he could start preparing the subpoena right away. He hoped to have it served on the county attorney's office by the next day. It was decided to ask for only the files relating to the full skeletons.

After Kemp left Grant breezed through his interviews of Chovan and Browne. As he had suspected, they had no direct knowledge of, or involvement in, the tissue or skeleton collection matters.

Next came Dale Fisher. He was twenty-six, and had been working at the morgue since 1990. He volunteered nothing, but answered any question put directly to him. He corroborated Kemp's statement, and said that he also received his defleshing and boiling orders directly from Franz.

Grant had caught up on the interviews and actually had a few minutes before Dr. Johnson was due in. He checked his e-mail and found a note from George. An attorney for Dr. Samuels had called and requested a postponement of his clients interview. George had agreed. No new date had been set. Grant suspected that Samuels wanted to see how things played out before he committed to anything on the record.

Dr. Donald Johnson showed up exactly on time. He was thirty-six, five feet nine, one hundred eighty pounds, with brown hair and full beard. He was still out of work on disability, and walked with a cane.

Although Grant had serious misgivings about the mans veracity, he couldn't help but like him. He was very warm and outgoing, with a sense of humor.

He was difficult to control, however. He had a laundry list of grievances against Franz, and wanted to air them all. Grant was focusing on the skeletons and tissues. After a lengthy interview, Dr. Johnson could provide no direct information regarding those subjects. Everything he knew about them was second or third hand. He insisted on preparing a statement that included all his allegations and concerns. Rather than argue, Grant let him use his desk and told him to take all the time he needed. He then went to the reception area and found that Hargrove and Longo had arrived early, and together. They were sitting next to each other, looking dour.

Grant took Hargrove back to the conference room first. He didn't really expect any derogatory information from either him or Longo. In fact, no one had implicated either of them directly with the major issues. But he wanted to hear what they had to say and get a story down on paper. If they could be locked into a particular position, they would at least be neutralized. Their statements now, could be used to impeach them later if necessary.

Hargrove steadfastly maintained that he knew nothing about illegal tissue harvesting or body stealing. "Are you saying it didn't happen, or that you don't know if it happened?" Grant asked.

After a rather heated debate, Hargrove admitted that he didn't actually know what had, or hadn't happened. Grant made sure that this fact was included in Hargrove's statement, along with his praise for Dr. Franz.

309

Marcia Longo's attitude and story were almost identical to Hargrove's. Grant watched her as she spoke with great passion about the virtues of her boss. He had to admire her loyalty, no matter how misplaced.

She prepared a written statement similar in content to Hargrove's. As Grant walked her down the empty corridor to the exit, she stopped and turned to face him. "I've got to know something," she said. "Why are you out to ruin Dr. Franz?"

"I'm not," Grant answered. "I'm conducting an investigation. The facts will determine his fate, not me."

"Liar!" she snarled. "This is personal with you. He embarrassed you once and you're determined to get your revenge aren't you?"

"You're mistaken, Ms. Longo. I'm just doing my job."

"Don't try to hide behind that line, you bastard!"

They stood there inches apart, glaring at each other. Her eyes clearly revealed her emotions, both hatred and rage. They also telegraphed something else. Grant's left hand caught her right wrist, as the open palm flew toward his face. They stood like that for several seconds. When Grant felt her relax he released her wrist. "Your interview is over. I think you had better leave," Grant said.

Longo turned her back and walked away. "I'll find my own way out!" she said over her shoulder.

After she disappeared, Grant turned to find Dr. Johnson standing a few feet behind him, smiling. "Here's my statement,' he said, waving several sheets of paper. "I see you made a friend," he added.

"That girl can be a very dangerous playmate," Grant observed, a slight smile on his face. "With her temper, I'm glad she's not mine."

Johnson nodded. "A real powder keg," he agreed.

After talking with Massey, Franz had remained in his office, the door closed, thinking. He was unaware of what had transpired between Franchell and Kemp. But he did know that the end was in sight. Kemp wouldn't stall Grant for over a day or so without a settlement being reached. With that chance now seeming very doubtful, he had to plan the only way left to stop DOH, he had to resign. It was his understanding that the most DOH could accomplish through a full hearing, would be his removal, and possibly revocation of his state licenses. If he resigned and surrendered the licenses, the state would have no valid reason to proceed.

Resignation, something he would have found reprehensible only a few days ago, now looked pretty good to him. He'd have to talk with Gorsky and make sure such drastic action would do what he wanted. He had a little time, however. Kemp's foolish attempt to prove he was a man, was at least giving him that.

Franz was lost in these thoughts when an ashen faced June Miller burst in the room. She closed the door behind her and leaned against it, as though she was afraid someone would try to follow her in.

"What in the world.....," Franz began.

"Bill Franchell from the DA's office is here," she said, interrupting him. "He wants to see the inventory, all of it. What do you want me to do?"

Franz's color quickly matched Miller's. "How in the hell did he get involved?" he asked.

"I'm not sure, but I think he's working with Grant," Miller explained. "According to the girls, he came storming in here and scared the hell out of Melvin, sent him over to Grant's. Then he asked for me, he demanded that I show him 'every bone in the place'. Should we call Whitehurst? Maybe he can call this off."

Franz shook his head. "Whitehurst sent him over here, can't you see that? Franchell wouldn't be doing this on his own."

"So what should I do? Do you want to talk with him?" Miller asked.

The little color remaining in Franz's face drained at that thought. "No! You'll have to show him, there is no choice. If this was my private office he'd need a warrant. But this is a county building, we've got to let him look. But don't answer any questions! Refer him to me if he wants an explanation."

Miller seemed somewhat relieved that Franz wasn't asking her to explain the skeletons. "I'll have him see you if he has questions, then?"

"I said refer any questions to me, I didn't say I'd be here to answer them. I'll be leaving and I won't be available. I'll call you later on your private line. Understood?"

Miller shrugged. "I guess," she said without conviction. She left Franz's office and escorted Franchell to the back conference room, the one with the musty odor, to see the bones.

At five o'clock Miller's desk phone rang. It was Whitney Price. "Hi, June, I'm back," he said, jovially. "When are you going to send those items over?"

"I'm not," she answered somberly. "A DA's investigator was here today and saw them all. And the state has a complete inventory list. There's no point in moving them now."

"What? The DA?" Price asked, experiencing a sudden hot flash. "What's going on? Let me talk to Bob."

"I don't know what's going on with the DA. We all know what DOH is after, though. I think they are in this together. Bob isn't here. He lit out this morning and I haven't heard from him since. I'm waiting around for him to call."

"If you hear anything, June, anything at all, let me know right away," Price requested.

"I will," Miller promised.

Grant's Wednesday started off with upbeat news. An e-mail from George said that he had the latest subpoena ready. He had spoken with Pamela Ashley. She had agreed to accept service via fax, with the original to be personally served. The files would be available next Monday at her office.

That was followed by a call from Pat Murphy. Grant briefed him on the events of the previous day. "Did you hear anything back from Franchell?" Pat asked.

"About a ten second call late in the afternoon," Grant replied. "He just said, quote, 'he's got a regular cemetery over there,' unquote."

Pat laughed. "The noose tightens," he observed.

"It sure seems to me that we're building one hell of a case," Grant said seriously. "But two things bother me. First is the unexpected. Every once in a while you hear about somebody who is charismatic, being so convincing in his explanation of things, that people are willing to overlook overwhelmimg evidence. And Franz can be a charmer when he's not ranting.

"The other thing is Whitehurst. A lot of the stuff that's turning up appears to be criminal, well beyond anything DOH can handle. And, other than having Franchell contact me, Whitehurst has shown no inclination to get involved."

"What about the AG?" Pat asked.

"Not likely," Grant said. "From what I hear you'd play hell trying to get them to go into someone elses jurisdiction without being asked. Whitehurst would have to invite them in, citing potential conflicts in his investigating a county official. It doesn't sound right, but that's the way it is."

"With this case there's always another bridge to cross, isn't there?"

"Yes. Let's just hope this isn't like that movie, 'A Bridge Too Far'," Grant said.

"How do you plan to combat that?"

"My thought has been to produce so much evidence that Whitehurst won't be able to ignore it. I think we're nearing that point. Just a little more time and I think we'll be there."

"What are you doing after work?" Pat asked, changing the subject.

"Nothing special, why?"

"Can you stop over around six? I'll have some cold beer, you bring the snacks, okay?"

"What's the occasion?"

"I'd like you to meet someone."

"See you at six," Grant said in confirmation.

June Miller had slept very little Tuesday night, and she looked it when she got to the morgue on Wednesday. Franz had called her late on Tuesday. He had admitted that he would have to resign. He had attempted to see Peter Gorsky to have him set up a meeting with Bronson, but Gorsky was out of town until Friday evening. Franz had scheduled to meet with him on Saturday.

She told him that Franchell had completed his review of the bones, made some notes, and left without comment. There had been no further contact from the DA's office. Franz promised to call Whitney Price and said he'd be in the office sometime on Wednesday.

As far as Miller was concerned, it was now a case of every man for himself. She needed to change horses, but didn't want to appear disloyal. Her reputation for loyalty was well known in the circles where she would seek future employment. She wanted to cooperate with Grant, but it had to be his idea, not hers.

For quite some time she had suspected that there was a source of information leaving the morgue other than Samuels and Johnson. Hoping she was right, she summoned Belinda Bernal to her office.

"Belinda," she said, with all the sweetness she could muster, "I'm going to tell you something in complete confidence. This must remain our secret, do you understand?"

Belinda nodded. "Yes, Mrs. Miller."

"Good girl. As you know, Dr. Franz is under tremendous pressure with this state investigation. I know that you think as much of the doctor as I do. But I'm afraid that this stress is affecting his judgement. He has said some things to me indicating that he may conceal documents, or destroy them, to keep them from the investigator. In spite of our personal feelings, we know that is wrong, don't we?"

Belinda nodded again. "Yes, Mrs. Miller."

"I want to be prepared to fully cooperate with the state should they call me, and I don't want to see Dr. Franz get himself into further trouble. I'm asking you to let me know immediately if he asks you to remove or shred any documents, or does anything like that himself. Will you do that for me?"

"I certainly will, Mrs. Miller," Belinda said with enthusiasm.

"I knew I could count on you, Belinda," Miller said, dismissing her. If she was right, she'd receive a subpoena from the state very soon.

CHAPTER TWENTY - SIX

Carrying a bag containing pretzels and chips, Grant got to Pat's office at six o'clock. The door was locked, but Pat answered his knock after just a few seconds. "Ready for a cold one?" Pat asked, taking the bag from Grant.

"You bet," Grant said, following Pat through the office and to the kitchen.

As soon as he entered the room, Grant saw James Doyle and Belinda Bernal seated at the table, a can of beer in front of each. "Surprised?" Pat asked, after greetings were exchanged.

"I guess you could say I'm pleasantly surprised," Grant said. "I had considered that your source could be Belinda, but not very seriously."

Pat handed Grant a beer. "Things are moving so fast that I figured it was time you met her away from the morgue," Pat said. "Do you want to explain the situation to John?" he said to Belinda.

"Since you know most of the people involved, Mr. Grant, you may be able to appreciate what it is like working there. When I started Pat and Bill Maxwell were there. They are real human beings, we talked about things and got along very well. And the best thing was that they didn't act like dogs in heat. I felt like they respected me," she paused, looking at Grant for some response.

Grant smiled understandingly. "I get the picture, please go on," he said.

"Well, Pat and Bill ran a professional office," Belinda resumed. "They didn't allow the guys to hang around the office. If they didn't have business there, they couldn't loiter. That made for a pleasant environment. And the more I learned about the job, the more I liked it.

"I'm sure you already know the circumstances around Pat and Bill leaving. But after they were gone things got real bad for me. June Miller is as tough as they come, but she had no problem with the boys pestering me. I'm talking about Melvin

317

and Michael. She wouldn't let them neglect their work. But if they were caught up, she let them do what they wanted. They apparently both wanted to impress me. Almost every day I'd hear about their exploits, both on and off the job.

"Anyway, I used to call Pat once in a while just to vent. During these conversations I'd tell him some of the things that were going on. I could tell that he was interested. He never asked me to do it, but I decided that I'd keep him informed when I heard things that seemed a little odd or interesting. I guess that's how I happen to be here tonight," she concluded.

"I figure that maybe if anything important comes up you'd like Belinda to call you direct. If I'm not available, that is," Pat clarified.

Grant tried to keep his face expressionless, as he thought of his wife answering the phone and hearing Belinda's sexy voice asking for him. He mentally cleared that hurdle. "That's a very good idea," he said. "Provided we have one understanding, Belinda. I don't want you to do anything at all to obtain information that goes beyond your normal duties. In other words, don't look in any files, don't read any mail, don't copy any documents, don't do anything that exceeds your routine tasks. I don't want either of us to have problems over this, okay?"

"I understand perfectly, Mr. Grant. And I'll only call you if it's very important and I can't reach Pat," Belinda said.

"Now that the business is settled, let's talk about fun stuff," Pat said, passing out another round of beer.

"Not so fast," Doyle interrupted. "I want to tell John that I'll be running a story tomorrow."

"What have you come up with?" Grant asked him.

"A source more reliable than you!" Doyle said, feigning indignation. He was pleased when his comment drew laughter from his audience.

"Actually, I received a fax of the latest subpoena today. My new contact told me that these files represent entire skeletons that are being stored in the morgue. The state is going to try to

318

determine where these skeletons should be, and how they came to be resting on shelves at the morgue."

The "anonymous" Linda was at work again, Grant surmised. "How do you think that story will play?" he asked Doyle.

"What do you think?" Doyle asked back.

"I think it could be a bombshell," Grant answered. "A lot of eyebrows will be raised, a lot of people will begin to wonder."

"That's exactly what I think, and hope," Doyle said. "We'll know by tomorrow evening. If I'm right, our phones will be ringing off the hook, and the fax will be humming."

Grant turned to Belinda. "Before we get off track," he said, "do you know if there is anyone else I should talk to, or talk to again? Anyone who has more to tell?"

Belinda thought for a moment. "No, I don't think so. After what happened to Melvin, everyone knows that this is serious. Those who won't stick their necks out for Dr. Franz have been honest with you. The others aren't going to change. I know one thing for sure though, they're in a panic. There's a rumor that Franz might leave, but that's only a rumor right now."

"I see," Grant said. "What about June Miller. We've been leaving her alone, trying to put on a little pressure. Do you think she'd turn on him?"

Belinda stared down at her beer can. She thought of Miller's razor sharp tongue, her condescending manner. "I just talked with her today," she said, without looking up. "She's one hundred percent behind him. She'll go down with the ship before she'll be disloyal. I'm sorry, Mr. Grant, but your strategy didn't work."

"That's too bad," Grant said. "I could have used her."

Doyle's story was the talk of Grant's office on Thursday. People who had never spoken to him were asking for an audience with him to get the inside scoop. Grant was polite, but refused to go beyond what had already been printed. He believed that this new disclosure could so arouse the public that Whitehurst would be forced into action.

Grant's delight over the article was in stark contrast to the attitude at the county building. Whitehurst made a bee line for Bronson's office as soon as he finished reading. "Have you seen this?" he asked Bronson, waving the paper in his hand.

"Yes, I've read it," Bronson said glumly. "I'm already getting calls demanding that I fire Franz."

"And my office is getting calls demanding that Franz be arrested," Whitehurst said. "The state is playing dirty pool by giving these 'anonymous' comments.

"I've tried to make hay on this," Bronson said with a tight smile. "That's the way the game is played. Do you have any suggestions on what to do now?"

"I know what I'm going to do," Whitehurst declared. "I'm going to announce that my office will conduct a review of the situation to determine if it warrants a grand jury investigation. My suggestion to you is to get rid of him. This is an emotional issue. If it gets out of control.....," his voice trailed off, the thought left hanging.

"You're right of course, Reggie. Chuck Allen will be here in a few minutes to talk about it. Do you think I can still come out okay on this?"

"You? Yes, if you're decisive it's a win, win situation for you. Points were made when you defended Franz to begin with. When you realize how bad things are you take strong action. Getting rid of Franz won't put Barone out of the picture, but it can strengthen you."

"You're right again," Bronson said, this time his smile was broader. "I think I'll end up just fine."

Anthony Barone had also read the morning paper. He was sitting at the dining room table in his home, located in the Utica suburb of Whitesboro. This was the house he and his wife had always dreamed of. Two floors, four bedrooms, attached double garage, swimming pool, and all the modern conveniences. And best of all, it was paid for.

Barone was tall and slim, his hair was dyed a dark brown. That, and a tanning salon, made him appear to be in his forties rather than sixties. He felt great physically, the effects of his cancer treatments all but gone. Up until recently he had been feeling great mentally, also. He was getting his ducks on the pond for his political resurrection. Ronald Bronson, his former friend, turned arch enemy, knew what was going on but had been helpless to do anything about it. That type of torture amused Barone, everything had been going his way.

But this investigation of the morgue was causing problems. At first it wasn't much. Bronson, admittedly a shrewd politician, had turned it to his benefit. But not enough to reverse the momentum of the "Barone Express", as he referred to his latest political effort.

No, right now he wasn't worried about politics. He was worried about where this investigation would lead. He was also an accomplished politician, better than Bronson. And to get to the top you sometimes had to give and receive favors. That was all a part of it. But he was also human, and had human failings that went beyond the craving for power and wealth. He wouldn't be able to stand it if anything happened to bring shame on his pride and joy, his children. There was one son and one daughter, both married but living locally. They respected and admired him. He'd never be able to face them if he caused them harm.

He paused in his thoughts to listen to the voices coming from the living room. His wife was hosting the morning coffee klatch. He had been sitting with them until the morning newspaper article focused the conversation on the morgue investigation. The old biddies wanted him to do something to force Franz out. They were planning to call the DA and Bronson to demand action. He had escaped to the relative privacy of the dining room.

The women were right, though. He would do something to force Franz out, but not for the reasons they had in mind. He picked up the phone and dialed the morgue.

George Epstein called Grant at ten o'clock. "I've got some good and bad news," he said.

"Let's start with the bad," Grant suggested.

321

"Dr. Rudolph has a lawyer. If we want to talk with him we'll have to go the subpoena route and have the lawyer present or, more likely, get a stall job."

"How do you know all this?" Grant asked.

"That's where the good news comes in. I called Tom Sullivan at Crowne to ask him to help us set up the interview. They fired Rudolph yesterday."

"What? Why?" Grant asked surprised.

"Dr. Slater faxed Sullivan a copy of the letter he sent us. That was followed by a series of telephone calls. A decision was made that Rudolph had violated enough Crowne work rules to warrant dismissal. When they called him to Sullivan's office to confront him, Rudolph said he had an attorney and that he wouldn't answer any questions without counsel. They fired him on the spot. A security guard went with him while he cleaned out his desk and then escorted him out of the building."

First McAree and now Rudolph, Grant thought. "It's been a great week for people getting what they deserve," he said.

"I thought you'd like that," George said. "Now, I suggest we hold off on Rudolph for the time being. Sullivan is prepared to admit wrong doing by Crowne and wants to work out a stipulation. I think that's what we should do."

"Yeah, Rudolph can wait for now," Grant said. "I faxed todays article about the skeletons to Linda. Ask her for a copy of it."

"I've got it, she sent it right up. I understand that we've been getting a few phone calls about it. People who have had loved ones go to the morgue are wanting to know if they ever came out. This may very well be the straw that breaks Franz's back."

"Keep thinking the good thought, George," Grant advised. "And so will I."

Dr. Franz answered the ringing desk phone. "Leave the office and call me," the familiar voice ordered, then the line went dead. Franz immediately left his office and went to the pay phone at the drug store a block away. Anthony Barone was not someone to be left waiting.

The first ring wasn't even finished when Barone answered. "You've got to go, Bob. We've done well for ourselves, but it's time for you to move on."

"I realize that, Tony. Peter Gorsky is out of town until Friday. I'll see him Saturday and tell him what I want to do. He'll schedule us to meet with Bronson."

"Good. But don't wait for Gorsky to call Bronson. You call him today and set up an appointment for Monday. You don't have to tell him what it's about if you don't want to. I just want to make sure you get in to see him as soon as possible. And don't give any notice, make your resignation effective immediately. Tell Bronson to notify the state right away. That should settle things. Got it?"

"I understand," Franz said, fighting back the urge to tell Barone to go fuck himself. "I even have some ideas about what I'm going to do next. I think...."

"I'm not interested," Barone cut in. "Just do what I told you!" The click told Franz the conversation was over.

"What a day!" Woody said as he drove the DEC Blazer toward Watertown Friday morning. "The sun is out, it's going to hit seventy degrees and we've had a good breakfast. What more can we ask for?"

"A productive interview?" Grant ventured.

"We'll get it," Woody predicted. "I do have to tell you though, this is probably my last hurrah on this case."

"What are you talking about?" Grant asked, concerned.

"The county attorney's office contacted DEC to discuss a settlement. We told them the investigation wasn't completed yet. They wanted some kind of a time frame. My boss knows I've been milking this thing. As long as he wasn't getting any heat he let me go. Now he wants me to wrap it up. I'll still do what I can to help, but it will have to be unofficial."

"I'm sorry to hear that, Woody. I think we're nearing the end. You should be able to be there."

"I'm not so sure about that. I think I've opened a whole new can of worms with this skeletal course. I got hold of the court orders Franz used to exhume the 'John Does'. It's my guess the applications were falsified. He said that the reason for exhumation was to determine the cause of death. That would already have been done at the initial autopsy. And if these poor souls are part of his inventory, he'll be in violation of the orders. In each case he was told to conduct his business and return the bodies to their graves 'forthwith'."

"But these are John Does, will anybody care?" Grant asked.

"If that was the only problem, probably not," Woody admitted. "But I also got the check that our guy used to pay for his enrollment. It was made out to the Oneida County Health Department Auxiliary. I found out that in spite of the name, this outfit has nothing to do with county government. They're a non profit deal, and are not supported with county funds."

"What do they do?" Grant asked.

"Provide health related services to the needy. Flu shots to the poor and elderly, stuff like that. Good things."

"Where do they get their money?"

"Donations and fund raisers. They have all volunteer workers. The office is manned by a few old ladies who retired from the county health department."

"So, what are you thinking?"

"I'm thinking that the county had nothing to do with these courses. Franz uses the auxiliary as a slush fund. He raises and spends his own money, using county time, probably county employees, and bodies obtained through his official county position."

"Jesus!" Grant exclaimed. "Another can of worms is right!"

"The question being, who can we get to look at it?" Woody said. "This is very clearly beyond DEC and DOH jurisdictions, no matter how creative our bosses are."

That question was much discussed but still unanswered, when they arrived at the state prison.

"This is a depressing sight isn't it?" Grant said as they pulled into the parking lot. The tall cyclone fence topped with razor wire, guard towers and drab buildings all contributed to Grant's impression.

They got out of the car and went into the main entrance. At first glance this could have passed for any other office or government building. But the cleaners were trustees clad in green prison uniforms. And across the lobby was a control booth manned by uniformed officers. To the right of the booth was a sliding barred gate, ominous in its appearance.

Woody and Grant gave their names to the officer at the booth's window, and passed their ID cards in for examination. They received their ID's back and signed the visitors log. The guard promised that the lieutenant would be with them shortly. A few minutes later the gate slid back and a tall, rugged looking officer wearing lieutenant's bars approached them. After introductions he invited them to follow him back through the gate and to the interview room.

After passing through a metal detector, the gate slid back for them to enter. Once inside, a second gate was revealed a few feet past the first. They waited while the outer gate smoothly closed, with a loud metallic click. Then the inner gate slid back. Once they cleared that, they found themselves in a long, well lighted corridor leading into the bowels of the prison.

They passed a group of inmates lined up for a search after returning from some activity. Another group marched past them, being taken to who knew where.

Grant glanced at them while avoiding direct eye contact. Many of these were dangerous, violent men. The same types you might see on television true crime shows. This place couldn't be much fun for Rodney Flowers, not given the crimes he was here for.

At the end of the long corridor, a couple of more twists and turns brought them to the interview room containing Flowers. The lieutenant ushered them past the guard standing outside the door and into the room. "Your company is here Flowers," he said to the man seated at the small table. "You guys knock when you're done," he added to Woody and Grant. Then he walked out, closing the door behind him.

Flowers was thirty-five, with light brown hair worn long. He didn't stand up during introductions or offer to shake hands. Grant estimated he was probably around five feet eight. Unlike some of the other inmates they had seen, Flowers didn't look like he was into working out. He appeared to be soft. The buttons on his green prison shirt were stretched over a protruding stomach. Grant guessed that in this environment, Flowers favors would be in great demand.

Woody started the interview by asking about the bone boiling and the disposal of the resulting waste. Flowers readily admitted that he was one of Franz's main men concerning these special projects. His story was very similar to Kemp's and Fisher's, but contained nothing new.

That changed when he was asked about the skeletal course, including the one he had hosted on his farm. "Yeah, I helped out with those," Flowers said. "I was the set up man. I'd take the stuff out to where the actual evidence recovery portion of the course was going to be held. Either Franz's place, or mine the one time."

"What kind of 'stuff' did you take to the field site?" Woody asked.

"The folding tables and chairs, propane torch and boiling tub, coolers for the soda and water. Plus I'd run for sandwiches and coffee."

"Anything else?"

"Just the bodies, body parts and bones. I'd take them out and position them the way Franz wanted them. Some buried, some partially buried, and some right on top of the ground. Then the students would have to find them and process the scene. We did it to make it very realistic for the cops."

"When you say bodies, do you mean the skeletons?" Grant asked.

"No, they were part of what I called the bones. When it was getting near time for the course Franz would freeze a body or two that he was going to keep anyway. We just wouldn't deflesh it right away. These were always partially decomposed jobs, but with flesh left on them. At the end of the course we'd boil them, and the John Doe down, and take the skeletons back to the morgue for the collection. As I said, we made it very realistic."

"How did you transport the bodies and bones?" Woody wanted to know.

"Bodies went in body bags in the trunk of my car. Skeletons and bones were in boxes in the trunk or back seat," Flowers answered.

"So you moved these bodies around in the trunk of a private car?" Grant asked.

"That's right," Flowers said.

"Did you have any paperwork on them, burial or removal permits?" Grant said.

"Paperwork?" Flowers asked, a puzzled look on his face. "What's he talking about?" he asked Woody.

"Never mind," Grant said, "I guess that was a stupid question."

"After you boiled these bodies down out in the field, where did you dump the waste?" Woody inquired.

"Right there, wherever we were."

"How were you paid for your time?" Grant asked.

"This was all done as part of my job. I was on the county payroll. Any extra hours earned me comp time."

"How did you pay for the soft drinks and sandwiches?"

"Franz would sign a blank check and I'd fill in the amount. I always brought him back a receipt," Flowers explained.

"His personal check?"

"No, the health department auxiliary."

"How did you end up having the '91 course at your place?" Woody asked.

"Franz asked me if I would do it. I guess his wife was giving him a hard time about using their farm. He promised me a thousand dollars for using my place. That was in addition to my regular pay."

327

"How did he pay you the thousand dollars, cash or check?"

"Neither. The bastard stiffed me. He said expenses ran higher than he had expected, and he didn't have the money. He told me to take an extra three days of comp time instead," Flowers said, shaking his head as though he still couldn't believe what had happened to him.

A short time later Woody summoned the guard and told him the interview was over. "Come on Flowers," the guard said, leading him back to whatever hell awaited him.

"I must say that I think you're doing the right thing here," Peter Gorsky said. It was eleven o'clock Saturday morning. Bob Franz was in his office and had just stated his intention to resign.

"Your resignation and the surrender of your director licenses will stop the DOH investigation. Once they get all that they could hope to gain after a full investigation and hearing, there is absolutely no reason for them to continue. No matter how much more they might find, they would have already assessed the maximum penalty."

"Let's just go over a couple of things again," Franz said. "I'm surrendering my director licenses, not my medical license." Gorsky nodded. "Any fine will be paid by the county," Franz went on. Gorsky nodded again. "And I will be admitting nothing," Franz said in conclusion.

"And that is the beauty of it!" Gorsky said beamimg. "When we made our earlier proposal, you were going to admit some wrong doing. That would have been right in the stipulation of settlement. Now you're just going to resign and leave this in the county's lap."

"But what if the state still wants more? What if they want to come after me personally? Can they do that?"

"The technical answer is, yes they could. But as a practical matter they wouldn't, believe me. They have nothing to gain and everything to lose if they do."

"Okay," Franz said. "We have to see Bronson at nine-thirty on Monday. I guess I'll see you then."

"Wait a minute, Bob. There's something else we need to talk about. If you take off what will happen to Ione? Will there be a divorce to handle?"

Franz smiled. "I had thought about that too, Peter. I thought about trying to land another job with all this baggage plus an estranged wife. I went to Ione last night and laid it all on the line for her. There is nothing emotional left between us. Our talk was just like any other business meeting. When all the cards were on the table she made her decision. She likes my earning potential, she wants me to have a job. She's going to come with me, wherever I go, to start over. So that's one problem we won't have to deal with."

As soon as Franz left Gorsky's office he went to a pay phone and called Marcia. He asked her to meet him at eight o'clock, at an out of the way restaurant they frequented. She agreed, although she questioned why they had to take separate vehicles. Franz hung up, knowing that he had to sever his ties with Utica, all of them.

Marcia Longo arrived at the restaurant just after eight. Franz was already seated at their usual secluded table. She took the chair opposite him. A waitress appeared and took her order for a glass of beer. Franz asked for another ginger ale.

After their drinks arrived, Franz got right to the point. "I'm sure that you've heard the rumor that I might resign," he said.

Marcia laughed. "I know better than that," she said. "We'll get through this thing, you and me."

"The rumor is true," Franz said gravely. "I'm going to tell Bronson on Monday. The resignation will be effective immediately."

Marcia looked and felt as though she had the wind knocked out of her. She stared at him, unable to speak.

"I wanted to meet you in this setting to tell you that it's over," he said.

Marcia had regained some use of her brain and mouth. "The job is over, or we're over?" she asked

"Both," he answered.

"Why does it have to be over for us?" she asked, confused. "If you want to go someplace else I'll go with you. You mean more to me than that job! Is that what you want to do?"

"No, Marcia, not exactly. You see, I am leaving, but I have to get another position someplace. I have to continue my work, that's the most important thing. In order to do that I have to appear to have a stable family life. I'm taking Ione with me."

Marcia was beginning to get the message, and she didn't like it. "You're going to dump me just like that?" she asked, snapping her right thumb and index finger. "Then you ride off into the sunset with your wife?"

"Exactly. But I want you to know that I truly enjoyed our fling."

"You're serious aren't you?" she asked. "You think you can treat me like a whore, call an eight year relationship a 'fling', and have me accept that!"

"Marcia," Franz said, somewhat surprised at her reaction. "That's all it was, just a long fling. You never meant any more than that to me."

She glared at Franz with the same emotions she had felt for Grant on Tuesday. Unfortunately for Franz, he wasn't quite as quick as Grant. In the blink of an eye, ten ounces of cold Miller Lite hit him flush in the face. Marcia stood up, still glaring at him. He watched her lips silently form the words "fuck you", before she turned and went out the door.

CHAPTER TWENTY - SEVEN

At nine-thirty Monday morning, Dr. Franz and Peter Gorsky met with Ronald Bronson and Charles Allen in Bronson's office. Gorsky opened the meeting by explaining what Franz planned to do and what it was expected to accomplish.

Allen was the first to respond. "I can find no argument with your logic," he said. "All things considered, I think this makes sense. Ron?"

Bronson didn't respond right away, apparently deep in thought. "You said that we would negotiate the details of the settlement with the state, right?" he asked Gorsky.

"That's right. Any fine, or admissions, will be yours to deal with. Bob is sacrificing his career, that's enough," Gorsky answered.

"When are we going to do this?" Bronson wanted to know.

"When can you make the announcement?" Gorsky asked back.

"Probably tomorrow or Wednesday, right Chuck?" Bronson said.

Allen thought a second. "Let's go for Wednesday," he said.

"The county will pay Bob for his unused leave time, and continue his health insurance for ninety days, I presume," Gorsky said to Allen.

"That's the norm," Allen agreed.

"What about a replacement?" Bronson asked Franz. "What do you think of Samuels?"

Franz almost choked, but maintained a poker face. "May I give you my suggestions concerning several personnel matters?"

"Certainly, Bob, go ahead," Bronson said.

"Right now, public confidence in the morgue is very low. I think a clean sweep of the management is the way to go. Let the people know there is a clean slate. I suggest that in addition to me, Samuels, Johnson, June Miller, and even Dr. Massey should be removed."

Bronson and Allen exchanged a quick glance, which Franz noticed. "Is Mort already among the missing?" Franz asked with a grin, knowing the answer was yes.

Bronson ignored the question. "That may very well be the way to go," he conceded. "Who would run things until I can find replacements?"

"Dr. Richard Belge, the Lewis County ME, will help out on a per diem basis until you're straightened out. I've already touched base with him."

Bronson looked at Allen. "Chuck, what do you think?"

"I think Bob has made an excellent point. This will die down more quickly if we replace all those people. I say to do it," Allen said.

"Can we still be ready by Wednesday?"

"I'll make sure that we are," Allen said. "I'll get Human Resources on the horn, and you meet with your public relations people to prepare a release. If we get on it right now there's no reason we can't be ready by then."

"We aren't just going to issue a release," Bronson said. "We'll make the announcement right in the auditorium. I want the cameras there. I have to look the people in the eye and assure them that I'm in control, and am doing what needs to be done."

"Great idea," Allen said. "After I get the ball rolling here, I'll call DOH and tell them we're throwing in the towel."

"Before we leave, I have one more concern," Gorsky said. "I hope that you don't use this press conference to make Bob a scape goat. He's doing what's right, he deserves to leave with dignity."

Bronson pondered Gorsky's comment briefly. "I won't trash Bob," he said. "But keep in mind that the main thing now is to cover my own ass."

As soon as his guests had left, Bronson called Whitehurst. "This is great news for you," Whitehurst commented.

"For you too, isn't it?"

"Well, maybe. I'd like to take the podium after you on Wednesday. I'll announce that my preliminary review of the operation of the morgue has revealed some management problems and errors in judgement. Nothing worthy of a grand jury at this point. I'll promise a final report upon completion of the review. Okay with you?"

"Sure," Bronson said, after a short hesitation. "I'll put you on the schedule. Does this mean that it will finally be over with?"

"Unless a smoking gun suddenly shows up, and that's doubtful if the investigation is stopped, yes," Whitehurst said. "That's on my end. But Chuck Allen will be busy handling claims over the tissues and skeleton collection."

"Yes, the treasury will take a big hit, I'm sure," Bronson said sadly.

"But look on the bright side," Whitehurst said. "At least the worst is over."

Grant returned to his office at three o'clock Monday afternoon. He had spent the day at the county attorney's office reviewing the subpoenaed records and waiting for copies to be made. Unlike with the earlier subpoena, today there were no problems. Pamela Ashley had the copies made without protest. No morgue employee was present.

He sent Linda and George an e-mail, telling them that his mission had been a success. He then settled down at his desk and started poring through the documents.

Marcia Longo was passing through the main office on her way out of the morgue Monday afternoon. "Excuse me Marcia," Belinda Bernal said. "Dr. Franz would like you to stop in his office before you go."

Reluctantly, she went to his office, stopping outside the open door. Franz spotted her right away. "Come in," he said warmly, "and shut the door."

She did as ordered, then stood staring at him. "If this isn't official business, I'm leaving," she said.

"Oh, Marcia," Franz said. "It doesn't have to be like this. Can't we part as friends?"

"It didn't have to be like this! That was your choice!" she said with venom. "Let's get something straight. I don't want to be your friend! I don't want any part of you! So let's just keep away from each other for whatever time you have left here."

Franz glared back at her, his face flushing. "Okay," he said, "if that's the way you want it. Now, the real reason I wanted to see you is to make arrangements to get my personal belongings back from your apartment. Do you want to bring them in, or should I stop by?"

"I disposed of your stuff when I got home Saturday night. It went in the garbage, just like the last eight years of my life!" she hissed.

"Everything? You got rid of everything?" he asked.

She walked out and slammed the door without answering.

Woody picked Grant up at ten o'clock Tuesday morning. "I hope you're prepared to take some heat for this." Woody said. "If anybody complains we might be in deep shit."

"Yeah, but we are in agreement that it has to be done, right?" Grant asked.

"True, but it sounded like a better idea when we talked about it on Friday than it does today."

"If we're going to do this it's got to be now, while we still have open investigations. That way we can only be criticized for poor judgement, not disobeying orders."

Woody didn't respond, driving past the morgue and taking an on street parking place two blocks away. The two men got out of the Blazer and entered a one story brick office building, the headquarters of the Oneida County Health Department Auxiliary.

The first room was sparsely furnished. A kind faced, gray haired lady sat at a small desk in the center of the room. "Can I help you?" she offered.

Grant and Woody gave her their warmest smiles and flashed their ID cases. "We'd like to speak with the person in charge if

334

we can," Woody said. "We just need a little help with something we're working on."

"I'm sure Mrs. Finster will be glad to assist you," she said. "She's our treasurer, if anybody can help you, she can. Follow me please."

They went down a short hallway and entered a room on the right. Another gray haired woman, well dressed and intelligent looking, sat behind a desk. "Audrey, these handsome young gentlemen need some help," their escort said. "I told them you were the person to talk with."

"Thanks, Lorna," Mrs. Finster said. "Please sit down and tell me how I can help." She waved at the two empty chairs in front of her desk.

Grant and Woody sat down and again showed their ID's. "We're conducting a confidential investigation, Mrs. Finster," Grant began. "It would be a big help if we had an understanding of how an organization like yours operates. Do you have the time to enlighten us?"

"I'd love to," she said, launching into an explanation of how the auxiliary functioned. They were a non profit, tax exempt organization formed in 1989. Their mission was to provide health related services to those in the community in need. This included a variety of vaccines, transportation to health clinics, and coordination with related businesses and organizations.

Dr. Franz, the ME, and Anthony Barone, the county executive at the time, had been instrumental in getting the auxiliary off the ground. Mr. Barone had even furnished his personal attorney to prepare and file the necessary paperwork.

They had an all volunteer staff. The office workers, including herself, were retired county employees. They raised funds through donations and sponsoring events such as softball, bowling and golf tournaments.

"Do you raise sufficient funds to meet your needs?" Woody asked.

"There is never enough to do everything you would like," she said. "But our fund raising efforts are quite successful, actually."

"Do you have anything readily available that would give us an idea of what you do financially?" Grant asked. "A computer printout, perhaps?"

"Computers!" Mrs. Finster spat, waving her hand in disgust. "I do everything the old fashioned way, by hand. I keep ledgers showing every dime we receive and spend. Let the bank deal with the computer!"

Grant and Woody laughed. "Would you mind showing us one of your ledgers?" Woody asked.

"Any one in particular?"

"How about the one that includes June of '91?" Woody said, knowing that should include the check Mike Durant wrote to pay for the skeletal course.

Mrs. Finster got up and went to a large file cabinet that was against the wall behind her. She returned with a huge, green covered ledger book. "By the way," she said, putting the ledger on her desk, "you two are very mysterious. Am I in any trouble? Has someone complained about me?"

"Not at all," Woody assured her with a smile. "This contains June of '91?" he asked quickly, pointing at the ledger.

"Yes," Mrs. Finster said, looking forward to showing off her work. "You won't find any mistakes in here," she said as she shoved the ledger toward him. "I'm seventy-six years old and I've never been accused of being sloppy or inaccurate."

The ledger was split in two sections, "credits" and "debits". With Grant looking over his shoulder, Woody opened the book to the "credits" section.

Mrs. Finster had every reason to be proud. She had meticulously recorded the date monies were received, their source and amount, check number and date of deposit in the auxiliary bank account. A note on the bottom of the page told where the bank statements and deposit slips covering those transactions were filed.

Woody flipped to the page where Durant's check should be logged. It wasn't there. In fact, there were no entries matching the amount of the enrollment fee. Several of the students would have paid during that period, but none showed up.

Mrs. Finster caught the look that Woody and Grant exchanged. "Is something wrong?" she asked.

"We have reason to believe that Dr. Franz was running a course for police officers around this time, and that the tuition checks were paid to the auxiliary. I don't see any of them entered here," Woody answered.

"Oh, why didn't you say so?" she said, relief in her voice. "You want to see the special morgue account."

Mrs. Finster got up and returned to the file cabinet. "Dr. Franz has a separate account set up for the morgue," she explained, talking over her shoulder.

She brought back another ledger and set it down on the desk. "This is the one you want," she said.

This book also contained the two sections. Woody quickly located the page containing the entries for June, 1991. Durant's check was recorded, along with several others for the same amount. In addition, there were entries for other, larger amounts. Two were received from an individual named Gordon Kirk. Those checks totaled twenty-three hundred dollars. Another check from "JER, Inc," was for eighteen hundred dollars.

"Do you know who Gordon Kirk and JER, Inc. are?" Grant asked. "Were these payments for some type of services?"

"I don't know," Mrs. Finster said, becoming nervous. "I just keep the books. I don't know anything else about it. I'd better call Dr. Franz over here to answer your questions. I'm sure he can be here in a few minutes."

"No sense in bothering him," Woody said smoothly. "We have to be leaving now anyway."

Grant and Woody stood up and extended their right hands to Mrs. Finster. As they shook hands, each thanked her for her help. "Are you sure you don't want me to call Dr. Franz?" she asked.

337

"No, we have everything we need for now," Woody said.

When Grant got back to his office he found a message to call Linda right away. "I wanted to be the first to congratulate you," Linda said in her bubbly voice.

"For what?" Grant asked, fearing what was coming.

"Dr. Franz will resign tomorrow. You've done it, John! In less than two months you've gathered enough evidence to force him out! Congratulations!"

"What's it mean?" Grant wanted to know.

"Why it means you've won," Linda said, disappointed at his reaction. "Now we can get back to what we get paid to do, laboratory cases."

There it was, in that last sentence. "Are you saying that the investigation is over?" Grant asked.

"Well certainly, John. Franz is leaving and turning in his lab director licenses. There's nothing else for us to go after, no reason to continue."

"There are loose ends," Grant said. "I've gone through the files on the skeleton collection. One funeral director, Whitney Price, handled every one of them. Two were supposed to have been buried, the rest cremated. That requires further investigation. And just this morning Woody and I found out more about the skeletal courses and money going through the health department auxiliary."

"What did you find?" she asked with sudden interest.

"Franz has a special account where all the tuition money was deposited. On top of that, we saw a couple of fairly large checks from an individual with the same name as Dr. Rudolph's brother-in-law. I don't know for sure why he's paying Franz, but I can make a good guess."

"Where did you see this information?"

"In a ledger book at the auxiliary."

"I don't recall discussing any plans to visit the auxiliary. Did we talk about it?" Linda asked, her voice cool.

"No, it was kind of a spontaneous thing," Grant said, being partially truthful.

"Well, I admit that the information is interesting, and probably needs a closer look. But that won't be by us. Our investigation is over effective immediately. Finish up any reports that need to be done, then send all your case materials here for storage."

"It can't end like this, Linda. There's too much here, we can't just let it die!"

"You have a point, John. I'll tell you what, write up a nice referral to Whitehurst. State all your allegations, suspicions, and evidence. If it's going to die, we'll let Whitehurst kill it."

"That's just what he'll do, kill it!"

"Damn it, John! That's not our problem," Linda said, agitated. "Look," she went on more calmly, "It isn't that I'm not sympathetic. But my orders were clear. Whether we like it or not, it's over."

After Linda hung up, Grant called Pat Murphy and James Doyle to get their reactions. Pat had suspected that Franz would have to resign. He was only surprised that it was happening so quickly. He shared Linda's opinion that this should be considered a major victory. The county had never done anything about Franz, and couldn't be expected to take any action now.

Doyle was aware of the next days press conference. He had learned that Franz's resignation, and other personnel moves, would be announced. He was very pleased with developments. Grant's feelings were definitely in the minority. He began to wonder if he was wrong. Maybe he should just let go and enjoy the moment.

Grant was in his recliner at six o'clock, watching the local news. Faith was out shopping, so he had unrestricted use of the TV. The ringing of the phone interrupted him.

"You're so close," Paul said in his mechanical voice. "You can't stop now."

"Aren't you about eight hours early? You usually strike in the dead of night, don't you?"

"Don't crack wise! This is serious!" Paul snapped.

339

"I've got news for you, asshole," Grant responded. "I have stopped. My investigation is over, done, finished! If you've got a complaint, make it to my boss. I'll give you her phone number."

After a short silence, Paul spoke again. "Calm down, Mr. Grant. I'm trying to help you."

"I don't need any help. I'm not investigating anything. It's been nice talking with you."

"Don't hang up! You know that Franz has done a lot more than what the public has heard. He's a criminal! What are you going to do about it?"

"All I can do is send a referral to the DA. He'll have to handle it from there."

"He won't do anything, and you know it!"

"You're probably right," Grant agreed. "But there's nothing more I can do."

"Yes there is."

Grant didn't want to ask, but he couldn't help himself. "What?"

"Get to the bottom of the relationship between Franz and Anthony Barone, then tell the DA. Good-by, Mr. Grant."

The auditorium in the county building was jammed when Ronald Bronson walked to the podium at nine o'clock Wednesday morning. A hush fell over the audience of reporters and interested citizens as Bronson began to speak.

"Ladies and gentlemen," he said somberly. "This is not a pleasant day for the county, or me personally. As you are aware, Dr. Robert Franz and the morgue have been the subject of a state investigation. Accusations have been made by current and former employees. The state, through the press, has chosen to release certain information to the public. Unfortunately, this was done in the form of anonymous leaks, designed to inflame the public, and destroy confidence in the medical examiner's office. Even more unfortunate, those methods seem to have worked. Our citizens are upset and concerned. I have no personal knowledge of whether or not Dr. Franz has done anything wrong. But as of today that will be a moot point. Because effective today, Dr. Franz has resigned."

Bronson paused for effect, then continued, making eye contact with the two TV cameras. "But I don't believe that Dr. Franz's departure alone, will restore public confidence to what it should be. Therefore, I am taking this opportunity to announce that assistant medical examiners Harrison Samuels and Donald Johnson, Morgue Administrator, June Miller, and Commissioner

of Health, Morton Massey, are having their employment terminated today."

A collective gasp filled the auditorium as Bronson walked away from the podium. That was followed by applause from some of the spectators. They appreciated a man tough enough to make the difficult decisions.

Bronson had barely made it out of the room before the reporters headed for the exits. They had to get out their reports on what would be known as the "Wednesday Morning Massacre."

Whitehurst delivered his report to a few hangers on, including Marcia Longo.

Grant was in his office, trying to get himself motivated,

when the receptionist called him at eleven o'clock. "There's a Marcia Longo here to see you," she announced.

Puzzled, Grant went to meet her. "Good morning, Ms. Longo," he said evenly. "What can I do for you?"

"I'd like to talk with you in private," she said.

Grant shrugged. "Sure, come back to my office."

Once inside his room, Grant motioned Longo to the chair side of his desk. He then closed the door and sat down. "I'm sure you know that my investigation is over," he said with a thin smile. "I don't know that we have anything to talk about."

"I'd like you to take a look at this," she said, removing a white envelope from her purse and placing it on his desk in front of him.

CHAPTER   TWENTY - EIGHT

Grant glanced at the envelope, then looked questioningly at Marcia. Her expression revealed nothing. He returned his attention to the envelope. It appeared to be a standard, white, business size envelope, about an eighth of an inch thick. There was no writing on the front. He tentatively picked it up and flipped it over. The flap had apparently been sealed at one time, then opened. It was currently held shut with a piece of scotch tape.

Grant again looked at Longo. "Go ahead," she said, "open it."

He opened the flap, reached inside and removed the contents. He set the photos on the desk. There were eight of them, three by fives, in color. Grant slowly looked at each one, front and back.

He felt his pulse quicken, his stomach knot, as he saw the man in the pictures, the same man, making love to a young woman. A dead young woman!

After his initial examination he looked away for a moment, gathering his thoughts, reining in his emotions. He then went through the pictures again, even more slowly.

There were two shots each of four separate incidents, four different women. The poses were similar, the female laying on her back on a gurney, legs spread, dangling over the sides. Her hips were elevated by what appeared to be a pillow. One picture of each set showed a sexually aroused male, naked from the waist down, standing near the gurney. The second shot showed the man on top of the female. Actual penetration was not visible. But the faces of the participants were very clear. Printed on the back of each picture was a date, all in '89, name and morgue case number.

Grant put the photos back down. "Do you know who the man in these pictures is?" he asked Longo.

"Yes," she said without hesitation, "Anthony Barone."

"I've got a lot of questions, Marcia, But let me ask you the most important one first. Why bring these to me? You know this is well beyond anything DOH can handle. Why not Whitehurst, or the cops?"

"You know who Barone is, right?" Marcia asked. She continued after Grant nodded. "You don't fool with 'Boss Barone', not in this county! I was at the county building before I came here. Mr. Whitehurst said that he had reviewed the morgue situation and found nothing wrong, just some innocent mistakes. Give me a break! Would you take those to him under these circumstances?" she asked, pointing to the pictures.

"No, I suppose not," he admitted. "On the other hand, just a few days ago you made a sworn statement praising Franz, and saying nothing was wrong."

"That proves my point," she said, unruffled. "I tried to protect Bob, so is the county."

"But you don't even like me, do you?" he asked with a smile.

"Not particularly, but I trust you. You're like a bull dog, you'll make sure something is done," she said in explanation.

"One more question before we get back to the pictures. Why give these to anybody? Why the change of heart?"

"What difference does it make?"

"Mr. Whitehurst will probably question your motives," Grant said. "You realize that we're going to have to see him, right?"

"I understand that. I'll address my motivation if, and when he asks me," she said firmly.

"Okay," Grant shrugged. "Did you take these pictures?"

"No. I first saw them only a few weeks ago."

"How did you happen to come into possession of them?"

"As I'm sure you know, Bob and I were lovers. He kept some personal belongings at my apartment. This envelope was among his things."

"He knows you have it?" Grant asked.

"He knows it was there, sealed. He doesn't know I opened it. I told him I threw all his stuff out."

"Do you know who took the pictures?"

"I assume Bob did. The printing on the backs is his," she said.

"Can you definetly identify these as having been taken in the morgue autopsy room?"

"Yes, and I can do even better than that," she said. "They had to have been taken from a supply closet, probably with the morgue camera. After I saw them I checked the case files. Everything matches, including the photos in the folders. These were the same women."

"You're very efficient," Grant observed. "Do you think there are any other pictures, anything more recent?"

"These are the only ones I'm aware of."

"Was Franz blackmailing Barone?" Grant asked.

"I don't know. I can't tell you any more, I just don't know."

Grant put the pictures back in the envelope, and left Marcia sitting there while he sought out a phone he could use in privacy. Finding the conference room empty, he went in and closed the door. He started to dial Linda, then changed his mind. Instead he called Bill Franchell.

Rather than coming directly to the point, he decided to test the waters first. "My boss wants me to write up a referral for Mr. Whitehurst. I'm going to outline all the questions that still need to be answered, what I suspect and why. And I picked up some information yesterday about those skeletal courses Franz has put on. It looks like he wasn't just building his collection.

I think he was using the bodies as part of a private business, with money laundering and other things."

"Money laundering?" Franchell said with a chuckle. "I think you need some time off, you're getting burned out."

345

"I'm just telling you what I think, Bill. Will your boss be interested in this stuff?"

"To tell you the truth, John, I think this thing is pretty well over as far as he's concerned. You drove Franz out, what more do you want?"

This was about what Grant had thought. "The main reason I called though, is about some information that has come into my possession just a few minutes ago. I think you need to hear about it. Can I come over?"

"I'm pretty busy right now, John. Why don't you just include it in this referral you're going to send over?"

"This is kind of hot, Bill. Just take a look at it. If you're not interested I'll take it somewhere else."

The 'somewhere else' captured Franchell's attention. "Well what is it?" he asked, not happy about the veiled threat.

"I'll be right over," Grant said. "It will only take a couple of minutes."

"Well.....," Franchell hedged.

"I'll be straight with you, Bill," Grant cut in. "You did me a big favor with Melvin Kemp. I'm trying to return that favor now. You'll never forgive yourself if you don't at least take a look."

That did it. "Okay, come on over. I'll be waiting for you," Franchell invited.

Grant stopped at the computer and sent Linda an e-mail. He said he had come upon some new evidence in the Franz case and was taking it to the DA's office. He promised to call later with the details. With the envelope securely in his inside jacket pocket, he gathered up Marcia Longo and headed out for the county building.

Bill Franchell met them in the reception area. He eyed Longo with suspicion, then amusement. "You're together?" he asked.

"Yes," Grant said evenly. "Where can we talk?"

Franchell took them to his office and closed the door. He motioned Marcia and Grant to the visitors chairs, then took a seat behind his desk. "What's this all about?" he asked.

Grant removed the envelope from his pocket and handed it to Franchell. "Marcia brought this to me a little while ago. I'd like you to take a look at the contents and see if you think it's anything important," Grant said with a straight face.

Franchell looked the envelope over, much as Grant had done. Then he removed the pictures. The look on his face was priceless. He checked each photo carefully, front and back, then looked again. When he finished, he let out a low whistle. "Let's talk," he said.

Marcia's answers to Franchell's questions were consistant with what she had told Grant. He went through some of the questions a second time using different words, but Marcia didn't waver. In response to why she had decided to come forward, she simply said she and Franz had a 'falling out'.

"Are you doing this for revenge?" Franchell asked.

"Yes," she said with a cold smile. "I'm making no accusations. I'm only giving you the pictures, they speak for themselves."

Apparently satisfied, Franchell excused himself to take the pictures to Whitehurst. He was back in twenty minutes. "Mr. Whitehurst will see you in just a few minutes, Marcia," he said. "He'd like to talk with you alone first, John."

Franchell took Grant to Whitehurst's office, made the introductions, then left. Grant took a chair across from the DA. Whitehurst stared at him in silence for several seconds. "You have turned out to be my worst nightmare, Mr. Grant," Whitehurst said, breaking into a grin. "And I mean that as a compliment. You got your teeth into this and wouldn't let go. And now you've come up with something that I can work with, something that demands a criminal investigation." He paused, again staring at Grant.

"Oh, I'll have to eat a little crow. My handling of this will be second guessed. But I'll live with it. The important thing is that now I'm going to go to work on this. I'm going to do it right, and I need your help."

"How so?" Grant asked.

"I want you to work with Bill. Tell him everything you've found, or think you've found. Show him the evidence you have and where you think you can find more. Tell him who you've talked with, and who still needs to be interviewed. In other words, I want him to know everything you know or suspect."

"Does that mean you're going to start from square one, right from the tissues on through?" Grant asked.

"Yes, Mr. Grant. Everything is on the table, I don't plan to leave a stone unturned. Can I count on your help?"

"As far as I'm concerned, yes. But I was ordered to close my case. I should get an approval from Albany before I commit."

Whitehurst shoved his desk phone toward Grant. "Go ahead and call whoever you need to get permission from. Then give me the phone, I'll make the request personally."

Five minutes later, Whitehurst had obtained Linda's blessing. He next summoned Marcia to his office, where she told the same story for the third time that day.

After Longo left, Whitehurst spoke with Franchell and Grant. "I want you to get started on briefing Bill right away, John. And Bill, when you two are finished, get back to me with your investigative plan, and a list of any grand jury subpoenas you're going to need."

Franchell checked his watch. "This will take some time," He said.

"Don't worry about the time, I'm not going anywhere until we're off and running," Whitehurst said. "I want this done right, but quickly. As soon as word gets out about this," he fixed Grant with a warning stare, "and that has a way of happening, the shit will hit the fan. We need to be out in front, way out in front. Make it happen!"

After Franchell and Grant were on their way, Whitehurst called Bronson. "This Franz thing isn't over, it's only just starting!" he said.

"What? What in the hell are you talking about? It was over yesterday, you said so!" Bronson exclaimed.

"I said it was over unless a smoking gun materialized. Well it did."

"God damn it! Don't play head games with me! Tell me what's happened!" Bronson demanded.

"I can't say anymore right now. Just hang onto your hat, this may be a bumpy ride."

At six-thirty Franchell made it back to Whitehurst's office. He had a legal pad containing several pages of notes. "I think we should examine all the morgue files relating to the skeletal collection. It sounds like every one of those death certificates may have been falsified regarding the disposition of the bodies. The internal morgue documents showing the body was turned over to the funeral director will be wrong too. They'd be considered business records wouldn't they?"

"If they're kept in the normal course of business, and purport to reflect the activities of that business, yes," Whitehurst opined.

"They are," Franchell said. "And we need to find out how much Mr. Whitney Price got out of this. He prepared all the death certificates and supposedly handled all the bodies. It's not difficult to figure how he did the cremations. But two of them should have been buried. I'm assuming that Price charged for full funerals, caskets and the works."

Whitehurst shook his head. "There are no depths to which people won't sink to make a buck," he mused.

"Then we've got this whole skeletal course mess. From what John told me, it sounds like Franz was running these courses on his own. He used bodies that he acquired through his county position, used county time and county employees. The money he collected in tuitions went into a special account he had set up at the health department auxiliary. Franz and Barone set the auxiliary up, by the way. There were supposedly other monies deposited in that account. A couple of the checks were from a guy believed to be associated with Acme Pharmaceuticals. Grant thinks they may have been payments for research tissue."

"Jesus Christ!" Whitehurst exploded. "Nothing is sacred. You can't even die and be left in peace. These bastards were raping the dead, figuratively and literally."

"John also saw a check entry from 'JER, Inc'. This could likely be Dr. Joseph Rudolph, the one from Crowne. We've got to follow the money trail, see who is who. I suspect we'll find one or more dummy companies, companies set up by Franz and Barone. I'll need a subpoena for the auxiliary records. As soon as I get the name of the bank involved I'll want their records too."

"You think Barone was getting his cut too? You don't think he was just a blackmail victim?" Whitehurst asked.

"Right now this is only a hunch, but I don't think he ever knew that Franz had these pictures. I believe that somehow Franz found out about Barone's attraction to dead women. He exchanged access to the bodies in return for a free hand to run his side businesses. In addition to the necrophelia, he let Barone share in the profits."

"Then why the pictures?"

"I think that when this started Franz wasn't sure of Barone, he took the pictures just in case. But he didn't have to exert any pressure to get Barone to share the wealth. You know that there have been rumors about Barone for years. It's always been alleged that he's an entrepreneur of sorts."

"Your scenario makes sense," Whitehurst agreed. "It sounds to me like we might have the elements of bribery and bribe receiving by both of them, in addition to everything else. Is that all?"

"All?" Franchell moaned, rolling his eyes. "If even some of this is true, we'll have enough to lock both of them up and throw the keys away."

"You're right, Bill," Whitehurst laughed.

"Okay, before I get in gear, how do you want to proceed? Who do you want the most? Are we prepared to offer anything to the other players to flip them?"

Whitehurst thought for a few moments. "Let's move forward with Barone as the ultimate target. None of this could have happened, or at least not gone on for this long, without him. Next is Franz. I need him to authenticate the pictures and fill in the details. But I won't offer much, I think I can build the case without him if necessary. The public would lynch me if I gave him a break."

"What about Price, Rudolph and the guy with Acme?"

"For the lesser players I'd be willing to deal. But nobody walks! Even if I bargain down to a misdemaenor, they'll do some time in the county slammer. But nobody is going to walk!"

"I hear you loud and clear boss," Franchell said.

"Okay, Bill, let's get started. I'll get your subpoenas for you. And don't bother with Franz. I'm going to get him in here, I want to talk to him myself."

As soon as Franchell left Whitehurst called Peter Gorsky at his residence. "Have your client in my office at nine tomorrow," he ordered. He hung up without answering Gorsky's questions.

CHAPTER TWENTY - NINE

Peter Gorsky met Dr. Franz outside the county building at quarter of nine Thursday morning. "You told me last night that you don't have any idea what this is all about," Gorsky said. "Did you think of anything overnight that I should know about?"

"No, Peter. As we discussed last evening, this must have something to do with the skeletons. I can't think of anything else."

"That's hard for me to believe, Bob. The skeleton story broke in the paper before Whitehurst gave his preliminary report. He rushed the damn report so he could get it over with at the same time your resignation was announced. I can't believe he'd reverse himself the following day. Are you sure you've told me everything?"

"I can't think of anything else I need to tell you right now, Peter."

Gorsky eyed Franz suspiciously. "I sense an ambush," he said. When Franz didn't respond, he shrugged in resignation. "Okay, let's go."

Whitehurst's secretary led them to her boss's office. "Good morning, Reggie," Franz said, attempting to show good humor.

Whitehurst nodded, but didn't speak or get up to shake hands. He motioned them to take seats opposite him. There was a period of uncomfortable silence before Whitehurst opened the meeting. "I asked you here this morning to discuss some new information in the morgue situation," he said.

"How new?" Gorsky wanted to know.

"I just found out yesterday," Whitehurst answered. "This new information is certainly inflamatory, and incriminating."

"Incriminating for who?" Franz asked.

"Please, Bob, let me handle this," Gorsky said. "Kindly direct any questions to me until I find out what's going on here," he said to Whitehurst.

"Okay," Whitehurst agreed. "But in answer to your clients question, it's incriminating to him, for one."

"We're here, let's get on with it," Gorsky said.

"I'd like to ask about some pictures," Whitehurst said, taking an envelope from his desk and handing it to Gorsky.

Franz slid his chair closer to Gorsky as the attorney removed the pictures. He held them in his lap, looking at them one at a time.

Whitehurst watched their faces closely. He quickly becameconvinced that Gorsky was totally surprised, and confused. Franz was also surprised, but not confused.

Gorsky finished his examination, then put the photos back in the envelope, and returned it to Whitehurst. "Disgusting to say the least," he commented. "But I represent Bob, not the man in the pictures. I don't see where this has anything to do with him."

"Those pictures were found among some of Bob's personal belongings. I'd like him to explain their background, how he happened to be in possession of them."

"Can I have a moment to talk with Bob?" Gorsky asked.

"Sure, Peter. I'll step into the hall, call me when you're ready." Whitehurst got up and walked toward the door.

"Wait a minute! Is this all you wanted to see us about? Is this the only issue?" Gorsky asked.

Whitehurst stopped and faced his guests. "No, it's not. I'm going to want to know about an account he has at the health department auxiliary, who put on these skeletal evidence courses and where the tuition money went, who Gordon Kirk and JER, Inc. are, and what went to the crematorium or grave on the forty-eight occasions when he kept the body."

The always cool Peter Gorsky was at a loss for words. Franz looked like a man who had just found out he had a terminal disease. Whitehurst controlled his urge to laugh. "I think I'll get a coffee. I'll be back in twenty minutes or so," he said.

Whitehurst returned to his office in a half hour. To his surprise, Gorsky went on the offensive. "About these pictures," he said, "I'm not going to talk about them until I have more information."

"What type of information?"

"I want to know on what basis you obtained a warrant to search Bob's private belongings. You did have a warrant, didn't you?"

"Warrant?" Whitehurst said. "Why would we have needed a warrant?"

"Bob tells me that the envelope in question may have been at a friends apartment. However, Bob spent a great deal of time there over several years. His friend provided him with certain space to store his private property. Bob's right of privacy applies to that location just the same as it would to his own home. Therefore, the permission of the tenant of that apartment is not sufficient to search Bob's things. You needed a warrant."

Whitehurst shook his head and gave a sarcastic laugh. "I'm not going to debate that issue with you now. That's a matter to be decided by a court. But, just for your information, the pictures were turned over to me right here. There was no search." Whitehurst waited a second to see if Gorsky intended to pursue the matter further. He didn't. "Now, let's cut the crap," he continued. "You don't have to posture in front of Bob, he knows you're a good lawyer. And there's nobody else here for you to impress. You know that neither of us is bound by anything that's said here unless we reach some kind of agreement. At this stage this is an off the record conference. We can both talk freely." Whitehurst made this statement for Franz's benefit.

"You don't have to tell me the rules, Mr. DA," Gorsky bristled. "Let's hear your offer."

"I don't know all the details of Bob's criminal activity yet. Any agreement will be contingent on full disclosure. If my investigators find that he's held anything back, all bets are off."

Gorsky nodded. "Continue."

"Bob will tell us exactly what he did, when, where, and with who. He will agree to testify against others as necessary. In return, and this assumes his being totally honest with us, he will plead guilty to one count of every crime. He'll serve the maximum on the most serious felony. All the lesser sentences will run concurrently."

"Plead to every count? Serve the maximum sentence?" Gorsky sneered. "That's no deal! Bob is a professional. He's never been in trouble before, and you're treating him like a common criminal!"

"That's because he is," Whitehurst said coldly.

After another hour, and two more private sessions between Franz and Gorsky, an agreement was reached.

"Now that we have an understanding," Whitehurst said, "I'm going to start asking you some questions, Bob. After that we'll do an interview on videotape. And remember, if you hold anything back the deal is off."

Whitehurst studied Franz, wanting to make sure he fully understood his situation. He was shocked at the way the man looked now, compared to when he had entered the room a couple of hours earlier. The arrogant, self-assured, cocky individual was no more. Franz actually looked smaller, his chair now seemed too big for him. Stoop shouldered, he looked straight ahead. The once smoldering green eyes were now dull and lifeless.

"I understand," Franz said. "Ask your questions."

"Did you take pictures of Anthony Barone having sex with dead women?"

"Yes."

"Tell me about that. How did it happen?"

"In late 1988, Barone and I attended a conference on emergency preparedness in Buffalo. It was a three day meeting. After the session ended on the second day we went to the hotel bar with several of the others. Barone got into the scotch. He had several drinks then, and continued drinking through dinner. After that, he and I adjourned to his room, where he had a bottle. By midnight I knew an awful lot about him."

"You weren't drinking?" Whitehurst asked.

"Just soda," Franz answered. "Anyway, he asked me if I ever got excited when I saw an attractive young woman naked

356

on my table. It was obvious to me that he was turned on by the thought.

Under some gentle prodding, he admitted that he had a fantasy about having sex with a dead woman. I told him that I had a fantasy too. I wanted to make Oneida County into a forensic center. A center controlled by me. I suggested that maybe we could help each other. I didn't know if he'd remember, but I wanted to plant the seed.

"A few weeks later he called me. We agreed to meet for dinner at a restaurant in Lewis County. This time he didn't drink. After dinner he said he remembered the conversation we had in Buffalo, he wanted to know what I had in mind. I told him that I could arrange for him to live his fantasy. I assured him it could be done at virtually no risk to him. In return, I said I would need his help in getting my expansion plans through the legislature.

"Barone said that was a problem. Money was tight, budgets were public information and well scrutinized. He said he could help some, but the best way to get started was to keep right away from the legislature, not to ask for anything. Out of sight, out of mind. He told me to think of a way to raise money on my own and get back to him.

"I called him a few days later. I told him that I had always wanted to run a skeletal recovery course, to train cops on the proper way to process a scene involving skeletal remains. There was no such course in the entire country that used real human remains. This training was needed and would be a money producer. I figured the courses would appear to be a county function, but they would actually have nothing to do with it. I just didn't know how to set it up so I could use the proceeds."

"Why aren't there any of these skeletal courses available any place else?" Whitehurst cut in.

"There are crime scene courses, but none using human remains. That's illegal in every jurisdiction I know of, including here." Franz explained.

"Anyway, I knew I could provide the bodies and body parts necessary. And as long as it seemed that the course was being run by the county no one would question it. No one did, not the cops who attended, or the instructors I used. One thing I want to make clear, this was a top notch course! Just because it was illegal doesn't diminish the quality."

Whitehurst didn't know whether to laugh or cry. He did neither. "Go ahead," he said.

"Barone said that he knew a way to handle the money. He said that once he got something set up, something that sounded like it was associated with the county, it could be used for any other money making ideas I came up with. That's when he first cut himself in. He said 'we' would be able to use the money as we wished."

"Did that bother you?" Whitehurst asked.

"A little, but not much. I wanted to go ahead with my plans.

I figured that I might be able to run two courses a year. Expenses would be minimal. Along with the money I'd get in my budget, I figured I'd be in good shape. My only concern was that Barone might want too much. But I felt that he'd settle for the girls and leave the money alone.

"So, we went forward. I took care of Barone's craving within a few days. But I wasn't sure how far I could trust him. Suppose he found that he didn't like having sex with the dead girls and wanted to back out? Suppose he got greedy? I decided to protect against those possibilities by making sure I was in a strong position to bargain. I took the pictures while Barone was preoccupied, he never suspected. After a few times I knew that he was hooked. Plus, he got more involved in the money end. I decided to hang on to the pictures though. I mean, you never know, do you? Unfortunately, I stored them at Marcia's."

"What do you mean that Barone got more involved with the money?" Whitehurst asked.

"Well, we set up the auxiliary. We stuck the county name in there and got started. But Barone said that the auxiliary had to have a legitimate purpose too. They had to do positive things, be

358

popular with the public. Since we had to keep our money separate from theirs, we set up a morgue account. Barone must have done something like this before. He knew all the answers, right down to using assumed business names to pay ourselves."

"Your courses didn't produce that much income," Whitehurst said. "Not for two of you. Where did the other money come from?"

"The tissues," Franz said. "When I first took over the morgue I made the rounds introducing myself. I let it be known that I didn't agree with the restrictive regulations placed on research. From time to time I'd get a call from someone wanting me to ignore the regulations to do them a favor. I'd help whenever I could, but these were isolated, one shot things.

"In early '89, Joe Rudolph called me from Crowne. He said they were starting a bladder project that would require a large volume of tissue from a targeted age group. This would also be a long term arrangement. He said that if I would provide the tissue he'd make it worth my time."

"But your reputation has been that money means nothing to you. You're simply committed to research. Why the sudden interest in money? To keep Barone happy?" Whitehurst wanted to know.

"The reputation you referred to was true, it still is. Money for Barone was a factor, yes. But I saw this as a chance to put myself in a position to dump Ione. I'm sure you've heard the rumors about our so called 'marriage'. Try to imagine yourself in my position, getting an 'allowance' of twenty dollars per week out of your check. I know that I made that bed myself. But I had absolutely no money of my own. I was totally dependent on Ione to pay the bills, buy my clothes and personal items. I had no idea where the money went, no say in it. Granted, I had agreed to that. But it's very unsettling to be in that position as you enter middle age. I saw Rudolph's offer as a way to gain some independence, a chance to create a financial security blanket."

"Is Rudolph JER, Inc.?" Whitehurst asked.

"Yes," Franz said with a weak smile. "He refused to have his own name on his checks. He opened up a checking account using that name."

"How did he make the money to pay you? He certainly didn't get it from Crowne?"

"You'll have to get the details from him. But it's my understanding that he was working with his brother-in-law at Acme Pharmaceuticals," Franz said. "Rudolph convinced Crowne to do the research. That way he was receiving his regular pay and his time was accounted for. Of course he was actually working on behalf of Acme all along. It was a good arrangement for Rudolph, and Acme. At least until now."

"If that was the set up, why did this Gordon Kirk pay you too?"

"Once we got started, things worked out so well that Kirk decided to help an Acme researcher obtain tissue as well."

"From kids?"

"It wasn't age specific. He wanted spinal cords from any donor."

"Wouldn't taking the spinal cord make the body difficult for the undertaker to handle?"

"It was the spinal cord, not the spinal column. No, its removal made no noticeable difference."

"Let's move on to your relationship with Whitney Price and how you built your skeletal collection," Whitehurst suggested.

"Whitney and I met when I first arrived in town. We didn't really get to know each other until we worked together on developing plans for dealing with a major disaster, an airplane crash, for example. We hit it off well and became friends. After I struck my deal with Barone I wanted to start gathering bodies and skeletons for my courses and collection. I knew that cremations would be the perfect opportunity. The poor and the elderly with no close family, were especially attractive. The next of kin often didn't want to be bothered with making funeral arrangements or incurring the expenses. They'd frequently accept my offer of a cremation at county expense. Whitney agreed to handle those cases. He got paid a small fee by the county. But I steered a lot of business his way. I got him appointed to a couple of county commitees, with the related prestige. I did him other favors from time to time."

"But two of these people were supposedly buried. How did he pull that off?"

Franz chuckled. "Those were old people who were found badly decomposed. Their next of kin were old and senile. But for religious reasons they wouldn't agree to cremation. I fixed them up with Whit. He knew there'd be a closed casket and no one would ask to look at the body. There was really nothing to it."

"So he charged them for everything and buried an empty casket?" Whitehurst asked.

"You'll have to ask him what he charged and what was in the casket. I can only tell you that the body wasn't."

"Let's take a break," Whitehurst said. "Then we'll start the videotape."

The following Tuesday morning, May fourth, Grant met with Whitehurst and Franchell at the DA's office.

"I just wanted to bring you up to date on where things stand, and thank you again for your help," Whitehurst said.

"A few days ago you said I was a nightmare," Grant laughed. "I'm glad to see that I'm forgiven."

Franchell and Whitehurst grinned. "Actually," Whitehurst said, "once we got into this it has been very interesting, and satisfying."

"Good. That's the way I felt about my piece of it," Grant said.

"The current situation is this," Whitehurst said, getting down to business, "we've reached agreements with most of the principles. If I have your promise that what I tell you will stay in this room, I'll share the terms of those agreements with you."

"You have my word," Grant assured him.

"Okay, let's start with Dr. Franz. He will be indicted on one count each of bribery, bribe receiving, falsification of business records, official misconduct, rewarding official misconduct, receiving a reward for official misconduct, defrauding the government and conspiracy. He will plead guilty to all counts. He'll do seven years for the bribery conviction. All the other lesser sentences will run concurrently. He is also providing testimony to the grand jury against Mr. Barone."

"I won't ask you to repeat all that, but some of those charges sounded like duplicates," Grant said.

"Yes, I guess they do," Whitehurst admitted. "They have to do with the relationship between Franz and Barone. They both gave and received benefit to and from each other. They were both public officials. For the bribery and official misconduct statutes they get charged for both giving and receiving."

"I understand, thanks" Grant said.

"Rudolph, Kirk and Price all got the same deal. This may sound a little light to you, so let me explain where I was coming from on this. My main target is Barone. I was willing to give Franz a little break on his sentence in return for his current and future testimony. My second priority was Franz. I cut these other guys some slack to lock them in against him. Do you understand my logic?"

"I understand why, but how far did you go?"

"Those three will plead to one count of bribery. There will be a sentencing recommendation of one year, to be served locally."

"What about Barone?" Grant asked.

"He hasn't expressed an interest in coming in to talk. On the other hand, we don't have a lot to talk about. I'm not inclined to give much away in his case," Whitehurst said.

"You're proceeding with getting an indictment then?"

"Yes. Pretty much the same as Franz, except without the business records. The big difference will be the sexual misconduct charges, for having sex with the corpses."

"When will all this hit the press?" Grant asked.

"We'll announce all the indictments at once, as soon as we're finished with Barone. That should be within a few days. Then they'll all have to report for booking and arraignment."

"What about Dr. Massey? I hear he's taken off," Grant said.

"Yes he has," Whitehurst laughed. "Along with a young lady named Gloria Daniels, his secretary. With Franz's help we're going to get an indictment against him for obstructing governmental administration. That is for trying to get Dr. McAree to interfere with your investigation. We won't chase him, but it will be hanging over his head if he comes back."

"Speaking of McAree, did you hear that he made a plea to official misconduct in Albany County?" Grant asked.

"Yes," Franchell answered. "He's going to get a couple of years probation, right boss?"

"That's right," Whitehurst said.

"I guess that covers it," Grant said.

"Not quite," Whitehurst corrected him. "We still have June Miller. We can't find that she actually participated in any of this stuff. She may have known about it and looked the other way. But that's a county work rule and ethics type thing, and she's already been fired. However, Bill tells me that she tried to block you from doing your investigation at Crowne. She tried to intimidate you didn't she?"

Grant laughed. "She threatened to have me arrested. I consider that to be intimidation."

Whitehurst nodded. "We can go after an indictment for obstructing governmental administration against her too. Is there any reason why we shouldn't?"

Grant thought briefly. "No, she never gave me anything but a hard time. She stuck with Franz to the bitter end. She wanted to go down with the ship I guess."

"We'll need to run you in front of the grand jury to tell them what happened. They're meeting today. Can you hang around a few minutes while I prepare the paperwork? Then we'll get you right in and out."

"I'll be happy to," Grant said with a smile.

A week later Whitehurst held a press conference to announce all the indictments. Although it had been rumored that Barone was in trouble, the nature of his crimes rocked the county from one end to the other. Particularly devastating were the sexual misconduct charges. They were only misdemeanors, the most minor charges on the indictment. But they caused a firestorm of outrage. Reporters and TV camera crews put Barone's house under immediate siege. Protestors gathered carrying signs demanding Barone's head. The crowds, and the cops sent to control them, created a circus atmosphere. They fed on each other.

Even the Barone children were hounded. Had their father ever sexually abused them? Did they know he had this sickness? The reporters wanted to know.

On the following Friday morning Grant got a call from Doyle. "I just heard from our reporter camped over at Barone's," Doyle said.

"Don't tell me he went outside and confessed to the mob," Grant said.

"Not quite," Doyle answered. "They found him dead this morning, hanging from a beam in his garage. I just thought you'd like to know."

CHAPTER THIRTY

Within four weeks the morgue story had played out. Initially, the public had difficulty believing that such horrible things had happened in their county. Then came acceptance, and appreciation. Thankfully the county residents had dedicated people like Ronald Bronson and Reginald Whitehurst to protect

them. Men who didn't rush to judgement. Fair men, but men who had the courage to do what had to be done. The radio talk shows and editorial pages were filled with accolades honoring them. Then, nothing.

Grant was suffering from Franz withdrawal. Linda gave him enough to do. But nothing was quite as interesting as the morgue investigation had been. He still smiled when he thought of what Franz had called his dummy company, "The Bare Bones Shop".

On a Friday morning in early June, he was sitting at his desk struggling with the daily crossword puzzle. The ringing of his desk phone granted him a reprieve.

"Mr. Grant, this is Kay Christensen from Ronald Bronson's office. Do you have a moment?"

"Sure, go ahead," Grant said with interest.

"Mr. Bronson asked me to call you, and others who were involved in the morgue investigation. He has been concerned because emotions ran pretty high during that episode, and things may have been said that shouldn't have been. As Mr. Bronson says, we are all in this community together and we have to get along."

Grant's interest was fading quickly. Maybe Bronson was looking for a donation or an endorsement, he thought.

"Because of that," Kay went on, "he thought it would be a good idea if the key participants got together informally. He feels that if people get to know each other away from the heat of battle, they may actually like each other."

365

"Okay," Grant said, "I take it the county is going to host some kind of get together?"

"Not the county, Mr. Bronson is inviting you to a get acquainted session. It will be at his home and is being hosted by Mr. Bronson personally."

"When is this shindig going to be?" Grant asked.

"Please, Mr. Grant, don't consider this to be a party," Kay admonished him. "In view of what has transpired recently, there is no reason to celebrate. It's more of a business get together. It will be a week from today, at seven o'clock. Will you be there?"

"Have you contacted Lt. Woods yet?" Grant asked.

"Yes, I just spoke with him. He plans to attend."

"I'll be there. Let me have the address."

The next Friday, Grant arrived in front of Bronson's north Utica home at twenty after seven. This was an upper middle class neighborhood. Although not mansions, the houses were newer and well maintained. He found a parking spot and settled back to wait for Woody. They figured that showing up at seven-thirty would make them fashionably late.

Woody arrived promptly at seven-thirty. It was a warm late spring evening. They were each wearing short sleeve shirts and dress slacks. Ronald Bronson answered their knock at the front door. "You must be Lt. Woods and Mr. Grant," he said. "I've been hanging around the door waiting for you to get here."

Grant and Woody introduced themselves. Bronson treated them like long lost friends. "I'm so glad to meet you," he beamed at them. "I certainly came to respect you two over the past several weeks."

They followed Bronson through the living room and kitchen, then out the back door. "The weather has cooperated," he said as they walked. "We're able to use the back yard."

The yard was large, and fenced. Three folding tables were set up together with several chairs around them. Multi colored party lights created a festive atmosphere. Grant did a quick head count and came up with ten people in addition to him and Woody.

"Help yourselves to a beer," Bronson said, motioning to a cooler on the ground near the tables. "Or there's hard stuff and mixer on the table. After you get your drinks I'll introduce you to the others."

Grant and Woody each grabbed a beer. "We're ready," Grant said.

They followed Bronson up to the tables. "Can I have your attention please," he said. "This is Lt. Woods and Mr. Grant. I'll let you do your own introductions." Bronson headed for the cooler and got himself a beer.

Whitehurst and Franchell were at the table, sitting on either side of James Doyle. Pamela Ashley was sitting a few places from them. Grant didn't know the others. That was soon remedied, however. As he walked around the table he met Charles Allen, Kay Christensen, another lawyer from the county attorney's office, and two assistant DA's.

Introductions completed, Grant and Woody joined in the conversations. The next two hours passed very pleasantly. Franchell kept everyone laughing with his endless stories. The beer was plentiful and cold. Snacks were passed around regularly.

Grant had to admit that Bronson had come up with a good idea. He was even beginning to believe that Pamela Ashley wasn't the witch he had thought. But Bronson himself was another story.

Although he tried to come across as Mr. Personality, Grant couldn't quite warm up to him. The way Bronson had trashed him in the press, no matter the reason, was not easy for him to forgive.

At a little after ten Grant went inside to use the bathroom. As he came out the back door he found Bronson standing there, sipping a beer and looking across the lawn at his guests.

"This was a nice idea," Grant complimented him.

"Thanks. I'm glad you came," Bronson said.

They stood there in silence. Listening to the murmur of conversation.

"Your success in this investigation, your tenacity, must have done a lot to enhance your career prospects," Bronson said finally. "They'll probably ask you to handle bigger things. And you'll owe it all to Bob Franz. At least that's the way he feels. I went to see him before he went away. He thinks you've got one coming."

Angry, Grant felt obliged to respond. "Let me straighten you out on something," he said. "I'm in a civil service position. I won't get any promotion unless I'm on the right list. And right now nothing is open for me. I may have earned a little bit of a reputation, but that's as far as it goes. Franz can go to hell! It seems to me that you did okay for yourself with this deal, though."

"What do you mean by that?" Bronson asked, still looking at his visitors.

"I mean that you were on the ropes politically. You ended up as a hero, your challenger gone, and with a job you can keep for as long as you want. I'd say you're a very lucky man."

"Luck? I don't believe in luck Mr. Grant. I believe that a man makes his own luck. Losers sit back and wait for something to happen, and hope that it's good. Winners don't leave things to chance, they push, they make things happen. Do you believe that, John? It's okay if I call you John, isn't it?"

"Suit yourself," Grant said. "And I'm not sure I agree with your argument, Mr. Bronson. At least not entirely."

Bronson didn't respond right away. "Please, John," he said finally. "There's no need to be so formal. There's just the two of us standing here. You might be more comfortable calling me by my father's name. You can call me Paul."

ABOUT THE AUTHOR

Dennis Griffin was born in Rome, New York in 1945. He joined the U.S. Navy in 1962. After being honorably discharged in 1966, he returned to central New York. He is married and has four adult children.

Mr. Griffin began his career in investigations and law enforcement in 1975, when he was hired by Pinkerton, Inc. as a private investigator. His duties included insurance fraud, missing persons, financial and background investigations, as well as undercover operations. In 1979 he was hired by the Madison County New York Department of Social Services as a Senior Child Support Investigator. He was responsible for locating and conducting financial investigations of persons failing to provide legally mandated child support.

In 1981, Mr. Griffin joined the Madison County Sheriff's Department, and attained the rank of sergeant. He was a shift supervisor and public information officer. During the same time period, he moonlighted as a part time patrolman for the Village of Chittenango Police Department.

In 1987, Mr. Griffin was hired by the New York State Department of Health as a Director of Investigations, Wadsworth Center. The primary mission of his unit was to investigate violations of the Public Health law relating to clinical and environmental laboratories, and health care fraud. He was responsible for hiring and training investigators, case assignment and general supervision. In addition, he personally handled the more difficult and complex investigations. Many of these cases received both local and national media attention. He retired in 1995.

Mr. Griffin attended Onondaga County Community College, Mohawk Valley Community College and the Central New York Regional Academy for Police Training. He is a member of the Las Vegas Writers Guild and is currently working on a second novel. RED GOLD will focus on trafficking in human blood, was part of a major Medicaid fraud ring operating in New York City in 1991.